Nicola Doherty grew up in Morl in book publishing before leaving ing career. Her first novel *The Out* the Romantic Novelists' Association edy category. Her second novel *If I Could Turn Back Time* was highly acclaimed. Nicola lives in Highbury, north London with her husband and no cats (yet).

To find out more visit www.nicoladohertybooks.com, follow her on Twitter @nicoladoherty_ or visit her on Facebook at NicolaDohertyBooks.

Praise for the *Girls on Tour* series:

'Nicola Doherty is one of my favourite chick lit authors for a reason and *Lily Does LA* only made me love her style of writing even more . . . The girls in this series are fun and full of life and energy which really lifts your spirits'   *Reviewed the Book*

'A great story with new beginnings, new friends, new city and finding things that you actually weren't looking for'   *On My Bookshelf*

'It's got everything a great chick lit novella is supposed to have – interesting and oh-so-not perfect heroine with big dreams, giggly moments as well as some serious ones . . . Can't wait to see what Nicola has got in store for us next'   *This Chick Reads*

'It had everything that I love in a great book – humour, wit, life-like characters, light-hearted romances, a fast pace, twists and a beautiful setting'   *Dreaming with Open Eyes*

'With its likeable characters, gorgeous sights and amusing moments, I loved everything about *Poppy Does Paris*, so much so that I didn't want it to end!'   *23 Review Street*

'Nicola Doherty has managed to create a character who I wanted to be – flaws and foibles included'   *Lisa Talks About*

By Nicola Doherty and available from Headline Review:

The Out of Office Girl
If I Could Turn Back Time

Girls On Tour ebook series:
Poppy Does Paris
Lily Does LA
Maggie Does Meribel
Rachel Does Rome
The Girls Take Manhattan

Girls On Tour

Girls on Tour

NICOLA DOHERTY

headline
review

First published in paperback in 2015 by
HEADLINE PUBLISHING GROUP

1

Cataloguing in Publication Data is available from the British Library

ISBN 978 1 4722 1880 3

Typeset in GiovanniITC-Book by Palimpsest Book Production Limited,
Falkirk, Stirlingshire

Printed and bound in Great Britain by
Clays Ltd, St Ives plc

Headline's policy is to use papers that are natural, renewable and
recyclable products and made from wood grown in well-managed
forests and other controlled sources. The logging and
manufacturing processes are expected to conform to the
environmental regulations of the country of origin.

MIX
Paper from
responsible sources
FSC® C104740

HEADLINE PUBLISHING GROUP
An Hachette UK Company
338 Euston Road
London NW1 3BH

www.headline.co.uk
www.hachette.co.uk

THANK YOU

A big thank you to Sherise Hobbs, Christina Demosthenous, Vicky Palmer, Frances Gough and Beau Merchant at Headline – a dream team indeed. Massive thanks also to Mari Evans. Thank you to Queen of Agents Rowan Lawton and to Liane-Louise Smith. And thank you to Adrian Valencia for a stunning cover.

Many, many thanks as well to all the readers who have got in touch to tell me they liked my books, and to all the amazing bloggers and reviewers who spread the world about books. As Jenny would say: you're all amazeballs.

POPPY DOES PARIS

Hi. I'm Poppy.

I stare at the blinking cursor. Where to start?

I'm a fairly normal girl.

Hah! I delete that right away. Bland Central Station, also not true.

I'm confident and outgoing.

No, that's even worse – makes me sound totally conceited. This is *awful*. Right. Start again.

Hi, I'm Poppy. On an average day you're likely to find me with my nose deep in a book, cycling home from the farmers' market in Hackney with my basket full of goodies, or at a vintage fashion fair. I love soul music, baking, Smarties, the sea, the 10th arrondissement in Paris and the Dirty Burger from MEATliquor—

Oh God. I sound like a revolting parody of middle-class hipsterdom: bike, farmers' market, Dirty Burger and all. It's all so cringe-worthy; I feel like I'm listing myself on eBay. Also, I forgot I'm going to need a pseudonym. Patricia? Penelope?

I tap my fingers for a few minutes, and then decide to just type the truth and see how it looks.

Hi, I'm Poppy. I work really long hours in an office full of women, and I haven't had a proper boyfriend in almost two years. I tend to rant on about things I find important and not many other people do. I'm addicted to cake and I'm like a demon when I'm

1

hungry. I'd like to meet someone creative, intelligent and sensitive.
I seriously doubt that I'm going to find such a gem on the internet,
but I've tried all the other—

'I've finished with these proofs,' says Sorrell, breezing into the office. 'Did you want to see them before they go up to production?'

'Oh, thanks, that was quick. Yes please – just leave them there,' I say, quickly minimising my screen. I don't want my assistant to see me composing my internet profile, though probably Sorrell could give me some excellent tips.

'Hey, I like your leather trousers,' I add, as she turns to leave.

'Thanks,' says Sorrell, doing a little twirl. 'Sample sale. Alasdair says they remind him of *The Avengers*!'

Good lord. I was here a year before I even spoke to our managing director, let alone cracked jokes with him about my leatherwear.

'Oh!' I laugh. 'Yeah. Very Emma Peel.'

'Who?' says Sorrell.

'Emma Peel, you know. From *The Avengers*.'

'Oh,' says Sorrell. 'Sorry. I don't remember them first time around.' And she's gone, leaving me wanting to explain: I don't remember them either! I was born in the eighties, like you! Except I'm twenty-nine and Sorrell is probably twenty-three, at most.

As I watch her leather rear depart, I have a guilty, resentful thought: once *I* was the zany, confident assistant with the memorable name and the quirky style, who made friends with all the senior people. But that was six years ago and I'm starting to feel like part of the furniture – and not a very shiny part either.

Right: that's enough of the pity party. I save my dating profile and start making myself presentable for today's editorial meeting. I'm in one of my favourite dresses: a fifties-style party frock I made myself from some red Liberty-print silk my mum found in a charity shop in Hastings. And my curls are looking frizz-free, thank God. I nearly cried when they discontinued the only leave-in conditioner that stopped me looking like one of the Supremes circa 1970, but I think I've found a replacement. I look in the mirror to check I don't have pen marks on my face and I'm good to go.

Until I stand up and hear the unmistakable rip of a seam. A quick feel confirms that the entire side of the dress has gone. Wonderful. I'd love to be able to blame the delicate vintage fabric, but the sad fact is that I've put on half a stone in the last six months. Too many work lunches, and too much time sitting at my desk. I quickly do a repair job with safety pins, throw on a spare cardigan that doesn't really go with the dress, and scuttle off to the meeting.

It's a long time since I've felt nervous when attending the editorial meeting, but today I do. There's a book that I'm really passionate about and today I'm going to find out whether anyone else agrees with me.

'Let's make a start,' says Ellen, our publishing director and my boss. 'Ooh, what are those?'

'They're *pastéis de nata* – Portuguese custard tarts,' I say, putting the box down in the middle of the table along with some paper napkins. 'Help yourselves.'

'Don't let me have one,' says Ellen. I know how she feels – I probably shouldn't have brought them either, but it was in a good cause.

'Oh yum. Thanks, Poppy,' says Melanie, the sales director, who's rake-thin. 'Can I take two? Where did you get them?'

'Bar San Marco. You know, the little snack bar down the road?'

My reason for bringing these in today was twofold. One, I think everyone will be more into my book if they're high on sugar; and two, a bit of product placement. The San Marco is a little gem, but it's struggling to compete against all the huge coffee shops, and the owner has told me he's not sure how much longer he can keep paying the rent.

'Is that the dingy little caff by the Tube?' asks Charlie, one of the marketing guys. 'I had a terrible coffee there once. Never been back.' He takes a slug from his PretACostaBucks paper cup.

I just smile. Charlie is nice enough, but he's a bit of a lad. If it's not in *Metro* or sponsored by Nike, he doesn't want to know.

'OK, let's begin,' says Ellen. 'Any new business? Poppy?'

I walk over to the hot seat, and the room goes quiet. I sit up straight and make sure I sound poised, enthusiastic and – above all – confident.

'Last week I circulated to a few of you a very, very exciting debut novel. It's a coming-of-age story set in London and Lagos . . .' I recap my pitch for those who haven't read the book, and wrap up with, 'So what did people think?'

There's an awkward pause while they all look at each other; it's as if I've put a dead frog in the middle of the table. Melanie speaks first. 'I thought the writing was beautiful, but . . . it felt like a difficult sell.'

Ellen nods. 'Same here. I did like the voice, but I wasn't one hundred per cent convinced either.'

I nod, trying to swallow my disappointment; if Ellen and Melanie don't like it, it's probably a lost cause.

'Anyone else read it?' Ellen asks.

'I read it,' says Charlie, to my surprise. I didn't even send it to him.

'And?'

'I thought it was really well written,' he says, making me even more surprised. 'I could see it getting great reviews, good publicity, maybe even winning prizes . . .'

I'm leaning forward, amazed. I wouldn't have thought the book was up his street at all. Have I completely misjudged him?

'. . . and selling about ten copies.'

Everyone laughs; he pretends to look regretful but he obviously thinks he's been funny – idiot.

'Well, that sounds like a pass,' I say, as lightly as I can. 'Thanks for reading, everyone.'

'Who's next?' Ellen asks.

'Me,' says Camilla, one of the non-fiction editors. 'I have a lead on a book by Katie Chipping.'

Katie Chipshop, as she's known, is a singer having her fifteen seconds of fame.

'Fabulous! Yes please!' says Melanie, and they start discussing it enthusiastically.

I do understand how important these books are to the business, but it's depressing all the same. I look at Charlie,

4

who's now talking about Katie's Twitter followers, and doing a partnership with a clothing brand, and think how unfair it is that we're turning down a really talented writer for someone like Katie Chipping.

'All other business,' says Ellen. 'Poppy, anything?'

'Yes. I'm very excited to say that we have made an offer for a new novel by Jonathan Wilder.'

I'm pleased that the reaction is at least as positive as it was for Katie bloody Chipping. I continue, 'His agent has been reviewing the offers, and they've asked a shortlist of editors to go and meet him, including me.'

'Where does he live?' asks one of the new publicists, whose name escapes me.

'Paris,' says Ellen. 'And he grew up all over – Switzerland, Italy, the States. His father is of course Michael Wilder, very famous too as a writer. Poppy, do you want to add anything?'

'Yes – well most of you will know his first book. It was set in a private school in New York and made into a film; the critics called him the new Bret Easton Ellis. And now he's back with his second book, which is about an American diplomat in Paris who wrecks his career with an affair.'

'Sounds great,' says the publicist. 'When are we doing it?'

'The deal's not done yet. He has other offers, so Poppy has to meet him and charm him,' Ellen says.

'The beauty parade,' says Melanie. 'You'll win that, Poppy.'

Which is very nice of her. But as we walk out of the meeting room, I'm still disappointed about the book I wanted to buy. Charlie strolls by me for a minute, saying, 'Fingers crossed for Jonathan Wilder. Melanie's right; you'll definitely win the beauty competition.'

'Thanks,' I say briefly. He can flirt all he likes but I'm still miffed at him for cracking jokes about my book.

As if he's reading my mind, Charlie continues, 'Sorry about that other book – I did think it was good, just a hard sell. I wasn't trying to be funny.'

'Oh . . . that's all right. Thanks for reading it.' Mollified, I give him a quick smile to show there are no hard feelings. He's not a bad guy, Charlie; he just lacks imagination. He's about to say something else when Melanie collars him, and I slip on ahead.

I would never admit it to anyone I work with, but when he first joined a year ago, I actually fancied Charlie. He is very handsome: he has a sort of young Viking look, with piercing blue eyes and blond hair. But then I began to notice things like his obsession with football, the way he dresses as if he's in a boy band, and his habit of tossing peanuts into his mouth as if he's training a seal. We did a bit of flirting at our last Christmas party and I was very briefly tempted, but now I'm so glad I didn't go there. I later found out he'd slept with at least three girls at work, which is just . . . icky. As practically the only single straight male in the entire company, it must be like shooting fish.

Back at my desk, I write an email to the agent about the novel I have to turn down. I'd love to have another little cake to cheer myself up, but I make myself put them in the kitchen because soon I'm going to be meeting Jonathan Wilder, in Paris, and I want to be able to get back into my size twelve jeans.

As a compensation for not having the cake, I treat myself to a quick look at the GQ shoot Jonathan did to publicise his first book. Dark hair, soulful eyes, high cheekbones, bit skinny. I click on a more recent picture; he's had a few protein shakes since then and he looks even better. Cut me a slice of that, as my friend Anthony would say.

'Poppy?' It's Ellen. 'Can I talk to you for a second?'

'Sure,' I say, quickly closing the screen. 'What's up?'

'It's about your trip to Paris,' she says. 'I thought it would be good if Charlie went with you.'

'Oh. Really?' I know Charlie's been involved in the marketing plans, but I didn't think he was that central to the pitch. And an irrational part of me thinks: this is *my* project – why does he have to come?

Ellen continues, 'I just think you could do with some backup, to talk about all our marketing plans.'

'Of course! That would be great. Really helpful,' I say, telling myself not to be so silly. It will be good to have Charlie's perspective, and show Jonathan the whole team is on board.

It's just weird that I'm going to be spending two whole days in Paris with him. Aside from work, what on earth are we going to talk about?

'Wow. A trip to Paris to meet Jonathan Wilder . . . how great is that?' says Alice. 'It's like going to LA to meet James Franco.'

'Or going to Italy to meet Luther Carson?' I say, smiling. I can't resist reminding Alice of the eventful work trip she went on when we worked together, before she left our company to work for a literary agency. 'Jonathan's not quite James Franco famous. Just as well or we couldn't afford him.'

Alice and I are sitting outside Bar Celona in Soho, the start of many a fun night in the past back when we were penniless assistants together. This evening, though, we're having a quick after-work drink before Alice goes home to her boyfriend and I go home to Don Draper on DVD.

I don't mean to moan, but I can't help adding, 'It's ironic really that I'm going to Paris. I'll be knee-deep in mini-breaking couples when I'm . . . well, let's just say it's been a while.'

'I know,' Alice says. After a minute she asks curiously, 'How long exactly? I mean, I know it's been a while, but . . .'

I swill the wine around in my glass. 'Coming up to a year,' I admit.

'Oh,' she says, taken aback. 'Well, that's not so long . . .' she adds unconvincingly.

It's funny. Where once it would have been shocking to be a single girl sleeping around, now it's the *not* sleeping with anyone that raises eyebrows.

'Why don't we just hit some bar together, see who you meet?' she suggests. Which is sweet of her, because picking up men in bars really isn't Alice's scene. Or mine, for that matter.

'It's OK, honestly. Call me old-fashioned, but I don't like one-night stands. I like to get to know someone first. But generally, by the time I've been on a few dates with someone, either he's gone off me or vice versa.'

Alice looks sympathetic.

'Well, you're sure to meet someone online,' she says encouragingly.

I've already told her about my foray into internet dating and she's all for it.

'Let's hope so.' I hold up crossed fingers. 'I'd prefer someone in real life, but I just don't seem to meet people any more.'

'What about the running club? Were there no men in that?'

'There were, but they were too fast. I was in the slower group and it was all women.'

'I think triathlon clubs are meant to be good for that reason,' says Alice. 'The abilities are more mixed up together, and it's more social. My cousin Lily's friend Maggie met her boyfriend in a triathlon club.'

I look at Alice in dismay. 'I'm not being funny, but . . . is that what it takes these days? Do we have to become triathletes to meet men?'

She laughs. 'No, of course not. What happened with that guy, you know, the comedian you met at that gig?'

'Oh, him. We were emailing, I made some joke, and he said I was being disrespectful to comedians and stopped writing back. And that's that. I don't know a single single man.'

'You must know *one*,' Alice says. It's sort of equal parts touching and annoying, the way all coupled-up girls are convinced that there must be eligible men around somewhere we haven't looked. Like, at the bottom of our sock drawer, or at the back of the cupboard behind the baked beans. 'What about Charlie from work, for example? I know you don't like him, but he is single . . .'

'Yes, he is single. And probably will be for ever, if he can help it. Definitely not relationship material.'

'But you used to think he was cute. And he flirts with you,' she reminds me.

'He flirts with everyone,' I reply automatically. But she's right; he does.

'I'm not saying he's the one for you,' she continues. 'But it shows you, there might be people around who you've overlooked.'

An idea is forming in my brain. Charlie. I have to admit, I do think he's attractive – in a seriously guilty-pleasure way, like Taylor Lautner or one of the *Made in Chelsea* boys. And I'm pretty sure

8

he finds me attractive too, judging from that Christmas party, and other little things he's said. But I'm not interested in him as a boyfriend, and he's definitely not interested in me as a girlfriend. Which means . . .

'Alice, that's a brilliant idea.'

'What is?'

'I'm going to try and have a fling with Charlie in Paris. In fact, we're staying for two nights, so who knows. It might be a whole dirty weekend!'

'What? Poppy, that's crazy! You don't even like him!'

'But that's the whole point. We don't want to go out with each other, but there's an attraction there. So we can have a fling, and neither of us will get hurt.'

'Are you sure? I mean, you work together – it could be awkward . . .'

'No, it'll be fine. Don't you see? If I wanted a fairy-tale romance with him, that would be one thing, but I don't, any more than he does. And also, I'm initiating it, which means I'm in control. He is right now packing his Chelsea boxer shorts and he has no idea what I'm thinking.'

'But what if you end up liking him after all?' Alice asks. 'Or vice versa?'

I think of the fact that Charlie uses more hair product than I do; the fact that he owns a Porsche key ring; the fact that he's at least three years younger than me and completely commitment-phobic. 'No, I think we'll be OK.'

Of course, by the time I'm queuing for the Eurostar late on Wednesday evening, I'm having second thoughts. What seemed like a great idea after a few glasses of white wine is different in the cold light of day.

'Evening! I just walked right by you. Are you in disguise?' Charlie asks me, as he joins me in the queue for check-in.

I don't know what he's on about. I'm in black pedal pushers, a black polo neck and a vintage trench, plus enormous sunglasses. I've added a big necklace of vertical silver spikes, just so it doesn't look as if I'm in fancy dress. 'Well, no . . . I was hoping more for Audrey Hepburn in *Funny Face*.'

Charlie is wielding a huge cappuccino coated in chocolate powder, and an even huger muffin, which he inhales almost whole before wiping his fingers on his double-breasted trench coat.

'Remind me,' he says. 'Which one is Audrey Hepburn?'

I raise one eyebrow. 'The one from *Breakfast at Tiffany's*.'

'Oh, right. Is that your suitcase?'

'Yeah, why?'

'It looks like something you'd take on the *Titanic*.'

I roll my eyes at him. It's a genuine vintage trunk case, heavier than modern ones, but it's beautiful, unlike Charlie's Red Bull sports bag.

But then again, I think, as we shuffle through security, isn't that a good thing? The more different we are, the more regret-free sex with him will be. As I watch him hoist his bag off his shoulder to put it in the plastic tray, his jumper rides up, revealing a very sexy midriff – not too flat. I find myself staring at that trail of hair that leads up from his tighty-whities. Aha. Briefs, not boxers. Which makes sense really. Once you get over a certain size, boxers just don't provide enough support, do they?

'Miss, come forward, please,' says a security woman, distracting me from my reverie.

As we find our seats, I feel awkward. I've never spoken to Charlie for longer than three minutes, and now we're stuck side by side in a train for more than two hours. As I sit down beside him, I notice his aftershave, strong but not unpleasant; I bet it's Dior Homme or something equally flashy. Then I see that I have a message from my mum. I stand in the aisle to listen to it, because I know that whatever it is, I won't want Charlie to hear.

'Hi, love, it's only me. Listen. I was talking to my friends at the bead shop, about your problems meeting men. And one of them suggested something called tag rugby? I looked it up and there's a club in Finsbury Park, which is very handy for you, I'll send you the details. Also, I'm going to come up to London for a demonstration against GM products on the fifteenth, so put that in your diary – we can have lunch afterwards. Oh, and have fun in Paris! OK, bye, love.'

I love her to bits, but honestly, Mum drives me around the

bend sometimes. I don't want to play tag rugby. And I feel like I spent my entire childhood on marches. There were so many pictures of Nelson Mandela in our house, I used to think he was a relative.

'Poppy?'

'Sorry, what?'

'I thought maybe we should go over the details of the publicity and marketing plans again,' Charlie suggests, wedging his coffee cup into the bin. 'Maybe divide them up, decide who says what.'

'OK. Though we don't want to sound too rehearsed. He has all the facts; now it comes down to whether or not he likes us.'

'Chemistry?' suggests Charlie.

'I suppose so.' I look up to find his blue eyes on me. Is he flirting with me? 'Well, partly. I imagine he'll want to hear that we love his book. You *have* read the book, haven't you?'

'Of course. We talked about it the other day, remember?'

'And what did you think?'

'I think it would sell,' he says. 'He's pretty good.'

'Is that it? For God's sake, don't overwhelm him with your enthusiasm, whatever you do.'

Charlie pats my arm reassuringly. 'Don't worry, I won't.'

I look down at his retreating hand, thinking: I wasn't imagining it; he does fancy me. Well, in the same way that he probably fancies everyone.

Across the aisle from us, a French couple are already getting their seduction on. Her skinny-denimed legs are slung in his lap, and he's trailing his hands lingeringly through her wavy dark brown hair. I stare at them and try to remember how long it's been since I sat in anyone's lap – not counting my gay friend Anthony when we were in someone's car coming back from a weekend in Brighton. Then I notice Charlie looking at me in amusement; he's obviously caught me staring at them.

'What? Nothing,' I say in confusion, and bury my head in my e-reader. It's a misconception that people of colour don't blush: I'm mixed race and I'm a chronic blusher. I don't see how I'm going to be able to seduce him if I'm this easily embarrassed.

It's always amazed me that in less time than it takes to get from London to Manchester, you can be in a completely foreign city. The Gare du Nord isn't that different to the new, revamped St Pancras – aside from being smaller – but it feels different; even the platform announcements sound sophisticated and mysterious. It's much warmer than London too; it's properly July here, where it still felt like March in London.

'Now what? Should we get a taxi?' says Charlie, gazing at the pert skinny-jeaned rear of the French girl, who's walking away with her boyfriend, still glued together like a three-legged race. 'Where's the hotel again?'

I immediately go off him once more as I realise I'm going to have to look after him the whole time we're here. Why are men all so useless?

'No, let's get the Métro – much quicker and cheaper,' I say, nodding towards the entrance to the station.

'Lead on, Captain Poppy,' he says, trailing along after me. 'I've never been to Paris before.'

'Are you serious? Not even on a school trip?'

He shakes his head. I suppose stag weekends in Ibiza are probably more his style. We head down into the Métro, where I find a free machine and start feeding euro coins – left over from the Frankfurt Book Fair last year – into the slot, getting us two *carnets* of ten adorably old-fashioned paper tickets.

'Thanks, Mum,' Charlie says, as I hand him his tickets. 'That's a thought. I don't have any euros.'

I recover from the 'Thanks, Mum' just in time to say, trying to keep my voice friendly, 'There's a cashpoint upstairs, where we were before. I'll wait for you here.'

Maybe this seduction thing isn't such a good idea after all, I think, as I watch the crowds sweeping in and out of the station. People dashing home from a late evening at work, pile-ups of tourists; it's just like London, except with subtitles. And except for that person who really is carrying a baguette.

Charlie rejoins me and we descend into the Métro, with its distinctive and not unpleasant smell, almost flowery, with base notes of hot metal. It takes me right back to my last trip to Paris, with my ex, Crippo. He spent three hours contemplating an installation in the Pompidou Centre, and then dragged me to a 'party' at his friend's place, where they spent the entire evening smoking weed and watching an experimental silent film set in a coal mine. Good times.

'Are you sure we're going the right way?' Charlie says, looking at the map of the line on the carriage wall. I nod. After spending a year here as a student, I like to think I know my way around and could maybe even be mistaken for a local. I'm probably deluding myself, but still, a girl can dream.

Twenty rattling minutes later, we arrive at Odéon. I sigh with pleasure as we come out of the Métro and see all the beautiful familiar sights: the glamorous, leggy students exchanging cheek kisses by the statue of Danton, the cinemas with huge queues outside, the broad boulevards of tall white buildings lined with cafés with names like Le Danton and L'Odéon. Everyone is very chic and intense-looking; as we pass people sitting at the little cane tables and chairs you can tell they're talking about philosophy, life and the universe, not last night's TV.

'Here you go,' says Charlie, handing my trunk back to me. I was so distracted, I didn't even notice that he just carried it up the stairs for me along with his own.

'Oh. Thank you.' I look around, trying to get my bearings. We're staying at the Relais Saint-Germain, on rue Saint-Sulpice. I know exactly where that is; I just need to orient myself.

'I've got a map in my bag,' says Charlie. 'And we're on . . . Boulevard Saint-German?'

'Saint-Germain,' I correct him. 'It's this way – come on.'

I'm pretty sure we're going the right way, and I keep expecting to see the rue Saint-Sulpice on the right, but then we find the Jardins de Luxembourg where they're not supposed to be, and have to turn back. My case is getting really heavy now.

'Let's stop for a minute. My phone's not working . . . I'll get out my map,' says Charlie.

'No, it's fine. I know where we are now; it's just down here, past this square and left. I've been here before.'

Ignoring me, he crouches down and there on the pavement he starts rooting in his sports bag, which seems to be mainly full of underwear. An elegant woman carrying a huge Yves Saint Laurent carrier bag steps over him and gives me a reproachful look. I can't even meet her eye, I'm so mortified. Then we end up getting directions from an American couple armed with maps, bum-bags and sensible walking shoes. It turns out we were looking for the wrong hotel: we're at the Relais Saint-Germain, which is right by Odéon, and I had the address for the Relais Saint-Sulpice. So much for me being like a local.

At least the hotel is lovely: lots of dark wood, exposed brickwork, tapestries and heavy velvet curtains. Charlie barrels up to the desk and starts talking in English to the pretty girl.

'Ah yes,' she replies, when he tells her our names. 'I have two rooms – a single and a deluxe suite?'

'Oh, but it was meant to be two singles,' I say, dismayed. 'Can we change?'

'I'm sorry, *madame*, we are fully booked,' she says apologetically. 'Victor will show you the rooms, and you can choose.'

There being not much choice, we stump upstairs after Victor, who looks like a resting model, as he carries my massive trunk.

'I'll take the single,' Charlie says.

'You don't have to do that – we can toss for it.' It doesn't seem fair for him to have the single just because he's a boy.

The single is perfectly nice, with pink striped wallpaper, flat-screen TV and a nice view over the Carrefour de l'Odéon. The deluxe suite, on the other hand, is *gorgeous*, with dark wooden beams on the ceiling, a seating area and a gigantic bed with a red counterpane and a fur throw. Behind a curtained alcove, floor-length windows lead on to a balcony with pink geraniums and a view over the jumble of metal roofs towards the two towers of Saint-Sulpice.

I look at it longingly. Gender equality be damned; I want this room! 'You can leave us the keys,' I tell Victor, in my best French. 'We'll arrange it between us.'

I'm quite proud of that construction, but Victor isn't fooled, and replies in English: 'Of course. Have a pleasant stay.'

I fish out a twenty-cent coin, trying to decide which is heads and which is tails. 'Let's toss for it, OK?'

'I tell you what,' Charlie says. 'Why don't you just take it, and in return I get to choose where we go to eat tomorrow night.'

'But we're not going out tomorrow night. We're meeting Jonathan in the morning, right? For coffee?'

'Sure, but you're going to want to eat at some point, aren't you? I know I am.'

This would certainly aid my seduction plan. But I'm not sure about that plan any more, especially if it means spending an entire evening with him. I don't want to be rude or hurt his feelings so I try and think up a quick excuse.

'Oh, sorry . . . I have plans with a friend.' This is a total lie, but he won't find out, I hope. 'My friend . . . Nicole. She lives in Paris. Didn't I say?'

'No, you didn't,' he says amiably. 'Nicole, huh? What does she do here?'

'She works for . . .' I look out of the window for inspiration. 'Renault. She works for Renault.'

Charlie shrugs, and says, 'OK. Well, let's flip for the room, if you insist.'

I wish I'd just accepted his offer of the bloody room, but it's too late now.

'Here goes. And it's . . .' I lift my hand. 'Oh. Heads. You win.' I watch as he flops happily on to his massive bed.

An hour later, having unpacked and gone for a stroll by myself, I open the window of my room and look out at the stream of people walking up and down the street. It's a quarter to ten in the evening. I can't quite erase the sight of Charlie lounging luxuriously in the four-poster bed.

Hmm. Am I actually going to try this seduction thing? Tonight?

While I think about it, I get out of the polo neck and trousers, which are way too hot for this evening, and have a quick shower. I ran out yesterday lunchtime and had a Brazilian and full leg wax – I lied and told Sorrell I had a work lunch, in case anyone asked. And I bought some brand-new underwear: a cute, frothy little black and pink bra from Coco de Mer and matching frilly knickers that cost as much as a full outfit. It seems a pity to waste them.

OK, I'm going to do it. I'll pop next door and see what happens. The key to the whole thing, obviously, is alcohol, so I'll ask Charlie if I can have a drink from his minibar. And if it all goes wrong, I can just blame it on my hay fever medicine – tell him it makes me go crazy.

I pull on a seventies denim baby-doll minidress and some low wooden mules. I spray a bit of Vivienne Westwood Boudoir on my pulse points and between my legs for good measure. I'm just on my way to the door when I remember to grab my handbag and put in a condom. In a spirit of optimism, I take two. My pulse is hammering in my throat; I can't believe I am actually doing this!

Charlie answers the door with no top on, which seems a promising start. 'Oh, hi,' he says. 'Sorry, I just got out of the shower. Wait a sec.' He pulls on an Adidas T-shirt over his track-suit bottoms. 'What's up?' The TV is on in the background.

'Not much. I feel like a drink and I don't seem to have a minibar in my room,' I say, trying to sound nonchalant.

'I have one, help yourself.'

'Do you want one?' I ask as I pour myself a vodka and tonic, hoping my legs look OK in this dress.

'Sure,' he says, sounding distracted. I turn around to find he's lying on the bed, eyes glued to golf on the TV. 'I'll have a beer, please.'

Feeling less and less like a seductive siren and more like a waitress, I retrieve a can. I'm guessing he won't want a glass.

'Thanks,' he says, barely looking at me as I hand him the beer. 'Sorry. Big match tonight, it's just starting.'

'Oh. I don't really follow—' I'm about to say 'golf' when Charlie shushes me and holds up a finger. 'I just want to see this . . . Go on! Get it in there! Get in the hole!'

Unfortunate choice of words. I sip my vodka and tonic. I wish I could just leave but it would look too obvious, so I have to sit through half an hour of the most agonisingly boring sport ever invented – with the most hideous clothes, too. The sleeveless wool vests! The visors!

'Not a golf fan, no?' Charlie says, when finally there's an ad break.

'Oh, I don't mind a bit of golf,' I lie. 'When does it finish?'

'A couple of hours. Do you want another drink?'

A couple of hours! I'm not that desperate.

'No, I think I'll head to bed. I'll see you tomorrow – meet in the lobby at a quarter to eleven?'

16

'Great. See you then,' he says. 'Oh, here we go. What's he doing now?'

Charlie barely looks up as I leave the suite. Back in my bedroom, I bury my face in my hands and let out a stifled shriek. What was I *thinking*? That was excruciating. I rip off my cute dress and seduction underwear, and get into my nightie. I thought Charlie fancied me, but he rates me somewhere below golf on the scale of attraction. Honestly, if it was football or Wimbledon it wouldn't be so bad, but golf!

I shudder as I remember how he called me Captain Poppy. And another memory I blocked out: the way he said 'Thanks, Mum.' Aargh. He obviously sees me as some kind of *parent* figure. So much for our one-night stand; it looks like this weekend is going to be all work and no foreplay after all.

The next morning, Charlie and I set off from our hotel on foot to meet Jonathan. We're not going far; he's suggested a rendez-vous at the bookshop Shakespeare and Company, which is right by the Seine, opposite Notre-Dame. I adore this place. I haven't been since I was a student, but I remember it having so much character; it's crammed from floor to ceiling with dusty old books, and there are chairs everywhere so you can sit peacefully reading.

Unfortunately, the peace and quiet I remember is nowhere in evidence as we squeeze ourselves into the shop. It's still crammed from floor to ceiling with lovely books, but also with tourists, most of whom are manically taking pictures despite the signs everywhere telling you not to. I lead Charlie upstairs to the second-hand section. There are two Japanese girls photographing each other in an alcove, but it's more peaceful here at least.

'Is that a *bed* over there?' Charlie mutters.

'Yeah. You can sleep here for free, as long as you read a book a day, and do chores I think.'

'Yuck. No thanks.'

Shrugging, I check my reflection in a tarnished mirror beside a bookshelf. I'm wearing a blue silk jumpsuit by Katherine Hamnett, which my mum wore in the eighties. I could see Charlie doing a double take when I appeared in it this morning; like me, it's obviously not his style. I am *so* glad nothing happened between us last night. Never in my life have I barked up such a wrong tree.

We edge into a side room, where two guys are playing chess. I watch them for a minute, smiling. Then I spot a dark head bent over a book. A tall frame curled into a chair.

'Jonathan?'

He looks up, frowning, and then slowly the mists seem to clear. 'Poppy,' he says, closing the book and standing up. 'Of course.' He leans forward to kiss me on either cheek, which I must say I wasn't expecting. Nice aftershave. 'I hope you haven't been searching for me for too long. It's dangerous to let me loose in here.' His dark-blue eyes, behind his black glasses, hold mine for a long minute.

'No, we just got here,' I say, taking in his height, the broad shoulders under a T-shirt and linen jacket, navy cotton scarf thrown loosely around his neck. He's well-built, like an American, but he definitely has a sort of French style going on. 'This is my colleague Charlie, our marketing guru.'

'Good to meet you both,' he says.

For some reason I'd expected Jonathan to be a bit aloof, but he's charm personified, leading us out of the bookshop and talking about taking us somewhere nearby for coffee.

'Was that your book?' Charlie asks, as we're about to head out the door. 'Or did you need to pay for it?'

I glare at him, but Jonathan just looks down at the ancient Penguin Classic in his hand and frowns. 'Oh, yes. Hey, Georgie,' he says, to a leggy girl descending from a ladder. 'Put this on my account, would you?'

'Sure, Jonathan. No problem,' she says, in a chirpy American voice. I love the fact that he has an account at his favourite bookshop.

'Stealing from a bookshop,' Jonathan says as we step out of the dark building into the sunshine. 'That's a crime that should land you in the lowest circle of hell.' He has a beautiful voice: deep, sexy and a little hoarse, with a transatlantic accent like Robert Pattinson's. His writer father is English and his mother is American, which of course explains it. Actually he looks a bit like R-Patz. Nothing wrong with that.

'It was our fault. We distracted you,' I offer.

'No, it was the book. I'm always in a daze after reading Kafka, aren't you?' He gives me a charming sideways smile, and I laugh.

'Me too,' says Charlie. 'Total daze.'

I give him another glare, but Jonathan doesn't seem to have noticed. Instead he leads us past an ancient church and down a few narrow, winding little medieval streets, crammed with restaurants and T-shirt shops, and then around a corner.

'That looks like a lovely place,' I say, observing a blue-painted café on our left.

'Well spotted,' says Jonathan. 'It's La Fourmi Ailée. It's where we're going. One of the best tea shops in Paris.'

I notice that his French accent is excellent, and that he really emphasises it, rolling his 'r's – he doesn't just swallow them up with the rest of his English words.

Inside the café is charming, with old yellow leather booths, a high ceiling with lots of bookshelves and what look like lines of poetry written up on the walls. There's a fireplace and even a Buddha statue; it's airy, peaceful and bohemian, the kind of place where you could spend a few hours sipping tea, reading or writing – though thankfully, there are no MacBook Airs in evidence.

'This is such a wonderful place,' I exclaim, as we sit down. 'It's so individual.'

'It's named after a quotation from Virginia Woolf,' says Jonathan. 'It's a line – I think it's in one of her letters – where she talks about wanting to write a light, feathery book with wings, after doing ant work. And "la fourmi ailée" means—'

My finger's already on the buzzer. 'The ant with wings?'

'Very good,' he says. 'Bonjour,' he adds to the waitress, who's just joined us, and orders un grand crème.

'Pour moi aussi,' I say.

'Très bien,' says the waitress, who's looking very chic and bohemian in denim cut-offs and a big floral shirt. I'm just thinking how nice it is that we're not being dumb tourists when Charlie says, 'Coffee, please.'

'Sure,' says the waitress, switching to perfect English. 'Latte, cappuccino, Americano?'

'I'll have what they're having,' Charlie says, smiling at her in a flirty way.

'So what made you decide to move to Paris, Jonathan?' I ask, when she's gone. 'Aside from the fact that it's the most beautiful city in the world, of course.'

'Aside from that? Well, the thing is, I write well here. And so many of the writers I love have lived here – Hemingway, Fitzgerald, George Orwell . . .' He shrugs. 'Anyway, I've never felt completely at home either in England or the States. Paris seems the natural place for exiles.'

'Your girlfriend is French, is that right?' asks Charlie.

What? I *happen* to have scanned the acknowledgements of Jonathan's new book for any sign of a girlfriend and there's nothing. To my relief, Jonathan replies, 'My ex-girlfriend was, yes. That is, she still is. We're still friends.' We all exchange the grown-up smiles of people who stay friends with exes.

'So,' says Jonathan. 'Tell me what you've got in mind for my book.'

Charlie and I talk him briefly through our ideas, and I'm pretty pleased: we sound enthusiastic but we're not sales-pitchy. I must admit, Charlie's impressive, and he's done his homework on all Jonathan's previous activities, including his modelling stint.

'Oh, it was hardly modelling,' Jonathan says modestly. 'One photo shoot for *GQ*.'

'Would you be willing to do it again?' asks Charlie.

'Sure. Whatever it takes.'

'I'm glad you don't see promoting your book as a chore,' I tell him.

'Absolutely not,' says Jonathan. 'There's no point in being the reclusive *auteur*. That was fine in Salinger's day, but not now.'

'Even Salinger would have to be on Twitter today,' says Charlie. 'And Pinterest.'

Jonathan laughs heartily. 'That's funny. Yes, I like Twitter. It's a good way to network, there's no doubt about it. Sometimes I just pour myself a Kir and pretend I'm at a cocktail party.'

Our coffee arrives, rich and dark, with a dense foam topping. I sip it, trying to savour this moment of having coffee in Paris with Jonathan Wilder.

'Great coffee,' Charlie says. 'Is the food good too? What's your favourite place to eat in Paris?'

'Probably . . .' Jonathan seems lost in thought, then smiles. 'Well, not the place you'd expect. A tiny, crappy-looking Algerian joint in the 20th arrondissement. No sign outside. Fluorescent lights, everyone chain-smoking. No menu. The food is out of this world.'

'It sounds great,' says Charlie. 'Why don't we go there tomorrow?'

Jonathan just laughs again, as if he's made a great joke. 'No, let's just book somewhere more conventional, like maybe . . . Le Meurice?'

'Le Meurice,' says Charlie. 'Sounds good. We'll book.'

'Where are you both staying?'

'Near Saint-Sulpice,' says Charlie.

Jonathan doesn't understand, and frowns. 'Where? Ah, Saint-Sulpice,' he repeats, giving it the full French. 'Great choice.' He gets to his feet. 'Excuse me, please.'

Charlie and I stay quiet for a minute after he's gone, then I let out a sigh of relief.

'Well, that seems to be going well. He's nice, isn't he?'

'I'm glad he likes our publishing plans,' says Charlie.

'You don't think he's nice?'

'Sure. Bit pretentious, maybe . . .'

I roll my eyes. 'Don't be ridiculous. You can't be pretentious if you're a genuine talent.'

'"Sometimes I just pour myself a Kir and pretend I'm at a cocktail party",' says Charlie.

'Shhh,' I hiss.

'Poppy? Charlie?' says a voice beside us.

Standing before us is Clémence Poésy, or a dead ringer thereof. A petite vision in black, with tumbling waves of mink-blond hair, a pouting pink mouth, a leather biker jacket sliding off her shoulders, and the most astonishing pair of legs ever poured into skinny jeans. No danger of deep-vein thrombosis in Paris: I've never seen such tight jeans anywhere.

'I am Constance,' she says, putting out a hand.

'Of course! Hi!' It's Jonathan's agent – I wasn't sure if she'd be joining us today. And I didn't expect her to be quite so glamorous.

'Great to meet you, Constance,' says Charlie, getting to his feet and shaking her hand. 'I'm Charlie.' He's brightened up quite a bit.

'I am so sorry I was so late. I couldn't find anywhere to park my motorbike,' she says. Her accent is adorable: 'park' comes out as 'purrk'. I can't believe how chic she looks considering she's just stepped off a motorbike. Even her helmet is cute, swinging neatly beside her tiny Chanel bag. I can't go anywhere on my bike without looking like a total nerd, with a helmet that makes me resemble a giant insect (extra-large to accommodate all my hair).

'Motorbike?' says Charlie. 'Fantastic. What kind?' Forget brightening up; he's looking at Constance as if she's something to eat.

'You must be really brave to ride it around Paris,' I say.

I'm sort of assuming Constance will say something like, 'Oh no, I'm a real chicken' or 'I'm very careful'. Instead, she startles me by putting her head on one side, appearing to consider and then smiling and saying, 'Yes, I suppose I am.'

'Constance. *Te voilà enfin*,' says a voice behind us.

Jonathan and Constance exchange cheek kisses.

'*Salut, Jonathan! Excuse-moi, impossible de trouver un endroit pour garer mon scooter . . .*'

We watch as they catch up with much shrugging and gesticulating. I feel like an extra in a very glamorous French film. Then Jonathan slaps his forehead.

'So rude of us,' he says. 'I sometimes forget that I'm speaking French, not English. You've all met?'

'Yes – we were just wondering how much of our spiel Constance needs to hear again,' Charlie says. He looks as if he'd be happy to tell her any amount of spiel.

'I've got an idea,' says Jonathan. 'Constance, why don't you let Charlie bring you up to speed on their very exciting publishing plans . . . and Poppy and I can take a stroll?'

Charlie and I exchange glances. I can tell that we're both thinking: what is the catch?

'That sounds an excellent plan,' says Charlie. 'I can talk you through the whole thing, flipcharts and all. And later, you'll have to show me that motorbike.'

'*Sans problème*,' says Constance. 'We can even go for a ride if you want, why not?'

'Great! I'd say you know Paris like the back of your hand.'

'I know it very well,' says Constance without a trace of false modesty.

Jonathan and I walk out of the café and I try to hide my smile as I put my sunglasses on. I've got Jonathan all to myself: what a result! Charlie has clearly got the hots for his agent, but she looks as if she can handle him. I can't believe I wanted to seduce Charlie last night; Jonathan is so much more attractive. Of course, this is a professional meeting and Jonathan is totally off-limits. But it reminds me that I have standards. Intelligent conversation; someone who's interested in culture and not afraid to be a bit different – that's much more me.

'There's just something about the light here, isn't there?' I say. 'It's that creamy colour of the buildings . . . the river . . . Wasn't Paris called the City of Light?'

'That's exactly right,' says Jonathan. 'About a hundred years ago. Can you imagine? Picasso, Matisse, Hemingway, Chanel, all working away together in a few square miles, all inventing the twentieth century.' He shakes his head as we start to drift towards the river. 'It's humbling, really. I feel very audacious even trying to write anything here.'

I make a non-committal murmur and Jonathan laughs. 'I must sound like a pretentious idiot.'

'Of course you don't,' I say sincerely. 'Honestly. What are we coming to if we can't mention bloody Picasso without being thought pretentious?' I'm really talking to Charlie, but of course he's not here to hear my words of wisdom. It's wonderful to be in Paris again and I'm drinking it all in: the old buildings with their dove-grey shutters and lanterns, the flowing brown river, the green stalls on the quays with their collections of second-hand books and prints.

'Ah, the *bouquinistes*,' Jonathan says when I point them out. 'It's impossible to imagine the river without them, isn't it?'

To our left is the peaceful grey bulk of Notre-Dame, rising out of the clumps of greenery. Below us are quays where couples are sprawled and intertwined. No point in telling people in Paris to get a room, I muse. The whole city is their room.

'Where do you want to go?' he asks, as we approach a bridge. 'Over to the Ile Saint-Louis and the Marais? Or do you want to head back towards the Latin Quarter and the Pantheon?'

I laugh. 'I feel spoiled for choice . . . Let's head towards the Marais. I love it there.'

'Do you know Paris well?' Jonathan asks, as we walk towards a bridge.

'Yes – I spent a year studying here, and I used to come here a lot with my ex. Good lord, what are these?'

The whole side of the bridge is covered with what I thought was a bronze wall of some kind, but in fact is little padlocks bolted to the bridge, with messages engraved on them. People are walking up and down taking pictures of them and examining the messages, most of which seem to be in English. *Snicky and Snuffy for ever. To Maria, my angel: will you marry me? 17.08.12. 18.08.12: She said yes!*

'The *cadenas d'amour,*' says Jonathan. 'It started on the Pont des Arts but the *mairie* took them all away overnight. Now they've popped up here.'

I shake my head. 'Is there anywhere on earth more obsessed with love and romance?' I say before I realise how weird that must sound.

'I hope not,' says Jonathan enigmatically. 'Tell me about the year you were here as an *étudiante.*'

We walk over the bridge towards the Ile Saint-Louis, and I tell Jonathan about my Erasmus year in Paris, when I stayed in a firetrap of a sixth-floor studio on the rue Soufflot, living off crêpes and Nutella and two-euro bottles of wine, and having the time of my life.

'I shouldn't really have been here – I was studying English in Manchester and a year in Paris wasn't totally relevant – but I just couldn't pass up the opportunity. It was such a great place to be a student. It didn't matter that we had no money. In summer we used to have picnics on the Pont des Arts, and in winter we used to spend hours in cafés nursing one drink . . .'

'Wonderful,' says Jonathan. 'Yes, Paris is almost better with no money. Especially for writers. It's like Hemingway says: "Hunger is a good discipline." Sometimes I envy him that . . . I worry that I'm not hungry enough.' He looks despondent.

'Oh no! Don't think that. You know, we haven't talked enough about your book yet. I loved it.'

'That's great. What did you . . . I mean, did you have any notes, for the book?'

I'm thrilled that he's brought this up. As we stroll through the quaint old streets of the Ile Saint-Louis, dodging groups of tourists queuing outside Berthillon for ice cream, I tell him everything I loved about his book, and make a few editorial suggestions, which he takes very well. When we arrive at the Place des Vosges, Jonathan stops walking, pulls off his glasses and turns to me.

'I am pathetically grateful to you for telling me all that,' he says. 'Those are outstanding suggestions, and I feel like you really got the book. Thank you for saying those nice things. You know how needy authors are, so I know you won't judge me for it.'

'No judging,' I say, smiling. If Charlie could see him now, he would know that he's not pretentious; he's *lovely*.

'Let me get you a Perrier Menthe,' says Jonathan. 'Or something stronger? The French don't have any Anglo-Saxon hang-ups about drinking at lunchtime, you know.'

We take a seat at a café in the arcade that runs around the square. It must be one of the most elegant in Paris, with its red and cream buildings and the garden with its topiary chestnut trees, white gravelled paths and black railings. The shade of the arches is delicious after the heat of the streets. I'm getting pretty hungry, but I don't know whether to suggest lunch; he might not have time.

'Can you believe it's nearly two p.m.?' says Jonathan, looking at his watch. 'Time flies. Do you want food?'

'Yes, definitely.' I love it when a man knows you're hungry.

I'm slightly disappointed to notice that most of the people sitting around us are tourists – a group of English women and an American couple, and a handful of Germans. It's not exactly my Parisian café fantasy. But at last the waitress addresses us in French. Jonathan orders a beer, and I order a Kir.

'Would you like your Kir with Sauvignon or Chablis?' the waitress asks me in English.

'*Avec Chablis, s'il vous plaît,*' I say stubbornly. 'Why did she do that?' I ask, when she's gone. 'I know my French is a little rusty, but I'm capable of ordering a drink.'

Jonathan smiles. 'They do it to me too. I think they're just not used to foreigners who speak such good French.'

I make a face. 'It's nice of you to turn it into a compliment.'

The waitress appears back in record time with our drinks.

'To your Paris trip,' Jonathan says, clinking my glass.

'To your book.' I clink Jonathan's glass.

'Thank you. And to getting to know each other.' He clinks mine again.

I'm so happy we got rid of Charlie; I can only imagine how much he would take the piss if he could see us toasting Paris and ourselves.

As if reading my mind, Jonathan says, 'You and your colleague are quite different, aren't you?'

'Well,' I say diplomatically, 'we do different things.'

Jonathan looks even more serious. 'For me, there's no contest. I'm sure he's very, ah, competent but I feel as if you understand me much better. If that doesn't sound *trop égoiste.*'

'Not *égoiste* at all,' I say, smiling.

Remembering my greedy breakfast of croissants at the hotel, I decide to order a salad, which isn't a penance at all; it's utterly delicious. It's just goat's cheese and tomatoes and salad leaves; it's simple but so fresh and tasty, and the tomatoes are mouth-watering.

'Oh my God, this salad is to die for,' I say, closing my eyes briefly. 'They just do not serve salads like this in London. It's incredible.'

Jonathan has ordered a croque-monsieur, which seems a bit boring, but I suppose he can eat here whenever he wants. 'So when's the last time you were in Paris?' he asks.

I was prepared for Jonathan to be somewhat self-obsessed, but he's the complete opposite. He listens intently as I end up telling him all about myself; how long I've been doing my job, and the studio flat in Hackney I managed to buy by the skin of my teeth.

26

I even end up telling him about my mum and what a kick she gets out of seeing my name in the acknowledgements of my books.

'Of course she'd have preferred me to be prime minister. Well, she'd have settled for me being an MP. Or a human rights lawyer or some sort of social activist. I went on a *lot* of marches when I was a kid.'

'What does she do now?'

'She's a social worker. Very dedicated. Lives in Brighton, still marching. She has boundless energy, all thanks to coconut oil, apparently. She's always forwarding me petitions and articles from the *Guardian* about nuclear power and women being oppressed. She's kind of exhausting, but she's great. We get on really well now.'

My glass seems to be empty. Jonathan lifts a finger and within minutes, two more Kirs have materialised. He obviously doesn't have any Anglo-Saxon hang-ups about drinking at lunchtime, either.

'So you didn't always get on so well?' he says.

Wow. It's honestly been years since I've met a man who was so great at asking questions. 'Well, when I was a teenager, we used to clash over all the usual things – boys, drinking, staying out late. Oh, and my hair.'

'Your hair?'

'Yeah. I went through a phase of experimenting with weaves, or relaxing my hair – you know, straightening it. She wanted me to wear it au naturel, the way I do now.' I indicate my mop. 'So I did the opposite just to wind her up. But now I love my hair.' I smile, and take a sip of my drink.

'I think she was right,' Jonathan says, smiling. 'Your hair is gorgeous.'

Now I'm blushing. And this second Kir is definitely going to my head.

'And what about your dad?'

'Well, I don't see him very often. He lives in Saudi now, working for a big corporate law firm. He's sold out, in my mum's view. They split up when I was seven.'

'I'm sorry.'

27

'Oh, it's fine. It's actually a miracle they lasted that long. They met at a CND demonstration when they were students and moved in together a week later. Mum's parents were very strict church-going Jamaicans and they were furious with her – running off with a long-haired white boy, even if he was training to be a lawyer.'

'I see.'

'Sorry, I didn't mean to ramble on. Bad habit of mine.'

Jonathan leans back in his chair, and takes an assessing look at me. 'Don't be sorry. It's very interesting. *You* are . . .' he smiles slowly, 'very interesting.'

Whoa, Nelly. I don't even need to get out my Flirt-o-Meter: that was easily a nine. Jonathan Wilder is flirting with me. Outrageously. And I really want to flirt back.

'What about a coffee?' I say weakly.

'Sure.' He pauses, then continues, 'Actually, my place is pretty close to here. Do you want to have coffee there?'

Hm. He's suggesting coffee at his place – when we're actually *in* a café. Now what? If I blush and say, 'That doesn't seem like such a good idea,' then it's all out in the open that we're flirting, and then he'll have to say something and I'll have to say something and then where will we be? But if I say yes and go back to his place for coffee . . . I'm old enough to know that coffee doesn't always mean coffee.

'What kind of coffee are we talking about exactly?' I say, playing for time.

'I have one of those Italian machines that cost as much as a small car,' says Jonathan. 'I love showing it off. So you'd be doing me a favour.'

OK, fine. This sounds like genuine, actual coffee. As opposed to the kind of coffee that never gets made. It might be my imagination, but looking at the French couples walking by us, it seems like they're drifting off back to their tiny wooden-beamed attic rooms for some afternoon delight.

'Poppy?'

'Sorry. Yes, sure. Coffee sounds great,' I say. 'Don't be silly,' I add as he makes to pay the bill. 'I can expense it.'

That was the perfect thing to say, I decide, as we leave the

28

elegant arcades of the square. It puts us right back on a work footing. I am not going to mess up this book deal just because he's gorgeous and I'm a few Kirs to the wind. Anyway, it's the middle of the day; nothing untoward is going to happen.

'Watch out, Poppy,' Jonathan says, and pulls me back by my arm. He's just saved me from nearly getting knocked down by a couple of people wobbling by on Vélib bikes. Shaking his fist at them, he yells after them in French, sounding very Gallic and indignant.

'Thanks,' I murmur. Was it my imagination or did his hand leave my arm a bit reluctantly? Oh God, this is unfair. Why does the most attractive man I've met in ages have to be off-limits because of work?

Weirdly, Jonathan seems on edge as well. He's suddenly become very chatty, pointing out landmarks as we walk.

'So,' he says. 'This is the rue des Francs Bourgeois – it was almshouses originally, but now it's the home of the real bourgeoisie; they've got every shop here from L'Occitane to Ted Baker. Oh, that's the Musée Carnavalet . . . it was the home of the Marquise de Sévigné. You must read her letters . . . this is a great ice-cream place – want one? No? Me neither . . . and this is me, to the right.'

We turn on to a quiet side street. Jonathan punches the code of number five and the huge, heavy door swings open. I step over the lintel and we enter a peaceful cobbled courtyard, with actual white doves pecking around the middle. The contrast between this and the bustle of the street we just left couldn't be greater.

'Wow,' I breathe. 'These courtyards are so magical – I love that sense that you just enter the code and step into a hidden, private world—'

'*Bonjour, Monsieur Villder,*' says a loud voice. '*Bonjour, mademoiselle.*' A tiny figure in flowery overalls pokes her head out of a cubby to the right.

'*Bonjour, Madame Gibert,*' Jonathan says.

'*Bonjour, madame,*' I add.

She takes a good look at me before ducking back into her cubby, where the TV is blaring. Jonathan says, 'Not so private really . . . but I love the fact that this is one of the few buildings still in Paris with a real *concierge*.' He leads me to a broad flight of steps to the left: dark polished oak, worn smooth by countless feet over the centuries. Jonathan gestures me to go ahead – what a gentleman – and I walk up the stairs ahead of him, hoping I look OK from behind.

'How old is this building?' I ask.

'Seventeenth century. Hence we're *sans ascenceur*.'

No lift. Well, that puts it in perspective. People must have climbed these stairs hundreds, thousands of times, during the Revolution, during the war, probably lots of them in order to do stupid things. Including sleep with the wrong people. Maybe the reason people go so crazy in love in Paris is because you're surrounded by the evidence of hundreds of years of bad behaviour. With every step I feel as if I'm coming closer to doing something very foolish, and not caring one bit.

'Here we are.' He holds the door open for me and ushers me in.

It's my dream apartment. Whitewashed walls, low leather sofas, and two huge windows that overlook the street. Dark wooden beams on the ceiling. Two sides of the room are lined with bookshelves filled with paperbacks, hefty-looking hardbacks and art books. There's a cinema poster for *Les Liaisons Dangereuses* – the 1950s version. His desk overlooks the street. To the right, there's a cosy galley kitchen with a table and two chairs.

'I love your place.'

'Just a simple *deux-pièces*,' says Jonathan, handing me a glass of water. 'I've had it about a year. It's not big, but it suits me.'

'Good lord, is that a Matisse?' I ask, looking at the wall behind him.

'Just a lithograph,' he says. With a smile, he adds, 'I'm not *that* successful.'

I can't exactly remember what a lithograph is, and I don't want to ask Jonathan. I perch on the edge of a sofa and sip my water. He's even added ice and lemon; colour me impressed.

'Now. Chopin, or Duke Ellington?' he asks, lifting up two records.

'Either,' I say, even though to be honest I'm not a huge jazz fan; soul music is more my thing.

'The Duke, I think. It's too hot for Chopin.' He puts the record on, then looks at me and adds, 'I think . . . I think I'll open a window.'

There's something in the air here. I haven't felt it in a very long time, but I'm feeling it now and I know I'm not imagining it. I walk slowly, following him to the window, and watch as he wrestles with the latch. There's a drop of sweat on his forehead. I have a mad urge to lick it off.

'Finally,' he says, getting it open at last. 'Just a second . . .' He turns aside to write something down in a notebook.

'Nice breeze,' I say, fanning my hair with my hand.

He stares at me and seems to swallow. 'That's a pretty bracelet,' he says. He reaches out and brushes it with his fingertips. 'Or is it a bangle?' His fingers close gently around it.

Now it's my turn to swallow. 'Actually, it's more of a . . . cuff.'

'Such a rich vocabulary,' he murmurs. His hand is still on my arm. And then he's pulling me forward . . . and Jonathan Wilder is kissing me.

Instantly, we both go wild. All the pent-up frustration seems to explode and I'm kissing him back, running my hands through his hair, grabbing his body and pressing it against me. I don't care any more about his book or how dangerous this is: I just want him, now.

'Let's go next door,' he murmurs. He leads me into the bedroom, where we fall back on to his pristine white sheets. He slides the straps of my jumpsuit down, and I slip out of it, revealing the black and pink bra, which he takes off skilfully before kissing me all over and reducing me to jelly. Now we're kissing again, and he's driving me mad by sliding his hands up my thighs and slowly, delicately, stroking me between my legs, through the thin material of the jumpsuit, until I feel as if I'm going to explode. Sitting upright, I wriggle out of it completely, wishing I hadn't worn something so awkward to take off. He pulls off his own clothes and I see that yes, you can spend all day writing the important literature of our time and still have a great body.

There's a brief interruption while Jonathan produces a condom from beside the bed. Then he kisses me again, lowers himself slowly on to me . . . and then we're moving together and it is incredible. He's muttering all the most flattering things – about how sexy and gorgeous I am – in *French*. I feel as if I'm in a film or a music video, complete with four-poster bed and billowing white sheets. Or maybe this is a dream; I can't quite believe it's happening.

Afterwards we lie together, breathless and flushed, and wait for our heartbeats to subside.

'That wasn't exactly how I expected the afternoon to go,' I murmur.

'I know.' I can feel him grinning; his cheek is beside my forehead. 'We never did have that coffee. Would you like some?'

'I would. But not yet – you don't have to get it yet.' I know it sounds sad, but this is something I've missed just as much: not just the sex (though yes, I missed that), but being close to someone, lying together afterwards. With Jonathan's arm around me, and his leg thrown over mine, I'm in a state of utter bliss.

'Poppy Desmond,' he murmurs, stroking my back, 'you were not what I expected either.'

I have to admit, I love the sound of him saying my name. I also love it when, later on, he fetches me a blue silk kimono to wear and we lie curled up on his sofa, drinking his coffee.

'This is really good,' I say, sipping it. 'That machine's worth whatever you paid. The coffee's good, too.'

'Thanks. I get it from a little Italian shop near the Bourse. I've run into Carla there, so I suppose that's a good sign.'

'Carla?'

'Oh, sorry – Bruni.' He knows Carla Bruni. Of course he does; he's Jonathan Wilder. Oh God. I can't believe what we've just done.

Somewhere in the distance, a church bell is striking. Five o'clock. Any minute now, reality is going to come flooding back.

'What is that expression – *cinq à sept*?' I ask quickly, to prevent any awkward realisations. 'Isn't it something to do with affairs?'

'It's the time when French men traditionally saw their mistresses, in between leaving the office and going home.'

'How sexist,' I sniff. 'What about the women having affairs?

32

Also, have you noticed how obsessed French cinema is with adultery? Every single French film I've seen is about an affair, it's unbelievable.' I could easily continue ranting but I stop myself just in time.

'Yes, perhaps,' says Jonathan. 'I think it's because they're more tolerant of shades of grey – they're not moralistic like American films.'

As we chat, I think: maybe this could actually work. I could publish him and have a relationship with him. There's no law against it, is there? Plenty of couples work together . . . And then I thank God that he's presumably not psychic, and has no idea what I'm thinking.

'So,' he says, after a while. 'What are you doing this evening?'

'This evening?' I wish I knew what he had in mind before answering. If I tell him I'm free and he doesn't ask me out, I'll feel bad. Ditto if I make up some story and then he says he has tickets to the opera.

'Well, no specific plans. Charlie suggested getting some dinner somewhere, but we haven't pinned anything down . . .' When he doesn't say anything, I add lightly, 'What about you?'

'I'm heading out to dinner with some friends. It's way out in the burbs – Saint-Germain-en-Laye. It takes forever to get there, on the RER.'

God, he sounds so sexy when he speaks French. I can just picture the evening: a small civilised gathering, all sitting outside on a candlelit terrace, talking about art and politics and books . . . but I think that was a subtle hint.

'I suppose I'd better get back to my hotel. Check that Charlie hasn't killed himself on Constance's motorbike,' I say as casually as I can, standing up and hunting for my clothes.

'You know, Poppy, I'd invite you, but I haven't seen these guys in a while . . .'

'Of course not,' I say quickly. 'Anyway, I'll be seeing you for lunch tomorrow.' I finish pulling on my jumpsuit. 'Now, where are my shoes?'

Jonathan goes back into the bedroom and re-emerges with them. 'Let me walk you downstairs.'

'It's fine, honestly.'

'Poppy,' he says seriously, as we walk to the door. 'Do we need to talk about this?'

'No, of course not,' I say again. 'It just happened and it was great, and I'll see you tomorrow.'

He nods and bends his head and kisses me again. I feel my insides melt, but as soon as I can, I force myself to pull away.

'OK, I'd better go. Have a good evening. See you tomorrow.'

'*A demain*,' he says. He reaches out, kisses my hand, gives me a last, regretful look, then closes the door.

Back down the stairs I go, in a daze. But I'm not thinking about centuries of history now; I'm thinking about tonight, and lunch tomorrow and . . . oh shit, I just slept with the author.

I can't figure out how to open the door, so of course Madame Whatsit has to come and help me, devouring me with curious eyes as she does. I hope her manic interest means she hasn't often seen Jonathan with a woman before. As I step back over the threshold, I feel a bit like a cat that's been put out for the night. Was he trying to get rid of me? But then I tell myself not to be paranoid. He's just going out this evening. That's allowed!

Back on the rue des Francs Bourgeois, the shadows are lengthening. The city seems to have a new energy, and people are coming alive for the evening. I gaze at all the couples going past me, intertwined. I'm sure lots of them started under dodgy circumstances: working together, already attached . . . But that's dangerous thinking. I can't allow myself to believe that Jonathan and I will be a couple. This could well have been just a one-off thing. In which case we'll handle it like grown-ups.

As I walk along, I find myself humming a tune. I realise it's Air's 'Sexy Boy'. Oops. My subconscious isn't exactly subtle. I hope I can appear normal tomorrow, in front of Charlie and Constance. Suddenly all my paranoia is back and I'm wondering: what is Jonathan thinking now? What's it going to be like seeing him tomorrow for lunch? And what am I going to wear?

Walking past a shop window, I catch sight of my reflection and feel a moment of doubt. Is this jumpsuit as cute as I think, or do I actually look as if I'm in fancy dress? I've never been interested in expensive designer clothes; I've always wanted to have fun with what I wear. I'm used to looking at clothes in shops and thinking that I could make something nicer, or find the original that it's ripped off. But the clothes here are something I could never make.

One dress in particular catches my eye – a simple sleeveless shift in a zingy orange colour. I walk into the shop and try it on. The size 40 fits me perfectly and the material is so lovely: a smooth silk–cotton mix.

'I have the bigger size, if you would like it,' the sales assistant says – in English, to add insult to injury. Surprised, I go back and check my reflection from different angles, but it seems to fit perfectly. What a cow. I tell her the 40 is just fine and take it to the till. It's more than I've spent on a dress in a long time, but I tell myself it's a professional investment. Also, it's euros, which don't count.

After walking home the long way round – via the Louvre (well, via a *millefeuille* pastry at Angelina's next door), the Tuileries and the Pont des Arts – I arrive back at the hotel and run straight into Charlie in the lobby.

'How's it going? I see you've hit the shops,' he says.

'What? Oh, yes.' I sit down on one of the couches to rest my aching feet, and he sits opposite me. 'We had lunch and then coffee . . . and then I walked home. I think it went well. We talked about the book and he liked my suggestions.' I pick up a flyer for the Louvre and fan myself with it, hoping he'll attribute my blush to the heat. 'How about you, how did you get on with the lovely Constance?'

'It was fantastic! I talked her through our publishing plans, and then we went for a ride along the quays – it's a scooter she's got, not a motorbike – as far as the Eiffel Tower and back. We stopped off at this amazing little café and had the best lunch . . . and then I went up to this park near here called the Luxembourg Gardens, that Constance told me about. Why did no one ever tell me about all this before?'

I don't even know how to begin to answer that one.

'Um, well, Paris is quite popular . . .'

'All anyone ever talks about is the Louvre, though. But

Constance says it's too big, and she much prefers the Musée . . . d'Olay or something?'

'The Musée d'Orsay. Yes, that is a great museum.' My head's beginning to hurt from a combination of sun, Kir and anxiety, and I decide I have to get away from Charlie, have a cold shower and lie down somewhere.

'Anyway,' Charlie says, 'when are you meeting your friend?'

'What? Oh. Not till later. I'm just going to have a little freshen-up first. What are you doing?'

'I'm going to head out with Constance. I would have asked her if you could join us, but you said you were busy. I booked us a restaurant for tomorrow, by the way. Not the one Jonathan said – that was a bit pricey – but another one.'

'Great. Lovely. Look forward to it,' I say, and flee up the stairs before he can ask me any more questions. Let him go out with Constance; I'm staying in tonight and ordering room service, before I get into any more trouble.

'Are you nervous?' Charlie asks me the next day, as we go up in the lift towards Les Ombres restaurant. It's on the roof of the ethnographic museum on the Quai Branly, which seems an odd place to find a great restaurant, but Constance recommended it and presumably knows what's good.

'Nervous about what?' I say, edgily.

'About whether they're going to accept our offer? I get the impression they're going to tell us over lunch.'

'Oh. Of course not,' I say. And it's mostly true. I think it's going to be OK. Jonathan loved my editorial suggestions. Constance loves our publishing plans. And Jonathan and I will figure all the other stuff out.

The terrace has a fabulous view of the rooftops of Paris, domi-nated by the Eiffel Tower. It's so close that you can see people going up and down in the lifts. The other diners are mostly men and women who I presume work in the government buildings nearby – though in their designer suits, they look considerably more dashing than British civil servants.

'You look great, by the way,' says Charlie. It's nice of him to throw a bone my way when he's so clearly got a crush on

Constance. He's made an effort himself, wearing a self-consciously trendy shiny navy blue jacket with the sleeves rolled up over a grey T-shirt. Then Jonathan and Constance arrive. Constance looks lovely in a white high-necked blouse and skinny black trousers. I can't take in what Jonathan's wearing, other than it's some kind of jacket and tie; I concentrate on making sure that I smile, stand up to receive his cheek kisses and generally act normal.

Occasionally when I'm in an important meeting or other formal situation, I get a mad urge to say something completely inappropriate. This is one of those times: I wonder what would happen if I told everyone, 'Hey! Jonathan and I slept together yesterday.' Luckily I'm prevented from doing so by our waiter, who wants to know about drinks.

'Actually,' says Jonathan, 'why don't we make it champagne?' He shoots me a modest look. 'We certainly feel like celebrating.'

For a surreal moment I wonder if he's about to tell everyone we're an item or something, but then I see that Constance is smiling too. She says, 'We'd like to accept your offer to publish Jonathan's book.'

Praise the Lord! As the waiter comes back with our champagne, I thank baby Jesus and all the angels that what happened yesterday obviously didn't mess anything up. Or . . . A very icky thought strikes me. Could it actually have *helped*? Does Jonathan think he's landed himself an editor with benefits? Surely not.

'That's great news. We're thrilled. Well, Jonathan, here's to your book,' I say, holding up a glass.

'To the book.' Jonathan holds my eye as he toasts. Then he pauses, glass mid-air, and thinks for a while before adding, 'And to our partnership.'

The conversation turns to writers we might send the book to for an endorsement. Jonathan has lots of celebrity and literary friends, but Constance also seems to be on first-name terms with all sorts of big fish.

'Wow, Constance, you have great contacts,' I say.

'Yes, I do know lots of people,' she says calmly.

This reminds me of her reaction to my inane compliment

yesterday, about her being brave to ride her motorbike. I'm not used to people – especially women – accepting compliments with such ease instead of contradicting them or apologising. Maybe it's a French thing.

'How about Denis Last?' Charlie is saying. 'He could be a good person to endorse the book.'

'Denis Last?' Jonathan recoils. 'He's very popular, of course, but . . .' He makes the word 'popular' sounds like a skin condition. Which seems a bit odd. Jonathan writes really well, but he is on the popular end of the literary spectrum, after all.

'I love his books,' says Constance. I find myself warming to her more, especially when she tells me how much she admired my 'costume' of yesterday.

'We have some great shops for antique clothes here,' she says. 'There's Kilo Shop in the Marais, which sells things by the kilo, and Odetta.'

'Is there still that place in Clichy – I used to go there all the time – what's it called again?'

'Ah, Guerrisol!'

Jonathan and Charlie are talking about something, but it's a bit stilted, and I get the impression Charlie's waiting to jump in as soon as the clothes talk stops.

'So,' he says. 'Do you all have nice summer holiday plans?'

'I will go to my parents' place in Provence for three weeks in August,' says Constance.

'Three weeks!' Charlie and I say in unison.

'Yes, normally it would be four weeks, but we have to work so much lately, we are becoming like Americans.'

'Nice,' says Charlie. 'I've got a golfing holiday in Portugal with some mates in September. I can't wait.'

'I love Portugal. I went to Lisbon last year for the Disquiet International festival,' says Jonathan. 'I ended up staying up all night drinking *vinho verde* with Ian.'

'Ian?' says Charlie.

'Oh, sorry – McEwan.'

Everyone murmurs politely. I'll admit, I've begun to notice a certain amount of name-dropping in Jonathan's anecdotes. He's also one of those people who reads out the entire name of the dish when ordering food: he's having the *filet de boeuf, pommes Pont Neuf, jus lié au foie gras*. But nobody's perfect.

'How was last night, Jonathan?' Constance asks. 'How is Calyxte?'

'Fine,' says Jonathan briefly. Very briefly, in fact.

'Who's Calyxte?' Charlie enquires.

Jonathan replies, 'A friend,' at the same time as Constance says, 'Jonathan's girlfriend. Her parents live near me, in Saint-Germain-en-Laye, which is just outside Paris.'

'Your girlfriend,' I repeat, staring at him blankly while thinking: *his girlfriend? Her parents?*

'It's complicated,' he says, looking harassed. 'We were together for a while, then we broke up, then we became friends . . .'

'Jonathan, you don't have to complicate your life with these categories,' says Constance, laughing. 'In French we have one expression: *l'homme, ou la femme, de ma vie*. The man of my life, the woman of my life. Very simple. Calyxte is *la femme de ta vie*.'

'Have you met Calyxte?' I ask Constance, concentrating on sounding calm.

'Oh yes, she's very charming and beautiful. She is the editor of a literary magazine.'

'Sounds perfect,' I say icily.

Jonathan is pretending to be absorbed in reading a wine label. 'I think I've been to this vineyard,' he murmurs. 'It's near Johnny's place.'

'Johnny?' Charlie asks.

'Sorry, Depp.'

I get to my feet. 'Will you excuse me a minute?'

As I walk towards the loo, I think: stupid, stupid, stupid. I am so stupid. I've been played, and now I'm in the most effed-up position ever. I slept with an author, who has a girlfriend. Who hosted him for dinner, with her parents, last night, while I was in my tiny hotel room watching badly dubbed *Friends*!

Now I have to work with him and talk to him about his book and hold his hand when he gets a bad review, and I just can't do it. I splash cold water on my wrists, wondering if there's any way out. Maybe I can hand him over to Ellen. But I'd have to explain why, and . . . Aargh. I feel like such a stupid idiot. After all my plans to have a fling with Charlie, I had mindless, meaningless sex with *completely the wrong man.*

I'm so humiliated I'd happily stay in here all day, but I have to go back out and face the music. I'll have to grin and bear it, and as soon as we get out of here I'll figure something out. The elegant surroundings actually help; as I walk towards our table, I decide to channel Glenn Close in *Dangerous Liaisons.* Specifically, the bit where she practises smiling as she sticks a fork into her hand under the table.

However, only Charlie is left at the table.

'They've gone over there for a smoke,' he says. 'Did you just drop something, Poppy?'

He hands me a small black Moleskine notebook. It looks like mine, but I think Jonathan has one like it. I open it up to check, thinking I'll know as soon as I see the handwriting. I find myself reading this:

> *'Isn't Paris the City of Light?'*
> *Cuff, bangle, bracelet – rich vocabulary*
> *Skin the colour of ~~coffee mocha~~ café au lait*
> *Clashes with her mother – father complex?*
> *'Why are all French films about adultery?'*

'Are you all right, Poppy?' says Constance, sitting down again.

'Hey – is that mine?' says Jonathan.

'Yes, it is,' I say, handing it over to him. 'And so's this.' I pick up my half-full wine glass, and empty it over his head. I take one satisfying look at his stupid gaping face, drenched in red wine, and then grab my clutch and walk out, ignoring the scandalised looks from everyone in the restaurant.

Outside, I stab the buttons of the lift and get myself to the ground floor. I emerge into the groovy landscaped gardens of the museum, which has a living wall that I would find really interesting at any other time. I hurry across the road and find myself on a bridge, I'm not sure which one. I'm very tempted to throw myself off it.

'*Excusez-moi, vous n'auriez pas une cigarette?*' I ask a man passing by.

'Yes, of course,' he replies in English, handing me one.

'Thank you, but if you don't mind, I am TRYING to practise my FRENCH!' I scream at him irrationally.

'Poppy!' Charlie rushes up behind me, out of breath. The guy leaves, looking scared. I don't blame him; I am completely losing the plot.

'What the hell was all that about? Hang on a sec.'

He taps the shoulder of a passing intertwined couple – another one! – and gets a light from them.

'I didn't know you smoked,' he says.

'I don't . . . This is sort of an emergency.'

Raising his eyebrows, Charlie steers me off the bridge and down on to the quays, where we find a seat on a bench.

'Did something happen yesterday with you and J-Wild?' says Charlie.

I take a drag of my cigarette and try and get my voice under control. 'Yes.'

'What . . . Oh.' There's a pause, and I can see the penny dropping. 'Oh.'

'I know,' I mutter. 'Please don't tell me how awful it is. I've never done anything like that before in my life.'

'No wonder you flipped when Constance mentioned his girlfriend,' he says.

'It wasn't just that, it was the notebook. He'd been taking notes on me – writing down things I said, things about my life. It was so horrible.'

'Well . . . but he's a writer; that's what they do.'

'Yes, except this has happened to me before,' I say. 'My ex-boyfriend devoted an entire art installation to our relationship. It was called *Bitch Done Me Wrong*.'

'Oh,' says Charlie.

I stare at the murky waters of the Seine, thinking: what is it about me that makes men want to use me for material? Am I just some kind of 'exotic' character to them? And is that whole lunch going to appear in a novel, complete with the drink in the face?

'Oh God, I'm so embarrassed,' I mutter, as the horror of the thing begins to sink in. 'I can't believe I threw a drink in his face.'

41

'I was quite surprised myself,' Charlie says.

I moan again and sink my face into my hands. Then I think of something else. 'Did you pay the bill?' I ask.

'No, I did not. Jonathan can pick up a bill for once in his life.'

'Oh no, Charlie – poor Constance will end up paying. And did the waiters look shocked?'

'The waiters? Not particularly. This is Paris, don't forget. I bet half the women in this city have slung red wine in someone's face at some point. Or *vin rouge*, as Jonathan would say.' He starts to laugh.

'I really can't see what's funny here,' I say coldly.

'I'm sorry, Poppy, it's just . . . His face was so priceless. I know he's a good writer, but he's a bit of a twat, don't you think? With his French phrases and Johnny Depp's vineyard and getting drunk with Ian McEwan.'

I finish my cigarette. I'm tempted to flick the butt into the river, but, ever my mother's daughter, I stub it out and find a bin for it. I'm beginning to feel as if Charlie has a point.

'What kind of things did he jot down in his notebook?' Charlie says. 'If that's not a rude question.'

I groan. 'Just stuff I told him about my mum and dad. And random things I said. And something about mocha-coloured skin, in case I was in any doubt.'

'Seriously? Isn't that a Ricky Martin lyric?'

I start to laugh.

'That's better,' Charlie says. 'Look. We're not going to salvage the whole book thing, are we? Unless you want to go back to Jonathan and tell him you have Tourette's, or you had a flashback to when you were in Vietnam, or something. Do you?'

I shake my head violently, feeling panicked at the thought of having to see Jonathan ever again.

'And our train isn't until tomorrow morning. So we might as well enjoy ourselves. I still haven't been up the Eiffel Tower, you know.'

'Charlie, I can't swan around pretending I'm on holiday. I've got to figure out what I'm going to tell Ellen. And what is Constance going to do, and Jonathan? If the whole thing gets out, I could be fired.'

'You won't be,' says Charlie. 'I promise. Don't forget, he doesn't come out very well from it either. Now, how about you show me some of the sights of Paris?'

Six hours later, I'm sitting at a table in a bar near the Eiffel Tower, flipping through my Instagram pictures of our day out. There's one of me flattening my nose against the window of Ladurée; me afterwards with a box full of *macarons*. There's Charlie having a huge pistachio ice cream on a *bateau mouche* river trip down the Seine, which he insisted on us taking although I told him it was a rip-off, strictly for tourists.

'But we *are* tourists,' he pointed out.

To my surprise, the *bateau mouche* was great, dodgy loudspeaker commentary aside. And there's the two of us at the top of the Eiffel Tower, my hair blown vertical by the wind. Charlie claimed to be scared of heights and said he needed a drink afterwards, so we're now having very overpriced gin and tonics off the Champ de Mars. The trauma of lunch has receded, and I'm actually having a great time. Charlie doesn't quote Virginia Woolf, and he's not going to expand my horizons or anything, but he is fun.

'I'm sorry we didn't have time to go into the Musée d'Orsay,' I say archly as he rejoins me, wondering if he'll remember that this was a tip from his beloved Constance.

'The what? Oh, the art museum. To be honest, I don't see the point of hanging around in art museums when you're in a foreign city. I mean, they have lots of art in London, right?'

I smile, thinking: he is sweet, but he's still a bit of a philistine.

'Much more important,' he says, 'is where you want to eat tonight. I've heard good things about a place across the river.'

'Sure.' I'm about to ask where he got his tip from before remembering: of course, it must be from Constance. I wonder what the deal is with them. When they went out together yesterday – was that a date? I might ask him over dinner. Not that I'm curious, of course.

After a short Métro ride, we get out at the Pont d'Iéna, and start walking down one of the massive avenues that run parallel to the Seine.

'Are you sure we got out at the right stop?' I ask doubtfully. I should have known better than to trust him with something as important as dinner. I'm now starving, and if we have to trek for hours before we eat, I'm going to be very bad company. I'm like the Incredible Hulk; you wouldn't like me when I'm hungry.

'Here we are,' he says, sounding pleased with himself. We're outside a vast stone modernist building right by the river.

'Wait. Is this the Palais de Tokyo? It is!' I remember this place: it's a gigantic space dedicated to experimental art. Outside, it looks like a 1930s stone palace; inside, it's all unfinished, like an aircraft hangar or Battersea Power Station.

'Apparently it has a very good restaurant. Art museums always do.'

He's absolutely right. The dining room is a huge, buzzing space, with Manga cartoons decorating the windows and futuristic-looking giant red lanterns hanging from the high ceilings. The menu looks very exciting – we've barely sat down before I'm eyeing up a caramel chicken dish. Screw the diet; I'm in Paris.

'It seems a bit of a waste not to look at the art,' I say guiltily, as we take our seats. 'I saw a sign for some kind of pop-up exhibition about Chanel Number 5 . . .'

'I wouldn't understand it. I haven't seen Number 1, 2, 3 or 4.'

I laugh. I'm relieved to see, in the mirror opposite, that the orange dress is still going strong after a day trekking up and down towers. I wish I'd thought to bring my make-up bag to do a touch-up – but it doesn't matter, I remind myself. It's just Charlie.

'I might have a cocktail,' he says, as the waiter comes over. 'What about you? One of your Kirs?'

'Definitely not.' I shudder. I order a glass of white wine, and for once the waiter doesn't reply in English. This is now officially my happy place. When our drinks arrive, Charlie lifts his glass to me.

'To Paris,' he says. 'And to you. And to me. And to publishing. And to world peace. And to Manga—'

'OK. Very funny.' But I'm laughing. He does sound a bit like Jonathan. 'What are you going to have?'

'Hm. Difficult, but probably the cauliflower soufflé, and the seared liver.' He frowns. 'They've put cow's liver in the English menu, but they must mean calf's, no?'

'I'm sure they do. Beef liver is practically inedible, isn't it?'

'It's not inedible, but it's very gamey. I wouldn't cook it myself. It would need a strong sauce. Whereas calf's liver just needs a dash of sherry, some butter and a very hot pan. And maybe some sage. And maybe some crispy little matchsticks of bacon.' He puts his menu down. 'I'm obviously hungrier than I thought.' And leaning sideways from his seat, he waves frantically, as if he's hailing a cab: gauche but very effective, as the waiter comes straight over.

After we've ordered, I say curiously, 'I didn't know you were quite so into your food.' What I mean is: I've seen him stuff it down himself at every opportunity, but I didn't know he could actually make it himself.

'I love food. Can't you tell?' He pretends to pinch an inch. Two girls beside us see him doing so, and I notice they're blatantly checking him out. I suppose his blond, blue-eyed looks are even more potent in Paris, because of the novelty value.

'Don't be silly, you're not fat,' I say.

'I will be if I keep going to MEATliquor.'

'Oh God, I love MEATliquor! I just wish I didn't have to deal with the queues. That's the annoying thing: so many of the places with good food, you have to queue at. It drives me crazy. I mean, do they do it to create hype or what?' I continue in this vein for a while before I realise he's smiling. 'What?'

'Nothing, I just like it when you rant on about stuff. I eat at home mostly, anyway.' He makes a tragic face. 'Nobody to eat out with.'

'So do you cook a lot?'

'Almost every evening, for me and my brother. He's in the police force, so he's not always home of an evening. But I like to think he's the only bobby on his beat who comes home to fried polenta and mushrooms with parmesan crisps . . . or a goat's cheese soufflé with a fennel and almond salad . . . or a really good steak and chips.'

'Do you make the chips?' I ask, mentally adjusting to this new picture of cordon bleu Charlie.

'Of course. We even have a deep-fat fryer.'

'I don't think I could trust myself with a deep-fat fryer,' I admit.

'I know. When I first got it, everything we ate was crispy brown. What about you, do you like cooking?'

'I love it. Sometimes I'm a bit lazy when it's just me, but I love having people round. Especially for brunches. I do a big frittata with feta and spring onions, and make a batch of mimosas. You should come sometime,' I add, impulsively.

'I would love to,' he says, looking pleased. 'This is excellent, by the way. Would you like to try some?'

I'm relieved that he doesn't try to feed me, but puts a bit on my plate. 'Wow. Yum. So where did you learn to cook?'

'Well, my dad was a cook.'

'Where?'

'Wormwood Scrubs.'

'What, the prison?'

'Yep.' He takes a sip of wine. 'I used to cook at home with him. And then when I left school, I got work in a restaurant kitchen in Richmond. But I wasn't cut out for kitchen life, so I decided to escape it for something clean and dry. I applied to college and did my English degree . . . and here I am.'

Good lord. So Charlie, who I always took to be a middle-class boy putting on a mockney accent, was basically raised in a prison. I shake my head.

'I wish Jonathan had been listening to you yesterday, not me. He'd have found a lot more to put in his notebook.'

'Well,' he says, 'you're a lot prettier than me.'

I don't know what to say to that, so I change the subject. 'So what's the story with you and Constance?' I say coyly. 'You seemed to take quite a shine to her.'

'What – you mean romantically?' He looks blank. 'No. She's a nice girl, and she *does* have a scooter, but . . . I suppose I like a woman with a bit more fire in her belly.' He grins at me, and my stomach does a backflip. I'm a little nervous for some reason; I think we need another subject change.

'So,' I say, 'don't you think it's unfair that Katie Chipshop's books are going to sell billions of copies when my novel got turned down?'

'Not really. I think if your novel was good enough it would have spoken to more people there. And Katie . . .' He reaches out and pulls a bit of wax off the candle. 'She may not have had much education but she's had lots of interesting experiences. I think it's good that she's able to tell her story, and that people who wouldn't read otherwise might be tempted to read because they know her.'

I hadn't thought of it that way before and I have to admit he makes a good point. I like the way he's thinking about it. And I like his blue eyes and the stubble on his chin. In fact there's no point in denying it any more: I like him. I like Charlie. And it's not just because he's so handsome; it's because he's so much brighter, and more interesting, than I'd realised.

'Why did you diss the coffee at my pet sandwich bar?' I ask him suddenly. 'I was trying to support them, by bringing in their cakes.'

'Oh. Sorry about that. I shouldn't have kicked them in the nuts while they were down. But seriously, you have to admit their coffee is rank.'

'Hmph.' It is true their coffee isn't great. It's sort of thin and watery. 'Well, maybe. But you have to admit their *pasteis de nata* are sublime.'

'The cakes were delicious,' he says solemnly. 'Best I've ever had. I'll write to the *Times* about them. Get Giles Coren to do a review.'

'Don't take the piss.'

Charlie leans forward. 'Poppy,' he says softly. 'I'm truly sorry I dissed the café. The cakes really were delicious.'

I look down and see that his hand is lying very close to mine on the table. He moves it closer, until our fingers are touching. I glance up to find him still looking right at me.

'*Désirez-vous un dessert ou un café?*' asks our waiter.

We both shake our heads. When the bill comes, Charlie insists on paying it.

'Make sure you keep the receipt, so you can expense it,' I remind him.

'No, I want to pay,' Charlie says illogically.

I can't think of anything to say to that. We walk out of the restaurant and take a stroll down to the Seine. The sun is setting, sending pink streaks across the sky, but you can still see the *bateaux mouches* going by all lit up, the Eiffel Tower with its lights coming on too, and even the Musée Branly, site of our disastrous lunch. I'm racking my brains for something cool and normal to say, but before I can think of anything, our hands are brushing together and I'm holding his. Then he's turning me towards him. And just like that, we've become one of those Parisian couples, kissing the life out of each other, oblivious to everyone around them but themselves.

We get back on the Métro and make our way to the hotel, stopping every so often to kiss again. He's exactly the right height to walk beside me with his arm draped around me.

'Suite 105,' Charlie says, at the hotel desk.

'And room 106,' I add. I want him to know that I'm not going to sleep with him tonight. Not after what happened with Jonathan; I can't – though I really, really want to.

However, there doesn't seem to be much harm in going into the suite with him. He sits on the chaise longue, pulls me on to his lap, and we start kissing again. I'd forgotten how exciting kissing can be. He's so gorgeous, and his lips are so firm and soft and he smells so nice: faint aftershave, and laundry detergent, and boy. Now his hand is inching up my leg . . . If I don't leave now, I won't be able to leave at all. I *should* leave.

But I can't. I physically can't tear myself away from him. And I don't want to. Instead, we continue kissing, and then I help him pull my dress down, all the way. I take off his jacket and his T-shirt, and kiss his chest while he wriggles out of his jeans. He has lots of trouble with my bra strap, so I have to help him take it off, which makes us both laugh. And then we're on the floor of his suite, and it's far too late to stop. It's not soft-focus and perfect, like it was with Jonathan; it's passionate and raw, and I probably look sweaty and unglamorous but I don't care; it feels so amazing that I lose all my inhibitions, and soon I lose control completely, right before he does.

'I'm parched,' he murmurs later, when we're lying curled up together in his bed. 'Do you want anything to drink from the minibar? Some water?'

'Oh, we shouldn't. The minibar's so expensive. I shouldn't have had anything from it.'

He smiles. 'Given how badly we've behaved already this weekend, I think a mineral water from the minibar is the least of our problems.'

He goes and pours us both a glass of Badoit. I'm half admiring his naked body, and half ruminating on what he said: given how badly we've behaved already this weekend.

Of course, what he really means is how badly *I've* behaved. Sleeping with two men in forty-eight hours.

'Come here, gorgeous,' he says, handing me the mineral water and pulling me into his arms for another kiss.

But I can't relax. I keep thinking, what if he thinks I'm easy because I slept with Jonathan and now him? I couldn't blame him. What if he has the same idea I had when I came on this trip, and he just wants a one-night stand?

'When you say how badly we've behaved, you mean me, right?' I ask, sitting up.

'What? No! I was joking.' He pulls me back down beside him.

'Well I could say the same thing. What about whatshername in publicity – and those other girls?' I know I'm being insane, but I can't seem to stop myself.

'What about them? I'm single, they were single . . .' He looks angry now. 'Look, I can forget about Jonathan – why can't you forget about them?'

I sit bolt upright again. 'I *knew* this would end up being about Jonathan. You can't get over the fact that I slept with him yesterday, and you think I'm a complete slut. Don't you?'

'Poppy, of course I don't think that.' But he doesn't sound completely convinced.

'Yes you do. I'm out of here and this never happened. OK?' I pull on my dress quickly, pick up my underwear, and jam my feet into my mules, forgetting that the stupid things take ages to put on. I decide to shuffle with them out of the door, but the shuffle goes wrong, and all at once the floor is flying towards me and I'm lying on the carpet with Charlie standing over me looking worried, and something very wrong with my ankle.

*   *   *

'It's just a bad sprain,' I tell Ellen for the millionth time. 'I'm honestly fine, but it's easier for me to work from home for the next few days, if that's OK.'

'Of course it's OK! I feel awful that you got injured in the line of duty.'

'No, believe me, this was totally my fault,' I say, staring down at my ankle.

The trip home from Paris was pretty unpleasant. Charlie and I weren't really speaking to each other, though he did help me with my stupidly heavy bag and with the crutches supplied by the hotel doctor. But at least I get to avoid the office for a few days.

'I'm sorry about Jonathan Wilder,' I add to Ellen. 'Did the agent say, um, anything else when she rang you?'

'No – she just said he felt you weren't suited.'

Whew. I send a little prayer of thanks in the direction of Constance in Paris, who has proved herself a real sister under the skin. It seems my secret is safe – until the mocha-skinned, hot-tempered heroine of Jonathan's next book makes an appearance. I've also decided to take a leaf out of Constance's book and take compliments in my stride – if I ever get one again, that is.

'Which reminds me, Poppy. That first novel you raised last week, the one set in Lagos?'

'Yes?'

'The film rights have sold! Can you believe it? I heard from the scouts. It's the same production company that made . . . well, it's all in an email anyway, which I'll forward to you. I think you should bid for it.'

'Seriously? You don't think it's too late?'

'Well, it might be – but it's worth a try.'

'Wow. Thank you, Ellen.'

We discuss the amount I can offer and then I put a call through to the agent, who says they're reviewing offers right now and she'll get back to me. It's funny: last week they were probably biting their nails, and now they're fighting off interest.

It's like me. Before I went to Paris, I'd had zero interest from, or in, men for the best part of a year. It was as if I'd developed a sort of force field that prevented anyone from approaching me. And then in the space of three days I was with two different men. It's a pity that one of them was someone I really liked, and I screwed it up.

I still feel sad about Charlie and I'm kicking myself. Why did I have to pick a fight with him over Jonathan and the girls at work? Now I'll never know if things would have worked out with him or not. I know that on the face of it, it doesn't look promising. We are very different; not to mention I'm twenty-nine and he's twenty-six, which is like sixteen in boy years. But I feel as if there was something there – or there could have been.

Suddenly I make a decision. I'm going to swallow my pride and email him, and tell him I'm regretting the way things worked out. I agonise over it for twenty minutes before sending a short email saying I'm sorry I acted like a nutter, and asking him if he'd like to go for a drink when I'm back at work. He might just ignore it, of course, but at least I'll know one way or the other.

'When I accused Charlie of not being able to get over the fact that I slept with Jonathan, I think it was really that *I* wasn't able to get over the fact that I slept with Jonathan,' I explain to Alice when she calls me the following evening. 'Two guys in two days: I felt like such a slapper.'

'Don't feel like that. I think you did the right thing emailing him,' she says. 'Have you heard back at all?'

'Not yet. I'll keep you posted.' I'm trying to sound cheerful, but I know that an email silence of twenty-four hours doesn't bode well. 'Anyway. How about you? What's your news?'

'Well,' Alice says. 'You know that American literary scout I had an interview with?'

'Yes! Did you hear anything?'

'Yep. I got the job. So we're going to move in September. You'll have to visit us in LA!'

'That's brilliant!' I say. 'Fantastic news, darling! Congratulations!' I am thrilled for Alice, but when we hang up, I feel deeply doomful. She's my best friend and I am going to miss her horribly. And also, I can't help noticing how her life is evolving, while mine is like a CD stuck on repeat. She's jetting off to LA with her boyfriend, who I'm sure she'll end up marrying, and I have trouble getting through a pint of milk by myself before it goes off.

Well, never mind. Onwards and upwards. I have my career, and my friends, and a new sewing machine. And there's always online dating. I take out my computer, intending to log on and work on my profile, but instead I end up checking my email yet again to see if Charlie's replied to my olive branch.

Nothing. Not a peep. And if he hasn't replied by now, he's probably not going to reply at all. Feeling miserable, I decide I can't face internet dating tonight; instead I'm going to run a hot bath and read a good book. I have the whole Booker shortlist to get through, but tonight I think I'll treat myself to my favourite guilty pleasure: an Enid Blyton book. Maybe *First Term at Malory Towers*. I keep them stowed in a secret box under my bed, even though there's nobody to see them but me.

First, though, I have to make myself some dinner. Except there's absolutely nothing to eat except half an avocado, a tin of lentils and some dried pasta. I hazily contemplate avocado lentil pasta, before I realise I'm going to have to phone for a takeaway – again. Getting around with the crutches is so knackering, I can't face walking down four flights of stairs to go to the shops. It's one of the many down sides of living alone: when you're sick, you have to rely on airlifts of food aid from your local Indian or pizza place.

I'm just rummaging in the kitchen drawer for the Spice Palace takeaway leaflet when I hear a ring at the doorbell. I assume it's one of the neighbours or someone selling something, but it's Charlie, out of breath from the stairs and holding two big Tupperware containers.

'Hi there,' he says. 'How are you?'

I stare at him in shock for a few seconds before I manage to say, 'I'm fine! What brings you here?'

'I thought you might want some provisions while you're still hopping.'

'Wow. That's amazing – come in.' Dazed, I watch as he walks in, puts his containers on the table and takes a loaf of brown bread, a bottle of white wine and a pint of milk out of his Red Bull bag.

'I didn't make the bread,' he says. 'But I did make you a chicken pie . . . and this is a *cassoulet*. In case you were missing France. Thanks for your email, by the way. I'm sorry I didn't reply – I took the day off today to do some cooking.'

I look at him unpacking his provisions. I can't believe he cooked all this stuff for me, and came all the way over to my place with it. I thought only girlfriends would schlep across town and bring you food when you're sick, but I was wrong about that. I was wrong about a lot of things, it seems.

'Charlie, this is so nice of you. Thank you. How did you even know where I lived?'

He puts a finger to the side of his nose. 'That's the advantage of having a brother in the Force . . . No, I'm joking. I asked Sorrell.' He digs into his bag and produces a white cardboard box. 'Here's something else I thought you might like . . .'

I open it up and find four *pasteis de nata* from the Bar San Marco. I look up at him and just grin stupidly, because I can't think of anything adequate to say.

'If I were you, I'd have the pie tonight, and the *cassoulet* will reheat nicely for tomorrow,' he says. 'And before you ask, yes, I did make the pastry. Ever noticed how, any time you produce a pie, people ask you if you made the pastry? What's that all about?'

I realise he's nervous, which makes me love him even more.

'I hope you can stay and have some with me,' I say. 'Do you want to open up that wine? The glasses are above the hob, on the right.'

'Great,' he says, looking happy. 'I'll just stick these cakes in the fridge . . . we can have them for dessert.'

I crutch over to him, take his face between my hands and kiss him. He looks surprised at first, but then he kisses me back passionately, putting one arm around me to support me so that I don't need the crutch. I decide that we might not get around to having those cakes for dessert, but it doesn't matter; they'll also be very nice for breakfast.

POPPY

You know it's not going to be the most productive day when you're googling 'George Clooney pet pig' before 10 a.m.

But it's that kind of day. It's the middle of August, the heat-wave is in its second week and the office air conditioning keeps breaking down. All the bosses are away and nobody can cope with any mental challenges greater than choosing between a Solero or a Mint Magnum. I feel like I'm losing an IQ point with every degree the temperature rises. But that's OK: I read an article in the *New York Times* recently saying that stupid people were happier. Or was it that being happy made you stupid? Something like that. I re-read one of my college essays recently and I wasn't at all sure what it was about. Though I know the real reason I'm so happy and it has nothing to do with the temperature or my IQ . . .

I'm startled by a brisk knock at the door. Charlie's standing in the doorway. He nods to me and Sorrell, who sits in the cubby right outside my little office.

'I just wondered if you'd had a chance to read my draft report on our email campaigns?' he asks, very formally. His sleeves are rolled up and his arms are all tanned against the white cotton of his shirt. Raaaaaawrrr.

'Oh yes,' I say, in the same formal tone. 'It was . . . very interesting. Particularly the bit about the . . . click-through rates.'

'Yes?' he says, almost sternly. 'And what about the section on test emails?'

'Yes, I thought that was good,' I say, clearing my throat. 'Very helpful. Especially the ones with one key link versus . . . lots of links.'

'Don't forget to send me through anything you want to add – from your perspective.'

'Will do,' I say, very crisply.

'Great. Thanks. Bye, Poppy.' He strides off and I find myself staring at his rear before I turn back to my computer, hiding a smirk.

Charlie and I decided this morning, as we took the Tube in together from my place, that we'd better continue having conversations in the office – just so as not to arouse any suspicion. Then I got off a stop early and went into Bar San Marco to get a coffee (though I really just wanted a *pasteis de nata* cake and the coffee was an excuse). We never walk in to work together: that's rule number one. And we never stop by each other's desks and chat – except on a few strategic occasions like this one. We're basically acting as if we're spies on opposite sides of the Berlin Wall in 1981. It's *so* much fun!

It's been three weeks since Paris and nobody suspects a thing. Except maybe Sorrell. She must be able to see that there's a suspicious new shimmy in my step and a sparkle in my eyes, plus I've stepped up my grooming dramatically. No more shaving just my lower calf when I'm wearing cropped trousers, or repainting my big toenail instead of doing a full pedicure. I'm wearing fake lashes almost every day. And I'm constantly distracted during important discussions because I'm busy thinking about Charlie and what we did the night before . . .

I turn back to my work, sternly telling myself I need to prune my inbox before it becomes completely overgrown. But then my phone rings. It's Alice; she never rings me at work, so I answer it, instead of letting it go to voicemail.

'Hi darling,' I say. 'What's up?'

'I've got some news,' she says. 'Is this a good time?'

'Absolutely,' I say, smiling to myself because I can tell from her voice exactly what this news is going to be. But when she tells me 'We're engaged!' I still find myself shrieking. 'Aaaaaaaaagggggh!'

Sorrell pokes her head around the door in alarm and I give her a thumbs-up so she knows I haven't spilled a caramel frappuccino all over my keyboard – again. I got in trouble with IT over that (and over the vintage hatbox collection I keep under my desk, which they claimed was a fire hazard).

'Oh darling, I'm thrilled for you. For you both! Sam's a lucky man.'

'Thanks!' she says. 'I'm so happy, Poppy. I keep leaving the milk out of the fridge and missing my stop on the Tube and everything. The other day I tipped a tenner in Starbucks by mistake.'

'That's interesting! I read that—' I'm about to share the happiness-equals-stupidity theory when I remember Sorrell sitting right outside. I don't want to corrupt my assistant (or look like an idiot myself).

Alice tells me how it happened – Sam proposed on the Millennium Bridge, and she was so discombobulated she almost dropped the ring in the Thames – and I ask if they've made any wedding plans.

'You'll hardly have time to get married before you leave London, will you?' She and Sam aren't leaving until September, but that's not long now.

'No. We're going to do it in Los Angeles, on October the tenth. And I know it's really far and I understand if you can't make it, but if you possibly can . . . I would love you to be one of my bridesmaids.'

'Aaaaaaaargh!' I scream again, but this time Sorrell doesn't bother to investigate. 'Of course I will! I've got holiday to use up anyway, and . . . What am I saying! Even if you were getting married in the Antarctic I'd be there with Gore-Tex on. I'm so honoured you want me to be your bridesmaid!'

'Thank you! I'm also having my friend Ruth, who you know, and my cousin Lily. You've met her, haven't you?'

'Of course! She's fun.' Lily is a willowy blonde clone of Alice – physically at least. Where Alice is gentle and sweet, Lily is a bit of a live wire; bridesmaiding with her should be entertaining. 'Isn't she an actress? She's going to love Los Angeles.'

'She's an aspiring actress really,' Alice says. 'I'm a bit worried about that aspect of things, to be honest. I don't want Sam to be put under pressure to find her a part.'

'I'm sure she wouldn't overstep any boundaries.'

'You don't know her like I do. Overstepping boundaries is her favourite form of exercise.' Alice laughs. 'But she's an absolute sweetheart. I'm really glad you two are going to get to know each other better. And if you wanted to bring a date . . .' I can hear the smile in her voice. 'You'd be very welcome to ask Charlie.'

'Oh no, I don't think so,' I say. 'Thanks, but that would be way too soon. I mean we've only been—' Again I remember that Sorrell can hear me from outside. 'I've only been, um, using that sewing machine for three weeks,' I say in an extra-loud voice. 'That's too soon. Isn't it?'

Of course now I'm imagining jetting off to Los Angeles with Charlie and going to Alice's wedding with him on my arm. It's a nice fantasy, but it would never happen. Or would it? Charlie and I are such an unlikely couple, I sometimes think I'm going to wake up and find I've dreamed the whole thing, Paris and all.

'Well, he's your sewing machine,' says Alice. 'Why don't you have a think about it and let me know?'

'Oh God, this is amazing,' I moan as Charlie leans over me. 'No, that's too much. Stop! Just . . . OK, fine, cut me the whole quarter.'

Charlie slices carefully through the Spanish tortilla he's just made. Glistening and yellow, with a crispy brown top, it looks like the most delicious thing I've had since the warm duck and fig salad he made me last time. In the first two weeks we were together, I was so keyed up that I could barely eat a thing when he was around. I lost three pounds, in fact. Now my appetite's back, and I can see myself putting that weight right back on.

We're sitting on my tiny balcony, which is just about big enough for an iron table and two chairs if we keep the door open and one of us sits in the kitchen. It overlooks the car park outside and all the neighbours' washing lines, and there's a certain *eau de* traffic fumes in the air. But we're having a feast worthy of a five-star restaurant: Spanish omelette, little roasted green peppers and manchego cheese, and a salad with hazelnuts and toasted breadcrumbs, all washed down with glasses of ice-cold home-made sangria – my contribution. I've always thought of myself as a good cook, but now that I've seen what Charlie can do, I've turned bartender.

'You know I'm going to turn into Jabba the Hutt if you keep feeding me like this,' I say, taking my first bite. 'Oh my God. This is *divine*.'

'That's OK. I mean the Jabba the Hutt thing,' Charlie says. 'More of you to love. I mean, to like.'

We stare at each other in alarm, before we mutually agree to act as if it was just a turn of phrase and resume eating happily.

'So,' he says. 'What was all the shrieking about this morning? I thought you'd seen a mouse or something.'

'Oh! It was really nice news. Alice and Sam are getting married, in Los Angeles in October.' I sip some sangria. 'And I'm going to be a bridesmaid.'

'Excellent! You'll have a great time. I've always wanted to go to California.'

'Have you really?' I ask, curiously. Charlie's never struck me as much of a world traveller. He's been to Spain on package holidays, and that's about it.

'Oh God, yes, are you kidding? Tasting Californian wines . . . breakfast at roadside diners . . . tacos and lobsters . . .' He looks dreamy. 'You'll have to make a holiday of it.'

'I will.' Suddenly I have a picture of me and Charlie eating lobsters beside the sea in Los Angeles, wearing giant bibs and clinking glasses of white wine. Before I can think twice, I say recklessly, 'I don't suppose you'd like to come too?'

He looks surprised. 'To California? Or to the wedding?' Which is silly. I'd hardly take him to Los Angeles and then leave him in the car while I attended the wedding, would I?

'Well, both. Alice told me I could bring . . . someone.' I was about to say 'bring you' but I don't want him to know I've been discussing him with my friends. Although I totally have.

'I'd love to, but I've got this golf trip with my mates in September,' he says. 'A week in the Algarve.'

'Oh! Of course. Sure. No problem.' I smile to hide my embarrassment. Yikes. That was keen of me – asking him to come to a wedding in Los Angeles with me when we've only been together three weeks. We haven't even discussed whether we're boyfriend and girlfriend yet. Let alone come out to people at work! Now I feel like one of those girls in films who wakes her boyfriend up in the middle of the night by staring at him and tracing circles on his chest.

Charlie's concentrating on one hazelnut that keeps escaping his fork. Looking up, he says, 'Although . . . I do have some holiday to use up. And there's no rule against going away at the start of September, and again in October, is there?'

'Not that I'm aware of.'

Charlie clears his throat. 'And I'm sure the boss would understand – if I say I'm going to California with my girlfriend . . .'

'With – wow. Yes, I'm sure she would,' I say. I'm excited, but also nervous. He's used the G word! He's also almost used the L word! This is all happening pretty fast, isn't it?

'So yeah, I'd love to come,' Charlie says.

'That's great! I'll tell Alice you're in. I was thinking of taking a week off – how does that sound?'

'Fantastic. We could spend a couple of nights in LA, explore around there . . . maybe have a couple of nights in Vegas . . . and obviously Disneyland.'

'Disneyland?' I repeat. He's joking, right?

'Of course!' he says. 'The one in California is the oldest *and* the only one built directly under Walt Disney's supervision. It's got all the old-school stuff like Tom Sawyer's Island and Main Street. And then there's the Tower of Terror – and the new Marvel Universe thing, of course . . .' He goes on for another five minutes about various aspects of the place, including how they elect the Disney mayor, before concluding, 'It's not just for kids, you know.'

I look at him in consternation, thinking: that's exactly who it's for. I haven't lost *that* many IQ points. My vision of this trip involves the John Paul Getty Museum and as many vintage fashion fairs as I can find. Have I just made a gigantic mistake?

Maybe I've rushed things – including telling my mum about him. She was pleased for about five minutes, before she started badgering me about when I was going to bring him down to Brighton to meet her. She wants to check out his posture and see how firm his handshake is, and quiz him on his views on private education and the gender pay gap. If I tell her he wants to go to Disneyland, she'll think he's an irresponsible, overpaid man-child. And who knows? Maybe she's right!

Charlie's still having trouble scooping up his hazelnut with his fork. So he picks it up with his fingers, and tosses it into the air, catching it in his mouth like a performing seal. I've seen him do this before, but I sort of . . . blocked it out.

'I tell you what,' he says. 'I'll ask the boss if I can have the time off – and then we can hatch more plans, look into flights and so on. Sound like a plan?'

'Sure,' I say, trying not to sound as worried as I feel. 'Sounds perfect.'

The following night, I meet Alice and Lily at one of the bars on the South Bank for an engagement-drink-slash-bridesmaid-summit. Ruth, our third musketeer, can't make it for some reason. Her loss: it's a hazy, golden evening, perfect for sitting outside and watching the world go by. Alice and I have already had a glass of Prosecco, gazed at her ring (massive but conflict-free diamond – Sam did well) and started discussing her wedding dress, when Lily comes flying along to meet us.

'Sorry I'm late!' she says breathlessly. 'Couldn't get away in time.'

'Rehearsals?' I ask, then kick myself, remembering Alice saying she was mainly aspiring.

'Sort of. You could say I'm rehearsing for my real life.' She looks mysterious, then explains, 'Temp job.'

We pour Lily a drink and start talking bridesmaids' dresses; Alice is super-organised and has even brought along some pictures.

'I do quite like this one, but it's strapless . . .' Alice looks at me questioningly; I shake my head apologetically. On the rare occasions when I go jogging, I have to wear two sports bras, one over the other.

Lily, though, doesn't seem too bothered either way.

'I'm sure whatever you guys pick will be fine,' she says, shrugging.

Lily certainly couldn't be called a clothes horse. Her outfit is a bit of a scroll-down disaster: it starts out fine, with a fitted black T-shirt, but then she's got denim shorts that she obviously created herself by taking scissors to a pair of jeans, and one-strap green Birkenstocks that have seen better days. But she's stunning: even prettier than Alice, with the same long blond hair and gorgeous wide-set green eyes. The two men beside us keep sneaking looks at her, proving my theory that men do not care about fashion. They use X-ray vision instead. But when Alice asks Lily if she wants to bring someone to the wedding, she shakes her head.

'No thanks. I don't have to, do I?' she asks.

'Of course not! I just didn't know . . . Are you still seeing that guy Calvin?'

'God, no!' she says. 'He was such an airhead. Spent all day updating his Wikipedia page.' She breaks off, hearing her phone. 'I think this is about an acting job! Excuse me a sec.' And she dashes off towards the edge of the terrace.

'How about you, Poppy?' Alice asks me. 'Any more thoughts about bringing Charlie?'

'I did ask him, but now I'm not so sure,' I confess.

'Why? Didn't he want to come?'

'No, quite the reverse. He started planning an entire trip around it, involving Las Vegas. And Disneyland. I don't want to go to Disneyland! I'm worried now that we've rushed into all this. What if we have a screaming fight in Sleeping Beauty's Castle – or end things in the middle of a desert in Nevada? It could be like the finale of *Breaking Bad*. Without the guns.'

She shakes her head. 'I think you're worrying over nothing.'

'Really?'

'Yes! Look. You like him, don't you?'

'I do like him,' I admit. 'A lot. So much.' I break off, picturing Charlie's eyes and the way they crease up when he smiles. And the way he kisses me, and the way his shoulders look from behind when I see him at his desk, looking all manly and hard at work . . . Also, even if we *do* break up mid-trip, I trust him not to be a dick about it. It's like Nora Ephron said: make sure you marry someone you wouldn't mind being divorced from.

'So just tell him you don't want to go to Disneyland. Or go! You might like it. If we went out with people who liked the exact same things as us, we'd be dating ourselves. Quite honestly, I would worry if your new boyfriend just wanted to go to vintage fashion fairs and museums with you. That sounds more like your friend Anthony. Your gay friend Anthony,' she adds unnecessarily.

'Don't stereotype! Anthony hates shopping, and he would love Disneyland. Maybe I should send him away with Charlie.'

'You know what I mean. Poppy, I haven't seen you this happy in ages. Don't do what I used to do.'

'How do you mean?' I ask.

'I remember you telling me that whenever a nice guy showed an interest in me, I would run a mile. Could that be what's happening with Charlie? Now that he's getting serious, you're starting to question things?'

'You could be right,' I admit. 'Oh God, you're completely right. I'm turning into one of those men we hate. How did that happen?'

Lily reappears. 'What did I miss?'

'Just firming up the guest list,' Alice says, raising her eyebrow at me. I taught her that trick! 'Was that good news, on the phone?'

'Didn't get it.' She tries to sound nonchalant, but she's obviously gutted.

'Oh dear. Did your agent give you any feedback?' I ask.

'Oh, I don't have an agent,' she says, sounding even more nonchalant, as I kick myself again. 'That was just the producer returning my call . . . my calls. Anyway. Alice, we haven't discussed the most important thing. Your hen party! If you want strippers, I know some very good ones. Reliable, too.'

While Alice tries to explain to Lily that she doesn't have enough time for a hen party, and definitely doesn't want strippers, no matter how reliable, I think about Charlie. It doesn't matter how different we are, or what my mum might think about him: I'm crazy about him. I would love to go on holiday with him. And I'll admit, it would be nice to have a date for Alice's wedding, instead of being seated beside the bride's twelve-year-old nephew, like at the last wedding I went to. I can cope with a day or two in the Magic Kingdom.

A few days later, I'm peacefully eating lunch at my desk, watching a video of a kitten riding on the back of a tortoise, when

Claudine, my most annoying colleague, rocks up to ask me if I've written my blog post yet for our website. I'm like a wildebeest: I don't like to be disturbed during feeding time. So I answer as briefly as possible.

'Yep – almost.'

She frowns. 'It's really important we post them at the same time every week, Poppy.'

This is typical Claudine. She herself does nothing all day but phone estate agents and look at pictures of horses online, but she also loves to crack the whip.

'Sure. I'll finish it right after I've eaten this,' I say politely, and turn back to my tortoise video.

But Claudine doesn't seem to get my hint; she's obviously in the mood for a chat and hangs around irritatingly. She's looking pristine, with a crisp white sleeveless shirt, a knee-length navy jacquard skirt, and smudge-proof red lipstick. How does she do that? These days, my make-up has all vanished by 10 a.m. I don't know where it goes, but it must go somewhere.

'So is Alice Roberts really getting married to some Hollywood hotshot in LA?' she says, picking up my stapler. 'I can't quite picture it.'

'Why can't you picture it?' I ask, smiling through gritted teeth.

Claudine shrugs. 'Just, you know Alice. Always getting dumped. Permanently single. You know what that's like.'

I fight the urge to grab my stapler from her and hit her around the head with it.

'When is it exactly, the wedding?' she asks.

'October the tenth. I'm going, so I can take pictures if you'd like proof.' I smile even more widely so she can't say I'm being rude. I don't know why she's so obsessed with Alice's wedding. Well, maybe I do. She's very insecure about her own boyfriend; in her Facebook profile picture, she practically has him in a headlock.

'October the tenth? That's funny – everyone seems to be away then.' She pauses. 'Charlie's going on holiday then as well.'

'Is he?' I ask indifferently, forking up my quiche. But I know I'm blushing. Damn! If anyone is going to be nosy enough to rumble us, it's Claudine.

'That quiche looks good. Actually . . .' Narrowing her eyes, she leans in, and I find my hands closing around my lunch protectively. What a psycho! How do I get rid of her?

'Sorry, Claudine, I've just remembered I need to make a call . . .' I reach for the phone. But she's already scuttled off.

A little worried, I send Charlie an instant message.

Can you chat?

Sure. What's up?

I think the C-dawg is on to us.

There's a pause, then he writes, *Maybe we should put her out of her misery so she can get back to work. Those pictures of horses won't look at themselves, you know.*

This makes me laugh out loud. Though I'm one to talk, with my kittens riding on tortoises.

He types, *Hang on a sec. I'm coming round.*

Minutes later, I hear footsteps approach, and turn around in happy anticipation. But it's not Charlie. It's Claudine.

'I knew it!' she says triumphantly. 'I just walked by Charlie's desk and he is eating the exact same quiche as you. And it's clearly home-made!'

'Oh Claudine,' says Charlie, walking in behind her. 'You are wasted in publishing. You should have been a forensic detective. *CSI: Bloomsbury.*'

'Oh my God,' she says. 'So it's true! This is *so* weird. I would *never* have pictured you two together.' She stares at us in turn as if we're a monkey and a Labrador or some other bizarre combination.

'Well now you can,' says Charlie. 'Feel free. Let your imagination run wild.'

'Ew! Gross,' says Claudine, and flounces out. Charlie and I look at each other, and start laughing.

'Well, I suppose we've told the whole office now.'

'Good,' he says. 'Now we can start planning for California.'

'Yes,' I say, reaching for my little Moleskine notebook where I've scribbled down some ideas. 'About that . . .'

Fifteen minutes later, we've worked out a rough itinerary we're both happy with. We're going to need ten days rather than a week, but that's fine. I'm looking forward to it. In fact, I can't wait.

Charlie goes back to his desk and I turn back to my email, to find a message from Lily.

Hi Poppy. Great to see you again the other night! I was thinking: even if Alice doesn't want a hen party, why don't we organise a little afternoon tea, just us bridesmaids and her? Do you think she would like that? Though if she changes her mind and does wants strippers, I know some out-of-work actors who would be totally up for it . . . Let me know! Lx

Laughing, I start typing back to say that afternoon tea sounds perfect. I've realised that Alice's departure is going to leave a really big friend-shaped hole in my life. I'm looking forward to spending more time with Lily.

LILY DOES LA

This is going to be an exciting phone call, I can tell. It *could* be J. J. Abrams asking me to audition for his new thriller. Or even Jake Gyllenhaal. He's single now, and he did take my number at that party last week. I allow a slow smile to spread across my face.

'Good afternoon, my name's Lily,' I say warmly into my headset. 'Have you got a minute to take a quick survey about your leisure activities?'

'I've had enough of these fucking calls! Stop calling me!' the voice snaps, and the phone is slammed down.

'Certainly, sir, I'll take you off our list at once. Have a lovely day,' I tell the ringtone.

Obviously I knew it wasn't going to be anyone thrilling, let alone a Hollywood director. But sometimes the only way I can make myself start a new call is by pretending it's going to be something good – or by practising an accent. After all, you never know when you might need it for an audition.

I'm sitting in a little grey cell with a computer screen in front of me. There are about 150 of us in the windowless room, which has a low ceiling, fluorescent lighting and stained grey carpets. All around me I can hear people saying: 'No, we won't sell your details', 'It can be as quick as ten minutes but it can take up to twenty', 'Can I ask your age? Are you: twenty to thirty, thirty to forty . . .' The irony of it: we've all got a script. It's just the wrong script.

I've just finished my sixth successful survey of the day (while taking the opportunity to practise my Scottish accent) when I get a tap on the shoulder. It's our supervisor, Gary. He has a horrible habit of creeping up on you and standing way too close so you have to breathe in his Lynx deodorant, and is generally a nasty little man, with over-gelled hair and a permanent frown.

'Lily,' he says. 'What have I told you before about those accents you put on?'

'I don't remember you saying anything,' I lie, with a confused look.

'Yes, I did. Twice. No more accents.'

He wags his finger at me and stands breathing down my neck while I make the next call. Bad idea, Gary. If you test me, I will test you right back.

'G'day, my name's Lily,' I say, in my best Australian accent. 'Have you got a minute to take a quick survey about your leisure activities?'

Gary squeaks and makes throat-cutting signs at me. I give him a friendly little wave back while the voice asks me how long it will take.

'It can be as quick as ten minutes but it can take up to twenty,' I parrot, still in Australian. Gary is going bright red in the face and waving his arms madly from side to side. I give him an innocent 'What?' look. Fire me, I think. If you're man enough.

'Twenty minutes! I don't have twenty minutes to spare. And what's it for?' the caller continues suspiciously. 'Are you going to sell my details to someone?' Great: a time-waster. He's going to spend ten minutes trying to catch me out and then refuse to do the survey.

'Hey, mate, relax,' I say. 'It's just some bullshit survey. Not worth bothering with.' I press the button to end the call and rip off my horrible headset, which I know is crawling with germs despite all the sanitising wipes I use.

'You're fired,' Gary splutters.

'No, I quit,' I tell him, pushing my chair under my desk. 'This is the worst job I've ever had, and I've had some shitty jobs. *Nobody* should have to do this.' I look around to see if I'm going to lead a walkout, *Jerry Maguire*-style. But everyone's still plugging away at their calls, oblivious. I stumble out, thinking: I can't believe I stayed three weeks in Gary's little battery farm. Now I just need to make sure I get paid.

As I trudge along through the rainy streets of Slough, I'm trying not to think about how many awful jobs I've had in the past three years. Meanwhile I'm desperate to get cast in something, anything. But you need experience to get work, and you can't get work without experience.

On the train back to Paddington, I pull out my phone and check for shout-outs on Spotlight.com, which is my main source of acting jobs. Today's new listings include a Global Circus Show – acrobatic skills essential – and a James Bond Murder Mystery Night in Cheltenham. Eighty-five pounds, no expenses paid. Also a Theatre in Education play about Hitler that's going to tour the West Midlands. They all look awful, but I'll try for them anyway.

I click on to my own profile, trying to see myself through a director's eyes. Age: 24. Hair: blond. Eyes: green. Height: 5'8". Weight: 9 st. That's all fine. But then my eyes move down to my embarrassingly scanty CV. Three years out of Central Drama School and all I've got to show for it is a tiny part in a community theatre production and two seconds on a Sofa Warehouse TV ad. I missed the end-of-year showcase, where most people get their agents, and I've never caught up.

Leaving the station, I head to Whiteley's shopping centre with the intention of looking for job signs in the shops. I trail around half-heartedly for a while, and then find myself on the escalator going towards the top floor, where the cinema is. I can't really justify the price of a ticket, but I need two hours' escape from my life. I hide behind a sign and jog on the spot for a minute, and then rush up to the guy at the entrance to the cinema.

'Hi, I left my scarf inside!' I say breathlessly, practically throwing myself on his little podium. 'Can I go in and get it, please?'

He stops chewing his gum and looks me up and down, smiling as if he knows I'm bullshitting him and is quite up for the challenge.

'Have you got your ticket?'

'No, I lost it! Please, I'll only be a minute.'

'What film was you watching?'

'*Spider Man*,' I say promptly.

He's obviously enjoying being counsel for the prosecution, because he continues, 'That ended ages ago. Did you only just remember your scarf?'

'No, I was on the bus, and I had to come all the way back. Please? It'll just take a second . . .'

'Hmm,' he says, his eyes twinkling. 'I don't think you was in the cinema today. I woulda remembered *you*.'

The admiring look in his eyes is as soothing as a hot bath, reassuring me that I've still got something going for me.

'OK, you're right. I'm sorry. I've had a horrendous day. I was fired.'

'For real? From what job?'

'Call centre.'

He winces sympathetically. His expression says: been there.

'But I'm an actor really. And I would love to go in and see a film, even if it's halfway through. I won't disturb anyone. Just this once.' I look at him pleadingly.

'OK,' he says eventually. 'But only because my manager's sick. And don't tell your friends, yeah?'

'I won't, I promise. Thank you so much! You're the best,' I say, thrilled.

'Remember me when you're a famous actor,' he says, waving me in with a gentlemanly flourish. 'Send me a ticket to your premiere.'

'Definitely,' I promise him sincerely.

'Hey,' he adds. 'Tell the guy at the popcorn counter that Ashraf said you could have a free popcorn. Regular size.'

Free film *and* free popcorn! Things are looking up.

I've missed the opening of the film, but it doesn't matter. It's a great reboot of the story and the script is fun. Emma Stone is also pretty bloody great. As the end credits roll up, I'm pinned to my seat with misery. I don't want to be one of those people who can't go to films or plays because they're jealous of the actors. But that's how I feel. Emma Stone is two years younger than me, and she's already a star.

I know the ages of all the Hollywood celebutants. Emma Stone is twenty-two. Jennifer Lawrence and Emma Watson are twenty-one. Carey Mulligan and Gemma Arterton are twenty-six. Emma Stone moved to Hollywood when she was *fifteen*. What have I been doing with my life? They say that if you haven't made it in your second year out of drama school, you won't make it at all. Maybe it's time to give up and do something else. But I can't think of anything else: when I try, my mind goes totally blank, like the screen in front of me.

'Excuse me,' says someone. The lights have come on, and they're tidying up the cinema. I look at the girl with her plastic bin bag, thinking: this is what my future holds. I'm never going to be up there on the screen; I'm always going to be down here watching. Or cleaning.

'Sorry,' I say, getting up. 'I'm just leaving.'

In the train on the way home to Bromley, I wonder what would have happened if I'd asked my parents to move with me to Hollywood at fifteen. My dad would have taken my temperature, and then he would have explained about things like visas and mortgages and National Insurance contributions. Mum, though – I bet she would have considered it. She was always up for an adventure. She might even have gone back into acting herself. And if we'd lived in the States, she wouldn't have had the accident . . .

But I can't bear to think about that. Instead I remind myself that Chris, my older brother, would have had the casting vote, and he definitely would have vetoed it in case it interfered with his Duke of Edinburgh Award.

Just then I get a text. *Hi love. Do you want a lift from the station? Lol Dad.* I hope he never finds out 'lol' doesn't mean 'lots of love'; it's too cute. I text back: *Yes please.* Poor Dad must be sick of giving me lifts. When I was at school, he used to drive me there with my bike in the back so I could cycle home. And if I didn't feel like it or it was raining, he would drive me home as well, with the bike in the back again. My friend Maggie, who cycled every day in all weathers, called it my 'comfort bike'.

'Thanks for picking me up, Dad,' I say, piling into the Volvo and kissing his cheek. He's wearing a brand-new pair of jeans and a primrose-yellow jumper that looks to me as if Fi bought it for him. She's very into her pastels and brights.

'That's quite all right, love . . . it's a rotten night.' He checks behind him and moves off carefully, wipers working. 'How was your day?'

'Awful. I got fired.' I think this sounds better than 'I quit'.

'Fired? Why?' He sounds horrified. But honestly, what did he think? That I was going to end up drawing a pension from my call centre job? Probably. He wants me to succeed at acting, but he's also keen on pensions.

'Because it was a living death and my manager was a dick.'

'Lily . . .'

'He was! He didn't like the fact that I was practising an accent, so he fired me.'

Dad sighs.

'What?' I say brattishly. 'I'm sorry, OK? I'll get another job.'

'That's . . . never mind. Let's wait till we get home.' Before I can ask him what he means, he adds casually, 'You know, we'll have to get you driving again one of these days.'

I stiffen. He's not going to bring that up now, is he? But thankfully he drops it, obviously sensing I'm not in the mood for a talk about how driving is a life skill, and Mum wouldn't want me to be scared off the roads because of what happened to her. Which is good, because that talk generally ends with both of us in tears.

When we get home, the kitchen is looking nice and cosy, with the rain lashing the windows outside. The beef stroganoff I made at the weekend is heating up on the stove, and Dad's cooked some wide noodles to go with it. I set the table quickly while Dad chooses the music.

'Ella Fitzgerald sings Cole Porter or Ella sings Rodgers and Hart?' he asks.

'Rodgers and Hart please.' I love 'The Lady is a Tramp' and 'This Can't Be Love' And I need show tunes to cheer me up.

This is a routine we got into a few months after Mum's accident, when Dad said we had to eat properly instead of having toast while slumped in front of the television. So we started taking turns cooking and choosing music, and we sometimes have wine and even flowers on the table. Weirdly, it's more date-like than anything I ever did with Calvin, my ex. Calvin's real name is Kevin, but he changed it, supposedly because there's another Kevin Jones with an Equity card. I personally think that was just another red flag, along with him having a poster of himself in his bedroom and complaining about being typecast because he was so good-looking. Oh, and the fact that he rang NHS Direct when his dog was sick.

'So Fi was saying she's been watching your YouTube videos,' says Dad, as we sit down and start on our beef stroganoff. 'She said they're really good; she's forwarding them to her niece who's doing English A level.'

'Oh. Tell her thanks.' I've uploaded a few self-tapes of Shakespeare monologues – Lady Macbeth, Cleopatra and Juliet – but so far they've only had about a hundred views. There are kittens in cardboard boxes with more hits than that.

'She was wondering if you'd thought about emailing them to directors. I know that's a little unrealistic, but perhaps you could tweet them, or . . .'

I count to ten to stop myself telling Fi where to stick her emails, and mutter, 'Maybe'.

'Don't give up, Lily,' he says gently. 'One day you'll have your break. You were so unlucky missing your showcase the way you did. It was bad timing, with . . . everything that was going on.' He stops short as we both remember the horrible week that followed the accident, when I couldn't get out of bed, let alone go to my end-of-year showcase. 'But you have talent; you will get there.'

'Thanks, Dad,' I say, feeling a lump in my throat. 'I'm sorry I was being a brat earlier.'

'That's OK. Look . . . there's something I want to tell you. I have good news and bad news. Though *I* think it's all good, as they say.'

I look up, and just like that I know. I know from his expression: guilty but also weirdly happy.

'It's you and Fiona. You're getting married,' I whisper. 'Is that it?'

'No, no,' Dad says, sounding relieved to be reassuring me. Then he says, 'We're moving in together.'

'Into her place?'

He looks uncomfortable. 'Actually, I'd like her to move in here.'

'Here? Into our house?' I swallow with difficulty. My beef stroganoff has turned into salty cardboard. Ella's mellow tones in the background sound like a car alarm.

'It makes more sense, as her place will be much easier to rent out. Obviously this is your home, and you're welcome to stay here as long as you want . . .'

'No, I'll find somewhere else,' I say quickly.

There's no way I can stay here and see my home invaded by Fiona's kitsch Buddha statues and potpourri and hideous pink and purple 'wall art'. I think of her sleeping in my parents' bed, and using my mother's wardrobe, and I feel ill. How could Dad do this to us? It's only been three years since the accident. How can he wipe out his entire family history like this?

'I know it's hard, Lil,' he says. 'But I think it will be good for all of us. You should be living with people your own age, not your boring old dad. When's the last time you had a night out with your friends?'

I shrug. I don't really see people from drama school these days; they're all busy being on TV or doing plays. The only person I see regularly is Maggie, and she spends a lot of time doing outdoorsy things with her boyfriend.

'Does Chris know?' I ask. He's sort of half-heartedly Team Fi – at least he doesn't think she's as awful as I do and he's said unforgivable things about Dad 'moving on'.

'Chris? No, no. I wanted to tell you first.'

Poor Dad looks so miserable at breaking the news to me. I know how lonely he's been; I get it. I just wish he'd got a dog or something instead.

'What's the good news?' I say faintly, hoping it's that Fi has had a complete personality transplant. There's nothing wrong with her, except she wears too much perfume and has a poster of a baby monkey saying 'Hang in there!' in her kitchen, and she can't eat anything vaguely calorific without saying 'Ooh! Naughty!' She tries too hard, and she makes me feel guilty for not trying hard enough.

'The good news!' Dad says, sounding relieved. 'You know your cousin's wedding in Los Angeles?'

'Of course!' This is the one thing I've got to look forward to. Alice is my favourite cousin and I'm thrilled for her – and very excited that she wants me to be her bridesmaid. And I'm equally excited to see LA. I wish we could stay longer than a few days, but Dad has to go back for work and I won't really know anyone else there except Alice and her friend Poppy, and they'll both be with their boyfriends – fiancés, I suppose, in Alice's case.

'We should really book our flights, shouldn't we?' I ask Dad. 'Do you want me to go online after dinner and have a look?'

'Hold on a second, Lily. Alice rang up earlier today, and asked if you could come out a week early and stay with her and Sam. Apparently she needs help with various wedding things, so if you were happy to do that, she'd be really grateful. I'll look after the flights.'

'Seriously? Thanks, Dad, that's amazing,' I say, feeling happy for the first time since he dropped the F-bomb. 'Can you imagine? An entire week in Los Angeles!' I'm picturing sunshine, palm trees, celebs . . . Who knows who I might bump into? 'Wait, what about Aunt Emily? And Erica?' Alice's mother and sister must know more about weddings than I do.

'Well it's all quite unfortunate timing. Erica will be having her baby around then. So Emily doesn't want to fly out too early, and Erica can't fly at all.'

'Oh, I see. Well, I'd love to help her.'

'There's just one thing,' Dad says. 'Alice doesn't want Sam to be put in an awkward position.'

'Sam?' I say blankly. 'What – like seeing me in a towel or something? I can bring a dressing gown. But I honestly don't think he'd notice; he only ever looks at her.'

'No, Lily. She meant because he's an agent. A film agent.'

I drop my knife with a clatter on the plate, scattering the remains of my dinner. 'He's a *film* agent? As in, he represents actors? I thought he was an *estate* agent!'

'Well that's what I thought too,' Dad admits. 'I must have misunderstood. I could have sworn your aunt said estate agent.'

'But I've met him a million times! He knows I'm an actor! How come Alice never told me? She knows I'm desperate to get an agent . . .'

'That's probably why,' Dad says drily. 'Alice said that she's sure Sam would give you advice at some point, but she doesn't want him to be put on the spot. Especially not the week before their wedding.'

'OK.' I nod. 'I understand. Of course I'll go and help her, I'd love to. And if Sam *happens* to mention that someone's dropped out of a film—'

'Lily!' Dad says. 'No. No putting yourself forward. No mentioning parts, producers, directors, acting, or anything related to the above.' There's nothing like a solicitor for fine print.

'Fine! I get it. I won't mention acting.'

But secretly I'm pretty sure there will be a way around Dad's prohibitions. And if I *did* get a break . . . I know Dad would be really happy. And Mum would have been so happy too. I'm sure the wedding stuff will be straightforward enough, and it'll leave me plenty of time to investigate some leads. Especially if I'm staying with a Hollywood agent for an entire week!

Six weeks later, I land at Los Angeles International Airport. LAX! I'm a little disappointed to find that it looks like any other airport: sleep-deprived crowds, screaming children, shiny floors and baggage carousels.

But then I see them: the paparazzi. Four or five guys with cameras, all pointing them right at me. They've hardly seen my Sofa Warehouse ad, have they? Or have they mistaken me for someone else? I'm thrilled, obviously, but also panicked that I'm being photographed right now. I didn't wear any make-up on the plane, and I'm bound to be all puffy and piggy-eyed. I'm not one of those girls who look naturally gorgeous, I need all the help I can get.

'Move aside, miss,' one of them says to me. I look and see that he's actually trying to snap someone behind me – some E-lister from a reality show, I think. Now I feel like a total airhead. Did I *really* think I was getting papped on the basis of one Sofa Warehouse ad?

'Lily!' Alice is bounding across to me, blond hair flying, looking very pretty in a pale blue wrap dress, with huge sunglasses perched on her head, and high-heeled sandals. I feel like a slob beside her in my Topshop T-shirt, cardigan and jeggings. 'It's so great to see you! Welcome! Is this all you've brought?' She gives me a huge hug and we both jump up and down with excitement. I'm so happy to see her, and also to have somewhere to be and something to do, even if it's only for a week.

Walking out of the airport, I'm rendered speechless by the warmth. It's October, but the sun's blazing, the sky is blue, there are palm trees. It's like heaven. And this is only the airport!

'It's as if the heating is on full blast,' I say, pretending to stagger and fanning myself. 'But we're *outside*. How can this be?'

'What's it like back home?'

'Like living in a damp Tupperware box at the bottom of the fridge.' It's hot in the car too, and it's a relief when Alice turns the air conditioning on and we drive out of the airport.

'I am so glad to see you, I can't tell you. Thanks for coming out early. This wedding . . . let's just say it's time-consuming.' Alice glances in her rear-view mirror. 'Am I OK to change lanes?'

I look behind me and it seems fine, so I say, 'Sure.' Alice pulls out, to the sound of furious honking. I'm not nervous, though; for some reason, I'm never nervous if other people are driving. Only if it's me.

'Aargh. Maybe that was a bit tight. Oh well, it's not far to our place. I can't wait to show it to you,' she says, sounding proud. 'You're going to love Venice. It's the nicest part of LA by miles.'

I had pictured a huge beachside mansion, like in *The OC*, but Venice looks like an ordinary neighbourhood, even run-down in places. Lots of low houses painted olive green, grey or cream, or made of clapboard. True, we're very close to the sea and there are palm trees on every street corner, but there are also lots of giant blue and green bins. There are fewer cars here and the streets are quiet; a woman goes by us on a bicycle, with a rolled-up yoga mat on her back. It's not exactly the Beverly Hills-type scenario I'd envisaged.

'Here we are,' says Alice, pulling up at a grey-green building covered with a pink-flowered bush.

I follow her up some steps to a spacious terrace overlooking a canal, lined with picturesque little bridges and paths. The houses are all painted pink and blue and green, and several even have boats tied up outside them on the water. The terrace is beautiful too, with hardwood decking and a concrete pond filled with water lilies. I'm beginning to see what all the fuss is about.

'Oh my God, do you have a boat?'

'We do actually, it came with the house. We just haven't had time to take it out yet,' Alice says. She makes a face. 'Sad, I know. Come inside.'

She opens up sliding glass doors to lead me into an open-plan kitchen-living room that looks like something from a magazine. Two luxurious grey sofas, with yellow chevron cushions, face each other near a high-tech fireplace. An antique chess set sits on a low glass coffee table. The room is on two levels: the kitchen, on the upper level at the far end, has a breakfast bar and a sleek oval dining table. If it wasn't for the piles of cut-up paper all over the coffee table, and another basket full of pieces of paper, I would think it was a show home.

'You've come a long way from Hertfordshire, girlfriend,' I say, hiding my awe with a joke. 'This crib is dope, yo.'

Alice beams. 'Isn't it? I especially love *this*.' She strokes the exposed brick wall above the fireplace. 'Let me give you the tour. This is our bedroom . . .' She opens a door to a beautiful room with olive-green walls, white paintwork, and glass doors on to a flower-filled balcony. 'And this is you.'

It's small but perfect, with grey and cream walls, a double bed, a small silver-lacquered chest of drawers and a dressing table with a yellow-cushioned footstool. One side opens completely on to a little garden.

'The bathroom's next door. It's all yours; we have an en suite.' Alice puts my case down. 'Bathrooms are very big here. In both senses. One of Sam's clients has seven in his house.'

I'm still gazing around the room. 'I have to warn you, I may never leave.'

'Come on, let's go back on the terrace and I'll get you something to drink,' says Alice. 'Do you want some iced green tea? I know it sounds dubious but I've got addicted to it. Go out, sit, enjoy the sun.'

I watch Alice swish over to the giant fridge, heels clacking on the floor. She's wearing much more make-up than she used to, but it suits her. I can't believe this is her actual life. When we were younger, I was always so impressed by Alice's achievements. Four years older than me, she could ride a bike without stabilisers, do up her laces when I was still on Velcro, and tell the time on a proper clock when I could only do digital. She could even do cartwheels. Sitting on the terrace, and looking out at the canals, I feel as if I'm seven years old again and she's cartwheeling all around me.

'So how are things going with the wedding?' I ask, as she sits down opposite me and hands me a tumbler of iced green tea. I take a sip; it's surprisingly delicious.

'Fine! Fine. Great,' she says brightly. A tad manically, in fact. 'It's just, you know, a lot of work. And we've both been so busy settling into the house and our new jobs and doing visa and immigration stuff – I'm frightened at how much there still is to sort out wedding-wise.'

I nod understandingly. I've seen the rom-coms; she probably just needs help making her final eyeshadow decision or reassurance that the swan ice sculptures won't melt. 'Well, I'm here to help. Call me Lily Wedding Services, Inc. In fact, let's make a list right now.'

'Are you sure, Lil? You're just off the plane.'

'No, it's fine! I feel really awake now. Let's do it.'

'If you're positive . . . I'll go and get the spreadsheet.'

A *spreadsheet*? Is she joking? But sure enough, she reappears with a laptop and opens up a forbidding-looking Excel file.

'So,' she says, opening it up, 'there are things that only we can do – like, we still haven't agreed on the song for our first dance, or written our vows . . .'

'You have to write your own vows?'

'Yes! That's what they do here; it has to be all personal and heartfelt. But we've been so busy and knackered, we haven't been able to face it. Which doesn't seem like a great omen.' She looks so despondent that I'm even more determined to sort everything out for her.

'What else? Tell me the essentials.'

'Right. I need to find a make-up artist, because the lady I'd booked has broken her hand; pick up all our dresses from the alteration place; organise a hair appointment for Mum and the aunts; find a canopy for the ceremony; organise flowers and confetti; call the chair hire place for some extra chairs; call the venue again with the final numbers, but first chase a few people who still haven't RSVP'd . . .' She reels off about a hundred other tasks before adding, 'Oh, and I need to get some drinks and snacks in for tomorrow evening. Cynthia – that's Sam's mum – and his sister and various other female relatives are coming over and we're making favours.'

'What are those?'

'You know – those presents they give away at weddings. We're making little jars of Californian olive oil, with the guests' names handwritten on the labels. And origami table decorations. Cynthia's suggestions.' She nods towards the basket full of paper inside the glass doors. 'I've been practising but mine all look like bus tickets.'

This all sounds like a major waste of time. 'Are you sure you want to spend a whole evening doing that?'

'Of course not! But I have to. Cynthia's really disappointed that we're not having what she calls a "real" rehearsal dinner. Our parents have never met before, so we wanted to have dinner, just the six of us, the night before in a restaurant.'

'But that sounds nice! Why's she disappointed?'

'Because that's not the way they do things in their family. They love having gigantic occasions where everyone pitches in and cooks cornbread with Great-Aunt Sarah's recipe, and makes home-made decorations, and I can tell she thinks I have no soul because I'm buying everything. Whereas I bet to all the film people who are coming, it's going to look like we're being cheap.'

'Alice, don't be crazy! How could they think that? The venue looks like a dream.' I've seen the website: it's called the Casa de la Luna, it's in Santa Monica by the beach, and it's stunning.

'Thanks. I think so too. We keep saying to each other: at least the venue is perfect. Anyway, what else? Oh. I need to book a hotel for Ruth and her boyfriend.'

I'm about to ask why Alice hasn't got herself a wedding planner when this stops me in my tracks. 'What? Wait, back up. Why the hell do you have to book a hotel for Ruth?'

Alice sighs. 'Because . . . I can't even remember why. She still hasn't booked her flights because she wants to get a last-minute deal, and she asked me to find her a cheap hotel in a good part of LA, but to wait till the last minute to book it. Which I genuinely don't mind doing, but it's one extra thing on the list and I feel like my head is going to explode as it is.'

Ruth might be one of Alice's oldest friends from school, but it sounds as if she needs a good slap around the head.

'Is she always such a pain?'

'I never would have said so, but lately, yes. She . . . Oh, never mind. I'm being bitchy.'

'Go on, have a vent. Family doesn't count.'

'She's been odd since I got together with Sam, to be honest,' she says reluctantly. 'She kept saying how hard it must be that he worked such long hours, and not many girls would put up with it, and wasn't I worried that he might move back to the States. And then when I told her we were engaged, she said, "Because of Sam's visa?"'

'No!'

'Yes. And did you see what she wrote on my Facebook page?'

'No, what?' I love a good Facebook drive-by shooting.

'She wrote, "Congratulations Alice, I'm so pleased for you, you've FINALLY found your happy ending!!!" Don't you think that's weird? FINALLY in caps? It made me sound desperate. And why wouldn't she congratulate Sam too? Am I the only one getting something out of this?'

'So why did you ask her to be bridesmaid?'

Alice looks at a loss. 'Well . . . I didn't exactly . . . No, forget it.'

I sit bolt upright. 'You didn't *ask* her?'

'She sort of assumed. But it was understandable because we've talked about being each other's bridesmaids in the past. Lily, please forget I said any of this.'

'You should uninvite her,' I say decisively. 'You don't need that toxic stuff at your wedding. Cut the cord.'

'I can't do that. It would be really rude, and she would go mental.'

She looks so stressed out that I decide I'd better change the subject. 'What about Sam? Can't he help? I don't know much about weddings, but I know they're not supposed to be a surprise party for the groom.'

'He has, he's done loads of stuff. He drove thirty miles recently to taste-test a tagine. But he's working round the clock these days, and also he doesn't care about it. Any of it. He just wants us to be married, and every time I forward him something to do he doesn't understand it or he asks if we can do without it, so I end up doing it myself.' She sighs. 'Anyway. That's enough about the wedding. I haven't even asked you how you are! How is the acting going? And how's your dad? I'm looking forward to meeting, um . . .'

'Fiona. But she prefers Fi.' I will never call her Fi.

'What's she like? Do you get on with her?'

'She's OK.' I'm not going into any more detail. 'You'll meet her at the wedding. Speaking of which: would you like me to call the chair hire place? And make hair appointments?'

'Yes! Would you do that?'

'Of course. And I can pick up your dress, too, and the brides-maids' dresses.'

'That's great! Let's see. You could hire a car . . .'

'Oh – sorry. I'm not really driving these days.' I know it's stupid of me. I wasn't even involved in Mum's accident. But I've tried sitting behind the wheel of Dad's car, and I still find it so frightening that I can't even make myself start the engine.

Alice looks as if she understands.

'We'll figure something out,' she says. She gets to her feet. 'I've got to go out for an hour or two, I'm afraid, I've got a meeting.' Alice has told me she works as a literary scout; I don't know what that is exactly but it sounds very cool. 'Here's a spare key, and you can borrow my bike. Why don't you cycle down to the ocean? You should try and stay awake as long as you can, to avoid jet lag. I'll be back around seven thirty and we can have dinner. Sound good?'

'Perfect! What about Sam?' I ask casually.

'He should be home early tonight. He's looking forward to seeing you.' A dopey, radiant smile breaks out across her face. 'I'm sorry I was moaning about all the wedding stuff. It is a pain, but you know what? It doesn't matter, because I'm marrying the man of my dreams.'

She gives me a hug and rushes off, leaving me wondering if I'll ever feel that glowy about anyone. Probably not – since Calvin cheated on me, I've become quite cynical about men. In my experience, either they're so keen that it's off-putting, or else they're players. But I'm happy for her.

I fire up Alice's laptop and order the extra chairs, so at least there's one thing off her list. Then I google hairdressers near the hotel where her parents are staying, and book in four appointments. Next, I decide to send Dad a quick email to let him know I arrived safely.

Alice is still signed in to her gmail. I'm about to sign her out when I see there's an unread email from Ruth. I know it's bad, but I can't resist having a peep. It says:

Hi Alice,

 Quick question. I know we talked about booking the hotel for two nights, but now I'm wondering if we should stay somewhere else the second night so we see more of California. The flights are still looking so expensive, and having flown all that way it seems a shame just to see LA, which everyone says is horrible anyway! And since you're not organising any events for the day after the wedding it might be dull hanging around. Or would there be stuff to do?

 Maybe you could organise a spa day for us hard-working bridesmaids? If you can suggest a few cool things for us to do on a Sunday in LA then I'll stick with the two nights, otherwise let's leave it at one. Maybe the second night in Santa Barbara? Or if that's too expensive (like all of California it seems!!) do you have other suggestions? Let me know asap!

 xo Ruth

I read the email again, open-mouthed. I literally cannot believe this shit. A spa day for us hard-working bridesmaids? LA is horrible? Who *is* this monster? My blood boiling, I start typing back.

Hi Ruth,
   I am sorry that my wedding is such a giant pain in the arse for you. You'll be pleased to hear we've decided to scale it back to immediate family, so you don't have to come any more. Enjoy Monica's hen weekend!
   Alice xo

Ah, if only. 'Having flown all that way it seems a shame just to see LA.' WTF? This isn't some sightseeing trip. This is my cousin's wedding. Which means she's not only disrespecting Alice, she's disrespecting our whole family. Specifically, my mother's family; Alice's mother is – was – Mum's sister. Still, I can't interfere. I try and delete my draft message, but Alice's computer is configured differently to mine, and somehow I end up making the screen go tiny, then huge, then it freezes. I click for a few minutes until it becomes normal again.

And then a message flashes up: *Your email has been sent.*

What? No! I didn't press send! I click frantically on the outbox to see if I can delete it there, but it's empty. I check the 'sent' folder, and there it is: a full-fat crazy email from Alice Roberts, courtesy of me.

Now what? I'll have to immediately message Ruth, apologise and say it was me and it was a joke. But I don't want to! She's been a cow to Alice. And even if I do apologise, surely the damage has been done?

I drum my fingers, then decide to email my dad first and write to Ruth later. It's the middle of the night in England anyway; she won't read my/Alice's message for hours.

But once I've signed out of Alice's email, of course, I can't get back in, and I don't know Ruth's email address. Damn. Well, she'll probably think the message is a joke . . . hopefully. I agonise for a while before deciding there's nothing I can do for the time being; I'll have to think of something later. Pushing the whole fiasco to the back of my mind, I go and do my make-up before leaving the house.

The sea – or the 'ocean', as Alice calls it   is about five minutes away. I lock up the bike, run down to the sand and paddle my feet in the Pacific. The water's freezing but everything else is perfect, with a light sea breeze and not a trace of smog. There's a crowd of surfers dotted on the gentle waves. To my right, in the distance, there's a long pier with an amusement park and Ferris wheel. Suddenly I have the kind of painful thought that often hits me out of the blue: Mum would have loved this. Whenever we went to the beach, she was always the first one out of the car, while Dad was re-parking more neatly and Chris and I were arguing over whose turn it was to use the boogie board.

To distract myself, I hop back on the bike and start cycling towards the pier. Signs tell me this is the way to Santa Monica. Santa Monica! I can't believe I'm actually here. Nor can I believe what I see on the cycle path along the way. There are people talking on their mobile phones while rollerblading, women riding what look like mobile cross-trainers, dogs on skateboards (being pulled by their owners, but still) and a man on a bike with a poodle in his backpack. I cycle past a synagogue called 'Shul on the Beach' with a sign outside that says: *Because there's more to Judaism than bagels*.

The epicentre of Venice Beach is a tacky-fabulous boardwalk, with graffiti-splattered buildings, pizza parlours, buskers, a skateboard park, rollerbladers and a roped-off area on the beach given over to body-building. Muscle men gleaming with oil are doing acrobatics on hoops and trapezes. Hearing music, I turn around and find it's coming from a man in a loincloth, with two snakes in a basket in front of him. A family nearby are eating lunch at an outdoor table, with a King Charles spaniel sitting up beside them like a person. This place is fantastic! I never want to leave!

I lock my bike, buy a slice of pizza and a Diet Coke from a

little hole-in-the-wall, and consume both while enjoying the sun and watching a rap artist busking. Then I wander down to the sand, where I notice a guy jogging towards me wearing a pair of navy shorts. He's cute. Not *Baywatch* exactly, but still: dark hair flopping over his brow, suntanned chest . . . He's also jogging barefoot, which intrigues me. He's got dark blue, slightly slanted eyes and looks deep in thought. Oops, he's noticed that I'm staring at him. Is he looking back? I think he might be.

'Hi,' I say, on a mad impulse. After all, Americans chat each other up all the time, don't they?

'Uh – hi,' he says, sounding surprised, as if he's not used to women approaching him. And jogs right by me. My cheeks flaming, I immediately turn around and hope nobody saw me get the brush-off.

'So how was your afternoon?' Alice asks when I get home. I stayed out so long, she's back already. She's setting the table for dinner out on the terrace, which looks beautiful with the sun sinking lower in the sky, casting its light on the canal. 'Did you do anything exciting?'

'Yes!' I start gabbling about body-builders and snakes in loincloths as I help her set the table. I'm wondering whether to confess about my email to Ruth, but it doesn't seem the right time. Better to wait and see what Ruth does.

'Sam will be home any minute,' Alice says. 'Are you OK to eat in? I'm sorry if that's boring, but he sounded exhausted on the phone. You must be tired too.'

'Of course! Let me change first.'

'You don't have to change. Come and have a glass of wine with me on the terrace.'

'Oh no – I feel kind of sticky after the plane. I'll be quick.'

Although I've met Sam several times, I feel acutely anxious about what to wear to see him now. I'm not a big clothes person – I live in jeans and T-shirts and Converse. But now everything I've brought seems too casual and shabby. Having thrown about five different outfits on the floor, I go with jeans, a navy tank top, silver earrings and my hair tied back in a bun, so he can see my bone structure.

I walk into the living room to find Sam picking Alice up and swinging her around. I didn't know people did that in real life.

'Honey, Lily is here.' Alice points out, looking pink.

Sam looks embarrassed too. 'Lily! Great to see you,' he says in an extra-hearty voice, putting Alice down and giving me a quick hug. 'How was your trip?'

Sam is very handsome, though I certainly don't fancy him – aside from being my cousin's boyfriend, he's a bit too all-American and serious and polite for me. Also he wears T-shirts under his shirts, which I find weird. But now I'm seeing him in a whole new light.

'It was great. I've been awake for,' I look at my watch, 'twenty-two hours now, but that's not a problem. I'm good at long days. Ten, twenty hours, makes no difference to me at all. Lots of stamina.'

'Good for you,' he says, looking bemused. 'I hope you like Italian food.'

'I love it! And I hear you're a *great* cook.'

'I do like to cook, but actually I picked something up. From the new place on Abbot Kinney,' he adds to Alice.

'We haven't used our kitchen once since we moved in,' Alice admits. 'Oh no, you got pasta! I'm not supposed to be having pasta until after the wedding.'

'Don't be ridiculous,' Sam and I say in unison. But all the same, I take a very small portion myself, and lots of salad. I shouldn't have had that pizza slice. I've been keeping thin for non-existent auditions for so long, it would be stupid to put on weight just as I might be about to get a break.

I had thought there might be some celebrity gossip over dinner, but instead Sam and Alice are arguing over what kind of music to have at the reception.

'I just don't think my Aunt Diane is going to want to dance to Cyndi Lauper all night,' Sam is saying.

'Well, I promise you nobody will dance to all your film soundtracks.' Alice turns to me. 'Can you believe Sam wants to have the theme tune from *The Godfather* for our first dance? I still don't know if he's joking or not.'

'I still don't know if *you're* joking,' Sam says. '"Waiting for a Star to Fall"? If it was junior prom in 1986, sure.'

'Which would you rather dance to, Lil?' Alice asks me. 'Cheesy eighties music or the *Cinema Paradiso* soundtrack?'

The real answer is definitely cheesy eighties, but I don't want to insult Sam. 'Well, I love eighties music, but film soundtracks can be pretty cool too . . .' I say, trying to be diplomatic but feeling weaselly.

'Thank you,' says Sam.

'You're welcome!' God, I sound like an idiot. I add quickly, 'Just out of interest . . . did you ever think of getting a wedding planner?'

'We tried,' Alice says. 'We met one who was lovely but booked out, and two who were scary. They kept talking about mood boards and signature cocktails and asking us what theme we wanted.'

'We said we wanted a wedding theme,' says Sam. 'They didn't seem to go for that.'

'I'm sure you're better off without them,' I say, trying to be reassuring. 'I booked the hair appointments and sorted out the chairs, by the way.'

'Brilliant! Thank you so much. Lily's also offered to pick up the bridesmaids' dresses, and my dress, but unfortunately she doesn't drive,' Alice adds to Sam. 'What do you think, could we hire her a driver for a few days? Or is that madness?'

Sam thinks. 'Maybe Jesse can help you out.'

'Who's Jessie?' I ask, picturing some assistant of Sam's.

'My cousin. He's one of my groomsmen, visiting here from Colorado. He'd probably be happy to help.'

'Great,' Alice says. 'And do you mind helping me to host this crafting evening tomorrow, Lil? People are coming from seven. I'd love a hand with it.'

'Of course! Anything you need. Absolutely anything at all. Nothing is too much trouble.' I hope Sam is noticing how helpful, reliable and all-around fabulous I am.

'How was your meeting with Brock today?' Alice asks Sam.

'Who's Brock?' I ask before I can stop myself.

'Wilson,' Sam says, shortly. 'He's a director. He's casting for a new film.'

I put down my knife and fork. 'Brock Wilson? As in *Apocalypse High*?'

'You've seen it?'

Does Sam think I was raised in captivity? Of course I've seen it, and I love it, along with the entire world. It's one of the greatest TV shows of all time. Brock Wilson is famous for having the wittiest scripts *and* the best, most kick-ass heroines ever.

'What's his new film about?' I ask eagerly.

'It's a Western.'

'But with a twist, right?' says Alice.

'Yep,' says Sam.

'It's about an English girl who travels to the Wild West and becomes an outlaw,' Alice adds, before looking as if she wishes she hadn't.

I literally cannot imagine a more thrilling part. I *have* to audition for this film. Even to be an extra would be a dream come true.

Sam glances at Alice and then says, as if reading from an autocue, 'It's nice that you're a fan. You'll be able to meet him at the wedding.'

'At the wedding?' I ask faintly. 'He's coming to the wedding? To *your* wedding?'

I cling to the edge of the table to stop myself falling over. 'How?' I croak.

'Just, you know, as a guest,' says Alice. 'Have some more wine, Lily.' She looks anxious, as if she thinks I'm about to demand that Sam drive me to Brock Wilson's house, right now. Which I'm not going to do. Yet.

'Could you introduce me?' I ask boldly.

'You'll meet all our guests,' Sam says, in a sort of ominously polite tone. 'Lily, you know I'd be happy to talk to you about acting while you're here, and give you some advice. But first, you should relax. You're on vacation.'

The meaning is clear: do not ambush our wedding guests, or there will be trouble. It's such a pity. But then it occurs to me: if Brock is a guest, his address will be on the guest list . . .

'Would anyone like some dessert?' Sam asks. 'I got tiramisu.'

'Not for me,' I say quickly. If I'm going to be meeting a director

– or even be seen by him in the distance – I can't afford to look anything other than match-fit.

'Really, Lil? You've hardly had any pasta,' Alice says, in a motherly way. 'You're so thin . . . Have you lost weight recently?'

I shake my head, smiling. I don't even give the tiramisu a second glance. I'm focused, like a laser beam, on meeting Brock Wilson somehow.

'Jesse's texted me,' says Sam. 'He can drop by tomorrow at two, and take you wherever you need to go.'

'Great!' I say enthusiastically. I'm sure we can power through the wedding jobs in no time, and then . . . I know where to find Brock's contact details. Now I need to get my hands on that script.

I'm almost dead with exhaustion by the time dinner ends, but I keep myself awake long enough to sneak out of my room when the others have gone to bed and flip through Sam's man bag, which he's left lying by the sofa. I'm doubly lucky: the script is here, and it's a paper copy. I do feel bad for rifling through Sam's bag, but he'll never know.

The script is fantastic, and Ella, the main character, is a dream: brave, funny and vulnerable. I skim through it as quickly as I can to get the gist of the story, and then I choose one of her best speeches. I'm too shattered to learn it now, so I take a photo of the page, like in *The Bourne Identity*, before finally crawling off to bed.

By lunchtime the next day, I've memorised the speech and found Brock's contact details on the guest list. I'm dressed in denim cut-off shorts and my flannel check shirt – just the outfit for running wedding errands and (hopefully) auditioning for a film set in the Wild West. I'm thinking of having some food when there's a knock at the door. It's already two. Damn. I always think arriving bang on time is as rude as being late. It doesn't give people a chance!

I open the door and find myself face to face with a familiar-looking dark-haired man. He looks different today – he's wearing shoes, for a start, and glasses, and is rather formally dressed in a blue shirt, tie and chinos – but he is definitely the guy I said hello to on the beach yesterday. *How* embarrassing.

'Hi,' he says, giving me a strange look. 'Lily?'

'Um – yes!' I think frantically about how to cover up my pick-up attempt yesterday. 'Jesse! Hi! Nice to meet you! Sorry, I'm not one hundred per cent ready yet. Can you give me a few more minutes?'

'OK . . . I'm parked illegally, I think, so I'll wait in the car.'

'Are you sure? Alice says they never come around here.'

'No, I don't want to get a ticket. I'll see you outside.'

I run inside and do a little dance while I bite my fist. Of all the strange men I could have said hi to on the beach, it had to be Sam's cousin. I touch up my make-up, scurry around gathering the addresses and printouts Alice has left me and then, when I can't delay it any longer, walk outside to find him sitting in a red convertible.

'So! I *thought* that was you yesterday,' I say, getting into the passenger seat. I think that's a neat way of covering up.

'You did?' he says, looking confused. 'But we've never met before.'

'Thank you for driving me,' I add quickly, pretending I haven't heard him.

'That's OK. All part of a groomsman's job.' He slows the car at the junction at the end of the street. 'The alternative was taking my sisters to some mall with a fountain that plays in time to Lionel Richie music, so you've saved me from that at least. Where to first?'

I show him Alice's map. 'We need to pick up the dresses from this place on Abbot Kinney Boulevard. We should probably bring them straight back here, and then we need to go to the flower market, or rather the flower district, which is all the way over . . . there.' I peer at the map. 'Oh. That looks a long way away.'

'It's fine,' says Jesse. He turns on the stereo; some classical music is playing. 'Do you like Beethoven? Or would you prefer NPR?'

I know NPR is the equivalent of Radio 4, so I shake my head. 'I love your car, by the way.'

'Oh, yeah. It's a rental . . . I got a special deal on it.' He sounds embarrassed. 'People in LA don't generally drive convertibles, because of the smog.'

'Really? It's not smoggy here.'

'That's because we're right by the coast. I hope you're not asthmatic?'

'Nope.' Gosh, he's a worrier.

'So,' he says, as we drive off, 'do you have a chauffeur in London as well?'

'I wish! No, I use public transport.'

'You don't have to drive to work?'

'I just got fired, so no.' I have to admit, I do like the way that sounds. It's dramatic.

'How come?'

'Because I was practising accents to make my job less mind-numbingly boring . . . I was working in a call centre. So they fired me over that. It was completely unfair, because I got better results when I used my accents. I could probably take them to court, actually.'

'That sounds like it would be a landmark case,' he says.

I look over suspiciously to see if he's taking the piss, but he's looking straight ahead innocently.

'What do you do?' I ask.

'I teach English at a high school. It's a public school, right outside Boulder. And I coach the girls' football team.'

I can imagine what kind of teacher he is: cute enough that all the girls have crushes on him, but upstanding and law-abiding enough that the parents trust him. I still feel embarrassed about yesterday, but I don't find him that attractive any more. He's perfectly nice, but he seems a bit serious, even uptight. And why is he wearing a tie?

Now we're driving along Abbot Kinney, Alice's Mecca, which is full of cool shops and cafés. I'm dismayed by the number of gorgeous girls drifting along clutching giant Starbucks cups and juices; I hope they're not all actresses.

One girl, in black ankle boots and tiny white denim shorts, is obviously a model; she has the longest limbs I've ever seen, like a daddy-long-legs, and her tanned skin looks completely poreless. And right behind her . . . I do a double-take. It's Scarlett

Johansson, wearing a blue T-shirt and black yoga trousers. She's got sunglasses on and has her head down, eyes glued to her phone, but it's definitely her. She's even tinier and more perfect in real life. After twisting around in my seat, I whirl back to Jesse.

'Did you see her? That was Scarlett Johansson!'

'Oh. No, I didn't see her.' After a minute, he adds in a clunky, deliberate way, like a bad actor being fed a line, 'My girlfriend likes her movies.'

I think that's a hint for me. I know I spoke to him yesterday on the beach, like the shameless hussy I am, but does he think I'm not going to be able to control myself unless he hangs the girlfriend garlic around his neck?

'Is she coming to the wedding?' I ask, just to be polite.

'No, she has to work.'

'What does she do?'

'She volunteers at an animal sanctuary.'

I instantly picture her: perky, blond hair in a ponytail, freshly scrubbed face with no make-up, loves handicrafts, goes hiking on weekends. But wait: is that her whole job? How does she earn a living?

'She must be very dedicated,' I say. 'I mean, to volunteer full-time . . . it must be hard financially.'

'We work it out,' Jesse says evasively.

Hm. Maybe not so saintly after all. I love our furry friends as much as the next girl, but it seems poor form to flake out on your boyfriend's family wedding for some unwanted pets.

'What do you do when you're not getting fired?' Jesse says. When I tell him I'm an actor, he asks the dreaded follow-up question. 'Have you been in anything I've seen?'

'I've been doing mainly commercial and theatre work,' I say: my standard response. I find myself continuing, 'It's hard. The people from my drama school who've got parts in television and film all seem to have gone to public school together, or they're related to the director or something. I know that sounds like I'm jealous, but it's true.'

'Well, maybe Sam can help you out.'

'Oh, he already has,' I say, thinking of Brock Wilson's script.

'I think this is where your dressmaker is at,' Jesse says, parking beside a row of shops. 'Do you have any change for the meter?'

'No, but it doesn't matter. We'll only be a minute, won't we?'

But he insists, and makes me wait by the car while he goes into the nearest shop to get change. *Very* law-abiding. I lean against the car, practically purring as I bask in the sunshine. I can't believe that a few days ago I was standing at a bus stop with wet feet, wondering if we had any Lemsip at home.

Just as I'm thinking that, I notice a little sign on the window of a place called The Farmacy: *Do you suffer from anxiety, stress? Medicinal marijuana available here.*

A thought strikes me. Alice is under an insane amount of stress. This could be exactly what she needs, and it won't even give her a hangover!

Jesse is back now, and feeding coins into the machine.

'Hey,' I say. 'Is pot legal here? I might get some for Alice.' I'm not sure if Alice will be totally up for this, but if it's legal it must be OK.

Jesse looks shocked. 'Forget it. Those places are incredibly sketchy and scammy. They could end up charging you hundreds for repeat prescriptions. And also, really?' he adds reprovingly. 'I doubt Alice needs that.'

I should have known better than to consult a teacher on buying drugs. I find his tone to be rather judgey, and it immediately makes me want to disobey him. But he's clearly on to me; he sits in the car watching me, leaving me no choice but to abandon my idea and go straight to the dressmaker's.

The dressmaker is a very severe-looking lady straight from central casting, complete with a tape measure around her neck and an indecipherable Russian-sounding accent. All I can make out is, 'Four dresses, yes? One bride and three bridesmaids.'

Oh God. I feel a cold chill as I think: there might not *be* three bridesmaids once Ruth has checked her emails. And I'm pretty sure she'll have done that by now. That stupid email feels like a ticking bomb; I don't know how to defuse it and it's only a matter of time before it explodes.

'Bride,' she says, handing me the dress. I almost stagger from the weight of it. It's heavy ivory crêpe, sleeveless but not strapless, with the kind of simplicity that can only have cost many, many dollars. 'Bridesmaids.' I put out my hands and take the dusty-pink-taupe-biscuit armful of chiffon. Alice is so nice: I'm sure not every bride would give us such gorgeous, flattering dresses.

'Do you mind if I make a phone call?' I ask the dressmaker, who shrugs. Using the mobile Alice lent me, I dial the number I got from the guest list, and wait. My palms are sweaty and my pulse is hammering, but I'm committed now.

'Wilson residence,' a female voice says, just like in the movies.

I take a deep breath. 'Hi, I'm calling from Sam Newland's office for Mr Wilson. I'm sorry, I meant to dial the office number but I think I must have got the home number by mistake.'

'OK, you should try his office,' says the voice. 'Do you want the number?'

Yes! It worked! I'm about to thank her and say goodbye when the voice says, 'But he'll be home in a couple of hours, so you can try him then if you want to set up a call.'

'OK, great, thanks. Good to know,' I say as casually as I can. 'Bye.'

This is incredible! I have the address, I have the speech memorised, and I know he's going to be at home. Fear pinches my stomach: am I really going to do this? But then I think: of course I am. Because what's more scary – going to Brock Wilson's house and asking for an audition, or going back to rainy Bromley and being the third wheel with Dad and Fi at dinner?

I make my way back to the car, weighed down by the armful of dresses. Jesse gets out and takes them from me, handing me a coffee in return – he must have got it while I was inside. 'Do we need to drop these home now?' he asks.

'Thanks. Yes, we should. But first, can we buy some snacks and drinks for this crafting evening tonight? That'll be one less thing for Alice to do,' I add virtuously.

'They look pretty,' Jesse says, glancing over the back seat as we stop at a red light.

'They're gorgeous,' I say, gulping the last of my coffee. 'I'm going to wear mine again. And do you see, each of them is a different design and shade to boot. Very cool.'

Jesse doesn't reply; he's looking at the floor of the car in front of me, where I've put my empty coffee cup. I wasn't planning on leaving it there, but now I nudge it with my foot to see what he'll do. He winces. Taking pity on him, I stash it away in my bag, feeling more and more sympathy for his wedding-dodging girlfriend. I can picture their life together: jogging every morning, watching the news together, recycling; they probably compost. No wonder she wanted to break free for a weekend.

It's fun browsing the grocery store; I love seeing all the weird products, like Mountain Dew and Green Goddess Yogurt Power Drink. I'm taken aback by how expensive it is here, though. I end up spending about $100 on some crisps, dips, cakes and little mini quiches, plus two bottles of wine – I was going to get six but Jesse convinced me that two was enough.

'My mom doesn't drink, nor does Cynthia.'

God, poor Alice. Tonight is obviously going to be a riot. 'Well, weddings drive people to drink. It's well known,' I say, as we carry the boxes back to the car.

Jesse gives me a look; I have a feeling I'm beginning to get on his nerves. But all he says is, 'Let's drop these back to their place and then we can hit the flower market.'

Everything really is bigger in LA, including flower markets. The building itself is like an aircraft hangar, with people staggering out under massive armfuls of red roses the size of triffids. We have to pay an entrance fee, and I can see why: it's like Disneyland for flowers. Everywhere there are buckets and rows of flowers four times the size of the ones we get in England and a quarter of the price: peonies, sweet peas, roses, irises . . . Mum would have gone crazy for this place; she probably would have ended up filling our hotel room with flowers, and my dad would have pretended to grumble at what a waste of money it was but secretly not minded at all.

'Are you OK?' asks Jesse. 'Is it not what you expected?'

'What? Oh yeah! I'm totally fine.' I snap back into wedding mode and take a few photos of flowers I think Alice would like. I buy a bunch of peonies so that she can see how they look with the dress, and check with the sellers that they'll have more later in the week. I also find some massive bags of natural petal confetti, as requested (the Casa de la Luna doesn't allow artificial confetti).

'Here – let me help you.' Jesse comes over and takes the bags from me, as I pay the flower seller.

'Thanks. Now let's go and buy a canopy.'

'What do we need a canopy for?' Jesse asks, trailing me through aisles of gerberas.

'It's for the bride and groom to stand under while they say their vows. It looks good in photos.' I say this matter-of-factly; I don't want him thinking I'm some kind of sucker for all this wedding stuff. I'm just doing my job.

The canopies are gorgeous, though; delicate white trellis-y ones that come with real white roses, and simpler, tent-like ones with voile cotton. I consider taking some photos to show Alice, but then I think: what she needs this week is to not have to make more decisions.

'I'll take the voile cotton one,' I tell the sales assistant.

I put it on Alice's card, give them the instructions for delivering it to the venue, and go off to find Jesse, who is looking very sadly at some cactuses, a confetti bag still under each arm.

'A present for your girlfriend?' the seller asks him.

He looks startled. 'Right. No, I don't think so.'

'Why not?' I ask, as we walk away. 'I would have thought cacti were the unwanted pets of the plant world. Or does she prefer roses?'

'Oh yeah, definitely roses,' he says, sounding glum. 'Two dozen long-stemmed red roses, three times a year: birthday, Valentine's and a surprise.'

Wow, talk about being whipped. But Jesse is obviously a very obliging guy, which makes me hopeful about the next stage of my plan.

'So,' I say, as we get back in the car. 'If it's OK with you, we need to pick something up from an address in Laurel Canyon, and then we can head back.'

'Laurel Canyon? But it's already five, and you need to be back by six for the party.'

Damn, damn, damn. I feel guilty about being late for the party, but then I remind myself that this will be a quick detour. We'll be back by seven, latest, which is when it starts anyway. And once I've managed to meet Brock Wilson, I can be totally available to Alice on all wedding fronts.

'I'll call her.' I dial her number. 'Alice? Hi, it's me! Yes, we've been getting on fine, we've got everything done. And we got some drinks and snacks for this evening, they're in the kitchen. But listen, I'm sorry, but we're going to be late for the party. We've got car trouble! I know. I'll let Jesse explain.' I hand him the phone, ignoring his protests and frantic arm-waving.

'Hey, Alice. Yeah. Um, I think the . . . carburettor's gone.' I give him a thumbs-up; he glares at me. 'Yeah, I called the rental company and they said it could take a while, so . . . Yeah, sorry about that. OK. Yep.' He hangs up. 'What the hell was that about?' he snaps.

'Thank you! That was brilliant. Very quick thinking.'

'Are you meeting your dealer or something? Because if you are—'

'No! No, it's nothing like that, I promise. Please, will you take me there?' I gaze at him pleadingly. 'It's really important. I'll explain later.'

Jesse says, with an expression of deep dissatisfaction, 'What number in Laurel Canyon?'

'It's just off it – 8262 Marmont Lane.'

He plugs it into his GPS, and starts the car. Soon we're deep in the gigantic tangle of highways and underpasses, spaghetti junctions and skyscrapers. The smog hangs thickly over everything like a giant thumbprint. On and on we drive, past buildings, parking lots, palm trees and 7-Elevens. Jesse isn't saying anything – he still seems annoyed – and I'm too nervous to talk anyway.

'Where are we now?' I ask after a while.

'Hollywood Boulevard. Didn't you hear the GPS telling you?'

'Seriously?' I look out of the window in disbelief. It's all so ordinary – low-rise buildings and signs for things like 'Smoke Shop' and 'Suit City'. A homeless guy goes by pushing a big cart full of his tattered possessions. We could be in Bromley. But before long, the landscape changes and we pass the Chinese

Theatre and the Roosevelt Hotel. Impersonators, living statues. Crowds and crowds of tourists, taking photos of each other with their hands on the ground. Maybe, if today goes well . . . But I won't jinx anything by thinking about being on the Walk of Fame.

Now we're climbing a hill – it's like a country road, lined with firs and palm trees. Up and up we drive, the bends making me feel more and more nauseous. I've got the familiar pre-audition sick feeling in the pit of my stomach, but a thousand times worse than ever before. I sip water, focus on my breathing, and start reciting the alphabet backwards to calm myself. But I keep losing concentration, and I also keep yawning, which is something I do when I'm nervous. Scared. Petrified.

'Oh, I'm sorry, are you bored?' Jesse asks. 'I know it's a really long drive. Too bad you're not at the party, huh?'

'I'm fine,' I reply weakly. We've turned off Laurel Canyon and now we're on an even posher and more exclusive-looking lane, with beautiful mansions behind high walls, lush palm trees and bougainvillea growing everywhere.

'Arrive at destination on the right,' says the GPS's mechanical voice. We stop outside a wide dark red gate, behind which is a big Spanish colonial-style house with gabled windows. I wipe my hands on my denim shorts.

'Nice place. You want to tell me who lives here?'

'Oh, it's . . . a friend,' I say, getting out of the car.

'Hey, not so fast. I'm coming with you.'

'No, no. Stay here. I won't be long.'

'Forget it! This isn't *Driving Miss Daisy.*'

I ignore him and leg it to the gate, where I ring the bell and try to look confident. 'Hi, I'm here to see Mr Wilson. I called earlier from Sam Newland's office.'

'Sam's office?' says Jesse, following me. 'What the hell is going on? Whose house is this?'

'Shush!' I tell him.

Silence; I wait in suspense. Will it work? Will they answer? Finally a dark-haired woman wearing jeans, a navy T-shirt and sandals unlocks the gate.

'Hi, I'm Denise, Brock's assistant. I'll take you in to him.'

And just like that we're walking inside. I'm so scared I barely notice the surroundings; all I see is a swimming pool and a terrace where a kid is playing, watched by a nanny. There's a breathtaking view over the city from here, but I'm not in a state to appreciate it.

'You can wait here if you like,' the woman says to Jesse, showing him to a sofa inside. 'Would you like anything to drink?'

'I'll have a non-alcoholic beer. We're not staying long,' he says, giving me a warning look. I'm too scared to say anything back to him, or to notice what the house looks like except for the high ceilings and a huge candelabra above our heads.

'Sure. This way,' she adds to me, and I follow her around a corner to a door. She knocks, and Brock Wilson answers.

He looks exactly like he does on TV: a grown-up comic-book nerd with glasses, a round, friendly, slightly shiny face, and receding hair. Cuddly, in fact, is the word. But also terrifying.

'Thanks, Denise, you can leave us to it. You've got something for me? From Sam?' he asks mildly. He's so trusting! Isn't he worried about crazed actors breaking in and holding him at knifepoint until he gives them a part? I don't have a knife, of course, but I *could* have.

'I . . . hope so. I'm . . . I think I could be perfect for the role of Ella in your film.'

'Did Sam send you?'

He's clearly puzzled, but not furious. 'Not exactly. I'm . . . well, he's getting married to my cousin. I'm helping them to organise their wedding. That's how I got your address. From the guest list. I want to audition for you.'

He's not listening; he's walking away towards his desk. He's about to press a panic button and have me dragged out of here.

'You've got fifteen minutes,' he says, sitting down. 'Show me what you've got.'

Oh thank you, God. I am so lucky. Before he can change his mind, I start the speech. I block out everything but the character and how she's feeling and I give it my absolute best shot, and I think it goes pretty well.

After I finish, he says nothing. I stand there while the minutes tick by.

'Sit down,' he says, indicating a chair.

I lower myself into it, in an agony of suspense. Did he like it? Did he hate it?

'Look. I'll be honest with you.'

This doesn't sound good.

'You do look the part. Tall, blond, English rose. But you're just . . . not what I'm looking for.' He looks a little regretful, but fine about it on the whole, as if he'd like dessert but doesn't have room for it.

'No?' I say, my voice trembling.

'This is a character who's travelled around the world and left her whole family behind at a time when women didn't do that . . . and I didn't get that.'

'Oh.' Now I'm completely stung. I thought I *had* got that across.

'I need someone with more . . . presence. More charisma.'

'I see.' He can stop there and that would be fine, frankly.

'More fiery.'

'Of course.'

'But still vulnerable. Complex. That's what I need.'

I nod, feeling about a millimetre high. He stands up and walks me to the door.

'It's not that you don't have something,' he says. 'It's just . . . not enough. Sorry.'

'Thank you very much for your time,' I whisper. He closes the door.

I want to collapse on the floor, but I manage to drag myself back along the corridor and find Jesse.

'We have to get out of here, now.'

'Why? What happened?' He looks around, startled, and then follows me out as I stagger back towards the car, barely looking right or left.

He doesn't think I can act. And I can't dismiss him by saying he's a two-bit crappy ad man or am-dram director. He's Brock Wilson. He's my hero, and he thinks I'm not good enough.

'Do you want to tell me what all that was about?' Jesse asks as we get into the car.

I shake my head, and then I manage to say, 'I need a drink.'

'You can have a drink at the party. What *happened* in there?'

'Oh no, please. I need a drink before I can face them . . . please don't make me go to the party. Not yet.' I know we're really late, but I'm in bits; I can't face a room full of strangers.

Jesse ignores me, and starts typing Alice's address into the GPS.

'I texted Alice earlier, by the way,' he says. 'Told her we were still waiting for the repair guy.'

I stare out of the window as we drive back down the hill, trying to process what's happened. Soon we're back on Laurel Canyon, and we've turned right, past a drive-through McDonald's and giant billboards advertising things like Liquor Locker and Squidbillies: America's 4th Favorite Animated Family! The sun's getting lower, sinking into the haze of smog. Ahead of us, perched on a hill, I can make out a big building like a mock French castle, with a sign outside saying *Chateau Marmont*.

'Look, Chateau Marmont,' I say tentatively. 'They must have a bar . . . I could take you for a drink to thank you for driving me around.'

Jesse says nothing.

'Jesse, I know you're not happy with me, but I really, really need a drink, now. Just a quick one and then we'll go to the party. My treat. Please?'

I can tell he wants to strangle me, but he's too nice. 'Fine,' he mutters. 'One drink, and then I'm taking you straight back. And tomorrow you're on your own. I'm not running any more errands for you.'

'OK,' I say meekly.

It turns out the bar in Chateau Marmont is down the road from the hotel itself. We drive there and Jesse hands our keys to a valet, who's so good-looking I'm gloomily positive he's an actor-in-waiting. Inside, the bar is decadent and dimly lit, with red-fringed lamps above the polished wooden bar and a sort of kitsch opium-den atmosphere. Jesse slides into a booth while I go to the bar to buy a locally crafted beer for him, and two mojitos for me. I neck the first one back and then sip the second more slowly. I know I should be calling Alice to tell her where we are, but I can't face the explanations that would involve.

102

I'm so lost in my own misery that I'm startled when I hear a voice.

'I hate to crash your pity party,' Jesse is saying. 'But are you going to tell me what happened?'

I shake my head. I'm never telling anyone; it's too humiliating.

'Let me guess,' he says. 'It involves a guy. Someone you've been seeing long-distance? Or you met him online and you saw each other for the first time today, and he's two feet shorter and two hundred pounds heavier than he said.'

I roll my eyes. 'As if I would ever cry over some guy, let alone one I'd never met. Please.'

'Well it must be something pretty big to make you blow your cousin off tonight,' he says. 'And make me spend three hours chauffeuring you across LA when I could have been . . .' he pauses as if he's trying to think of something, 'sightseeing. You can't be that selfish.'

'I'm not selfish!' I say, stung, and thinking: am I? Oh God. I probably am. The mojitos and the lack of food all day must be getting to me, because I start crying. Jesse passes me a paper napkin, looking resigned, and says, 'Come on, tell me. I was joking about the guy. It was an audition, wasn't it?'

Nodding, I manage to recover myself and tell him: about how I got Brock's address, and the audition and what a disaster it was. I expect him to say how stupid it was or tell me off for stealing the address, but instead he whistles and looks almost impressed.

'You shouldn't have done that, but I have to admit . . . you've got some moxie.'

That makes me feel worse, because I do pride myself on having moxie.

'See, the thing is,' I say, sniffing, 'I always thought, if I could have a real chance, I'd be discovered. But now I have auditioned for someone good – and he thought I was awful.' I shake my head. 'It's made me doubt my whole sense of who I am.'

I look over at Jesse and see that he's hiding a smile.

'What's so funny?'

'Nothing! Just – wow. Your whole sense of who you are? You

should be an actress, definitely. You certainly have a sense of drama.'

'I prefer actor. And I'm not so sure. Maybe being a drama queen isn't the same as being a real actor.' I drain my mojito and start ripping up my napkin.

'Have you eaten today?' Jesse asks. 'We could order some fries or something.'

'I shouldn't,' I say automatically. 'I might have a salad.'

'You need more than that,' he says. He goes to the bar and comes back with two menus. 'My girlfriend's had us on the paleo diet,' he remarks.

'The pale-what?'

'It's where you eat like a caveman. Caveperson. So, nothing but organic meat, nuts, vegetables . . . no grains, no dairy, no alcohol. It's hardcore.' He looks at the menu. 'I think I'll have the truffle mac and cheese.'

'Make it two. Actually, no. I'll have the tagliatelle with ragu, and a glass of white wine. And the cheese puffs.' After all, what's the point in watching my weight if I can't act anyway?

Jesse orders our food at the bar. Looking at him from a distance, I think what an odd pair we must look: me in my Daisy Dukes and him in his neatly ironed shirt and tie.

'Why are you wearing a tie?' I ask, when he's come back with wine for me and a cocktail for himself.

'I was meant to be meeting my uncles for a drink in some swanky bar in Beverly Hills while you ladies were crafting. I've got a jacket in the car as well.'

'I'm sorry.' For the first time, I realise how much I've turned his day upside down.

'It's fine. Trust me, I didn't feel like it.'

'How come?'

He looks as if he's about to explain, but we're interrupted by the arrival of the food. My cheese puffs and tagliatelle with ragu are to die for: little melty balls of flavour, and sweet pasta perfectly al dente. I can feel the carbs and fat going straight to my brain. Jesse gives me some of his mac and cheese, which is so good it makes me bang the table with my fist.

'This is unbelievable,' I mumble between mouthfuls of salty, greasy goodness. 'I can't believe I've deprived myself for so long.'

'Me either.'

The way he looks at me makes me wonder if he's talking about more than mac and cheese. But he's hardly the type to flirt when he's got a girlfriend.

'If I keep this up, I'll definitely be too fat to go on Valentino's yacht,' I remark, wiping up the last of the pasta sauce with a piece of freshly baked bread.

'Excuse me?'

I laugh, feeling better. 'It's something I read once. There's a memoir by some celebrity's daughter where she talks about a trip that was being planned on Valentino's yacht when she was a teenager, and how excited she was – until a famous actress, her mother's friend, said to her, "You're too fat to go on Valentino's yacht." It's so camp and ridiculous, not to mention mean. But sometimes I use it as motivation when I'm tempted to pig out.'

'You use that as motivation? Some bitchy comment that scarred a teenage girl for life?' Jesse says.

'Yeah. I know it's twisted.'

A handsome blond waiter with frighteningly perfect teeth comes by to clear away our plates. 'You guys all SET here? How WAS everything?' he says. He's also obviously an actor, throwing himself into the part of Waiter this evening. I resolve to leave him a big tip.

'Can I ask you something?' Jesse asks, once he's gone and we've ordered another round of drinks. 'Why was it so important to you to get this part anyway?'

'Why?' I look at him blankly: isn't it obvious? 'Because I love acting.' But I find myself continuing, 'And also . . . my mother used to act, before she died. But she gave it up to look after me and my brother. She became a teacher because the hours were easier with a family. Before that, she did quite a lot of theatre, and she was in an ad for coffee – you still can find it online.' I've watched it so many times I know that silly ad by heart.

'What happened to her?' he asks gently.

'She was driving to a rehearsal, as it happens.' Tears are pricking my eyes and I blink to stop them. 'Just a little local amateur production, but it was her first part in years, and she was so excited about it. It was a horrible rainy night, and another car shot out of a side road without looking . . . and that was that. The other driver was killed too.'

'I'm sorry.'

'I just feel so sad for her that she didn't even get to do that play, and . . . maybe it sounds silly, but I feel as if I owe it to her to try and make it. And to my dad. I don't know if that makes any sense.'

I take a breath and another slug of wine. I can't believe I told him all that. I'm braced for more sympathy or questions, but instead he says, 'I know what you mean.'

'Do you?'

'Of course. I want to please my family too. Which is why this whole thing with my girlfriend . . .'

'What whole thing?'

He pauses before saying, 'I broke up with her. But I haven't told them yet.'

'Why not?'

'They're going to be disappointed and blame me and want us to get back together, and I can't deal with it, not this weekend, with Sam's wedding and everything. Do you want another drink?'

'I'll go. What would you like?'

I decide we'd better change the subject before we both spiral into a depression. So when I get back from the bar, we start talking about films and books and our families, and random nonsense like the reason he was jogging barefoot (he forgot his trainers) and the fact that his Aunt Cynthia, Sam's mother, has discovered she's one-sixteenth Navajo and wants the whole family to do a sweat lodge ceremony at Christmas.

'What is a sweat lodge ceremony?'

'I don't know how authentic it is, but it's meant to be a Native American custom. It basically means they pack you into a room and turn the heat up, and you see visions. Allegedly. My Uncle John has offered to take her to Paris instead, but she's not budging.'

106

'I'd take Paris over a sweat lodge any day.' I wave my wine glass to indicate our surroundings. 'We could almost be in Paris here, couldn't we? They even serve absinthe.'

'I wouldn't know. I've never been to Europe. I'm such a cliché: an English teacher who's never been to England.'

'How come? You must get good holidays as a teacher.'

'I do, but Wendy never wanted to leave her dogs. She adopted them from the shelter. They only have three legs each,' he adds, holding up three fingers to illustrate. 'Poor little guys.' He looks sad, and I realise he's pretty hammered.

I shake my head. 'She put her three-legged rescue dogs above a trip to Europe? And her name's Wendy? I hope you don't mind me saying, I think you dodged a bullet there.'

'You could be right,' he says, smiling down at me. I suddenly notice that he's sitting rather close to me, his arm propped casually on top of the booth behind me. His tie is crooked and his dark hair is ruffled. His eyes are gorgeous: sort of almond-shaped, with the kind of long, dark lashes that are wasted on men. Out of nowhere, I have the urge to undo his tie and run my fingers through his hair. Slowly, I move a fraction closer to him – and he moves a fraction closer to me.

'So you think I should take a trip to Europe?'

I have to clear my throat before I can reply. I'm finding it hard to meet his eyes.

'I think you might like it.'

And then my phone beeps at top volume with a text message, almost giving us both a heart attack. It's from Sam, and it says: *Where are you? Should we call the police?* I drop my phone in panic. Jesse picks it up, takes a look, and without a word we put down way too many dollars before racing out of the bar.

Once we're outside, it becomes obvious from the way we crash around that we're both properly drunk. Clearly we have to leave Jesse's car there overnight and find a taxi. It's a while before we're able to get on the road, but eventually we stumble up the steps to Sam and Alice's place. Sam answers the door looking like a thundercloud.

'I'm sorry we're late. Where's Alice?' I ask, feeling queasy with fear.

'She's gone to bed,' he says curtly, keeping his voice low. 'She was pretty tired after hosting this evening all by herself, and worrying about where you were . . . and we got a strange call this evening.'

He must have heard from Brock Wilson. Oh God, oh God, oh God . . .

'Her friend Ruth called. Apparently she got some weird email from Alice, firing her from being a bridesmaid. Do you happen to know anything about that?'

Aaaaarrrgh. 'Oh no. Oh Sam, I'm so sorry. Look, the thing is, I *did* write to Ruth, but only because she was being so horrible to Alice—'

'I don't want to hear it,' Sam snaps. 'Let me make it clear for you. Alice is upset. In tears. That needs not to happen. Ever. Do you understand?'

I nod, feeling like a total worm.

'If you can't help her properly, then stay out of her way. That goes for you too, by the way,' he adds, seeing Jesse behind me, apparently for the first time. 'My God,' he adds. 'What did you do to him?'

I look at Jesse, who seems normal; a bit bleary-eyed, maybe, and his tie is undone and he's swaying on his feet, but he's fine.

'I'm fine,' Jesse explains. 'We had car trouble.'

Sam looks at us both in disgust, and says to Jesse, 'You can keep her tonight. Just bring her back in the morning. Not too early.'

And he shuts the door in our faces.

'Whoa,' Jesse says loudly. 'He wasn't happy, huh? What was all that about an email?'

The last thing we need is to wake Alice up by drunkenly discussing the situation outside her window, so I drag him away from the house. I'm tempted to knock on the door again to try and apologise, but Sam's face was too scary.

This is like a nightmare, except it's real and it's my fault. I had hoped to be able to tell Alice that yes, I went missing, but I got a part in Brock's film; I thought she would be happy for me.

Instead I've made her cry. I can't believe I've done that and I don't know how I'm ever going to make it right again.

'We can walk to my place from here,' Jesse is saying. 'It's on the other side of Abbot Kinney.'

'OK,' I say dully. I turn to follow him, but we end up bumping into each other.

'Steady,' he says, holding my shoulders. 'Hm. Maybe we should sit somewhere for a while . . . to sober up?'

'OK,' I repeat. Then an even better idea occurs to me. 'How about the beach? It's just down here . . .'

I'm half expecting him to say the beach is really dangerous at night or something, but to my surprise, he hesitates for a bit and then says, 'Sure.'

The beach, so busy during the day, is deserted; just crashing waves and us. The sky is completely clear and as full of stars as Hollywood Boulevard. We don't say anything, just listen to the boom of the surf and the hiss as it retreats.

One of my favourite episodes in *Sex and the City* is the one where Carrie gets dumped by Post-it note. There's a bit where she says that this can't be the day when she was broken up with by a Post-it note; it has to be the day that something else happens. Which is exactly how I feel. This cannot be the night when I made my favourite cousin cry and spoiled her wedding. It *has* to be the night when something else happens.

'Jesse,' I say. 'How about a swim?'

'A swim? No way. It's super dangerous. And freezing.'

'A dip, then. It won't be freezing, it's really warm.' I stand up, and start unbuttoning my flannel shirt.

'Lily, you're crazy . . .' he says, looking away.

'Exactly. This way, this will be the worst thing I've done all day.' I drop the shirt on the ground – it's fine, I'm wearing a bra – and unzip my denim shorts.

'It will be if you drown. The currents here are really strong. Come on, put that back on,' he says.

Picking up my shirt, he puts his hand out to grab my arm – and then I don't know if he's pulled me closer or if I've come to him, but suddenly we're standing very close together. And then we're kissing. He kisses me, hungrily, holding my head in his hands. I can actually feel my knees wobbling. All thoughts of a swim have gone out of my mind. He presses me closer, and it seems as if things are about to get very unplanned indeed when suddenly we're blinded by a glaring white light. I let out a shriek.

'Sir? Ma'am? Can you stand up for me, please?' It's a very young-looking policeman, wielding a flashlight. 'The beach isn't safe at night. You need to get yourselves home.'

'No problem, officer,' Jesse says, covering me with my flannel shirt. 'Come on,' he says to me. 'Let's get you home before anything else exciting happens.'

I wake up the next morning to find Justin Bieber staring down at me from a poster on the wall. The duvet is pink, with fairies on it. I'm still in all my clothes and every part of me hurts, from my head to my throat. I'm completely disoriented for a minute before I remember I'm at Jesse's family's rented house.

Poking my head out of the room, I see a bathroom and slip inside. With my panda eyes and bed hair, I'm not what most families would want to see at their breakfast table, but I don't have anything to repair myself with, so I settle for scrubbing at the mascara with some baby shampoo, and make my way down the corridor.

There are voices coming from the kitchen, as well as the smell of coffee and something else delicious. Jesse, looking very grey and unshaven, is sitting at the table while an older woman with blond hair in a neat ponytail, dressed head to toe in hiking gear, is making waffles. Seeing me, she turns around and says in a super-friendly voice with undertones of menace, 'So this must be the mysterious missing *cousin*!'

'Lily, this is my mom, Diane; Mom, meet Lily,' Jesse says.

'Um – hi,' I say in a small voice, sitting down.

'So what happened to you two last night?' she says, looking me up and down. 'We were so *worried* about you. First we thought you were stuck in traffic, then we thought you might have been in a car wreck, or held up and robbed or even *killed*. I mean, this is Los Angeles.'

'I told you, Mom. The repair guy took hours to show up, and

then we had to get a cab, and then we ran into traffic. And my phone died.'

Jesse's story seems plausible to me, but his mum clearly doesn't buy it. 'And then you got locked out of the house? That seems so strange to me. Alice doesn't seem like the kind of girl who would let her cousin wander the *streets*.'

Jesse pours out some coffee for me. I sip it gratefully, unable to meet his eye. I'm trying not to think about how much I must have embarrassed Alice last night, as well as worrying her. Not to mention our escapade on the beach: what was I *thinking*? Thank God we weren't arrested. I can only imagine Sam's reaction if he'd been woken up again to bail us out.

'Hey, you're finally awake! We thought you were going to sleep for ever.'

I blink at the chirpy vision that's just bounced into the room and is looking at me curiously: around twelve or thirteen, tall, tanned, with a long brown ponytail. I'm not sure if it's a hallucination or what, but I feel like I'm seeing two of her.

'Claudia, don't be rude. Lily, these are my sisters, Carla and Claudia.'

'Are we ready to go hiking already?' asks Carla or Claudia, bouncing on one foot. 'I'm bored.'

'We're waiting for your brother, girls. Here are your waffles, Jesse.' Diane plonks them down in front of him. 'Lily, I'm afraid we don't have any for you. We weren't expecting extra guests.'

Jesse rolls his eyes and gives me half of the waffles on his plate. I start eating quickly before Diane takes them away from me.

'Did you sleep in your clothes?' Carla or Claudia asks me. 'You look sort of wrinkled.'

'How come you couldn't make the crafting evening?' the other one chimes in. 'And why didn't you stay at Sam's place last night?'

They both look so cute and healthy and clean; they make me feel like a public service announcement about the consequences of bad behaviour.

'We had car trouble. Stop asking so many questions,' Jesse says.

111

'You know who we needed last night? Wendy,' says Diane. 'Remember those little paper signs she made for my birthday that said "Yay"? So creative. I can't wait to see what she does for your wedding. Lily, did you know Jesse is getting married next June?'

My waffle seems to have got stuck halfway down. 'Ah – no, I didn't,' I say, looking at Jesse, who's busy pouring himself more coffee.

'We're going to be bridesmaids!' says Carla or Claudia. 'Wendy's going to get us both dresses from J. Crew. She says every girl deserves to be a princess for a day.'

I can't look at him. I feel so stupid. Not only did he not break up with his girlfriend; they're getting *married*.

'Well, Jesse, you'd better get ready,' Diane says. 'We're supposed to be meeting Cynthia and John and the cousins. For our hiking trip. Don't tell me you forgot?'

'I'm coming,' he says shortly. 'I just need to drop Lily home first.'

'She can walk, it's not far. You need to hurry or we'll be late. And since we're down a car, we all have to go together.'

Jesse hesitates before saying, 'Lily, do you mind?'

'Not at all.' I get to my feet. I've got to get out of here, and away from him. 'Um, thank you for the coffee,' I add to his mum.

She barely nods. 'One last thing: Jesse, will you sweep up the hallway before we leave? Someone seems to have tracked in a lot of *sand*.' She gives me another look and then she's gone.

I hurry out, Jesse following me. I wait until we're on the street before I turn on him. 'You're getting *married*?'

He looks uncomfortable. 'No, I'm not. We've broken up.'

'If you say so.' I don't believe him for a second. Calvin did the exact same thing: told me something was over when it was blatantly still going on while he was away shooting his stupid pilot. He might have been a better actor than Jesse, but I still know a lie when I hear one. I keep walking.

'Lily – it's the other way. Wait! Stop.'

I turn around, ready to hear a proper explanation if he's got it. 'It's left here,' he says, 'and then right on Abbot Kinney, and left again once you pass Intelligentsia Coffee. I'm sorry I can't drop you home. I'm sorry about all of this.'

That's it? Pathetic. Not only is he cheating on his fiancée, he's a wimp who can't stand up to his family.

'Don't be,' I say with as much dignity as I can muster. 'Yesterday was one giant mistake and I think it's best we forget about it.' And I march off.

I'm a nervous wreck by the time I knock on Alice's door. She looks awful: pale, hair scraped back, puffy red-rimmed eyes. I think of how she looked when she met me at the airport – glowing, smiling, hair bouncing. It's like a makeover in reverse, and it's all my fault.

'Come in,' she says quietly. I follow her, head down. I'm so ashamed. All the shenanigans of yesterday – getting Brock Wilson's address, the audition, getting drunk with Jesse, kissing him, not to mention emailing Ruth – seem like the actions of a stupid, selfish cow.

'Alice, I'm so sorry about last night . . .'

'It's OK, really. That's the least of my worries. I'm upset because we had a phone call from the Casa de la Luna this morning. They've had a fire and they're going to be closed for at least three weeks.'

'You're joking!'

'No, I wish.' She pads back to the sofa, where she's obviously been watching TV, though the sound's now on mute. The curtains are drawn and there's tons of mess from last night on every surface, including rows and rows of mini bottles of olive oil and piles of origami decorations and paper. 'We've taken the morning off work to try and scope out other places, but it's too short notice. I think we're going to have to postpone the wedding. I don't know. I can't deal with it any more.' She grabs a handful of nuts from a bowl beside her. 'Want some candied pecans? Cynthia made them. In her spare time, in a holiday house. Can you imagine? Sam's family is unbelievable. They're all doing a ten-mile hike in Topanga today, which is good because it gives us a few hours before we have to break the news to them.'

I feel very lucky that she's not more angry at me, but I'm also worried about her: I think this news has tipped her over the edge. 'Is Sam here?' I ask. I'm scared of facing him but I want him here to look after her.

She nods. 'We were just talking about whether we should go to the County Clerk's Office or fly to Vegas and try and have a party for everyone later. But everyone's here now, and we wanted all our friends and family to be there . . .' Her eyes start brimming over. I can feel mine pricking as well.

'Alice, I'm going to fix this.'

'Thanks,' she says, laughing and wiping her eyes. 'That's sweet of you, Lily, but you can't.'

'Yes I can!' I spot a pile of pink paper napkins with 'Here Comes the Bride' on them and hand one to her. 'I said I would help you with the wedding and I will. I'll find somewhere. Just give me your contact numbers and I'll do all the work. From now on, I am your wedding planner, and I'll do a good job. I promise. I'm sorry I've been so awful, but please, please let me make it up to you.' I'm so desperate for her to believe me, I'm almost in tears as well.

'How are you going to do that?' a voice says behind me. 'You don't even know the city.'

It's Sam, his hair damp from the shower, in jeans and bare feet, pulling on a white T-shirt. He pokes his head out of the T-shirt, and gives me an unfriendly look. I have to say, although he's frightening when he's in a bad mood, he is also rather sexy. Off-topic, Lily.

'Well – couldn't you have it at someone's house? People have massive houses here.' I'm actually thinking of Brock Wilson's place, but I don't mention that. I try to think of the other famous names I saw on the guest list. 'What about Luther Carson? Would he let you use his place?'

'Luther?' Sam says dubiously.

'I think he would, you know,' Alice says to Sam.

'You think? It seems like a big ask . . .'

'As long as it wasn't any hassle, I think he'd quite like it,' says Alice. 'It would make him feel like the star of the show.'

'That's all we need,' Sam says. 'I guess I could call him . . .'

'No, I'll call him,' says Alice, jumping off the sofa and looking more like herself.

After Alice leaves the room, I start clearing up while Sam sends messages on his BlackBerry, ignoring me. I'm relieved that the whole topic of Ruth and the crafting evening seems to have been shelved, but I'm not going to push my luck.

Minutes later, Alice comes back beaming all over. 'Luther said it's fine. We can have the ceremony in the back yard, and there's room for the reception there too. We just need to organise chairs and tables. Oh, and catering.'

A back yard doesn't sound so promising – it makes me think of some poky little area where they keep the bins and empty milk bottles. Seeing my expression, Sam says, 'It's about five acres, with ocean views. Anything else?'

'Yes, he said Jenna can do my make-up. Isn't that lovely? That's Luther's wife,' Alice explains to me. 'She's a make-up artist.'

'That's great!' I was hoping Alice would let me do her make-up myself. But this isn't about me, it's about Alice.

'He's given me his housekeeper's number, and he said we can make arrangements with her. So I suppose we call everyone and tell them to go there instead?' She looks at Sam.

'Let me call people,' I plead. 'The officiant and caterers and guests and everyone. I'll make an extra column in the spreadsheet to keep track of who I've called and to confirm they know. And I'll see if we need a special licence or anything. In fact, let's make a list now of everything I need to do, and then you can go back to work. What about parking at Luther's place? I can look into that . . .'

I look at them both, pleading silently with them to give me a second chance. Sam doesn't seem inclined to give me any such thing. But Alice says, 'OK.'

'I guess we don't have any choice,' Sam says ungraciously. 'Wait a second, though. How are you going to manage without being able to drive?'

I take a deep breath and look at them both. 'I can drive. I have my licence with me, and I can hire a car. I'll be absolutely fine.'

I've been thinking about this ever since I left Jesse's place, and

I've realised I'm going to have to face my fears and start driving again at some point. Mum would be the first person to tell me that. And I owe it to Alice to step up and do it now, if I'm going to be any use to her at all.

'Good idea, Lil,' Alice says, smiling at me. 'I think you'll be fine as well.'

After we've spent half an hour hashing out a plan of operation over coffee, I finish cleaning up and Alice goes to have a shower. Sam's about to leave too when I stop him.

'Sam, there's something else I've got to . . . confess. It's sort of the reason I was late . . .' Before I lose my nerve, I come clean about the entire Brock Wilson fiasco. I even tell him about filching the script from his bag; there's no point in leaving anything out as it'll only make things worse if it comes out later. Which, knowing my luck, it will.

Once I've finished, Sam regards me silently for a long time.

'Tell me something,' he says eventually. 'Do you think you can take all this . . . manic determination that you have, all this ruthless scheming and plotting, and channel it into working on our wedding? Because that would be good.'

I nod frantically. 'I promise.'

'What made you write that email to Ruth?' he asks abruptly.

'Oh.' I look down at my hands, noticing that my nails are bitten to pieces. 'Because she was being horrible to Alice. She was giving her extra stress and making her feel that her wedding was inconvenient.'

I'm realising now how stupid that sounds, given that I'm the one who ruined the craft evening. But Sam stays quiet, which makes me ramble on even more disastrously.

'And I thought, nobody messes with my family. Sort of . . . *Accept this justice as a gift on my cousin's wedding day.*' Then I kick myself. He's probably not in the mood for my Marlon Brando impression.

To my surprise, Sam laughs. 'You're a *Godfather* fan?'

'They're my favourite films! I've watched all of them, with my dad. He loves them.'

He smiles, and I begin to feel better for the first time since I

116

made Alice cry. 'You're right,' he says. 'Nobody messes with our family.'

Feeing weak with relief, I decide that Sam, like Alice, is an incredibly nice person. Unlike his stupid cousin.

For the next four days, I live, breathe and sleep wedding. Instead of it being a nightmare, I love it. It's hectic, but also very satisfying to tick things off the list, and figure out practicalities like signs to show people where the loos are, and who's going to put up the marquee and pack away all the chairs at the end of the night. It's no different to producing a play, except we don't even have to sell tickets. Best of all, I feel as if I'm finally helping Alice instead of sabotaging her. I love giving her regular updates about all the things that are sorted and that she and Sam don't have to worry about.

'Are you sure you don't mind me deciding things without you?' I ask her doubtfully, when we're talking about what time to serve dinner.

She shakes her head. 'We'd prefer it. Sam only cares about the ceremony, and I only care about the ceremony and my dress. And my hair,' she adds sheepishly. 'Everything else is over to you.'

One of my main jobs is to be a buffer between Alice and her future mother-in-law. Cynthia's not pleased at first to be dealing with the monkey instead of the organ-grinder, but I flatter her by asking advice and channelling her energy with every spare task I can think of, from organising car pools to collecting the last RSVPs. She and Diane have very strong feelings over the height and number of the flower arrangements, so I just ask them to give me a shopping list.

I put Sam's younger brother, Nick, in charge of favours. He's quite camp and very sweet and enthusiastic, and he's obviously very proud to be a groomsman. He's been poring over wedding websites and blogs, and he keeps trying to test me on minor points of wedding etiquette.

'What about escort cards?' he asks, when I'm at their rented apartment dropping off the baskets of favours.

'Are you serious? Who are you planning to give those to?'

It turns out that escort cards, instead of being ads for dubious services, are like name cards that people pick up when they get to the venue. We've already got place cards for the table, and a seating chart, so I decide we can do without those.

'Really? I saw some cute ones on Pinterest. And I think my mom will be bummed if we don't have them.'

'Then let's not tell her,' I suggest. God, it's fun to make decisions. I wish I got to do more of it in my normal life. As I rush off, I hear him muttering happily, 'This wedding is going to be the death of me.'

Then there's flower shopping with Sam's younger sister Melissa, who I like a lot. She's very pretty and spends lots of time texting her boyfriend and staring into shop windows, but she's also very laid-back and easy-going. When I ask her what she does for work, she rolls her eyes and says, 'Oh my God, don't even go there. Beyond boring.' She's so laid-back, in fact, that when Alice tentatively asks her if she'd like to be a bridesmaid, and wear a dress she hasn't even tried on, she says, 'Sure.'

'Thank God she said yes,' Alice says. 'Otherwise we would have had an uneven number of bridesmaids and groomsmen.' It's the day before the wedding and we're getting our nails done at a very chi-chi little place in Santa Monica, where they serve bubble tea and fortune cookies. Melissa was invited, but she overslept and couldn't make it.

'And darling, everyone knows the wedding isn't legal unless you have an even number of bridesmaids and groomsmen,' Poppy says, teasing her. Poppy is great. She and Charlie flew in a few hours ago, but she's wearing the most incredible pink vintage Chanel jacket with faded blue skinny jeans and high heels. She can also raise one eyebrow, which is something I've never managed.

'Well, it made Cynthia happy,' Alice says. 'This is her only chance at a traditional family wedding. Melissa will probably get married on the beach in flip-flops. Nick will have a big white wedding, but not quite the kind Cynthia wants. He told me he's going to have "We Found Love" by Rihanna for his first dance.'

'They're probably just relieved Sam's not marrying some airhead actress,' says Poppy. 'Oh. Sorry, Lily.'

'That's OK,' I say, amused. I haven't actually thought about acting or checked Spotlight in days, just because I've been so busy.

'I'm still not clear, though. Why can't Ruth make it exactly?' Poppy asks.

Alice and I exchange glances. 'I'm sorry,' I say for the millionth time.

'It's genuinely fine.' Alice explains to Poppy about my email to Ruth, and says that she called Ruth to apologise. 'And she actually said she was sorry too. She's been a little jealous because her boyfriend hasn't proposed yet. She admitted they were broke and flying here was a stretch for them, so I said not to worry about it. So I'm genuinely glad you emailed her, Lily,' she finishes. 'Honestly. Otherwise we would have been resenting each other, but this way we cleared the air.'

Poppy is looking at me with a mixture of fear and amusement.

'Talk about Ruthless. It sounds like you have been busy,' she says, as we walk over to the pedicure station. 'Anything else happen this week that we should know about?'

'Not really,' I say, crossing my fingers.

'In other news,' Alice says, 'Sam's cousin Jesse has broken up with his fiancée and it's caused a massive family handbag. Oh Lily, you've spilled your tea.'

My hands are shaking, but I recover myself slightly while Alice goes on.

'The family all loved her, and they'd set a date, and Jesse's mother and Wendy – that's the fiancée – had been dress shopping together and all sorts,' Alice is saying. 'Poor Jesse. It must be so hard to call off a wedding, but all Diane can talk about is their deposits and how they'd already sent their STDs.'

'Excuse me?' says Poppy, raising one eyebrow.

'Save-the-date cards, sorry. Wedding lingo. It's all a nightmare, especially since Jesse's father is in prison.'

'*What?*' Poppy and I say in unison.

'Yes – oh dear, that's very indiscreet of me. Don't mention it, obviously. He's doing four years for tax evasion. I do feel sorry for Diane, but she's not making it any easier – she keeps talking about how this was the only thing she had to look forward to, and the one good thing happening to their family . . . I must say, I'm glad she's not my FMIL.'

'FMIL?' asks Poppy.

'Sorry: future mother-in-law.'

I stare blankly at my feet in the soapy water, thinking: poor Jesse. He obviously wasn't lying after all. And no wonder he's so law-abiding – or was, before I got him drunk. Oh my God: imagine if we'd been arrested on the beach for public indecency or something!

'Didn't Jesse mention any of this to you?' Alice asks me. 'He drove Lily around the other day,' she adds to Poppy.

'Did he now,' says Poppy, giving me a sly look. 'Was that fun?'

'Did something happen with you and Jesse?' Alice asks, almost knocking her magazine into her footbath. 'That's great! Tell me more!'

'Ye-es,' I admit. 'He'd already told me about breaking up with the fiancée. But we were both drunk. No big deal.' I would normally be more open with Alice, but I don't want to run the risk of her or even Poppy saying anything to Sam that might get back to Jesse.

I can't help wondering if Jesse's announcement has something to do with me. Though if it did, surely I would have heard from him by now? Oh well. Even if he didn't live on the other side of the world, his life must be complicated enough at the moment, and he's completely on the rebound. All in all, I decide it's just as well that we're not talking.

'Who's in charge here?' asks a man in work boots and a hard hat.

'She is,' Nick says, pointing at me.

'What is it?' I ask, panicked. It's the morning of the wedding and we're well behind schedule. The chairs aren't set out yet, the caterers are late, and the canopy where Sam and Alice are meant to be saying their vows still looks like scaffolding. And now there's someone in a hard hat who seems to think I'm his foreman.

'We're trying to put up your marquee, but the ground here

doesn't match the plan we were given. We don't normally work to a plan, and this one makes no sense.'

I look at him blankly.

'What do you want me to do about it? I don't know anything about marquees. Just put it up whichever way you think will make it stay up.'

'We thought you wanted it done,' he points at his piece of paper, 'according to this plan.'

'I don't know anything about a plan! I've never put up a marquee in my life! Just please put it up and make it stay up!'

'Lily!' Poppy yells out of an upper window. 'They want to do your hair.'

'Give me five minutes!' I have to get this canopy up before I do anything else. I climb up the stepladder I borrowed from Luther's housekeeper and start wrestling with the poles, instructions in one hand. I didn't know the bloody thing would come in pieces; it's worse than Ikea furniture. Why oh why didn't I put it up yesterday instead of getting my nails done? Nobody will notice my nails, but they will notice if Alice and Sam have to get married on a pile of sticks.

'Do you want a hand with that?' says a voice behind me. It's Jesse, not in his suit yet. He's obviously come by to help. My heart thuds at the sight of him and I wish I'd been able to wash my hair this morning, or put on make-up, instead of keeping myself a blank canvas for the hair and make-up people. I must look a fright.

'God, yes please. Thank you. Um . . . great. Thanks.' I'm too nervous to say anything else, so I thrust the instructions into his hand and race off across the lawn and into the house.

Luther's crib, a gigantic mock-colonial mansion, is both massive and thoroughly pimped, with a vast hallway with marble floor and *Gone with the Wind* stairs, long silk curtains everywhere and tall windows that overlook the Pacific. I hope I'll be able to find my way to the Bridal Prep Command Centre without the help of GPS.

'We're in here,' Poppy calls from a landing. I do a double-take: her hair is looking three times its normal size, and not in a good way.

'I know, I know,' she says. 'I'll fix it when he's gone. But wait till you see Luther's bedroom. There are mirrors on the ceiling!'

'Is everything OK?' I ask, sliding into the room. 'Oh, Alice. You look gorgeous.'

Her hair is in a beautiful low chignon twisted at the back of her neck – very Old Hollywood. She's wrapped in a dressing gown and Jenna is doing her face; there's a lot of glow and dew going on and her eyes look enormous.

'How's it all going out there?' she asks anxiously, talking out of the corner of her mouth as Jenna blots her lipstick.

'Perfect! All good. Zen, Zen.' I wave my hands to indicate peace and calm. 'How are you?'

'I feel sick,' she says in a small voice. 'And I've just realised I have nowhere to put my lipstick or my concealer.'

'It's OK, I'll grab you for touch-ups when you need it,' says Jenna. Contrary to what I was expecting, she's a real earth-mother type, very calm and capable and gorgeous. She's also a size fourteen or thereabouts; it makes me think more highly of Luther that he's married to a non-lollipop.

'Do you want some more tea, darling?' says Aunt Emily, coming into the room looking smart in a bottle-green silk suit. She arrived yesterday, having left her flight until the last minute in case my cousin Erica had her baby early. 'Are you sure you won't have a banana? Lily! How are you? Help me persuade Alice to have a snack.'

'Mum, please, stop asking me.'

'You look beautiful, Emily,' I say, hugging her to distract her from thrusting bananas at Alice. Emily likes to be equipped with snacks at all times; I'm willing to bet the banana came all the way with her from M&S in Hitchin.

Next minute the hairdresser, Stevie, sweeps into the room. 'Well hello, Bridesmaid Two,' he says, snapping his straighteners at me. 'Is this Bridesmaid Two? Or Maid of Honour?'

'Oh God,' says Alice, looking nauseous. 'I honestly hadn't thought about it. I don't know who the maid of honour is. I'm sorry if that's really rude.'

'It's fine!' I say quickly. 'Poppy, you should be maid of honour. I can be a bridesmaid.'

'No, you're family! I'll be a bridesmaid,' says Poppy.

'Melissa, help me out,' says Alice to Melissa, who's playing games on her phone. 'What does the maid of honour have to do?'

'I think she walks down the aisle with the best man,' says Melissa. 'And the bridesmaids walk with the groomsmen. Can I please not walk with Jesse? He's my cousin and it would be weird.'

'I don't know who else you can walk with,' says Alice. 'You're related to Nick *and* Jesse, don't forget.'

Stevie is looking bemused; he's obviously not used to this kind of ad hoc scenario. We've just decided Poppy will be maid of honour but that Melissa will walk with the best man when the door bursts open and someone crashes into the room, soaked with sweat, dressed in workout clothes and plugged into an iPod. It's Luther Carson, looking even sexier in real life than he does on screen, if that's possible. Poppy, Aunt Emily, Melissa, Stevie and I all try not to stare at him as Alice introduces us. I don't know if I'm more discombobulated by meeting Luther Carson, or by seeing him in the same room as my Aunt Emily.

'What's going on?' he says, pulling off his sweaty T-shirt, seemingly oblivious to all our eyes riveted on him. 'Alice, you look very pretty – nice job, baby.' He goes to kiss Jenna, who swats him away distractedly.

'That was a sweet run. Eight miles, sixty-two minutes,' he says, flopping down on the bed, where all Alice's underwear and accessories are laid out. 'Well, what have we here? Sam's a lucky guy.' He's picked up Alice's garter belt and is looking at it with his trademark sexy smirk. Jenna glances up, finally seeming to notice him.

'LUTHER!' She stands up and starts shooing him away. 'Put that down! Get out of here! Go and shower in one of the guest bathrooms and then see if they need help downstairs. Sorry about that, hon,' she says to Alice, sitting down and applying a last dusting of translucent powder as if nothing's happened.

There's a knock at the door. Poppy goes to answer it, and comes back to say, 'The photographer wants to come in and do some getting-ready candid shots.'

'Now?' Alice says, looking green.

'You don't have to if you don't want to, darling,' says Aunt Emily. 'It could be rather nice, though. Erica had them at *her* wedding.' The look on Alice's face tells me this may not be the first time she's heard this phrase.

'I wouldn't mind a few minutes on my own,' she says faintly.

'Good idea,' says Emily. 'Everyone, let's clear out and give Alice some peace. You'll be super, darling. I'll come back in a while with your bouquet.'

I look at them both, thinking how lucky Alice is to have her mother there on her wedding day. Emily is obviously thinking the same thing. As we leave the room, she squeezes my arm and whispers, a catch in her voice, 'I do wish your mum was here.'

'Me too,' I say, squeezing her back. But there's no time to brood: Stevie is already asking me how I feel about a sort of Grecian goddess up-do, and Nick has run upstairs to say that his Great-Aunt Sarah, who shouldn't really be driving, has turned up early and managed to scrape one of Luther's vintage cars, and did anyone remember to order pizza for the band?

For the next hour and a half, chaos reigns as we frantically race to finish everything before the guests arrive. And then it's time, and Alice is walking up the aisle on Uncle Graham's arm, to the sound of 'God Only Knows' by the Beach Boys. Melissa follows with the best man, then Poppy with Jesse and me with Nick. The mess of this morning has disappeared and everything looks perfect: the canopy at the end of the lawn with stunning ocean views behind it; bunches of sweet peas at the end of each row of chairs; the marquee behind us where we'll be eating and dancing later.

The ceremony goes perfectly. Cynthia reads a Native American poem about two eagles soaring in the sky. Aunt Emily reads from Corinthians 13. When Alice and Sam recite the wedding vows I helped them find on the internet, and exchange the rings I picked up from the jeweller's, my eyes start filling up.

'Do you have a tissue?' Poppy asks me, as we wait to have our photos taken afterwards. 'Oh thanks, darling. I'm getting sentimental in my old age.'

'Good. Me too,' says a good-looking blond guy in a pale blue suit and white shirt, handing us each a glass of champagne. Poppy introduces me to Charlie, her boyfriend.

'Quite a place, isn't it?' Charlie says, indicating the rolling green lawn, the perfect sunshine and the beach and ocean twenty feet away. 'The last wedding I went to was in a sports hall in Dagenham. Bit different.'

'I love the mix of guests,' Poppy says. 'Look at that guy – I think he was in *True Blood* – standing beside Alice's mum in her hat. Have you met any celebs, Lily?'

'Not really.' I have already said hello to Brock Wilson and his wife – he said hi vaguely as if he couldn't quite place me, which was a relief.

'Sam must be annoyed those other three guys turned up wearing the same suit as him,' Charlie says. I'm about to tell him this was on purpose when I see the glint in his eye and realise he's joking. I think I might have temporarily lost my sense of humour in all the wedding panic.

I start talking to Charlie and Poppy about their hotel and the rest of their travel plans, which they're very excited about: Griffith Observatory and Palm Springs for her, Disneyland and Vegas for him. But the whole time, I'm conscious of Jesse in the distance, talking to a Natalie Portman lookalike. I really hope it's not the actual Natalie Portman. He doesn't approach me while we're having our photos taken, or during the drinks reception. It's textbook: the more he leaves me alone, the more I wish he would come over. And it's also textbook that our one conversation today had to take place *before* I had the benefit of my professional make-up, my beautiful up-do and my pale pink strapless chiffon dress.

I console myself with the fact that I'll be beside him at dinner. But as we go in, Alice takes me aside and tells me Sam's sister Melissa is upset that she's not at the same table as the bride and groom.

'She's in tears,' Alice says, looking worried. 'I know she seems laid-back, but she's a bit emotional and she adores Sam. Do you think . . .?'

'Of course! She can have my place. It's fine.' I don't want Alice

125

to be stressed about anything today. And if Jesse wants to talk to me, he can come and find me. I feel less saintly, though, when I realise I'm now sitting between some random couple who are friends of Sam, and my dad and Fi.

'Here she is,' says Dad, giving me a hug. 'We've barely seen you all day! Emily says you've been doing great work behind the scenes.'

My reply is cut off by Fi gushing about what a beautiful place this is, and how gorgeous Alice looks, and how handsome Sam is, and how wonderful to have the sunshine, and how exciting it is to be in a celebrity's house, and do I think it's OK to take pictures. Honestly, she brings out my dark side like no one else. She's also wearing a pink suit and an enormous purple hat, which exactly blocks my view of Jesse at the top table.

As the meal goes on, I catch up with Dad, and make small talk with Sam's friend Jeff about his web business and the app he's building. Then Luther, as MC, announces that the toasts are starting. Luther himself kicks off with a speech that's quite touching even though it's mainly about him, or rather, the book he wrote when Alice was his editor. He finishes up by saying, 'And if I hadn't written my book, I probably wouldn't have taken a part in the best TV series ever' – there are a few whoops – 'and most importantly, I wouldn't have met my adorable angel . . .' He raises his glass to Jenna, and everyone cheers. 'So here's to you two beautiful people for helping me change my life. May you always be as happy as the day I first caught you sneaking around together.'

The American and English contingents are pretty different in their speeches. Sam's father's speech is all about how much he's learned from watching Alice and Sam grow together as a couple. Uncle Graham's speech is mainly about Alice's A level results and Winston Churchill. Alice and Sam both speak, and are witty and touching and adorable. They thank everyone who made the wedding possible, from their parents to Luther's housekeeper.

Then, to my surprise, Sam says, 'Lastly I need to thank someone else who's worked really hard to put this entire wedding together – Alice's cousin Lily. She was meant to be doing a few light bridesmaid duties, but she's ended up coordinating the entire day like a pro. Lily, you've given us exactly the wedding we wanted, and you've saved us from going insane in the process. To Lily.'

'To Lily.' And the entire marquee full of people joins in a toast to me. No curtain call or applause from an audience has ever made me feel so special.

'Are you a professional wedding planner?' asks Gretchen, the wife of my new friend Jeff.

'Gosh, no. I just made a list and figured it out.'

'You did a great job. Which florist did you use?'

'We bought the flowers from the LA flower market. Sam's mother and aunt arranged them.'

She nods. 'And these place cards?'

'I ordered them off the internet.' I wonder why she's so interested. 'It wasn't hard. I mean, it *was* hard but it was fun.'

'What's that they say? Find a job you enjoy and you'll never work a day in your life!' pipes up Fi.

'You should think about working in event management,' Gretchen says. 'I run a company in Santa Monica – we look after all kinds of events: wrap parties, premieres, product launches. We can always use good people. Do you have a driver's licence?'

'Sure. I've been driving around all week.' I glance over at Dad, who's looking proud.

Gretchen hands me her card. 'Give me a call tomorrow, and maybe we can set something up.'

I'm about to tell her I'm just here on holiday when something makes me change my mind. 'I'd love to. Thank you.' I put her card away, thinking: I may as well call her. It might lead to nothing, but you never know. And I'm not exactly in a hurry to get back to rainy London.

'Oh look,' says Fi. 'They're setting up for the first dance! Let's go and see.'

Dad stands up, smiling at her Tigger-like enthusiasm. It occurs to me that he smiles a lot more now that she's around. I might not like her all that much, but he clearly does, and I suppose I'd better start getting used to it. I stand up too and come with them, wincing as I do – I'm not used to wearing heels, and after being on my feet all day, these are starting to kill.

'I do love your dress,' Fi says to me for the millionth time, as we make our way through the tables.

'Thanks, Fi.' I give her a properly genuine smile, and Dad gives me the same thing.

Sam and Alice never did agree on the kind of music they wanted for their wedding, so I found them a covers band that plays sixties and seventies music. I had assumed their first dance would be a slow number, but it's upbeat: '(Your Love Keeps Lifting Me) Higher' by Jackie Wilson. We've been listening to it for days and I know it'll always remind me of their wedding. Now more couples are joining them on the dance floor: Sam's parents, my dad and Fi, Luther and Jenna, Poppy and Charlie, Nick and some cute young guy who I bet is an actor. Aunt Emily is laughing as she dances with Uncle Graham. She doesn't look much like Mum except when she laughs, and then it's uncanny how similar they are.

Feeling a lump in my throat, I try and imagine what today would be like if Mum were here. I've done that so often: every birthday, every Christmas, even normal days. She'd have been livid with me for ruining the crafting evening – not to mention everything else – but I think she'd be proud of the way I helped put the wedding together.

'See, Lily?' I can almost hear her saying. 'You can do anything if you put your mind to it.'

What about acting, though? I ask her silently. I have put my mind to it, and it hasn't worked. Would she be disappointed? Would she be sad if I stopped trying, or if I went after that event planning job instead?

Obviously I'll never know, but I don't think she would. I think she'd say it didn't matter as long as I was happy. I feel a weight lifting as I remember: she always just wanted me to be happy. And I think she'd also ask me why I wasn't dancing and what happened with that nice boy who was driving me around.

'Hey,' says a voice behind me.

I turn around; it's Jesse.

'I'm glad I finally get to talk to you. Every time I've seen you today, you've been halfway up a ladder or shouting instructions to someone.'

'I've been working,' I say a little defensively.

'I know you have.' He comes closer and I notice again how handsome he looks in his suit, and how gorgeous his almond-shaped eyes are. 'I hope you're planning a quiet day tomorrow to recover?'

'Tomorrow . . .' I don't want to sound as if I'm fishing for a date. 'I'm going to help clear up a few things here in the morning, and then I think Dad wants to see this thing called Watts Towers, whatever that is.' I don't add that I have no intention of playing gooseberry with Dad and Fi.

'Oh, great idea. They look like the Gaudí buildings in Barcelona, except they were built out of garbage by an Italian immigrant called Simon Rodia. It took him thirty-three years. There's a great documentary about them, called *I Build the Tower*.'

I nod, thinking: I appreciate the architectural history, but isn't he going to mention anything about what happened?

His face changes. 'Well – enjoy,' he says, and turns to leave. For the first time it occurs to me that he might have been looking for signals too.

'Wait!'

He turns back.

'Jesse, I heard you ended your engagement – officially. I'm sorry.'

'Thanks. It's better to have it out there,' he says. 'I mean except for all the screaming and yelling and recriminations. That I could do without.'

I laugh reluctantly.

'Look,' he says in a low voice, 'I know I should have told you we were engaged. But the truth is, I didn't want you thinking I was an asshole for calling off the wedding. I guess I hate to be the bad guy. But I've realised that when you try to please everyone—'

'You end up pleasing no one?' I suggest.

'Exactly.' He smiles, and I smile back. I'd like to say I'm also sorry about his father, but I'm not supposed to know about that.

'Jesse!' Diane's joined us, right on cue. 'Carla's over-tired and we need to get home. Can you drive us?'

'No, Mom, I can't,' he says, without taking his eyes off me. 'I've spent all day trying to talk to Lily and I've finally managed to pin her down, so you'll have to drive yourselves.'

Diane looks at me suspiciously, then back at Jesse. 'Fine. But don't forget, we're doing the tour of Universal Studios tomorrow morning and then afterwards we've got the cookout.'

'Actually, I can't make the tour either,' Jesse says calmly. 'Or the cookout. I'm helping Lily clean up here, and then I'm taking her to see Watts Towers. And then in the evening I'm taking her out for dinner and drinks. I haven't decided where yet – somewhere nice. Do you like Japanese food?' he asks me.

'Love it,' I say, thrilled but with one cautious eye on Diane. I've never been asked out in front of someone's mum before; it's very odd.

'I never thought I'd say this, but . . .' Diane turns to me. I brace myself, but she continues, 'You did a good job with the wedding. We thought it was going to be a pretentious corporate LA affair, but you turned it into a family occasion after all.'

Jesse and I look at each other in wonder as she leaves.

'That's rare praise from my mom,' he says. 'Well, thanks for the alibi. It was nice talking to you.' He pats my arm and moves away; I stare at him, stricken.

He turns around slowly. 'Too much? Not funny?'

'Not even a *bit* funny,' I tell him, arms folded. He comes towards me again. The band has started playing 'Signed, Sealed, Delivered'. Behind Jesse, I can see Nick giving me a very unsubtle thumbs-up from the dance floor.

'Sorry. Do you want to dance?' he asks, grinning.

'I would, but my feet hurt,' I admit, holding up one foot. 'These are not the best heels to wear if you're running around doing errands all day.'

'Why don't you take them off? Or better still . . .' Suddenly I'm being scooped up in his arms and he's carrying me away from the dance floor, down the lawn towards the ocean.

'What are you doing? Jesse! Put me down!' I shriek, giggling like a fool. And then I can't say anything at all, because he's kissing me. I put my arms around his neck and kiss him back, at length. I don't even care that various members of both our extended families can probably see us: I'm feeling so outrageously, ridiculously happy I could burst.

'So, tomorrow,' he says, putting me down gently once we've stopped for breath. 'Are you free? I just want to make sure you don't have plans to go chasing off to the Hollywood Hills for another audition, or getting arrested on the beach . . .'

I'm laughing, but I'm also thinking about the fact that the wedding went well, that I've made my peace with Dad and Fi, and that I've finally realised there might be things I can do with my life besides acting.

'Yes,' I tell him, kissing him again and kicking off my shoes. 'I'm free. Come on, let's go and dance.'

24 October
From: Lily
To: Maggie

Maggiee!!!!!!!!!!!!!!!
I am writing to you from the 'deck' (that's what they call the terrace) of Alice and Sam's place in Venice Beach. The sun is setting. I am having a beer. There are boats going by on the canal. I think this is what they call 'living the dream'.

I've been house-sitting for Alice and Sam while they're on honeymoon in Sicily. Sam was lecturing me about not setting anything on fire or having parties and trashing the place, but as I said to him, I don't know enough people here to have a party. (Yet!)

I am sorry for waking you up that time. I was so excited that I got the job and I couldn't wait to tell you – I just got the time difference slightly wrong. My dad was pretty surprised about it all too, though he thinks it's A Good Thing and will be The Making Of Me, whatever that means. I hope you're not cross at me for skipping town without coming back to say goodbye.

I just had my first day at work and it was brilliant. I had to chase RSVPs for a children's birthday party where Selena Gomez will be singing, source 1,000 Mason jars (had to google those, no idea what they were but they're very big here) and think up ideas for a launch for a new organic cruelty-free make-up line from Alicia Silverstone. AS IN *CLUELESS*. I KNOW! It is so much fun. I'm going to have to work some evenings – on Thursday I'm doing the clipboard at a party in CHATEAU MARMONT. I KNOW! Sorry, I'll try and rein in the caps. It's kind of how the people in the office here talk.

I'm also house-hunting. I've met some 'interesting' potential flatmates, including one guy who told me he found his job, apartment and girlfriend all online before he moved to LA from Silicon Valley. That was in Silver Lake, where all the hipsters live. Tomorrow I'm going to see a place here in Venice, sharing with two other girls. It's more expensive but they seem nice, so fingers crossed. I'd like to stay near Alice and Sam and I could also cycle to work beside the sea. Or as they say here, 'bike to work beside the ocean'! I'll be bilingual soon.

What else? I got Alice and Sam a belated wedding present – two Koi carp to live in their pond. One is called Lily, after me, and the other is Monica because I bought them in Santa Monica. I hope they don't get stolen, they were pretty expensive.

And last but not least . . . Jesse is coming to stay with me this weekend. We've been emailing almost every day. I can't wait to see him and I think he'll be happy to get away from Boulder. There are still ructions over his wedding-that-never-was. His mum wanted him and his ex to design a special 'We're sorry we cancelled our wedding' card but Jesse put his foot down and said a group email was fine.

Write soon and tell me all your news. I'd love to Skype, but as this laptop can't cope with Skype, that will have to wait till after I get paid. Sam's lent me an old one of his for the time being. I'm also going to buy a car! I'm borrowing my boss's nanny's car at the mo, because she's home visiting relatives in Guatemala. She has a lot of religious medals in the car, which I find reassuring.

Lots of love,

Lily xxx

25 October
From: Maggie
To: Lily

Hi Lil,

It sounds as though you are having an amazing time! I'm so glad, and of course I'm not cross at you. You know I haven't really been cross at you since the great Hedgehog Hairbrush incident of '97. I was just surprised, is all – one minute you're going to a wedding in America and the next you've relocated. But on the whole I think I agree with your dad.

How can I compete? I'm so boring. I am writing from my desk in the lab office. It's raining outside and I've just been browsing Net-a-Porter while having a halloumi hot wrap from Pret (new in their vegetarian range, very nice). I'm banned from shopping, though, as I just bought the most gorgeous biscuit wool coat from Toast – looks like something Betty Draper would wear. What are you doing about all your clothes, incidentally?

Flat is falling apart as usual. The electric toilet in Fran's en suite broke, and we had to wait for five days before the landlord sent his dodgy handyman around. He was basically casing the joint – he even asked me if the place would be empty over Christmas. I should move, really, but the location's good and Fran and Christina are so easy to live with. Also, Leo and I might think about moving in together . . . we'll see.

Leo is great, busy as ever. The next three weekends are all booked up – we're at a wedding, then he's got a stag weekend and then the weekend after, he's going cycling in the Lake District. And then I'm away for work the weekend after that. So we're not going to have any time on our own until it's practically Christmas.

Speaking of which: I was thinking of getting him, for Christmas, a scrapbook with photos and ticket stubs etc., from all the things we've done together over the past year. I saw a lovely one in Paperchase. It's our first anniversary at New Year, so it could be a nice way to mark it. What do you think? Is that cute or is it psycho?

Also, when are you coming home for Christmas? It might seem like ages away, but I saw my first chocolate Santa in Sainsbury's today.

Mxx

1 November
From: Lily
To: Maggie

Hi Mags,

Greetings from Colorado, where I'm visiting Jesse! His place is great: he has a spare bedroom and a bonsai tree and a water filter thing and everything. Boulder is lovely, really chilled-out and outdoorsy. But small. We ran into J's ex-girlfriend last night, which was not awkward at all (I'm being sarcastic). She was exactly as I pictured her – very wholesome, also wearing make-up while jogging. I know you wear eyeliner for your triathlons, but that's different. You can't help being stylish.

Regarding Leo – that is a pain that he's so booked up; you've mentioned it before. But at least he has a life. I'm not sure about the scrapbook, though, Mags – it could be a little intense. It sounds more like a girl present. Feel free to make me a scrapbook of our friendship any time, but maybe get him a book or something?

It's so warm here, it's hard to believe it's November. Regarding Christmas . . . it's so expensive to fly home, I've decided to stay here instead. Alice and Sam are going to Salt Lake City to his grandparents' place, and Jesse will be heading there too with his family. So it looks like we'll all be spending Christmas together, which is weird but will be really lovely. I will miss our Christmas Eve Baileys in the Black Lion, though! And I'll miss Dad and my brother as well – and even, sort of, Fi. She and I have exchanged a couple of emails, you'll be glad to hear. Short ones. But still.

I must go now, as J and I are heading out for beers with some of his teacher friends. I'd better not have too many, as we're getting up at 6 a.m. tomorrow to go hiking. I know! I can't believe it either. We're spending the rest of the weekend in Canyonlands National Park, which is all the way over in Utah. It's where that guy dropped down a canyon and cut his arm off to escape. So if you don't hear from me, SEND HELP!

Lily xxx

PS When are you and Leo coming out to visit me? You would both love it – it's so outdoorsy and you could do some serious damage in the shops here. It turns out it's cheaper for me to buy stuff here than have my old clothes shipped over!

PPS Terrible news: Monica (one of the Koi carp) got attacked by a raccoon. She was nearly eaten but Sam saved her just in time. He's put a net over the pond but he's grumbling that he can't look after her for the rest of her life. I didn't realise they can live to be a hundred.

4 November
From: Lily
To: Maggie

Hey Mags,

Just following up quickly to let you know I got home from Utah alive. It was really great, though knackering – I hadn't realised we'd be walking for quite so long. Jesse and I had an argument about Aron Ralston (the guy who cut his arm off). He was saying how stupid he was for going out hiking alone and that he didn't respect the wilderness enough, and I was saying that surely that was the whole fun of it (not fun, but you know what I mean). Jesse can be a little judgemental, but I know he doesn't mean it.

In other news, I got the apartment in Venice! I'm so excited. The girls seem great. Amanda is a trends forecaster, and says that Mason jars are over and the new thing is coloured glass. So that's good to know. And you would like Megan, she's very sporty and jogs five miles along the beach every morning, but she's also very into her grooming. She even waxes her arms. It's a whole other world.

Lxx

PS I got a car! Here's the link. I really wanted a jeep, like in *Clueless*, but it's too expensive, so I'm having this one instead. Jesse says it will be a nightmare to get it serviced, but I've always wanted a vintage car.

15 November
From: Maggie
To: Lily

Hey Lil,

Congrats on the new flat *and* the car. And you're spending Christmas with Jesse! I'm so happy for you! And of course I'll visit soon. Leo is keen too – we just need to sit down and make plans, and as ever that's hard to do as we're both so busy (well, he is).

I wouldn't worry about arguing with Jesse, by the way. Sometimes I wish Leo and I argued more. The other day we were disagreeing about how to pronounce the word 'python' – I said it should rhyme with hyphen and he insisted it was 'pyTHON'. I went online and produced multiple examples of people pronouncing it the normal way, but he just said, 'I'm not convinced.' I should really have thumped him but instead I counted to ten.

However, we have made exciting plans for New Year. Some friends of his are going skiing – they've hired a chalet in Méribel, in the French Alps. I will send you the link separately, it looks very luxurious (and is costing an arm and a leg). I was worried it would be a massive group as per usual – you know how social Leo is – but it's just us and two other couples. Plus another girl, called Jenny. I've been there (i.e. single and stuck on holiday with a load of couples), so I'm going to be extra nice to her. Sorry if that sounds really patronising, you know I don't mean it that way.

I am so happy that Leo and I are finally going away together. Three whole days. Do you realise this is our first proper holiday together and we've been going out for a year? You and Jesse are putting us to shame – but I suppose you are long-distance.

Maggie xxx

PS Sorry to hear about Monica. I can't believe you live near raccoons! Take a picture for me.

21 November
From: Lily
To: Maggie

Hey Maggie,

Raccoons are nothing! I've seen lizards, hummingbirds and even a skunk (kept well away from that).

Bit of a shock in the apartment the other evening: Amanda (trend forecaster) revealed that she's polyamorous – 'poly' for short. This means she has sexual relationships with lots of people at once (though Jesse says it's just Greek for sleeping around). I feel so prissy but I'm alarmed – I don't want to come home from work and walk in on an orgy. Though as Megan pointed out later, Amanda's not actually seeing anyone at the moment, so she's only polyamorous in theory.

Anyway – the chalet looks AMAZING! So luxurious, and I can't imagine anything more romantic. And Maggie, you're totally right that the only reason Jesse and I go on so many holidays is because otherwise we'd never see each other! In fact, I'm spending Thanksgiving with him in Boulder next weekend. I wasn't sure about going to Boulder because we'll have to have dinner with his whole family, and his mum's not my biggest fan. But I'm sure it will be fine.

The other day as I was driving to Malibu (!) for work, I was thinking how quickly life can change. Three months ago, I was miserable, temping, living at home with Dad and cynical about men. And now I have a job I love, a wonderful boyfriend to spend Thanksgiving with, and I live by the beach with a polyamorous trends forecaster. It just shows you.

I have the same kind of feeling about you and this skiing holiday. Anything could happen. You could come home engaged! If you do, promise to let me help plan your wedding. I'm getting some very hands-on experience here and I could genuinely do a good job even from abroad. Will you have it in Bromley or in London, do you think?

Love,

Lily xxx

PS You can tell your fiancé from me, it's PYthon to rhyme with hyphen.

5 December
From: Maggie
To: Lily

Lily – get a hold of yourself! We are not getting engaged! Leo and I are SO far from getting engaged, you have no idea. Sometimes I feel like I'm in a long-distance relationship with him, even though we both live in London.

Anyway, it's not my life's ambition to get married. Last night we went out for drinks with a girl in my lab who just got engaged. She was showing everyone her ring and she seemed happy, but hysterically happy and almost relieved. Like she'd never thought her boyfriend would allow this great thing to happen and now he had. I don't want to ever look like that. And I'd much rather be happy in a relationship than engaged when it wasn't right. So for this holiday, I just want to have a nice time with Leo. And not get caught in an avalanche.

How was Thanksgiving in Boulder?

Mxx

10 December
From: Lily
To: Maggie

Hi Mags,

OK, I jumped the gun, I'm sorry. And you are totally right that getting engaged isn't the be-all and end-all. Jesse and Wendy were engaged: say no more.

But you're not in a long-distance relationship with Leo! You're just both busy and pursuing different interests. Jesse and I are completely different, you know. He bought an old dresser on Craigslist that he's restoring with special varnishes and sandpaper and everything. I keep my clothes on an Ikea rail. When we're driving, he wants to play NPR (public radio – very boring) and I want to play Rihanna. But we're happy.

Thanksgiving was actually really lovely. The food was fabulous – his mum, Diane, is a really good cook. It was just a pity that we were ten minutes late because I had to call Dad; I didn't realise ten minutes late is a big deal in Jesse's house.

But dinner was fun. There was a lovely moment where we all had to go around the table and say what we were thankful for. His little sister Carla was thankful that the film of *The Hunger Games* was so true to the book. Claudia said she was thankful she got such good grades this year (I know, what a suck-up). When it got to my turn, I was thinking about my mum and how she doesn't know I moved to California, and I started crying. I think it made Diane warm to me somewhat or think I'm less of a heartless minx in any case. Though I don't think she completely believes that Jesse broke off his engagement before he ever met me – somewhere deep down, she still reckons I'm to blame. But Jesse stands up to her if she ever drops hints, so it's fine.

Some good/bad news on the Koi carp front: it turns out that Monica and Lily are going to become parents. I could

140

have sworn the man in the shop said they were both girls. Sam's not happy but Alice says it's fine – they'll just get a bigger pond.

Lots of love,
Lily xxx

21 December
From: Maggie
To: Lily

Hi Lil,

Oh dear – that's unfortunate about the fish. But maybe it will be good practice for Alice and Sam in case they have kids. Or they could set up a Koi carp breeding business – it could be a good sideline?

I'm already home for Christmas, just got back to Bromley an hour ago. I had a very, very stressful journey. Just before I got on the train home, the landlord texted me to tell me not to use Fran's electric toilet, because it's broken again, and according to his dodgy handyman, this time IT COULD KILL US. Don't ask me why he didn't text Fran: he only communicates through me, because he knows I'm a pushover.

So I spent the whole journey home on a packed train with no reception, trying to call and text Fran – first to warn her, and then to check if she was alive. It isn't like her not to answer, and I was having visions of her dead on the bathroom floor. Death by toilet! I was about to call the fire brigade when finally she texted me back – she got drunk at her work Christmas party and stayed over with one of her colleagues.

Now I'm completely worn out and I'm also worried that the dodgy handyman *is* going to break into our flat over the Christmas holidays. Maybe the whole toilet thing was a ruse to keep us away? But there's nothing I can do for now. Instead I am going to go downstairs and have a gin and tonic with Mum and Dad although it's only five o'clock, and later we'll play Cluedo. They know how to live.

By the way, I didn't mean what I said about Leo and

me being in a long-distance relationship. I was hung-over and gloomy when I wrote that. But you were right about the scrapbook, it was nuts. I got him a scarf instead.

Mxx

25 December
To: Maggie
From: Lily

Happy Christmas! I'm at Jesse and Sam's grandparents' place in Salt Lake City. There are going to be twenty of us for Christmas dinner; every time I turn around, I meet a new cousin and they're all seven feet tall. I'm glad Alice is here or I'd be a little overwhelmed. They're all very friendly, though.

And I didn't tell you this earlier, but Sam paid for my flight here as I was broke after buying my car. I've offered to pay him back, but he just said I was family now and to call it a Christmas present. I couldn't believe it. I feel even worse about Monica and Lily now and I've decided I'm going to adopt at least one of their kids (Monica and Lily's, I mean, not Sam and Alice's).

Speaking of presents, I'm not sure you should take my advice, to be honest. I feel bad because I bought Jesse an Oxfam goat – I thought he would prefer that kind of present – and he bought me a beautiful pair of silver earrings. But he says he loves the goat and at least I didn't give him a Koi carp.

I hope you have a wonderful time skiing. You'll have to take loads of pictures. And by the way: I know I jumped the gun with the whole Leo-proposing-in-the-snow thing. But I do think this skiing holiday of yours will be special. You can quote me on that. Let me know how it goes!

Lots of love,
Lily xxx

MAGGIE DOES MERIBEL

'Ow!' Muttering under my breath, I glare after the tall blond girl who's just run over my toe with her very heavy wheelie suitcase. She ignores me and installs herself further down the carriage, putting her massive case on the seat beside her.

One of my new Rag & Bone suede boots has now got a distinct scuff, which is infuriating considering I only bought them the other day after getting up at 7 a.m. to brave the Boxing Day sale at Selfridges. I could go up to her and point out the damage, but it's not worth it. It's too early in the morning, and anyway, I'm not like my friend Lily, who will say anything to anyone. My preferred response to any conflict is always to avoid it.

Instead, I turn back to my *Vogue* and drool over a shoot of casual winter clothes: flat leather biker boots with buckles, hooded cardigan-coats with fur trims and luxuriously soft wool leggings – sort of *Game of Thrones* meets Burberry. I have a terrible habit of buying new clothes every time I go away somewhere, and I was itching to invest in some new outfits for this holiday. But the holiday itself was expensive, so I've made do with my Reiss camel-coloured belted wool coat, a couple of pairs of skinny jeans, my nicest angora and cashmere knits – and my poor, newly maimed suede boots.

'You don't need to buy a ski suit,' my boyfriend Leo reassured me. 'Just borrow one. Then if you like it you can invest in one, and if you don't, you won't be stuck with a load of useless gear.'

It's not that I don't think I'm going to like skiing – at least, provided I don't break my neck or make a complete fool of myself

– but I could see Leo's point. So I've borrowed a knackered old ski suit from my parents' next-door neighbours. It's pretty awful, but I'm hoping I won't be spending all my time on the slopes. Instead, I'm focusing on the après-ski: lots of bubbly in the snow, hot chocolate by the fire and strolling hand-in-hand with Leo through the narrow little streets of Méribel that look like something from a Christmas card.

The girl who attacked me with her suitcase is now shouting down her phone, telling the other person that she's on the Heathrow Express but will be there soon. I put in my earphones and turn up my music to drown her out, feeling very sorry for whoever she's going on holiday with.

Never mind: I'm finally spending quality time with Leo. He has to travel a lot for work since he's an engineer, and most of his weekends are already spoken for with football, cycling and running – and those are just the winter sports. I like to be active and I do sometimes join him on the odd day trip, but you'd have to be Jessica Ennis to keep up with all Leo's outdoor pursuits.

Of course, I'm busy too. I love my job as a microbiologist, and I have friends and a life of my own. I certainly don't want to make Leo give up his beloved hobbies. But sometimes I wish he wasn't quite so tied up with them, or with all his friends and teammates. One night in the pub, I ended up discussing it with his sister, Holly.

'The thing about Leo,' she said, 'is that he's a free spirit. You're the first proper girlfriend he's had in years. So he's used to going away with his sports buddies every weekend and travelling for work and not having to make plans with a girlfriend. He loves you and he'll adapt, you just have to be patient.'

I think it's ironic that Leo is called a free spirit for being single for five years, whereas I was single for two years before I met him and felt like the village spinster although I'm only twenty-seven. But I know Holly's right, and that I have a tendency to overthink everything – and to be too sensitive. I'm hoping this holiday will get me and Leo back on track. And if we do move in together – which I hope we will sometime soon – that will solve all our scheduling problems, as we'll see each other all the time.

Just as I'm thinking that, the train arrives at Heathrow and I see Leo himself waiting for me on the platform, skis propped up beside him and wearing the Paul Smith scarf I gave him for Christmas. I make my way down the carriage, waving at him through the window as I wait for everyone to get their luggage before me. Suitcase Girl barges out of the train ahead of me, flicking her long highlighted hair in my face as she does. To my surprise, she makes a beeline for Leo, who greets her with a big hug. What the hell? Seeing me behind her, he beams and starts waving.

'Mags!' he says, pulling me towards him for a quick kiss. 'This is my girlfriend, Maggie. This is Jen – Jenny,' he adds to me.

Great. So this is Jenny: the one single girl in our group of couples. I'd intended to be extra nice to her, but now I can see she's able to look after herself. As we walk towards the terminal, she elbows her way in between Leo and me and starts peppering him with questions. She has an obnoxiously loud voice, and I find myself looking around to see if people are staring at us.

'So how ARE you?' she asks him. 'It's been *ages*. How was your Christmas and everything? Did you do that swim on Christmas Day? I heard it was amazeballs.'

I try not to get annoyed, reminding myself that I'm used to girls paying Leo a lot of attention. He's very cute: tall and well built, with light brown hair that he wears very short (though I wish he'd let it get longer) and gorgeous blue eyes. But even though girls often flirt with him, the great thing about Leo is that he doesn't flirt back. He's just sociable; the kind of person who'll always get people together, or welcome someone who's new to a group. In fact, that's how we met. I'd recently joined his triathlon club and was skulking around on the edges when he chose me for his swim team. I must admit, seeing him in his wetsuit was a good incentive for those 6 a.m. starts.

'Hey, Maggie Moo,' he says to me, as soon as there's a gap in Jenny's monologue. 'Are you ready for your new addiction? Maggie's a skiing virgin,' he adds to Jenny; I think he could have phrased it better. 'But I think she'll love it.'

Jenny, however, isn't interested in whether or not I'll love

145

skiing. 'There they are. Dave! Over here!' she shrieks at the top of her voice, almost puncturing my eardrum. Waving madly, she strides across towards the check-in queue where the other two couples are waiting. I've never met them before; I know that the two guys are doctors, and that Leo knows them from his tennis club, but that's about it. I really hope they're not like Jenny.

'I might grab a tea quickly – do you want to come?' I ask Leo, thinking it would be nice for us to have a few minutes alone before we join the others.

'Wait, Mags,' he says. 'You can get one later, once we're through security. Come and meet everyone.'

This is typical of Leo: he's a social animal and a team player, whereas I can be more of a lone wolf. The others have obviously been here a while and Jenny has joined them, even though this means skipping the queue. 'We're together,' I hear her snap to a woman behind her, as Leo introduces me to the others, starting with his friend David.

David is short, blond and handsome. He's wearing a navy quilted jacket with a corduroy collar, and looks very preppy and serious.

'Great to meet you. David Fitzgerald,' he says. I find it odd when people give you both their names in a social situation – as if you're going to write a report about it or something.

'And this is . . . I'm really sorry. I've forgotten your name,' Leo continues, turning to David's girlfriend.

'Sorry, this is Nina,' David says. Nina is petite, pretty and dark; she looks as if she could be Spanish or French. She's wearing white jeans and has her hair in a French plait, both of which strike me as unusual – especially her hair: she must have got up very early to do that.

'And this is Rachel and Oliver – guys, this is Maggie. Hello? Guys?' Leo prods Oliver to attract his attention.

'What? Oh, sorry, we were just . . .' Rachel and Oliver look at each other and giggle. They're wrapped around each other in a kind of standing embrace, barely breaking apart even when we have to shuffle along in the queue. They're both tall and dark, but Rachel is definitely the more attractive half of the couple, with long glossy black hair and gorgeous pale skin. Oliver's a bit too tall, and his ears stick out, and his glasses are perched on the end of a big nose – but he looks friendly and fun.

'We were just saying . . . Never mind, it's not interesting,' Oliver says, gazing at Rachel with a dopey grin. Even if Leo hadn't told me they're a new couple, I think I would have guessed.

'It's lovely to meet you.' Rachel shakes my hand, beaming blissfully; it would obviously be lovely to meet me even if I were Jack the Ripper, she's so loved-up. I feel momentarily jealous that they're going on holiday so early in their relationship. But then I stop myself. What could be more romantic than celebrating my one year anniversary with Leo in the French Alps?

Unfortunately I have to make a rather unromantic purchase: tampons. With any luck, I won't need them during the holiday, but I'd rather be safe than sorry. As soon as we've passed security, I scoot over to Boots to sort myself out. I grab a box quickly, and then stop by the Rimmel counter to try a new cream eyeshadow that's been recommended by my favourite beauty blogger. I pick out a gorgeous bronzy shade that works nicely with my muddy green eyes.

I have a bit of an eyeshadow problem: I tried to count my eyeshadows recently, but I gave up when I got to fifty. In my defence, I always think you need more eye make-up when you have a short pixie haircut, like me – otherwise I think I can look like a boy. I had long hair for years but it got so wrecked from constant highlighting that I cut it all off a few months ago and let it go back to its natural light brown. I love it, though it is chilly in winter.

'There you are! Hurry up, our flight's boarding.' It's Jenny, startling me out of my hair/eyeshadow reverie. As she strides away, I hear her say in her foghorn voice, 'Found her, she was buying tampons.'

I'm still fuming when I leave Boots to find Leo waiting for me. He rolls his eyes when he sees I've bought another eyeshadow. He's always telling me that I don't need make-up. I've tried to explain to him that it's not a question of needing it, but it's a waste of time.

'Come on, Mags, we're boarding – the others have gone ahead.'
'I can't believe she said that!'

'Said what?' Leo asks, tugging me gently along.

'Told you all I was buying tampons! Is she always like that?'

'Maggie,' Leo says. 'Chill. We're on holiday. It's not a time for stressing.' He slings his arm around my shoulders and I feel myself relax a little. 'I didn't hear her,' he adds.

'I'd say they heard her in France,' I mutter, but I drop it. Leo's right; there's no point making a big thing of it.

On the plane, Jenny sits with David and Nina, and I can hear her going on about some hospital Christmas party, which was full of people David knows and Nina doesn't. Jenny seems to be a surgical registrar, like the other two boys. God help her patients: I can imagine her on ward rounds, bellowing out the gory details for all to hear. Rachel and Oliver sit together a few rows behind us and I can hear low murmuring and laughing, followed by a lively argument about euthanasia, of all things. Bizarre. Rachel is Irish, like David; I wonder if that's how they know each other.

'Sort of,' Leo says, when I ask him. 'Rachel's friend Zoë used to go out with David. That's how Rachel met Oliver.' He frowns. 'Can't believe I forgot David's girlfriend's name.'

'Oh, I wouldn't worry about it. I'm sure she didn't mind, she seems sweet.' I'm about to add, 'Unlike Jenny', but I stop myself.

'Rachel said something nice about you,' he says. 'What was it . . . She said she loved your hair and that it made you look like that actress . . . Jennifer something? Sorry, I can't remember who exactly.'

'Doesn't matter. That *is* nice.' That's what I love about Leo. He might look like a hearty, rugger-bugger type, but he's thoughtful. My previous boyfriends were both scientists, and both sporty and straightforward like Leo, but neither of them would have remembered to pass on a compliment like that.

'How're things at the Death Trap Crime Scene?' Leo asks, referring to my flat.

'Well, the good news is we weren't broken into over Christmas, and the toilet is fixed. But the latest thing is that the ceiling of my room has flooded.' It was while I was packing: water came pouring through the light fitting, making a sizzling noise like a horror film. It's made me even more determined to scrape

148

together a deposit for a flat. Realistically I couldn't buy one on my own, but if Leo and I were to join forces . . .

'And is the landlord going to sort it?'

'He can't, the handyman's gone on holiday now.'

'That's ridiculous! I'll call him for you if you want, and make him do it.'

'Thanks, Leo.' Now I feel bad for resenting Leo being busy. He really is a great boyfriend. Suddenly I remember something. 'Oh, guess what my brother gave me. Two tickets to that new play at the Royal Court! It's totally sold out.' I've already decided one of my New Year's Resolutions will be to do more cultural things instead of just going to the pub after work. 'It's on the twenty-fifth of January. Can you make it?'

'I'm not sure . . . I think there's something on that day.' Leo shifts in his seat and pulls out two diaries from his pocket – his old and new ones. 'Ah,' he says. 'I thought so. That's Brownie's thirtieth and he's planning drinks somewhere.'

'Who?'

'Nick Brown. Squash club.'

'Oh. Never mind, I can go with someone else.' I genuinely don't mind going with a friend, but I'm dismayed to see that the January pages of Leo's brand-new diary are already filling up, and it's still only 29 December.

'I tell you what, though,' Leo says. 'The play will probably finish by ten or so, won't it? So we can go to it, then on to Brownie's drinks afterwards.'

I smile at him. 'OK.' Compromise: the secret to all successful relationships, according to magazines and my mother. Although I wish just once we could have an evening entirely to ourselves without having to dash across town to some acquaintance's drinks. I wouldn't mind if it was a close friend, but I've never even heard of Brownie. But then I think of one of my lab mates who complains that her boyfriend never wants to go out anywhere, and tell myself how lucky I am that Leo is sociable and outgoing and up for doing things like the theatre.

We land late and Leo hurries to buy sandwiches for everyone so that we can have lunch on the bus. After about an hour, we've left the suburbs of Grenoble far behind and we're in the foothills of the French Alps. I've never seen the sky look so blue in winter, or snow so white. And the mountains! Soon they're soaring up on either side, higher than any mountains I've ever seen before, dotted with pine forests and blanketed with sugary snow . . . I hope to God we're not going to be skiing down anything like that.

The guys are now having a very competitive discussion about moguls, black runs and off-piste skiing. Everyone except me and Nina is clearly a skiing fanatic; even Rachel, who I was hoping might be a beginner too, seems to be experienced.

'Have you been skiing lots of times before?' I ask her.

'Twice, in Italy. I can do red runs, that's about it,' Rachel says.

'Red runs in Italy are way easier than in France,' says Jenny.

Rachel and I exchange glances at this and I decide we're going to get along. I'm about to ask her if she took lessons when Oliver says, sounding fascinated, 'I didn't know you'd been skiing in Italy. When?'

'Oh, did I not tell you? Well . . .' Rachel turns back to him and within seconds they're deep in conversation again. They're obviously at the stage where they can't wait to tell each other everything about themselves.

'How about you, Nina, have you been skiing before?' I ask.

Nina shakes her head, and I realise I haven't actually heard her speak yet. Can she speak? Of course she can; she's obviously just quiet.

'Maybe you'll keep me company on the baby slopes,' I suggest.

'You should both try ski school,' says David. 'Spend a day or two getting the basics down.'

Now Oliver, Leo and Jenny are talking about cross-country skiing. I knew Leo and I would be at different levels, but it's beginning to look as though we're basically going to be on different holidays.

'Oh, wow, look!' says Nina suddenly, in a surprisingly deep, sexy growling voice.

I look out the window and see that we've arrived in Méribel. It's adorable, full of wooden chalets and little winding streets knee-deep in snow. There's a huge Christmas tree lit up in the main square, which is lined with bars and cafés, their lights glowing invitingly in the purply winter dusk. Glamorous-looking people in full-length puffa and fur coats and even fur hats are parading up and down, lit up by the jam of Mercs and BMWs with foreign registration plates crawling along the narrow streets.

'Looks like a real dump, doesn't it?' Rachel says.

Though I've only just met her, I know she's joking, but Jenny seems to think she's being serious. 'Méribel's one of the nicest villages in the French Alps, you know,' I hear her saying reprovingly.

The bus parks in a car park off the main drag, where we're greeted by a blond English girl with a clipboard.

'Fitzgerald party? Come with me.'

We follow her along the slushy street. My feet are freezing and I've realised that it was stupid to bring these suede boots: they're going to get wrecked. Everyone we pass without exception is wearing snow boots. After about five minutes we turn off towards a group of wooden chalets topped with thick snow and lit by yellow lanterns.

We follow our rep up a flight of wooden steps. She unlocks a door and we all troop in, with Oliver holding the door open for me and the other girls. It opens straight into a big room with beams on the ceiling and a log fire surrounded by big sofas. Through the window we can see the last of the sunset casting a golden glow on the mountains. On a round table there's an array of mini smoked salmon sandwiches and bowls of pistachio nuts, and a bottle of champagne in a bucket, with seven glasses.

'Your chef, Gavin, has left a menu for you and he'll be here shortly to make dinner. Tomorrow you can either order dinner from him, or we can give you a list of excellent restaurants in Méribel, including several with Michelin stars!' She smiles and leaves us to it.

A chef? Michelin stars? I'm beginning to understand why this holiday ate up such a big chunk of my savings. Not that I'm complaining.

After toasting our holiday, we go off to explore the place, champagne in hand, and everyone starts shrieking over the facilities.

'Look, there's a jacuzzi!'

151

'This room has a heated floor and heated things to leave our boots on!'

'Look at the view from this bedroom!'

Opening the fridge, Jenny says, 'Dammit, there's no DC. We specifically asked them to stock it, Dave, didn't we?'

'What's DC?' Rachel asks.

'Diet Coke,' David says briefly.

'There's a supermarket in town,' Oliver says. 'But you'll have to call it CL: Coca Light.'

'I'm going to go and get some. Dave, will you come with me?' Jenny says.

David looks undecided, glancing at Nina and then back at Jenny. I watch the three of them, thinking how bizarre this dynamic is: it's as if David's got two girlfriends. Although I do have a glimmer of sympathy for Jenny's addiction. I brought a box of Twinings English Breakfast myself; I can't survive without at least six cups a day, or more when I'm in the lab.

'Wait,' says Oliver. 'First we need to decide which room everyone's having.'

There's one room that's much bigger and nicer than any of the others, with its own fireplace and a spectacular view of the mountains and sunset. Everyone clearly wants it, but because we don't know each other very well, we all hang back politely.

'You and Nina should have it – you organised the holiday,' Rachel says to David.

'Let's toss a coin for it,' suggests David. 'Or draw cards. I saw a pack of cards downstairs.'

We go back downstairs and draw a card each – including Jenny, which seems strange. It's a double room, and there are three doubles and one single. Which couple is going to take the single room if Jenny gets this one? I look at Leo, but he doesn't seem to have noticed anything odd.

In the end, Oliver draws an ace and there are jokes about the honeymoon suite; we assign the rest of the rooms painlessly. Then Jenny and David go out to buy Diet Cokes. I wonder if this bothers Nina at all, but she doesn't seem to mind, going into their room and shutting the door behind her.

'That was weird about the rooms, wasn't it?' I ask Leo when

we're in our bedroom, which is the smallest double, with blue-and-white painted walls and an attic ceiling; it's lucky I'm not tall. He could easily have taken the second-nicest one, which had an en suite, but he hung back and let David and Nina have it.

'How do you mean?'

I lower my voice. 'You know – how Jenny wanted it when it was a double and she clearly was meant to have a single.'

Leo shrugs. 'She probably just didn't think it through. Anyway, the couples had a double probability of drawing it.'

One of the things I like most about Leo is that he never bad-mouths anyone, no matter what they've done. But sometimes I wish he would just agree with me, especially when someone is blatantly being crazy.

I start unpacking, enjoying the sight of my perfect capsule wardrobe hanging up neatly together. I have to do this, even if I'm only staying somewhere for a night: I hate living out of a suitcase. In contrast, Leo chucks everything on the floor. He says it's a reaction to the enforced tidiness of boarding school, but I'm not so sure.

'I'm going to have a quick shower,' he says. 'And then we can have a drink with the others.'

'Sure. But wouldn't it be nice to . . . relax here together for a while?' I pat the duvet seductively. 'Relax' is our code word for sex. Which we haven't had in a while, what with being at home with our families for Christmas and everything.

Leo grins, then comes over and gives me a kiss that makes me weak at the knees. A proper kiss. A holiday kiss.

'I intend to do *lots* of relaxing with you,' he says. 'But it's the first night, and David and Ol were talking about heading to some place that does the best *vin chaud* in the French Alps, apparently. So I think we should go – to be sociable.'

I smile. 'OK, party animal.' He's right: it would be odd if we didn't emerge from our room. And there'll be plenty of opportunity to 'relax' after dinner.

The *vin chaud* is lovely, and so is the food that our chef Gavin has whipped up for us when we get back: scallops and black pudding to start, and beef bourguignon. I don't eat meat, but I can eat the

153

scallops, and the garlicky, crispy, creamy potatoes and green beans. I'm about to tactfully remind Gavin, for future reference, that I'm a vegetarian when Leo does it for me.

'Yes, of course,' Gavin says. 'I've made a mushroom bourguignon as well.'

'Oh, brilliant. Thank you!' I also shoot a grateful smile to Leo.

Jenny, of course, instantly wants to know why I'm a vegetarian.

'Do you think it's cruel to animals or something?'

The answer is yes, but I don't want to insult everyone else, so I murmur, 'It's just a personal preference.' My other personal preference would be for her to shut up, but I don't see that happening any time soon.

Gavin asks if we want him to stay and serve up, and thankfully the consensus is no.

'I'm pretty glad he's gone,' I confess, once he's left and we're all sitting down at the candlelit table. 'I'm not used to staff.'

Jenny gives me a puzzled look. 'Aren't you?' she says.

I don't know what to say to that, but luckily Oliver saves me.

'Come on, Jen,' he says, laughing. 'I'm not fooled by the rocks you've got. I know you're still Jenny from the block.' Jenny – who's clearly never been near any kind of block – rolls her eyes and says, 'Whatevs, weirdo,' while everyone laughs. I'm so relieved the others are normal; I don't know what I'd do if they were all like Jenny.

'Cheers, everyone,' David says, lifting his glass. 'Here's to blue slopes and red wine.'

'Blue slopes and red wine!' everyone chimes in, clinking glasses. Leo gives me a wink and I wrinkle my nose back at him, thinking: this is going to be the perfect holiday.

The next morning, we all get dressed in our ski gear and head out to hire our skis. I'm hating my bulky navy all-in-one, which last saw action circa 1998 and makes me look like the Michelin man. I hadn't realised that it's actually held together under one arm with bits of duct tape. Duct tape! I can't even bear to wear tights with ladders in them.

'Oh my God, I haven't seen a suit like that in decades,' Jenny hoots at me in her foghorn voice as we leave the chalet. Of course her outfit is like something out of *Harper's Bazaar*: cream-coloured separates with an enormous fur hat and Chanel sunglasses – cow. 'Where did you get it, an antique shop?'

I wish I could think of something cutting to say in return, but she's already bounced ahead to David, and is stuffing a snowball down his neck. She obviously has a crush on him; he doesn't seem to return it, but all the same, it must be very annoying for Nina. At least it's a gorgeous day: blue skies, blinding sunshine, crisp but not too cold.

'You don't have to do ski school,' Leo says, as we clunk around the hire place sorting out boots and skis for me, Rachel and Nina – the others have brought their own. 'I'm sure I could teach you the basics this morning.'

I'm tempted to take him up on it – it would be lovely to spend more time with him. Dinner ended so late last night that there was no time for anything romantic; we just fell asleep. But he's clearly dying to get out on the slopes, and I don't want to deprive him, especially as we're here for such a short time. Not to mention that I can't even figure out how to put these boots on, so I don't think I'm going to be a quick learner. I run and swim and go to the gym, but when it comes to anything involving balance, I'm like a baby hippo.

'Here – tighten them a bit more. They have to be tighter than normal shoes. That's it.' Leo gives me a pat on the bottom. 'I'll text you at lunchtime and we'll see you at that café at the bottom of the ski lift.'

'Which ski lift?' I ask, but he's already clattered away after the others.

Nina is doing ski school too, and the two of us clump off together to find our instructor. I'm envious of her cute little separates, which are black and white with a snowflake pattern, teamed with a pink bobble hat. She's as quiet as ever, and in my attempts to make conversation, I feel as if I'm practically interviewing her.

'So you and David both live in New York, is that right? What do you do there?'

'I'm a vet.'

'Oh, cool. I'm a clinical microbiologist.' Silence. 'What made you move to New York? You're not American, are you?'

'My mom is, so I have a US passport.'

'And did you know anyone over there before you headed over?'

'No.'

I wouldn't consider myself a chatterbox, but in comparison with Nina I'm practically Graham Norton. I'm relieved when our lesson begins and I don't have to try and talk any more. Our instructor is Roy, a middle-aged Yorkshireman with a pot belly and a moustache. He looks understanding, and the slope is reassuringly gentle; in fact I have to admit it's practically flat.

We start with snowploughs – aka stopping – which are reasonably easy, and then move on to going very slowly across the slope in a diagonal line, one after the other. Nina is pretty good and gets the hang of it quickly, but I keep grinding to a halt in the middle and holding everyone else up. They can't even ski around me because we haven't learned to turn yet.

'Knees bent and lean *forward*, Maggie,' Roy calls. I thought I *was* leaning forward, but apparently not, hence the stopping. All at once I feel an almighty shove from behind, and I'm zooming forward. The bastard: he pushed me! Surely that's not allowed. But everyone's cheering and clapping, and I realise I'm doing it! I'm skiing! This is a piece of cake! Until my skis cross over each other and I fall flat on my face.

'Well done,' says Roy.

As I pick myself up and dust off the snow, I'm beaming: I did it! And now that I've fallen over once, I've realised the snow is quite soft, and it's not the end of the world if I fall again. We move on to turning, and I can't believe how well I'm suddenly doing. I must be a natural! Left, right, up mountain, down mountain: it's all coming together. I can't wait to show Leo my new skills. I'm picturing us slaloming down a dazzling white slope together when I see Nina waving to someone, and I realise the others have arrived – they're leaning against the fence of our baby field, watching us with big grins on their faces. I hadn't realised we'd be getting an audience.

'One more drill before lunch,' says Roy. 'Just start up here' – he indicates with his pole – 'and go around each marker and finish here at the bottom.'

I can do this. It's the same as the drill we just did. But I'm feeling self-conscious, especially when I see Jenny's smirk under her huge sunglasses. She's still rocking her massive fur hat, even though it's warm and sunny.

Nina goes ahead of me: she glides down steadily and makes all her turns, only knocking one of the poles slightly. I start off reasonably smoothly, but as I approach the first pole I lose my nerve and my left foot starts sliding out of control. I lean back to try and get my balance, but my foot shoots away from me, and to my mortification I slide across the poles, knocking them all over, and skid the rest of the way down on my bum before landing at the bottom covered in snow. The others are all clapping and laughing, so I pick myself up and pretend to bow.

'Brilliant, Maggie,' Leo calls, wiping his eyes, as I join them.

'You'd better not have been taping that,' I tell him, giving him a little shove.

'I wasn't! You did great. Come and have some lunch.'

We click off our skis and stump across the road to the nearest restaurant in our ski boots, walking like people on the moon. My shins are aching now, and my thighs are shaking, and I'm starving. I notice that David is carrying Nina's skis as well as his own, and I wonder if I should mind that Leo's not carrying mine. But that would be unreasonable; Nina is smaller than me. Leo obviously feels bad about laughing at me earlier and has his arm around me as we wait in the queue to get into the café.

As we stand there, we see an incredibly cute sight: a group of young kids, no more than six or seven years old, zooming down the slope on their miniature skis. They're not even using poles, just bobbing along like little wind-up toys with their brightly coloured suits and helmets. It's depressing to think that they're already better skiers than I'll ever be.

'How sweet is that?' says David. He looks fondly at Nina and is about to say something else when Jenny jumps in and starts asking him some technical question about his skis.

I'm still watching the kids, and I notice one little girl at the end falling over and howling in despair. Within seconds the instructor is by her side. He pulls his visor off to talk to her, and I do a double-take, because he is *gorgeous*. He looks like a young lion: all messy tawny hair, bronzed skin and golden stubble, tall and lithe in his blue and white ski suit. And he is so cute with his little pupil, dusting her off and talking to her reassuringly until she's calmed down. I stare at him, thinking: that little girl doesn't know how lucky she is.

'Was your instructor anything like that?' Rachel murmurs to me as we go inside the café. I shake my head wordlessly. I'm tempted to stare at him again over my shoulder, but I don't want Leo to see me perving over the local talent.

'Let's order some beers, seven croque-monsieurs, a giant side order of *raclette* and some *frites*,' says Oliver, looking at the menus. 'And whatever the rest of you are having.'

'That's the brilliant thing about skiing: to hell with the diet,' says Rachel.

'You are the last person in the world who needs to diet,' Oliver says adoringly.

Meanwhile, David is quietly telling Nina that she looked 'sensational' on skis. I feel as if I'm on some kind of double honeymoon. Shouldn't Leo be telling me I don't need to diet, or that I look sensational on skis? But then I remind myself that that slushy stuff doesn't last for ever. It's much better to be able to laugh at each other.

We all order beers – I opt for a special raspberry one – croque-monsieurs and fries, and then chocolate profiteroles for dessert. All around us people are lounging at the tables, eating, drinking and chatting under the blue sky. I can't believe we're sitting outside in the sunshine, with our sunglasses on, in December. I don't even care when the tea I ordered with my profiteroles turns out to be lukewarm water with a tea bag bobbing on top, or when Leo makes us all pose for a billion photos; this is definitely worth some Facebook boasting.

'So what do you think of skiing?' he asks me.

'I like this part,' I say through a mouthful of profiteroles. 'No, I do like skiing . . . there was a moment there when I had it. Sort of.'

Leo nods. 'I'd say you could come out with us tomorrow.'

'Cool,' I say, thrilled.

I notice that Oliver and Rachel are both looking alarmed, though. 'There's no rush,' Rachel says. 'I did a week of ski school before I went on the big slopes.'

I'm thinking that maybe they're right and I should do a few more lessons when Jenny says, 'Yeah, don't push it. You've got a way to go.' Which makes me all the more determined to make her eat my snow dust. I notice that she's offering David, and no one else, her extra *frites*. She's pretty deluded if she thinks she can win him over with a few chips.

After we've finished lunch, we go our separate ways: the others to the big slopes and Nina and me back to ski school. Except Nina seems to have changed her mind about ski school.

'I'm going to go home and read my book,' she says in her quiet, growling voice, and off she trots, taking the key David left with us. I'm tempted to join her, but I want to pack in as much practice as possible while we're here.

On the way home after the lesson, I make a quick detour into a shop and buy myself some proper snow boots, black with a hot pink trim. It would be a false economy to let my suede boots get wrecked, and these are so much cosier; I love them.

I'm so knackered when I get in that I pull off my ski gear and crawl into bed. After what feels like ten minutes, I wake up to find Leo sitting on the bed beside me. It's dark; I must have slept for hours.

'How was ski school?' Leo asks.

'Fine,' I say, yawning. 'I think I'm getting the hang of it. How was your afternoon?'

'Great,' he says. 'We've got a good standard in the group.' He puts a hand on my thigh underneath the duvet. 'It's six now. I said we'd go for a drink with the others at seven. Which means . . .'

'Means what?' I ask blearily, rubbing my eyes and hoping I wasn't drooling.

'We've got some time to relax . . .' He slides a hand up my leg.

Oh. I want to relax with Leo, obviously, but I didn't realise it was going to be squeezed in so efficiently between naps, showers and drinks. Do we really have to meet the others at seven on the dot? But then Leo starts kissing me, and I feel the familiar thrill working its way through my body. The fact that we haven't been together in so long – since 15 December, in fact – makes it even more exciting.

It's just a pity we're on such a tight schedule and there's no time to lie around together afterwards, let alone get dressed up for dinner. I barely have time to pull on my favourite skinny jeans, a stripy grey and white knit from Maison Scotch and my new snow boots. My face is so flushed from the day outdoors that I tone it down with some colour-correcting base and pile on the mascara as a sort of distraction.

Rather than have dinner in the chalet, the others have decided to go out for a pizza. I could eat ten pizzas after my day on the slopes. We head to a big, noisy place off the main square, with red check vinyl cloths and bright overhead lights. It's perfect, except that Jenny is opposite us, going on and on at Leo about their skiing today. Her voice is so deafening, I would put my fingers in my ears if I could get away with it.

I'm dreading trying to make sure I get a meat-free pizza in my rusty GCSE French, but the waiter speaks reasonably good English. Nina surprises everyone by ordering in perfect French. I make a mental note to ask her how to say 'boiling water' so that I can get a proper cup of tea tomorrow.

'You never said you spoke French,' Jenny says in an accusing tone, as if Nina's some kind of spy. 'How come?'

'My dad is French,' Nina says. She's wearing a chunky white polo neck, which doesn't suit her quite as well as her ski gear; she has such a great figure, I think she should show it off more.

'*Oh là là,*' Jenny says sarcastically, drumming her fingers on the table. I look over at David, but he either hasn't heard or is pretending not to. I can't understand why he and Oliver are friends with Jenny. It's not as if either of them could fancy her. She's expensively put together, but her eyes are cold. She seems to be flicking her hair at Leo a lot this evening, but I'm fairly sure David's the one she's really in love with.

'What do you do, Maggie?' Rachel asks. When I tell her,

Jenny says, 'Really? You look like you work in fashion or PR or something.'

'I'll take that as a compliment,' I say, smiling, though I've heard this before and I think it's ridiculous – as if scientists can't take an interest in fashion or make-up. Jenny's a doctor, but those Chanel sunglasses didn't come out of a medical catalogue. Or that stupid fur hat.

'This is more like it,' Oliver says happily, when our pizzas arrive. 'Wipe-clean tablecloth, elbows on the table. All that silver service at the chalet makes me nervous. I keep thinking I'm going to break something.'

'Oh, come on,' says David. 'You must admit this is a lot nicer than that trip of yours last year – with the bunk beds and no electricity.'

'Ah, that was great. Ski trip in Norway,' he explains to Rachel. 'It was all off-piste and we skied from one cabin to the next, carrying our food with us in backpacks, cooking on camper stoves and making fires – it was brilliant.'

'But how did you dry your socks?' Rachel asks him gravely.

'They hung them up on the bunk beds,' says Jenny. 'Face it, Oliver. We're not students any more. You don't have to cycle to the hospital: you can afford the bus. Or even the Tube.'

'It's not the money, it's the adventure,' says Oliver.

This makes me smile. Oliver seems an appealing mixture of old-fashioned and down-to-earth: he's a stickler for holding doors open and I've noticed he never lets Rachel buy a drink, but at the same time he's not fancy.

'Ugh, it's work. Excuse me,' Rachel says, looking at her phone. 'I've got to take this.'

'What does Rachel do?' I ask, watching her pace around talking on her phone. She's wearing a shirt, a pencil skirt and flat boots; she looks almost as if she could be in the office, instead of being on holiday.

'She's a lawyer,' Oliver says, sounding proud. 'They're in the middle of a big case . . . I think that's one of the other associates asking her for advice.'

I nod, thinking that being a lawyer would be my worst nightmare: arguing for a living. Of course there are all kinds of politics in my lab – whose name goes on a paper, who gets the funding, who's flavour of the month with the professor – and we often collaborate, but my favourite part of the job is when it's just me, my bacteria and my microscope. I don't think I'm especially shy or antisocial; I just prefer working alone.

'I hope you remembered to switch off your phone,' David says to Nina, putting his arm around her.

'You'd hardly get calls from work, would you?' Jenny says to Nina.

'No, people do call out of hours,' Nina says.

'About a pet? Seriously?' Jenny says, pouring herself yet another Diet Coke.

'You're obviously not a pet person,' Nina says. Her tone is so mild that I don't think Jenny even registers that this is an insult. She loses interest in the discussion and turns to the others.

'So tomorrow,' she says. 'Who's up for going off-piste?'

'That would be fun,' Oliver says. 'Rachel might be up for it.'

'I'm not sure,' David says, looking at Nina. 'Didn't we say we'd aim for an easier slope tomorrow that we can all do?'

Nina shrugs, indicating that she doesn't mind either way. I look at Leo, who says, 'I'll go with whatever the group decides.'

'But . . .' I'm about to remind him what he said at lunchtime – that we could go out together – but I stop myself. I don't want to rock the boat if the others are all dead set on going off-piste.

'We were just discussing tomorrow,' Oliver says to Rachel, who's finished her phone call and sat back down. 'Which would you prefer: for us all to do an easy blue slope, or to go off-piste with me and Dave and Jen?'

'Oh, blue slope definitely,' Rachel says. 'Isn't that what we said? Blue slopes and red wine?'

Jenny pouts. 'You'll go off-piste with me, Dave, won't you?'

'Do you mind?' he asks Nina.

She shakes her head. 'No, not at all.' And she genuinely seems to mean it: she's munching away at her pizza without a care in the world. Either she doesn't notice Jenny's weird possessiveness with David, or else she's reached some kind of Zen-like state where it doesn't bother her. Whichever it is, she's taking it a lot

162

better than I would. I might find Leo too ready to put the group first, but at least he wouldn't let another girl monopolise him. Especially a nutter like Jenny. Earlier today she was talking about some new registrar she works with who keeps on trying to get people on her team out for drinks. 'I mean,' Jenny said, 'she's just got to accept that there comes a certain point where it's too late to make new friends.' I couldn't believe my ears.

'Jenny's awful, isn't she?' I say quietly to Leo when we're in bed later on.

'Shh,' he says automatically.

'Leo, she's not going to hear me. Don't you think she's a pain?' I know he doesn't like me saying mean things, but he's got to agree with me in this case.

'Chillax, Maggie,' he says, yawning. 'She's fine. Anyway, what's she ever done to you?'

I can't come up with an immediate answer to this, but something about Leo's tone really gets on my nerves, and I lie awake thinking of possible replies for at least five minutes, until I fall fast asleep.

The notion of a blue slope sounded so easy last night after a glass or two of wine, but the next afternoon, when we meet up after my morning lesson, I'm feeling much less confident. For a start, my thighs are screaming after yesterday, and also the ski lift itself looks terrifying. It's bigger than a ride at Alton Towers – a gigantic metal clanking thing that goes hundreds of feet up in the air. The tiny metal mushroom seat lands on the snow and then you have two seconds to jump on it before it lifts in the air again. I don't see how I can get on it, let alone stay on.

'Leo . . . I'm not sure about this,' I say quietly, hanging back. 'I think maybe I'm not ready.'

'Come on, Maggie,' he says. 'You said you wanted to do it, and we're all here now. I could have gone off-piste but I'm doing this so we can be together.'

'OK, OK,' I mutter. After all, if those tiny children can do it, surely I can.

I walk ahead and line up behind Oliver and Rachel, waiting for a mushroom seat with my name on it. It approaches, I manage to grab it, and then we're flying high in the air. I can see the café below and all the lucky, lucky people safe on the ground. I hope one of my skis doesn't fall off and kill someone. And that *I* don't fall off. My lunchtime croque-monsieur is churning in my stomach and I'm beginning to realise I've made a huge mistake. I've also realised the ski lift makes lots of different stops and I don't even know where we're meant to be getting off. I could end up in Switzerland if I'm not careful.

Up ahead, Oliver turns around and calls back to me, 'We're next, Maggie.'

'Remember to put both your skis on the ground and push with your poles as you get off,' calls Leo, from behind me.

The ground is approaching. Rachel and Oliver have both jumped off smoothly and are skiing away. Now it's my turn. I manage to hop off the seat but the stupid thing actually gets caught in the belt of my ski suit and I'm almost rear-ended by the people behind me.

'You OK?' It's Rachel, gliding up to me. 'Those button lifts are the worst. They're much harder than the actual skiing. You'll be grand once we get on the slope – let's go and take a look at it.'

We go and join the others, who are poised at the top of . . . a giant Everest-style mountain. I thought blue slopes were meant to be easy, but this looks practically vertical. We're so high up I can't see the bottom, and the slope below is packed with billions of skiers all bombing along at top speed. It's also clouded over, and I've felt several flakes land on me; we're obviously in for snow. Or a blizzard.

'Guys, I think I might walk down,' I say faintly. 'I'll see you back at the chalet.'

But this isn't a popular suggestion. 'Walk down! No, you can't. You can't walk down,' they all say at once. I get the message: no walking down.

'You'll be fine,' Leo says. 'It's ten minutes to the bottom, max. I'll stay with you.'

'This is the only steep bit,' says Rachel. 'Once you get round that corner, it all evens out and it's lovely.'

I'm clearly going to have to do it, so I nod, deciding I'll

snowplough down as slowly as possible. And if the worst comes to the worst, I'll slide down on my bum.

Leo offers to ski behind me but I tell him that would make me more nervous, so we set off in convoy: first Rachel and Oliver, then Leo, then me. I cautiously push myself along, keeping my skis as far apart as I can and trying not to look down. Ten minutes, I repeat to myself. Or maybe an hour, at the speed I'm going. Suddenly, something huge and yellow zips by me, missing me by millimetres. I shriek out loud, slip and go into a frantic cartoon-type slide before I can get my balance back.

'You OK?' Rachel calls back. She's stopped to wait for me. I can see that the guys have already gone way ahead. What happened to Leo staying with me? 'Stupid snowboarders – they're always bashing into people. They're not dangerous, though,' she adds, seeing my face. 'Let's take it nice and easy for the rest of this bit,' she continues tactfully.

But even her nice and easy is much too fast. I don't want to make her babysit me all the way down, especially because I have a horrible feeling I'm going to cry and I don't want to bawl on her ski suit.

'I think my boot is loose . . . I'm going to fix it. I'll catch you up, OK?'

'No, no, I'll wait.'

'Honestly, I'd much prefer you to go ahead.'

Seeing that I mean it, she nods and skis ahead slowly. I stand there and contemplate the slope below, which I can barely see as the snow's coming down more thickly now. This is a nightmare. I'm tempted to sit down and try and go down on my bum. Except it would take hours and I'm freezing now that we're up so high and I'm not moving. I start snowploughing again, and I'm making reasonably good headway until I realise I've completely lost the others. I can see that the path ahead splits – which way am I meant to go? I could easily take a wrong turn and end up on a black. I need to hurry and catch up.

Cautiously I bring my skis together to try and increase my speed, but then I start going too fast. Whizzz! I've hit a patch of ice, and I'm sliding towards . . . Oh God. Is that a cliff? I frantically try and stop myself by leaning back, forgetting that

that's what makes you fall, and then my skis shoot out from under me and I'm on the ground, covered in snow and very, very sore.

I'm giving up. I've had it. I'm going to lie here and they can just sweep me up when they tidy the slope in the evening.

'Are you all right?' says a voice. Male, French, unfamiliar.

I squint up and see through the snowflakes in my eyelashes that it's the gorgeous tawny-haired instructor, in black ski gear – he's out of uniform and obviously skiing for fun. He's also with two friends, who've stopped to watch. How humiliating.

He turns to the guys and says something to them in French; they nod and go on ahead, leaving him with me.

'Take my hand,' he says. God, his accent is sexy. 'OK, now straighten out your skis and stand up slowly. Don't worry, I've got you. Are you hurt?'

'Just my pride,' I mutter.

He laughs, showing heartbreakingly white teeth. 'That's funny. OK, we'll go to the bottom together, yes? I'll stay with you.'

'No, you don't . . .' But I don't have the heart to send him away. If I'm left here alone, God knows when I'll make it down. He looks like the kind of guy who could carry you down a ski slope. Or out of a burning building . . . OK, concentrate, Maggie.

'Here's how we're going to do it. I ski ahead, not too far, and show you the place to go.' Barely seeming to move, he turns himself around and skis effortlessly *backwards* until he's ten metres or so below me.

'Yeah? Easy. Forget about the rest of the mountain; you only need to ski to me.'

Backwards. The man can ski backwards. He's like Bond. Or Jason Bourne. Does Jason Bourne ski? I launch myself towards him cautiously, and end up right beside him. Very close to him, in fact. I'm suddenly out of breath, and not just from skiing.

'Great. Now again.' He glances behind him, and skis backwards another little bit. '*Eh oh, attention!*' he yells to a snowboarder whizzing past. 'Don't worry about looking behind you. I'm backwards so I keep a watch out behind you. OK?'

We repeat the process four or five more times, until the ground levels out and we're on a flatter bit of the slope. Everyone else seems to have taken the right-hand turn and this stretch is much quieter. It's even stopped snowing. I nearly slip when I reach him, and he catches me by the arm. He feels so . . . *strong*. Manly. *Get a hold of yourself, Maggie*, I tell myself sternly.

'OK, we made it through the hard part! You did good. How many lessons have you had?'

'Two yesterday and one this morning.'

He mimes surprise, pulling up his goggles. 'No way! You are excellent! Really, really, you did good. Now you want to ski with me to the bottom?'

We set off together, and he keeps an eye on me the whole time, giving me little tips occasionally. It's stopped snowing. The sun's beginning to sink down and it's turning the snow pink and orange. The air is so fresh and crystalline, it feels like you could drink it. The snow is soft, with just enough of a slope for us to glide along effortlessly. It feels as if we're flying through the white landscape, alone on the slopes under the darkening blue sky. I wish I could bottle this feeling: I think this is one of those moments I'll remember for the rest of my life.

'This is incredible!' I yell.

He laughs and nods as he skims along beside me.

'Skiing's the best feeling in the world,' he says. 'Nearly.'

Was that a sex reference? Is he flirting? Probably not, but I should be careful in any case. Leo wouldn't appreciate me discussing sex and skiing with a hot instructor. I see the bottom of the slope coming into sight; we're nearly there. I can hear the pop music they always play at the main lift getting louder and louder. I manage to stop myself with a more-or-less respectable snowplough and land beside him, both of us laughing and breathless.

'Congratulations, you made it,' he says, grinning at me and pushing his tawny hair out of his eyes. He's squinting in the late-afternoon sun. His eyes are dark green and there are little freckles across the bridge of his perfect nose. I hope I'm not staring at him.

'Thank you so much,' I say, slightly awkward now that we're

face to face. 'I don't know what I would have done without you.'

'Why were you skiing alone?' he asks. 'Where was your boyfriend?'

'Oh, he went on ahead,' I say without thinking. Damn! I've just told him I have a boyfriend. Maybe that was what he was trying to find out. But I do have one!

'*Tant pis pour lui*,' he says, with that lazy grin again. 'So where are you—'

'Maggie! There you are!' It's Leo. 'Where did you get to?' He's clumping towards us on his skis, looking concerned but also annoyed. I'm pretty peeved myself but I'm not going to get into it now, so I explain briefly that I got stuck on the mountain.

'And, um . . .' I turn to my rescuer. 'Sorry, I don't know your name.'

'Sylvain. And you?'

'Oh, I'm Maggie. And this is Leo. My boyfriend. Leo, Sylvain helped me down.'

'Nice to meet you.' Sylvain gracefully kicks his skis into a start position. 'Enjoy the rest of your holiday.' And he skis off, leaving me dazzled with a tawny vision. I love the way he says holiday. Ollyday.

'Maggie, what happened to you? I was worried!' Leo says, sounding annoyed.

I can't believe he's cross at me; I'm the one who should be cross. 'Then why didn't you stay with me? And why did you make me go up there in the first place? I told you right before we got on the lift that I wasn't ready.'

'I thought you were with Rachel! I was going to go back but I saw you were together. Then we lost you both, and we found Rachel but not you.'

He doesn't answer my second question.

'Well, I was fine.' I'm tempted to add 'no thanks to you', but I bite my tongue. I don't want a row. I start clanking towards the exit, feeling like a medieval knight in armour. 'But I'm exhausted. I need to go home and have a cup of tea and a bath, or a jacuzzi even.'

'But the others are still here – they're having hot chocolate. Don't you want to join them?'

168

'Leo, I'm knackered. Can't we just go home? We can text them.'

'I think that would be rude,' Leo says reproachfully.

I stop short and look at him indignantly. He abandoned me halfway up a mountain, and now he's worried about being *rude*?

'I'm sorry if I'm being *rude*, Leo, but I've had a horrible afternoon and I want to go home. I'll see you back at the chalet.' I moonwalk off towards the ski hire place, half expecting him to follow me, but he doesn't. God damn. If this is what happens on skiing holidays, then I wish we'd stayed at home.

'So what's happening now?' says Jenny.

We've just finished dinner and everyone's lying around in front of the fire. David and Leo are playing chess. Nina and I are both reading. Only Jenny is staring straight ahead, arms folded. I'm beginning to realise there's something properly wrong with her; it's as if her brain chemistry's amiss or something. I would feel sorry for her if she wasn't so mean. Her first words to me when she saw me this evening were, 'I hear you had an epic fail on the blue slope today.' I ignored her.

'This is called r'n'r, Jen,' says Oliver peacefully, from where he's sitting with his feet in Rachel's lap. 'Rest and recovery. Or is it rest and relaxation? Either way, I highly recommend it.'

'I know you do,' says Rachel, pressing his nose with her finger. He pretends to bite the finger and she pretends to shriek. I look away, sighing inwardly.

Leo and I have made up – sort of. At least, he said he was sorry and bought me some chocolates from one of the little souvenir shops, so I've officially forgiven him. I can tell he was surprised: I rarely get angry, and the way I snapped at him earlier was a major hissy fit by my standards.

Unofficially, though, I'm still annoyed, and now I'm thinking I shouldn't have forgiven him so readily. I could understand him leaving me alone on the slopes if he thought I was with Rachel, but it's not just that. I've always considered Leo to be so thoughtful, but how thoughtful is he being these days? He didn't listen to me when I said I wasn't ready; he would have gone off-piste without me if that was what the group decided . . . it's adding to the growing feeling that he's putting other people first and me last. I've had it for weeks – months, even. I thought it would be different on holiday, but it's even worse.

'Ouch,' says David, arching his back.

'What's wrong?' Jenny asks.

'Nothing – a twinge in my shoulders.'

Jenny immediately comes over and stands behind him, massaging his shoulders. Nina looks up from her book, expressionless. I am dying to meet Leo's eye but he's staring studiously at the chessboard.

'Ah – thanks, Jen, but I'm OK. I might go in the jacuzzi later,' David murmurs, and leans away from her, ostensibly to make a chess move. Jenny shrugs and sits down; Nina goes back to her book. We're all pretending not to have noticed, but I can tell everyone's clocked what just happened and can't wait to discuss it once they've left the room.

I've come to the end of my book, a thriller I grabbed in the airport and raced through on the flight despite it not being great. I go upstairs to get my other book, *One Hundred Years of Solitude*. I've been reading it for months and haven't got past page twenty, but I'm determined to get into it on this holiday.

I'm rounding the corner at the top of the stairs when I look out of the window and catch my breath. There's a full moon hanging low in the gap between the mountains, with a massive golden haze around it. It's so bright that you can actually see its light reflected on the forest and on the snow. It's spectacular.

I pad back downstairs. 'Leo,' I call out softly.

Leo turns around abruptly from his game. 'What?' he snaps impatiently.

I stare at him. 'Nothing.' I go back up the stairs and into our room, where I take off my sweatshirt and change into my most clinging pink angora jumper. After quickly piling on some eyeliner, I pull on my snow boots and coat and stuff *One Hundred Years of Solitude* in my pocket. There's a back way out, via the jacuzzi and the gear room, and I slip out, closing the door quietly behind me. I don't even know where I'm going; I just want to get out of here.

Méribel is even more adorable by night. The little wooden and stone-clad buildings are all lit up, their windows twinkling with red lights and white paper snowflakes. I pass by restaurants full of happy gatherings, and dark-panelled bars where smartly dressed couples are sipping *vin chauds*. I keep walking until I find a bar that looks more casual than the others, dark and full of barrel seats, booths and cheerful noise. I go to the bar and order a gin and tonic. It's twelve euros but I don't care. The barman doesn't even measure the spirit; he just sloshes it in, and tops it up with a generous handful of lime slices.

There's a big, rowdy group at one end of the bar, so I choose a seat at the other end, sliding into a candlelit booth and opening my book. But I can't take in the words on the page; I keep thinking about the way Leo snapped at me. I know I'm probably premenstrual, and overreacting, but I can't get over how *mean* he sounded.

It was all so different at the beginning. I remember how he kept on seeking me out at triathlon training until finally we got together at a New Year's Eve party thrown by someone in the club. And when I had a fluey cold right after and couldn't come to practice or see him for two weeks, he texted me every day or sent me funny videos from YouTube until I was better. I can't remember the last time he sent me a funny video.

Also, now that I think of it, he definitely wasn't as busy with all his activities in the beginning. I remember him cancelling a big cycling trip to spend time with me. And then there was the time when we were sitting together having coffee off Oxford Street and he noticed my watch strap was broken. He took it from me and went out, and came back fifteen minutes later having had it fixed at a jeweller's. Maybe that kind of honeymoon period doesn't last, but still. Am I being oversensitive, or is he being a dickhead? I take another slug of my G&T, which is incredibly strong.

'*Bonsoir*.'

Oh my God. It's Sylvain, looking even more gorgeous out of his ski suit. I burble out an incoherent greeting, caught completely off guard.

'You're here alone?' he asks, cutting right to the chase. 'No boyfriend?'

'No . . . I just felt like some peace and quiet.'

171

He nods. 'Ah, Gabriel García Márquez! He's a great writer. I also like Isabel Allende – have you read her books?'

I'm impressed, though it's a bit patronising of me to think a ski instructor wouldn't read. I shake my head, hoping I won't have to admit that I still haven't got past page twenty.

'Would you like a drink?'

I look down and see my glass is empty. I'm about to offer to buy him a drink to thank him for rescuing me on the slopes, but then I change my mind. I can tell he's younger than me, and I already feel like Mrs Robinson with my crush on him. If I buy him a drink, it will just make it worse.

'Sure,' I say, trying to sound casual, as if gorgeous French ski lions buy me drinks all the time. 'I'll have whatever you're having.'

As he goes to the bar, I can't help admiring his rear view. He's wearing a soft, worn-in white cotton shirt tucked into perfectly cut navy cords. And he's leaning on the bar in a way that shows off his lean torso and his snake hips. A very drunk and pretty blond girl in a tight blue T-shirt and jeans, with two long pigtails, comes up and starts attempting to dance with him. He laughs and gives her a twirl. I'm half expecting him to go and join her, but instead he extracts himself from her and comes over to me with two glasses of spicy *vin chaud*.

'I hope your friends don't mind you abandoning them,' I say, awkwardly.

He turns to watch the blond girl swaying back towards the big group. I'm not a hundred per cent sure, but I'm willing to bet she's not French: everyone knows French women don't get drunk.

'It's OK. I go out most nights with the other ski instructors. We're celebrating because one of them, an English guy, got his licence to teach here.' He raises his *vin chaud* and clinks it against mine. '*Salut*. Some of the French instructors are angry that there are too many English instructors in the Alps, but me, I don't mind.'

'Are you from this part of France?'

'Yes, I'm from a little village called Mégève, a few kilometres away. I learned to ski when I was three years old. We used to ski to school.' He smiles. 'And you?'

He leans forward, and I catch a light waft of expensive-smelling aftershave or cologne. Leo never wears aftershave.

'And me what?' I ask. He's so handsome it's hard to think straight.

'Where are you from . . . what do you do?'

Something is buzzing in my pocket. I take out my phone and see that I have two missed calls and a text from Leo: *Maggie, where are you? Everyone is really worried.*

Everyone is really worried? Is that what he cares about – that I've upset the group? I could honestly kill him right now.

'Excuse me,' I say, and start texting back: *I'm fine. Having a drink with a friend. Back later.*

I press 'send', feeling annoyed with myself again. Why didn't I just tell him to eff off? It's always the same with me: I bottle everything up inside or imagine it in my thought bubble.

I glance up to find Sylvain looking at me. Properly looking at me. In a way I haven't been looked at for months. Our little booth is dark and secluded, aside from the flickering candle on the table that throws Sylvain's beautiful features into even better focus.

'Sorry. What were you saying?'

'I was asking you about your life . . . where do you live?'

'In London, in Fulham. I'm a microbiologist,' I add, and brace myself for him to recoil or ask me if that means I study bugs; or my favourite: 'You don't look like one.' Which is ridiculous: what is a scientist supposed to look like? Judging from the cinema, the answer is Jennifer Garner.

Instead, his face lights up. 'Ah, that's great! Are you in a hospital? Do you study virus or bacteria?'

'Oh. Bacteria. I'm a research scientist – I'm studying resistance markers in a particular strain of TB.'

He nods. 'I am studying, ah, *biochimie*.'

'Biochemistry. That's cool.' Oh God, he's a student.

'I'm nearly completing my PhD, in Grenoble.' Good, he can't be that young. We talk about our work for a while, and it's really interesting: he's obviously very bright. And talented. And gorgeous. I should get up and go home soon, before my

173

crush on him rages out of control. Ten more minutes, and I'm gone.

'So,' Sylvain says. 'What are you doing tomorrow, for the *nouvel an*?'

'Oh, for New Year's Eve? I'm not sure actually.' I frown as I think of having to go home to the chalet and discuss New Year's plans with Leo. 'We'll probably have dinner in the chalet or something. What about you?'

'We are going to a bar, and then out to the main square. There are fireworks . . . it's nice. You should come.'

'That does sound nice,' I say, imagining a parallel life where I'm kissing Sylvain at midnight as fireworks explode above us. But back in my real life, I have a real relationship to sort out. I finish my drink and stand up, bracing myself for the confrontation with Leo that's waiting for me at home.

'I'd better go . . . thanks for the drink.'

'Goodbye, Maggie.' He leans forward and kisses me on both cheeks. As soon as I feel his lips on my skin, something happens. Maybe it's my misery over Leo, or downing that very strong G&T on top of the wine at dinner, or maybe it's just sheer animal attraction, but I find myself moving towards him again, and then he kisses me properly. I'm feeling horribly guilty and I know I should pull myself away, but I can't. His fingers are curling in my hair, and I can feel the strength and warmth of his shoulders and arms under the thin fabric of his shirt. He smells divine: spicy and warm, like the *vin chaud* . . .

'Maggie?'

I jump away from Sylvain, scared out of my wits. It's Leo, standing three feet away from us, looking devastated.

'I came to see if you . . .' He looks from me to Sylvain and back again. 'Never mind.'

He walks out of the bar. Oh God, what have I done?

'I have to go,' I blurt to Sylvain.

Sylvain looks pretty shaken up too, but I can't let myself worry about that now. I run outside, pulling my coat on. The freezing cold is like a slap in the face, making me realise how tipsy I am. Leo is walking slowly up ahead. 'Leo!' I call after him. 'Leo, I'm sorry. I didn't mean for that to happen.'

He turns around. 'You mean you didn't arrange to meet him, after he rescued you on the slopes?' he says coldly.

'No! I went into that bar to get out of the house, because you were so horrible to me.'

'Me? When was I horrible to you?' Leo sounds astonished.

'Earlier. When you were playing chess, and I called you and you snapped at me.' I wish there was a better way of putting it; I know it sounds lame.

'Right. So I "snap" at you,' Leo makes air quotes, 'which I don't even remember doing, and you turn around and *cheat* on me?'

'Leo . . .' This is a nightmare. He *was* being horrible, but I'm also totally in the wrong.

We're at the chalet. Leo unlocks the front door and we go inside. Everyone else seems to have gone to bed, thank God; this is hard enough without an audience.

'Leo, please – we need to talk,' I say in a low voice, following him into our room.

'I don't feel like talking. You can have the room tonight. I'm sleeping downstairs.'

I've never seen him so angry. He gets a few things from our bedroom and goes out, closing the door behind him.

The next morning, I wake up with a vague sense of doom. Then everything comes crashing back in slow motion: my near-death experience on the mountain, too much wine at dinner, kissing Sylvain – and the awful, awful fight with Leo. I slip downstairs and wash down two paracetamol with a cup of tea.

'Oh, there you are. Leo was really worried about you last night. Have you had a domestic?' It's Jenny, pouring herself a Diet Coke. I wait until she's left the room, and then grab a can for myself. I notice it's her last one, but I'm beyond caring about that: it's a small crime after what I did last night. I drain my glass, then go upstairs to our room, where I find Leo getting his ski stuff together.

'You can get changed in here,' I say tentatively. 'Leo . . .'

'I'd rather not,' he says shortly. He closes the door behind him as he goes out. I curl up on the bed and listen until the door slams downstairs and I'm positive everyone's gone out.

It takes me for ever to have a shower and get dressed. I didn't think I'd had that much to drink last night, but I have a stinking hangover today. Not only that, I'm aching all over as if I've been beaten up. I can't face skiing or any other snowy activity. I put on my coat and then go outside to get some air, with *One Hundred Years of Solitude* in my bag again – how appropriate. Trailing up the little street, squinting in the sunshine, I wonder how on earth I got myself into this mess. Leo and I have got some serious problems that we need to address, but I've made it a thousand times worse by kissing Sylvain.

'Maggie! Over here!'

I give a guilty start, but it's just Rachel, dressed in jeans and her coat.

'Oh, hi. You not skiing either?' I ask.

'No, I think I overdid it yesterday – I decided to take the morning off. I've had a sauna and I'm starving. Do you want to come and get some hot chocolate?'

I nod, grateful for the company. We wander down the street until we find a very cute bakery-café place with antique chairs and a chandelier, and order hot chocolate and some little doughnuts. The hot chocolate arrives as two little jugs of piping hot milk and some solid chocolate, which we blend together with a whisk to the consistency we want. It's a lot of work when you feel as bad as I do. Rachel has hers quite thin and liquid, but I let mine stay gloopy, like a rich chocolate sauce.

'It's hard to imagine that this used to be a tiny farming village, isn't it?' says Rachel, looking at two women in full-length fur coats standing at the counter comparing their diamond bracelets. 'It must have changed massively over the last fifty years.'

I nod gloomily, dipping my doughnut into my hot chocolate. Now I'm thinking of Sylvain telling me about his childhood in a little skiing village . . . and that kiss. It was quite a kiss. Electric. Explosive. But I also suspect hormones and alcohol had a lot to do with it. Sylvain is not my future boyfriend. Whereas Leo *is* my future – or I hoped he was.

'I don't want to pry, but are you OK?' Rachel asks gently.

She seems nice and I've got to tell someone.

'Promise you won't say anything?' I say nervously.

Her eyes widen, but she nods, and I tell her how Leo upset me yesterday and how I ended up kissing Sylvain in the bar.

'Do you think I'm a terrible person?'

She shakes her head immediately. 'Of course I don't.' I feel reassured, especially when she continues, 'I mean, it's not like you did it for fun or because you were bored. It sounds as if there might be other problems, with you and Leo . . .'

Though I feel guilty about complaining, after what I've done, I find myself telling her how frustrated I am in general about Leo's schedule – about how he devotes so much time to his friends and activities that there isn't much left for me.

'But maybe that's the kind of thing that happens after a certain amount of time. It's all lovey-dovey at the beginning, but then inevitably . . . Oh God, I'm sorry! I don't mean you and Oliver.' What is wrong with me?

'Don't worry,' says Rachel, laughing. 'I didn't think you did. Are we being completely sickening? I'm sure we are.'

'No, of course you're not! All I mean is,' I say, going red and changing the subject, 'relationships are never perfect, are they? They need work.'

'They do. But I think you're meant to enjoy it,' Rachel says. 'It's not meant to be like working in a coal mine.'

This makes me laugh for the first time today, and makes me feel better. Being with Leo can be challenging, but it's certainly not like working in a mine.

'Maybe you should tell him how you're feeling,' Rachel says. 'It sounds as if you're frustrated because you want to spend more time together, but he might not even know that.'

I sigh. I know this is the sensible thing, but I dread this kind of talk. 'Yeah. I will talk to him . . . Though I don't know if he'll listen, after what I've done.'

'Of course he will. You've been together long enough that he has to.'

'Maybe you're right.' I dip the end of my doughnut into my bowl and scoop up the last of my hot chocolate. 'How long have you and Oliver been together?' I ask curiously.

Rachel looks partly embarrassed and partly proud as she says,

'About two weeks. I know, it's mad. I've known him longer than that, but we got together just before Christmas, and then he invited me on this trip, and I thought . . . New Year in the Alps, why not? It beats paying thirty quid to get into some nightmare club in London and then being vomited on all the way home on the Tube.'

'That's true,' I say. Rachel's description sounds like an awful New Year's Eve I had a few years ago, when Lily and I went to the club from hell because we'd heard there were lots of single men there. There were, but they were all horrible and seemed to think that trying to grab your bum was a valid form of communication. I'd be ashamed to admit it to Rachel, but quite apart from my feelings for Leo, I'm not relishing being thrown out of the safe nest of our relationship into the single jungle again.

But I don't think that will happen. I'm not sure why, but I feel more hopeful about things now. I mean . . . Leo wouldn't be so upset that I kissed Sylvain if he didn't care about me. The kiss was a huge mistake, but maybe it will lead to something changing for the better between us.

After we've paid our bill – I insist on treating her – Rachel and I get changed back at the chalet and head out for a quick session on one of the easier slopes. When I see a group of kids coming down towards us, I look at their instructor to see if it's Sylvain. That would be very awkward. But thankfully, it's not. I'm sure he's forgotten about me by now; he's hardly short of romantic prospects. With any luck, I won't bump into him again.

'Oliver says the others are stopping for lunch now,' Rachel says, looking at her phone. 'Do you want to come and join them?'

I'm about to say no, that I'll wait for them back at the chalet – but then I change my mind.

'No. I'm going to call Leo and ask him to come and have lunch with me in the village,' I tell her. I exchange numbers with her in case Leo refuses to meet me and I need someone else to let me into the chalet.

But Leo agrees to come and have lunch with me, alone. I'm

encouraged: he obviously wants to talk. I choose one of the more casual restaurants – wooden chairs with heart-shaped cut-outs, red and white checked tablecloths, no Michelin stars – and wait for him at a table by the window, feeling as nervous as if this was a first date. I order a Perrier; no more boozing for me.

Not that I can blame the booze, of course. I never, ever thought I would be the kind of person to cheat on my boyfriend. The idea of trying to explain it to him suddenly feels really lame, as if I'm trying to justify myself. There's no excuse for what I did.

Looking out of the window, I can see Leo coming down the street – with Jenny. They're both in ski gear, walking slowly, chatting away. Suddenly she stuffs something – some snow I think – down his neck and shrieks with laughter. He chases after her for a few minutes, and puts some snow down her neck, before they go their separate ways. I don't like seeing this horseplay between them – it reminds me of the way she acts around David. But I'm not exactly in a position to complain.

Leo comes through the door of the restaurant, and manages to make his way to my table and sit down, all without meeting my eye.

'Leo . . .'

'Let me order some food first, will you?' he says, his eyes fixed on the menu. 'I'm starving.'

He orders tartiflette, which is basically cheesy potatoes with bacon. I'm not sure I'll be able to eat anything, but I order the same thing without the bacon, for the sake of having something. I still haven't tried fondue, but I think you have to share it, and this isn't the moment.

'I'm probably going to have to pay excess baggage if they weigh me at the airport,' I say. Leo doesn't even smile, and I kick myself for making a joke, however lame.

We sit in silence until our food arrives, and I make myself wait until Leo's eaten half of his before I start talking.

'Leo, I am so sorry about last night. There's no excuse, but I'm so sorry. I didn't mean to hurt you. I never—'

'Why did you do it?'

Oh. I wasn't going to try to justify myself, but it looks as if I'm going to have to. 'Well – it was because I was upset and lonely and annoyed at you.'

'At me? What did I do?' Leo sounds annoyed himself.

'I wanted to show you the full moon, but you snapped at me.'

'The full *moon*?' He laughs bitterly. 'Jesus, Maggie. And I didn't snap at you.'

'You did. You looked at me as if I was this horrible person you didn't even want to be around.' It sounds so pathetic and trivial now.

'I told you: I honestly don't remember doing that.'

'But it's not just that.' I really want him to understand. 'It's . . . Ever since we've come on this holiday, I've felt as if you'd rather spend time with the group than with me.'

'But it's a group holiday.'

If this is our break-up conversation, I may as well be honest with him. And it all comes pouring out.

'I know it's a group holiday, but I'm your girlfriend, and sometimes I feel as if I have to fight for scraps of your time. You're so booked up with all your friends and activities – every weekend there's something happening. And I love that you're so busy and active, I do, but sometimes it feels as if there isn't room for me in your life,' I finish, feeling almost breathless. Leo is staring at me as if this is all completely new information. How could he not have picked up on it? I suppose he just didn't.

'I didn't know you felt that way,' he says eventually.

I nod, and look down at my tartiflette, which I've barely touched. To my surprise, Leo says, 'What do you want me to do about it?'

He sounds resentful, but he did ask. So I recklessly start giving him suggestions.

'Well, maybe we could have a standing date night every week, the way you do with your poker gang . . .'

But he shakes his head. 'That would be too difficult.'

I decide to go all out. 'Or we could move in together. Then we'd see each other more.'

'Maggie – sorry. Yesterday I found you kissing another guy, and now you want us to move in together?'

I hang my head, feeling tears pricking at my eyes. He's right. But then he surprises me by saying, 'I *could* try and be less busy.'

'Really? You could?'

'Yeah. I mean, I can't do a weekly date night – I think that's unrealistic. But I could try and cut down on the cycling. And the football.'

'That would be great.'

'I can't promise anything, but I'll try.'

'Thank you.' I look down again and start ripping my paper napkin to shreds. In a low voice I continue, 'And can you forgive me?'

After an agonisingly long pause, during which he sips his beer, he nods. 'I suppose I can.' He squeezes my hand. 'New year, new start, right?'

I nod, grinning all over my face, and squeeze his hand in return. We're back together *and* he's agreed to try and be less busy. This is brilliant.

'So tonight,' he says. 'The others were talking about having dinner in the chalet, and then going out to the square to see some fireworks. Sound good?'

I nod again. 'Sounds great.'

Leo persuades me to go back to the slopes, and we do a blue run with David and Nina. Like my conversation with Leo, it's much easier than I thought it would be. I'm so happy that by the evening I'm singing tunelessly in the shower. I put on the new dress I bought for Christmas – a glittery forest-green number from Joy with a cut-out back and long sleeves, über-flattering – and my favourite stud earrings from Alex Monroe, in the shape of pears. And I finally take the time to do my make-up properly, giving myself big bronze smoky eyes with my new gel eyeshadow and lining them with my Stila smudge stick in Damson. I've even brought some individual fake lashes, which look great in photos.

'Mags.' Leo puts his head around the door. 'Come on. We're about to have some champagne.'

'OK – I'm coming. I just want to do my lashes . . .'

'But everyone's waiting for you.'

181

'OK, OK.' I don't see why they can't start drinking without me, but I don't want to pick a fight when we've just patched things up. I follow Leo down to the living room, where everyone's gathered around a table full of canapés.

'We've made Kir Royales,' David says, handing me a glass before putting his arm back around Nina. She looks great in a sleeveless red dress: much more grown-up. I notice that David doesn't have his usual shadow. Jenny is standing on the other side of the room laughing ostentatiously at something Leo's saying and flicking her hair at him. She's obviously trying to make David jealous; I wish she wouldn't use Leo as a prop.

'Cheers, everyone!' says Rachel. 'Happy almost New Year!'

We all sit down to dinner, which Rachel and Oliver serve up. Gavin has knocked himself out with a beef dish in pastry, with a tomato tart for me, and spinach savoury pancakes to start. I'm so full that I can't even manage the clafoutis – a kind of cherry pie – for dessert, but as Oliver points out, it will be nice for breakfast.

'Wow,' Leo says. 'It was only a few years ago that New Year's Eve meant wandering around in the rain looking for the house party of a friend of a friend. Now we're skiing and eating clafoutis. When did we get so old?'

I laugh. Rachel beams at us from across the table; she's obviously pleased that we've made up. The only person who doesn't seem full of New Year's cheer is Jenny. Aside from a few grumbles about what a nightmare she's having trying to sell her two-bedroom flat in Putney, she's been mostly quiet by her standards. I notice that she's given Leo half her dessert, which makes me edgy because it reminds me of her offering David her chips. But I'm probably being paranoid. It's just a dieting trick of hers, or else she's showing David what he's missing.

After dinner, we sit around drinking very strong Irish coffees made by David, until someone notices that it's nearly eleven and the fireworks have started. We all put our coats on and file outside. Leo and I walk along with the other two couples ahead of us. Jenny is lagging behind on her own. I've just noticed that she has the same Superdry jacket as Leo, teamed as ever with her gigantic fur hat. If it was anyone else I'd wait for her, or go and check on her, but I'm not that nice.

'What's up with her, I wonder?' I murmur to Leo.

He looks behind. 'Not sure. I'll go back and check.'

'Oh – OK.'

I'd prefer it if he didn't, but that would be mean, and anyway, I don't want to push it with Leo right now. I catch up with Rachel and Oliver and we make our way to the main square, which is packed with happy après-skiers and holidaymakers. The fireworks are arcing across the sky in starbursts of white, red, yellow, green and purple. Rachel and I stand near the Christmas tree while Oliver goes off to get us all some hot wine. I hope Leo finds me soon; I don't want to play gooseberry all evening.

'So,' Rachel says, turning to me with a smile. 'All good?'

'Oh yes – thanks. We sorted things out.' But even as I'm saying that, I'm thinking: did we? I'm still being rushed because 'the group' is waiting for me. Leo's dashed off to look after Jenny and I still don't feel I can say anything. We're no closer to moving in together than we were before we went away. Has anything genuinely changed?

'That's great! Where is Leo, by the way?'

'He's gone to check if Jenny's OK.'

'Oh yeah.' Rachel raises her eyebrows. 'Have you heard?'

'No! What?'

'I shouldn't be gossiping, but . . . Nina apparently walked in on David and Jenny in the jacuzzi this afternoon. Nothing was happening, except that Jenny was topless. Supposedly she forgot her bikini top.'

'Are you serious?'

'Yes. Nina didn't say anything, but apparently she took David to one side afterwards and told him his relationship with Jenny was weird and that he needed to choose between them.'

'Nina said that? But she's such a mouse!' I feel mean saying that, but it's true.

'The mouse that roared. Apparently she's laid down some ground rules and he's agreed to them. I don't know what they are . . . no more topless bathing together, I imagine.'

183

'How do you know all this?'

'Oliver told me.'

'I don't believe it,' I murmur. 'Was David annoyed?'

'I don't think so. He said that he's had this problem with Jenny before – which I happen to know is true – and now he's realised he needs to set some boundaries. I feel sorry for her, to be honest. This isn't all her fault: David should have sorted it out a long time ago.' Rachel pauses, looking as if she's thinking of something specific.

'So what do you think's changed?'

'I think it's Nina. He's crazy about her. The whole reason we're having such a deluxe holiday is that he wanted to spoil her, apparently.'

I look over at David and Nina, who are standing together a little way away. He's behind her, with his arms circled around her. He's just the right height to rest his head on hers; they both look very happy. Nina's obviously not such a mouse after all. Just because she's quiet doesn't mean she's weak; in fact it occurs to me that there's a certain chutzpah in not feeling you have to make conversation. And she wasn't scared of losing David. She told him what she wanted and I'm guessing she was willing to walk away if he didn't agree.

Whereas . . . what did I sort out with Leo exactly? I asked him to free up some room in his schedule for me, and he said he'd try. I know I cheated on him. But is that really all I deserve?

Oliver rejoins us with some mulled wine in paper cups, and we stand around looking up at the fireworks. I don't know where Leo's gone. But I do know this: what I did with Sylvain was wrong, but it doesn't mean I don't want a proper boyfriend. And it's finally dawning on me that Leo is not going to be that for me, ever. I'm going to end it with him.

'I've got to go and find Leo,' I tell Rachel.

Threading my way through the crowd is difficult, especially since it's dark and everyone's wearing massive puffa coats or full-length minks. As I dodge around, I'm getting more and more worked up about everything I've put up with from Leo. For example, the way he's always telling me to chillax. We only chillax when it suits him! Why can't we chillax about me getting lost on the mountain, or saying something bitchy about someone, or interrupting his chess game?

Just as I'm thinking this, I see the lettering on the back of Leo's navy Superdry jacket. His arms are encircled around another navy Superdry jacket, which belongs to Jenny, who Leo is kissing.

The sight hits me like a punch in the gut; I know instantly that I'll never forget it. It's horrible. When Leo turns around and sees me, he looks surprised, and guilty – but not that surprised, and not really that guilty.

Ignoring their shocked expressions, I hurry back into the crowd, my eyes blurry with tears. I can't believe Leo did that to me – and with someone so horrible. But then again, I did it to him.

'Maggie! Wait!' It's Leo. I turn around reluctantly.

'Look, I'm sorry about that,' he says. 'She was upset . . .' His voice trails off and I can tell that he's realising how lame that sounds.

'So you had to kiss her? Come on.' I put my hands on my hips. 'Leo, I know I kissed someone, but that was a stranger. She's on holiday with us! I'm going to have to see her at breakfast tomorrow!'

'Well, now we both know how it feels, so maybe we can put it behind us.'

He so doesn't get it. 'I don't think we can put this behind us. We wouldn't be going around kissing other people if we were happy together, but we're not.'

'Yes we are,' he says, sounding uncertain.

'No we're not, Leo. I'm not. I want to share my life with someone, and you won't even schedule a weekly date with me, like you do with your poker group.'

Leo doesn't say anything. All around us, the countdown to midnight has begun, in English and French, accompanied by the big screen. I think he finally gets it now.

'I'm sorry,' he says.

'Me too.' As the cheers for midnight break out, and people start singing 'Auld Lang Syne', I feel a lump in my throat. What a shitty, shitty New Year's Eve. 'I'm going home to the chalet,'

185

I say, trying to keep my voice even. 'I'll see you tomorrow, OK?'

He looks as if he's about to protest, but then he stops. 'There's a key under the mat,' is all he says. He steps forward and hugs me briefly.

'Happy New Year.'

'Yeah. Happy New Year,' I reply.

I turn around and walk away, crying properly now. It's one thing to break up with Leo; it's another for him to have a replacement waiting in the wings. I can't believe he told me he kissed Jenny because she was upset, as if he's some kind of snogging Good Samaritan. He kissed her because he fancied her, though how this is possible boggles my mind. She's *awful*! I wonder: does she really like him, or is she rebounding from David? Either way, at least I don't have to feel so guilty any more. I blow my nose on a paper napkin from the restaurant where Leo and I had our reconciliation lunch, thinking what a waste of time that was.

Out of nowhere, I'm remembering Sylvain again, and our fateful kiss. I completely misjudged things with Leo; what if I did the same with Sylvain? What if there was genuinely something there? Well, it's too late now.

Everyone's busy kissing and hugging, exchanging Happy New Years. I've had it: I'm going home. I'll sleep in our room and Leo can damn well bunk in with Jenny in her single bed. His feet will probably stick out of it but I can't help that.

As I trudge back to the chalet, I keep on having flashbacks of seeing the two of them together. And I keep on wondering what on earth he could see in her. But even though my feelings are bruised and my pride is dented, there's a part of me that feels as if it's coming awake after being asleep for a year. It's the part of me that would always rather be alone than with the wrong person.

'Maggie!'

I stop and slowly turn around, barely daring to hope. But it's him. I knew it from the way he put the accent on the second syllable. Ma*ggie*. He's wearing a Barbour-type jacket, with a scarf thrown around his neck in the way that only French men can. He walks towards me, hands in pockets.

'Alone again?' he asks, grinning. 'One hundred years of solitude?'

I nod. 'Alone again,' I agree. 'Alone for good.'

'*Bonne Année*,' he murmurs, looking down at me.

'Happy New Year.' I feel a stupid grin growing on my face.

We stand there for a minute longer, and then he leans down, and kisses me. I kiss him back, hungrily. His cheeks feel cold, but his stubble is so sexy and his lips are warm. He tastes of *vin chaud*, and I can smell that gorgeous faint aftershave again. When he puts his arms around me, I realise I'm shivering – but it's from excitement.

'You're cold,' he says, rubbing my arms. Then he adds, 'We could go inside . . . back to my place?'

Uh-oh. I barely know him, and I'm on the rebound, and he's younger than me, and he lives in France, and it's not going to go anywhere, and the others will worry if I stay out late. I definitely shouldn't go home with him.

'OK,' I agree.

As we walk, I pull out my phone and text Rachel. *All over with Leo, am with a friend. Will explain later. Tell the others I'm fine.* She'll probably think I'm a complete slapper, but I can't help it; I'm not coming home now.

I'm expecting Sylvain's digs to be in some giant cheerless apartment block, but instead he leads me to a chalet on the edge of the village that has been divided into studios. He unlocks a door and leads me into a cosy studio with a bed in one corner and a sofa and table in another. There's a fire burning low in the grate, and a sheepskin rug in front of it.

He takes my coat and hangs it up very carefully with his own, then puts a couple of logs on the fire before asking me if I want some tea with rum.

'I'd love some.' A Frenchman who drinks tea: is this a sign? He goes off into a little kitchen alcove and puts on a saucepan of water, and I find myself wondering how on earth the kettle hasn't made it to France.

'Do you like Saint Etienne?' he asks.

'Sure!' He walks over to the CD player in the corner, and I imagine myself walking up behind him and putting my arms around him.

Forget doing more cultural things: my New Year's resolution is to say things out loud instead of thinking them in my bubble, and to do things instead of imagining them.

I walk over to him and put my arms around him. He turns around and we kiss again as the music starts. God, this is magic. He kisses my throat and my collarbone while I run my fingers through his gorgeous, untidy tawny hair, inhaling the smell of his skin. We're so carried away that we barely notice the bubbling noise getting louder, until we look over and see that the saucepan of water has boiled over.

'I forgot the tea,' he mutters. His breath is fast and he looks as dazed as me.

'Don't worry about the tea.' He goes to turn off the gas, and when he comes back, we start kissing again. He's stroking my skin through the cut-out on my back; now he's undone the clasp of my dress, and he's kissing my shoulder.

'Let's lie in front of the fire,' I murmur, letting the dress drop around my waist. I don't know what's got into me, aside from some Kir Royales and a couple of *vin chauds*, but I like it. He takes my hand and leads me over to the fire, then lies down beside me on the rug. It's a little itchy, but I don't care: I feel incredibly sexy, half-naked and bathed in firelight.

'Ah, Maggie,' he groans, looking down at me. 'You are so sexy.'

It might be corny, but it's also irresistible. He starts unbuttoning his shirt, revealing the most gorgeous chest I've seen in real life, probably ever: strong and athletic without looking Photoshopped. I undo his belt and fly, tugging his trousers off. He pulls my dress down completely and lies on top of me, boxers still on, and we move together for a while, kissing and touching every inch of each other that we can reach.

'Are you sure?' he asks.

'Oh God, yes,' I say, panicked that he'll change his mind. And then he fishes a condom out of his trouser pocket, and pushes himself inside me, and I stop thinking about anything at all except how incredible we feel together.

Afterwards we lie together looking into the fire, my finger lazily tracing circles over his chest and stomach. From where I'm lying,

I can see a desk with some textbooks neatly laid out. Sylvain is obviously a conscientious guy: the perfect scientist. We have our work in common – sort of. Maybe there's something in this. Maybe we could visit each other . . . I could come back here and learn to ski . . . He could get a job in London . . .

'What are you thinking about?' he asks, drowsily.

'Oh! Um . . .' I'm wondering how I can reply without either lying through my teeth or sounding completely sad. 'How unexpected this is.'

'You're right. I didn't expect.' He drops a kiss on my collarbone. 'I hoped, but I didn't expect.' He sits up, and holds out a hand to me. 'Do you want to go to bed? To sleep?'

I don't even consider putting on my clothes and facing the cold world outside again; I just nod, and we make the short journey across the room to get into his bed. The sheets are icy, and we curl up together to try and warm up. It feels so incredibly weird to be with someone who's not Leo. Weird, but wonderful. I'd love to stay awake longer to enjoy being wrapped in his gorgeous arms, but I'm shattered after the dramas of today, and I know I'm going to be asleep within minutes.

Beside me, I feel Sylvain look up.

'Look, Maggie,' he says. I follow his gaze and see that he's pointing out of the window at the full moon. I smile to myself as I drift off to sleep.

The next morning, I'm completely disoriented for a good few minutes before I remember what has happened. I don't know which headline in the Maggie *Times* is most startling: that Leo and I are finished, that Leo kissed Jenny, or that I went home with Sylvain. Thank God I remembered to text Rachel, or else the others would have had the local gendarmerie combing the streets of Méribel for me.

Sunlight is coming in through the windows; I smell coffee, and toast. And there's Sylvain, dressed in his instructor gear, his tawny hair falling over his beautiful bronzed forehead as he prepares something in his little kitchen.

'Good morning,' he says, smiling. He brings over a big cup of milky coffee – practically a bowl – and some buttered toast.

'Oh, thank you,' I murmur. I sip the coffee and eat the toast, feeling awkward after my wild abandon last night. I must look a state, with all my make-up smudged and my hair on end; it's always crazy in the morning. Whereas Sylvain looks as gorgeous as ever, except his eyes are slightly tired. His beautiful greeny-gold eyes.

'Are you taking lessons today?' he asks.

'No. We're leaving today! Shit. What time is it?'

'Eight.'

'Oh God.' I know we're meant to check out at ten. 'Um . . . hang on a sec.' I throw on my dress, which was lying near the bed, and rush into the bathroom. I look every bit as awful as I'd expected: deathly pale, with smudged clown eyes. Thankfully there are some make-up removal wipes, so I clean the ruins of my make-up off my face.

Hmm. Make-up removal wipes? Unless Sylvain is a fan of make-up, which I don't think he is, surely these indicate the presence of some other girl . . . or girls? I rinse my mouth out with water and toothpaste and splash water on my face before going back out to him.

He's looking at his watch, but glances up as soon as I appear. I know it wasn't meant as a hint, but it's a good reality check. Make-up wipes in his bathroom are sort of irrelevant. I'm on a skiing holiday where I just broke up with my boyfriend, and Sylvain is a ski instructor-slash-student. I don't think either of us believes that this is the beginning of a new relationship. But it's a wonderful start to the new year.

'Sylvain, I'd better go.' A silly grin is spreading over my face again as I look at that sheepskin rug and remember what happened on it last night. I don't feel embarrassed any more; I feel sexy, and confident, and more grown-up than I did twenty-four hours ago – certainly more confident than after I saw Leo kissing Jenny.

He helps me find my tights and shoes, and then helps me on with my coat in a very gentlemanly way. Then he walks me to the door.

'So . . . good luck in your studies,' I say, and then feel an urge to giggle as I realise I couldn't have come up with a more grandmotherly way to say goodbye to him if I'd thought about it for weeks.

'And you. Do you want me to walk you home to your chalet?'

Part of me quite likes the idea of turning up at the chalet on Sylvain's arm, but I think the situation is complicated enough already.

'No, that's OK.' I reach up and kiss him on the cheek. 'Thanks for a wonderful night.'

In response, he bends down and kisses me properly. It's a truly passionate kiss . . . all the more so because we both know it's the last one.

He opens the door for me, and I trot down the stairs, turning to wave at him still with a silly grin on my face. He waves back, then closes the door. And I'm alone in the snowy street, under a bright blue sky on a beautiful winter's day. The snow is sparkling in the sun; the air is crisp. I should be devastated at the end of my relationship with Leo, but I'm not, because I'm beginning to realise how unhappy I was while I was with him. I'm sad, of course, but I also feel hopeful, as if life is full of possibilities.

I do feel nervous as I get closer to the chalet. I have no idea what things will be like with Jenny and Leo, or if everyone will know about what happened. I'm dreading the questions and discussions and odd looks. I'm getting up the courage to walk in when Rachel emerges wearing her coat, her dark hair gleaming in the sun.

'Maggie!' she exclaims, running down the steps. 'There you are! What happened to you last night?'

I explain briefly about breaking up with Leo and going home with Sylvain. I leave out the part about Jenny; if Leo hasn't mentioned it, then I don't want to either.

But something in Rachel's face tells me that Leo and Jenny have already taken care of that.

'Oh. Did they spend the night together? Actually, wait. I don't want to know.' I shake my head. 'I just want to go home.'

'No, no, they didn't. And I don't think the others know about any of this – I just wondered about it. I won't say anything. Look, why don't you go and have a coffee down the street, and I'll pack for you. You can come back here in an hour and we'll all get the bus.'

'What? Would you really do that?'

She nods. 'Of course!'

'You don't have to,' I say, touched. 'Honestly. I need to face Leo; I'll have to do it sometime anyway. But listen, would you like to swap contact details? It would be nice to meet up when we're back in London . . . if you're free . . .' I stop short, thinking that maybe Rachel will be too busy with work and Oliver, or that she might find it odd to keep in touch with me once Leo and I have broken up.

But she says, 'Definitely! Have you got your phone handy?' We exchange email addresses, and Rachel says she'll find me on Facebook too.

Next minute, the door to the chalet crashes open. It's Jenny, wearing Ugg boots, jeans and an Abercrombie and Fitch hoodie, hair practically standing on end with rage.

'My fur hat is missing!' she says. 'I had it last night when we came home from the fireworks . . .' She looks down at me and for the first time seems to realise who she's talking to. But she doesn't break stride. 'I definitely had it, and now it's gone and I can't find it anywhere. It cost two hundred quid! I'm not leaving until whoever has it gives it back.'

'I'm sure you're not suggesting that one of us is holding your hat hostage,' Rachel says in her most lawyerly, reasonable tone. 'You probably dropped it in the street somewhere. Maybe you should go and take a look.'

'No! I definitely had it!'

'Well it wasn't me,' I tell her. 'I wasn't even here last night. I was in bed with one of the ski instructors.'

She blinks at me and I grin back at her. I can't believe I just said that. This is a whole new me.

'Maybe you should ask Nina,' Rachel says. 'She might have seen it. Although she's quite keen on animal rights, so you might want to be careful . . . Was it real fur?'

'Of course it was real fur!' Jenny turns on me. 'You stole it! Because you're a vegetarian – and you're angry at me for stealing your boyfriend!'

This is just so ludicrous, it makes me snort with laughter. 'Jenny. Come on. I did not steal your fur hat. Any more than you stole my boyfriend. He's got a mind of his own and we've broken up for reasons that have absolutely nothing to do with you. So don't flatter yourself.' I feel more liberated with every word, realising that though I *do* mind that Leo kissed her, a lot, my night with Sylvain has definitely eased the pain.

'Hang on,' says Rachel. 'I see something.' She goes around the side of the steps and retrieves something from under a bush. 'Here is it! You must have dropped it when you were coming inside.' Her tone is almost soothing as she goes up the steps to hand Jenny the hat, and I realise that she must be feeling sorry for her. I do too, really: anyone who can lose their mind like that over a missing hat is a bit pathetic.

Jenny grabs the hat, dusting it down protectively. 'I'll have to dry it with my hairdryer. Probably ruined,' she mutters. After a minute she says, 'Thanks, though. And soz,' she adds to me. 'About the hat, and about . . . last night.'

I have to take a deep breath first, but I'm able to say the right thing. 'It's OK.' And I mean it. Eighty per cent, anyway.

Jenny mutters something else and goes back inside. Rachel and I look at each other and laugh, shaking our heads.

'God, that was nuts,' she says. 'Fur flying, literally. Look, I'm just going out to meet Oliver for a last hot chocolate. You're sure you're OK? Come and join us once you've packed.'

'Thanks. I'm fine! Go!' And it's true. Yes, I'm dreading the journey home – I can already picture the hours of awkward travelling, sitting beside Leo in silence, or worse, sitting on my own or playing gooseberry with the others while he keeps Jenny company. And yes, I wish my relationship with Leo hadn't ended the way it did.

But I feel free, and optimistic, and braver than I have in ages. As I watch Rachel going down the snowy street, I realise that Jenny was wrong about something else, too. It's never too late to make a new friend. Smiling, I run up the steps to the chalet, ready to face the first day of the new year.

2 January
From: Maggie
To: Lily

Well, you were dead right: New Year WAS special. Can we Skype this evening – maybe 10 p.m. my time (that's 6 a.m. your time?) Lots to tell you.
  Mx

2 January
From: Lily
To: Maggie

It was good to talk just now. I'm sorry, Mags, I didn't think your holiday would be *that* memorable. You seem in really good form considering. I'll let you know the dates I'll be over in Feb as soon as I've cleared it with work. And maybe I'll see your new apartment? I think your parents are right to insist on you moving house. I'm all for cheap rent, but not when you might die.
  Lots of love,
  Lily xxx

PS I just googled 'Sylvain ski instructor Méribel' and I found a pic. Is this him? If so . . . GOOD JOB, as they say here.

3 January
To: Lily
From: Maggie

Yes, that is him! Though the picture doesn't do him justice. I just found him on Facebook (didn't know his surname before!!) but I decided not to friend him. It's better this way. We'll always have Méribel.
  I am fine about Leo really. In a way it was such hard work dating him, the break-up is easy in comparison. I forgot to tell you Dad's theory. He reckons it was always

a bad sign that Leo doesn't support a football team (?) He says football teams are how young men learn loyalty and commitment and no wonder Leo was a wrong 'un because he never had that. I tried to explain that actually Leo was TOO team-spirited and always put other people ahead of me, but Dad's convinced he's right. Who knows, maybe he is.

Mxx

6 January
From: Lily
To: Maggie, Poppy

Hi girls,

Some dates for your diaries: I'll be in the UK from the 9th to the 18th of February. I am slightly in trouble because I'll be away over Valentine's weekend, which also happens to be Jesse's mother's sixtieth birthday. But that was the only time I could get off work, and as I said to Jesse, it's not as if we would have had time to do anything romantic anyway. It's typical Diane to have her birthday on Valentine's AND to mark it with a weekend-long festival of events. Quite frankly, I think I've spent more than enough time with his family over the past few months, they must be sick of me by now.

Anyway, bit of a tangent. The point is, I really want to see lots of you both while I'm home, and I want to introduce you two as well! I think you'll get on.

Love,
Lily xxx

7 January
From: Maggie
To Lily

Hurrah! It's in the diary. It will be so good to see you. And it will be great to meet Poppy, I've heard so much about her. One of my New Year's resolutions is to widen my social circle and meet more people. I won't bore you with the others because I know you don't do resolutions, but suffice it to say, this is going to be MY year. (Sorry if that sounds greedy. It can be your year too.)

If you're not doing anything on Valentine's Day, do you want to do something together? Dinner and a movie?

Mxx

7 January
From: Lily
To: Maggie

Hi Mags,

That's a great resolution, to meet new people. I'd like to do that here – I am meeting people through work etc., but it's tricky because I'm tied up almost every weekend travelling to Boulder or having Jesse here. For example, my flatmates are going out on Saturday night; Amanda's on the guest list of a new club. But I can't go with them, as Jesse's coming over and he's not keen. It's such a pity. I mean, of course it's not a pity that he's coming over, just that I haven't had a good girls' night out in ages.

And of course I will be your date on Valentine's. I won't want to be anywhere near Dad and Fi in any case.

Love,
Lily xx

PS Gretchen (my boss) is rather creative with the truth. Today I overheard her telling someone on the phone that I'm a good friend of Pippa Middleton's. I was going to say something but she's in such a foul mood from her detox I decided best not.

PPS Get this: my flatmate Megan has had business cards printed out – not because she needs them for work, but so that she can hand them out to guys she meets. I can't work out if that's a genius idea or not.

8 January
From: Poppy
To: Lily

Happy New Year darling! That's great that you're coming over, and I'll look forward to meeting Maggie too. And thank you for the Christmas card, that was so sweet of you and so clever to customise it. I liked the picture of the goldfish but I didn't quite understand who Monica is? I thought your flatmate was called Megan?

How was Christmas with Jesse and the whole clan? He's such a sweetie and we really enjoyed hanging out with you both in California. I had a nice Christmas in Brighton with my mum. I finally introduced her to Charlie – he came down for the day on the 28th. I should have done it months ago really (as she's pointed out). It went bizarrely well! She loved that his dad worked in the prison service, and then he got major points for agreeing to a walk on the seafront even though it was blowing a gale and we could easily have been swept out to France.

In a really weird development, she also ended up meeting Charlie's dad. He came down to pick Charlie up in the car and she insisted on him coming in for a glass of port. I kept thinking of *Ghostbusters* – you know, don't cross the streams – but they got on scarily well, and bonded big-time over their jobs (Mum's a social worker). Bill (Charlie's dad) has persuaded Mum to apply to join this independent monitoring board for prisons, which involves regular visits and making sure the prisoners are being treated correctly – essentially, poking around, which is my mum's idea of heaven. I shouldn't be mean, she is brilliant really. I just hope she and Bill don't . . . um . . . get on *too* well. I'm sure they won't. Although they have made friends on Facebook.

Did you get nice Christmas presents? Charlie got me the

most beautiful vintage silk nightie – I was very impressed.
I got him the new Ottolenghi cookbook, which was rather
cheeky of me, especially since I'm supposed to be on a diet.
Oh well, you only live once. God, I AM turning into my
mum.

Write soon, lots of love,

Poppy xx

PS You know how I ended up having a lot of fun at
Disneyland? Well, don't laugh, but Charlie and I have talked
about doing Euro Disney next. I know . . .

6 January
From: Jenny
To: Oliver, David, Leo
Subject: HAT

Hi guys,

Thanks for a great hols. Excellent powder snow and
moguls, good chalet, I'd go again.

We have a problem, though. My Chanel hat went missing
just before we left. I found it and packed it. But it has
completely vanished from my suitcase AGAIN. Someone
definitely took it and it's not funny. It's real mink, it cost
£300, and if I don't get it back I WILL take action.

Can you forward this to your girlfriends?

Thanks,

Jen

From: Oliver
To: Rachel, Maggie, Nina
Subject: FW: HAT

Hi all,

At Jenny's request, I'm forwarding the below email. That
fur hat was NOT a party favour. If you have any information
regarding its whereabouts, please come forward in confidence
to this email address, or call Crimebusters on 111 9999.

Hope you're all well.
Oliver

From: Rachel
To: Maggie
Subject: RE: FW: HAT

Is she for real?

From: Maggie
To: Rachel
Subject: RE: FW: HAT

For reals, you mean. What do you suppose has happened to her silly hat now? She can't have lost it twice. Do you think Nina might actually have taken it?
I'm innocent, I swear!
Also why is she saying 'girlfriends'? She knows Leo and I broke up.

From: Rachel
To: Maggie
Subject: RE: FW: HAT

She's fishing for intel – wants to know if you're back together. And her hat has obviously gone up in value; didn't she tell us it cost £200?
I'm innocent too. But how about Nina? She does love animals and is not keen on Jenny. Means, motive and opportunity . . . Well, she'll be safely back in New York by now. Unless the US extradites her to face charges.

From: Jenny
To: Leo, Oliver, David
Subject: FOUND HAT

False alarm. It was in the bottom compartment of my suitcase.

From: Oliver
To: Maggie, Rachel, Nina
Subject: FW: FOUND HAT

Call off the search.

From: Rachel
To: Maggie
RE: FW: FOUND HAT

THANK GOD! I thought we were going to have to get Interpol involved.
    How are you, anyway? We must go for a drink sometime!

From: Maggie
To: Rachel
RE: FW: FOUND HAT

I'd love to! How about next Wednesday?

MAGGIE

As I exit Piccadilly Circus Tube to meet Rachel, I'm as nervous as a fourteen-year-old boy meeting a girl outside McDonald's for his very first date.

Obviously it's not a date. But I don't often go out on a limb to make new friends in this way. My friends are all people I've known since I was a kid, like Lily, or else we met at uni, or we hang out in a group like in my lab or at triathlon club. We got on well on holiday, but what if Rachel and I don't have anything to talk about? What if she finds me really boring and hates me?

Of course, she was the one who suggested meeting up. Though now that I think of it, all she said was 'we must go for a drink sometime'. I was the one who pinned her down. What if she was just being polite?

That's enough: I am being ridiculous. We will have fun. And I think she'll like the place I suggested. It's funky and laid-back, with big leather seats to lounge in, and little candles on the tables, and dark wooden booths. And delicious cocktails. I must say, I feel like quite the cool-hunter, taking us here. Here we are – there's Rachel, waiting for me outside. But it's freezing; why hasn't she gone inside? Oh. That's why.

'It's closed down!' says Rachel, stepping forward, also swathed in a giant coat. 'So annoying. Never mind. Hello!' We exchange clumsy hugs, like Michelin men.

'Oh God, I'm so sorry,' I say. Not just closed, but closed *down*; so much for my cool-hunting. 'Such a bad choice. Let's see . . .'

We both look around helplessly; I feel extra responsible for finding somewhere but my mind has gone completely blank of every bar in Soho. Every bar in London, in fact. In the world.

'How about that place over there?' I say at last, pointing at a pub across the street.

Bad idea. The place is jammed to the rafters with Soho media monkeys wearing their ironic Christmas jumpers and yelling at each other over the thumping music. There's barely enough room to stand and it looks like the only way to get to the bar would be crowd-surfing.

'Hmm,' Rachel says, looking around. 'Bit busy. What do you think?'

I think it's terrible and we should leave. But I don't want to sound like an old lady who can't handle a normal Wednesday night in a pub, so I say cautiously, 'I'm happy if you are?'

'OK. What would you like?'

'Oh no, I'll get this!'

But she insists, and goes off to the bar. I seem to be right in the flight path between the front door and the bar, so I edge sideways until I'm in the flight path between the toilets and the bar. It takes Rachel so long to get served, I can almost see the hipster beards growing around me.

'Phew! Sorry that took so long,' she says, returning with two glasses of wine and a packet of crisps. 'Oh.' She wants to eat the crisps, but it's hard to do that and hold her drink while we're standing up. I tuck my drink under my arm to open the packet for her, but then there's nowhere to put them, so she just stuffs them in her pocket. This is all happening to a constant accompaniment of jostling; we're practically being lifted off our feet by the groundswell of drinkers.

'So,' she says, raising her voice to be heard above the racket. 'How are you?'

I don't know if it's just me, but this question sometimes leaves me completely stumped for any reply other than 'Fine.' Some people – Lily, for one – always seem to have some cocktail-ready headline, like they just saw a pigeon on the Tube or they've just got back from Marrakesh. Not me. I could tell her I just got back from skiing, but she knows that. So I just say, 'Fine! How are you? How's work?'

'Oh, you know,' she says, leaning back to let a guy with a tray of ten pints go by. 'The usual. People shouting at me for . . .' But what she says next is drowned out by screams from the group beside us. They've also just turned the music up.

'Sorry,' I yell. 'What was that?'

Rachel shouts in my ear. 'This is horrendous. Do you want to get out of here?'

Nodding agreement, I knock back my wine and we fight our way outside, abandoning our glasses by the door as there isn't a table in reach.

Now if we were on a date and this was a rom-com, we'd turn to each other and smile. Ice broken, we'd start wandering down a side street and find the perfect little spot, where soon we'd be perched on bar stools laughing over Cosmos, *Sex and the City*-style.

But no such little spot appears, and we're left with the problem of where to go – even more pressing now that it's raining. Rachel's being a good sport about it all and waves away my apologies, but I still feel very embarrassed.

'Why don't we get some food?' she suggests.

I agree eagerly, and we start looking for a restaurant. But there doesn't seem to be anywhere good – possibly because we're both being über-polite and keep deferring to each other, plus we're unsuccessfully trying to catch up and chat while finding a refuge from the sleety rain. Eventually we end up in a random Thai restaurant, at Rachel's suggestion. I'm not in the mood for Thai, but I've already made two bad choices for us this evening and I'm not risking a third.

The restaurant's quite full, so we end up sitting at the back, beside the swinging door to the kitchen.

'Whew! Finally,' says Rachel, unpeeling all her winter layers. 'So . . . how are things? Sorry, already asked you that.'

'Would you like to order some drinks?' says the waiter.

We both order Singha beers, choose something to eat, and

finally we're able to relax and start chatting more normally – initially, at least. First, of course, we discuss Jenny and the Case of the Missing Chanel Hat.

'My favourite bit was the subject line. HAT! Like she's a caveman,' Rachel says.

I laugh. 'Well, it is the right hat for a caveman.'

'How do you mean?' Rachel says, puzzled.

'Just, a fur hat . . . like the Flintstones . . . They wore fur, didn't they? Um, never mind.'

Oh dear. I remember us laughing loads on holiday, but maybe I'm just not funny. Thankfully there's a diversion when our food arrives. I start ladling my green tofu curry over steaming rice, trying to think of what to say next.

'How is Oliver?' I ask.

'He's fine!' she says. 'He's got a patient with a very interesting elbow fracture. Apparently her arms are so long that . . . Never mind, it's not that interesting. How is . . . um, have you heard from Leo?'

I shake my head. 'No – it's for the best really.'

We discuss the likelihood of Jenny and Leo getting together, and decide it's slim; he's not that crazy. And then, for some reason, silence descends. I'm sick of talking about Leo. But what else can we talk about? We can't exactly discuss the food; it's like every other Thai meal I've ever had.

'So do you . . .' I rack my brains. 'Do you ever have to defend any bad guys, at work? Like murderers and so on?'

Rachel looks startled; that was obviously a dumb question. 'No. We don't do criminal law.'

I nod intelligently, though I don't understand: surely all law is for criminals?

'How about you? How's work?' she asks.

I can't just say 'Fine' again, so I try and explain about the project I'm working on, how it involves collecting samples from lots of different hospitals and how difficult it's been. As I hear myself describe all the departments I've phoned up and the people I've emailed, I marvel at how boring I'm being. How is it possible for one person to be so boring all by herself? And yet I can't stop myself.

'Do you want some of my pad Thai?' Rachel asks, when I've finally dragged myself to the finishing line of my story.

'Oh, no, that's fine. Do you want to try my tofu curry? It's quite good.'

'No, it's fine. Thanks, though.'

Silence again. Why is it so awkward? We got on so well on holiday . . .

Suddenly it hits me. *This was a holiday romance.* We had a great time on the beach – well, the ski slopes – but now our tans are fading and we've lost our friendship bracelets and we have nothing in common any more. This Thai meal is the smoking ruins of our New Year's fling.

'Is everything OK with your food?' I ask, noticing she's abandoned her dinner halfway.

'No, it's fine . . . except I always forget how, with noodles, the first bite is the same as the last, you know? They just go on and on.'

Oh God. She could be describing our date.

'I thought it would come with more vegetables,' she says. 'That's one of my New Year's resolutions; get my five a day.'

'Really?' I say, looking up. 'That's one of mine! It's surprisingly hard, isn't it? What other resolutions did you make?'

Rachel starts counting on her fingers. 'Only one cup of coffee a day; stop eating Triple Berry Muffins from Pret; gym three times a week without fail; learn Spanish; and read the *Economist* every week. Oh, and wear less black. My friend Zoë works in fashion, and she's always telling me to wear more colours.'

'Those are great resolutions,' I say, admiringly. 'Mine are: get my five a day *and* eat more cruciferous vegetables . . .'

'Ooh, nice.'

'Thanks. Do more cultural things; no drinking at home on weeknights; no more than half an hour's TV a day; improve my contouring . . .'

'What's contouring?'

'It's where you give yourself cheekbones and sort of sculpt your face with powder.' I demonstrate with an imaginary brush. 'I can never get it quite right. What else . . . Take up indoor climbing, finish reading *One Hundred Years of Solitude*, and travel more. Leo was always away for the weekend; why shouldn't I be as well?'

'Brilliant!' says Rachel. 'Those are all great! I want to travel more too, I'm adding that. I don't understand people who don't make New Year's resolutions, do you? They're so satisfying!'

'I make them every year. And I also review my life goals.'

'Ooh, that sounds interesting. What are your life goals?' Rachel asks eagerly.

'Any coffees or desserts for you?' says the waiter, clearing away our plates.

'I'll have a coffee. No, actually – can I have a green tea?' says Rachel. 'Almost forgot!' she says to me.

'I'll have one too! That's a great idea!' I say enthusiastically.

Over green teas, Rachel tells me her plan to make friends with one of the female partners at work, in a bid to get made senior associate. In return, I tell her about my scheme to get on the property ladder by buying a beach hut in Brighton.

'See, I had hoped Leo and I would move in together, and eventually buy a place. But that won't happen, and I can't afford a proper flat on my own, so I've got to think creatively. A beach hut is the perfect solution. I'd have to commute, but imagine waking up every morning to the sound of the waves! And the value is only going to go up.'

'Wow! That sounds . . . Do they have central heating?' Rachel asks.

'I'm not sure. I think they have burner stoves.'

I have a feeling Rachel is dubious about the beach hut plan, but she just says, 'If you're interested in property in Brighton, I should introduce you to my friend Poppy. Her mum lives in Brighton and she knows it really well.'

I nod. I consider saying that I *am* going to meet someone called Poppy, when Lily comes home next month, but it's obviously not the same person and the name is hardly that exciting a coincidence.

Rachel continues, 'In fact that reminds me, I have one other resolution that I forgot to mention . . . Well. I didn't forget exactly, but it sounds so dorky.'

'Go on. This is a safe space,' I say, indicating the pink tablecloth strewn with the remnants of our Thai dinner. I'm quite a neat person, but when it comes to Thai food I always leave the table looking as if a toddler's thrown a tantrum.

'Well, I would like to make some new friends so my life's not just work and Oliver,' says Rachel. 'Not to make you feel like you're some sort of tick on my list, but . . .'

I put down my tea. 'Me too! That's one of my resolutions! Especially now that I've broken up with Leo. I mean, I will try internet dating and stuff like that, but it's always good to meet more people, isn't it?'

'Of course it is! Do you remember what Jenny said on holiday – something about how after a certain point in life it's too late to make new friends?'

'I know! I thought that was so stupid!'

'Me too! That's why I'm so glad we met up.'

'Oh good!' I add rashly, 'I felt like I was being really boring earlier . . .'

'No you weren't! I felt like *I* was being really boring!' says Rachel. 'It just shows you, doesn't it?'

We beam at each other happily. Finally the holiday magic is back! We stay longer than almost anyone else in the restaurant, chatting about anything and everything, and before we've even asked for the bill we've already made plans to meet up again. Rachel's going to come with me to the theatre next week.

'I was meant to be going with Leo,' I explain. 'Though he also had a birthday party that night, so we were going to squeeze them both in. Some guy called Brownie who I'd literally never heard of. Honestly, with all the acquaintances Leo has, if he did ever get married, I can't even imagine the numbers. It would be like a Katy Perry concert.'

This makes us both giggle. Rachel says, 'They'd have to have it in Hyde Park, with a big screen.'

'Leo and his wife would be tiny specks on the stage, in the distance . . .'

'Or they could just hire the Great Hall of the People in Beijing and be done with it,' suggests Rachel. We're now laughing so hard, she's wiping her eyes.

'Well, his loss is my gain,' she says, when we've both recovered.

As we signal for the bill, I decide she's right: Leo's loss is my gain too. And it looks as though this year, there's one resolution I'll definitely be able to keep.

RACHEL DOES ROME

I never would have thought it was possible to be this happy in February.

Normally I dread this time of year. Everyone's broke and grumpy from detoxing, Christmas is a distant memory, and the weather is bleakety-bleak. Plus, it contains Valentine's Day, which hasn't always been my favourite occasion. But this year I'm actually looking forward to it.

It's a Friday night in early February, and Oliver and I are having dinner in a little Italian restaurant near his flat in Queen's Park. Outside it's dark, sleety and miserable; inside, it's candlelit, warm and rosy – which is just how I feel.

'Now,' Oliver says, pouring me a glass of red wine. 'Aren't you glad we're not queuing in the cold with a load of bearded wankers?'

'I suppose,' I reply, laughing. I had suggested trying a new gin bar in Dalston this evening, but Oliver was too knackered. As an orthopaedic surgeon, he works as hard as I do in my law firm. Anyway, it's not as if we never do anything exciting; we did go skiing together for our fourth date. My older sisters both thought I was crazy; from their reactions you would have thought I was hopping off to Vegas to marry him. But five weeks later, we're still going strong.

As I catch sight of myself in the mirror opposite, I realise I even look different. My tan has faded and I'm back to my usual paper-white. But right now I'm actually glowing, and it's not only from the red wine. We've just finished a lively argument about the age of consent – the kind of nerdy debate we both enjoy – when Oliver picks up a folded card from the table.

'Book now for Valentine's Day. Fifty-five pounds for three courses, including a complimentary glass of Prosecco.' He shakes his head. 'Can you imagine? Paying three times the normal price to sit in a restaurant full of whispering couples. No thanks.' He pauses, looking at me doubtfully. 'You feel the same, don't you?' he asks.

'Totally,' I say, truthfully.

Oliver looks relieved. 'Oh good. You think the whole Valentine's thing is naff as well?'

I'm about to say, 'Sure.' But I'm not completely sure. I'm just as allergic to the whole pink-napkin, single-carnation thing as Oliver seems to be. But that doesn't mean that I don't want us to do *something*.

So I say, 'I totally agree with you on the naff front. I definitely wouldn't want a roomful of teddies and heart-shaped chocolate boxes. But I think it's nice to do something. A little token acknowledgement.'

Oliver smiles and nods. 'That sounds exactly right.'

I return to my ravioli, happy that we're on the same page. I don't have to worry that he's going to deliver a singing telegram to my office. But we will be doing something. Maybe he'll make dinner at his place; maybe we'll go to see a late-night showing of a classic film, or have a drink in a nice bar. The main thing is, we'll be together.

So I'm disappointed when, a few days later, the plan changes. It's around 9 p.m. and I'm coming home from work in a taxi; one of the 'perks' we get when working late. This is often my only chance to make personal phone calls, so I've got into the habit of calling people, especially Oliver, at this time. The Addison Lee drivers are now totally clued up on all the doings of my social circle. We've had a quick chat and I'm about to suggest a double bill of black-and-white films at the Curzon as our Valentine's Day celebration when Oliver says, 'I'm afraid I have to go to Bristol on the weekend of the thirteenth and fourteenth.'

'Oh. Really?'

'Yeah. I've been asked to give a paper at a conference.' He

pauses and continues, 'I know it's Valentine's weekend . . . I hope you don't mind.'

I do mind, because we said we'd do something. But I also know that writing papers and going to conferences is a really important part of Oliver's job; he has to get his name out there if he wants to become a consultant. One of the things I love about him is that he never complains about me working late, or on weekends; he gets it. So I'm going to be a good sport too.

'That's fine. Maybe we could meet on the Friday instead?'

'Well I'm actually going down on the Friday.'

'OK, fair enough,' I say quickly, not wanting to be whiny or unreasonable. I was really looking forward to doing something with him. But it can't be helped. And Oliver immediately asks when he can see me again, so I don't feel *too* neglected.

The irony is that in the beginning, I was barely interested in Oliver at all, and only went out with him in a spirit of experiment. If I'm being honest, I thought he was a bit geeky. He didn't fit in with the picture of a perfect boyfriend that I'd had before – sharp, successful, sophisticated and gorgeous. Or, as my friend Zoë used to describe my ideal man, 'a cruel millionaire'. Like my ex, Jay: urgh.

But then . . . it was like looking at one of those pictures of a vase that suddenly become two faces in profile. One night I realised that even though he *was* very tall and awkward, and his ears did stick out, I found him unbearably sexy. And fun, and passionate about the same sort of stuff as me – politics, current affairs, things happening in the world today. And with endearing random traits like an encyclopedic knowledge of early noughties R'n'B. I'll never forget seeing him dance around his kitchen singing and stripping off (well, his jumper) to the sound of 'Hot in Herre' by Nelly.

Back at my studio flat on Finchley Road, it is definitely not hot in herre: it's freezing. Bloody February. Every year I promise myself I'll go somewhere hot for a winter break, and every year I end up staring down the barrel of another February in London.

As I let myself in and turn on the heating, I reflect that for once, it would have been nice to do something on Valentine's

Day that didn't involve my tracksuit bottoms and Katherine Heigl films. And although I know it's stupid of me, I don't want to admit to people at work that we're not doing anything. They loved the story of our trip to France, and now they're probably expecting me and Oliver to jet off to the Maldives or something for Valentine's weekend.

I know! Why don't I organise a girls' weekend away? I'm sure there's someone else who would love to go somewhere hot and sunny for a fun weekend. But when I think of who to call, I realise that everyone's going to have romantic plans. My best friend Zoë is completely loved-up with her new boyfriend. Poppy, who used to be my wing-woman, is going to Paris with her boyfriend.

Then I think of Maggie. She's single and bound to be up for some fun. We met on a skiing holiday over New Year and hit it off, and have since met up frequently, most recently for the theatre (she had a spare ticket as she'd been planning to go with her ex-boyfriend, who she broke up with at New Year). She might feel it's a little early in our relationship to go away together, but it feels right to me, and when you know, you know . . . I decide to phone her right away.

Maggie answers after a few rings. When I ask her what she's doing the weekend after next, she says, 'Valentine's weekend, you mean? Nothing in particular. Don't rub my nose in it.' But she sounds happy; she's at the buoyant post-break-up stage where she's delighted to be single.

'How would you like to go somewhere for a weekend away? Oliver has to go to a conference, so I'm at a loose end. Oh God, sorry! I didn't mean it like that.' I know there's nothing worse than the friend or acquaintance who suggests meeting for drinks 'because Jonny/Jerry/Bill is away'.

'Don't worry,' says Maggie, laughing. 'I know you didn't. I'd love to go somewhere.'

'Really? Great! I know it's short notice . . .' Maggie is so sweet-natured that I could easily see her agreeing to a weekend away just to be polite, so I'd better give her an out.

'No, this is my year of saying yes to things. What about Rome?'

'Rome?' Instantly my head floods with visions: the Colosseum, the Forum, the Vatican; pizza, pasta, sunshine, red wine . . . 'Yes! Perfect!'

'Oh, wait,' Maggie says. 'Sorry. I just remembered, I do have a Valentine's date – with my friend Lily. She's home for a visit and we said we'd do something that weekend.'

'Do you think she'd like to come to Rome?' I know this is a bit mad – going away with someone I've never met. But since my New Year's impulse holiday with Oliver, I'm increasingly open to allowing madness into my life. In small, controlled doses, of course!

'Yes! I do, actually. She'd love that.' There's a pause while I hear tapping. 'Rachel. Do you realise it's twenty degrees in Rome right now?'

'Let's have a look at flights.' After scanning Kayak for a few minutes, we find a reasonable one leaving on Friday afternoon and coming back on Sunday afternoon.

'I can take a half-day on Friday. Where would we stay?' Maggie asks.

'I don't know. Do you want me to pick somewhere?'

'Sure, if you don't mind.'

As I search the internet, I wonder where Oliver would want to stay if we went to Rome together. I think he'd be more inclined towards the youth-hostel end of things. Our luxurious New Year's break was an anomaly; Oliver generally has frugal habits, even though he grew up with money. Whereas I grew up with money being very tight, and I'm careful with it – but I also believe in treating myself and my friends, otherwise why the hell am I working all these hours?

Soon I find what looks like the perfect hotel: Il Palazzetto. It's an old building with high ceilings and luxurious decor *and* a private terrace that overlooks the Spanish Steps. And best of all, they've got a last-minute promotion, which means it's within our agreed budget, provided the other two are happy to share a room. Maggie emails me back to say that Lily is up for it, and they're going to book flights this evening. We are go!

On my way to the airport, I'm wondering how we'll all get on. Maggie and I met on holiday, so I know her holiday style: she's pretty laid-back and I'm confident we'll get along. But Lily is an unknown quantity. All I know is that she's one of Maggie's oldest friends, that they grew up in the same street and that she's visiting from LA, where she recently moved. I'm hoping that I like her and that I won't feel . . . well, 'left out' makes me sound like a teenager, but I suppose I do hope I won't feel like that. I think this is a hangover from age fifteen to eighteen, when I was moved to a new school where I had no friends at all and spent all my time studying. That was a decade ago, but old habits die hard – with me, at least.

But as soon as I see them at the airport, any niggling concerns disappear. Maggie gives me a big hug and Lily is very friendly and excited about our trip. 'This was SUCH a good idea,' she says as we make our way to the departure gate. 'I'm so glad you saved me from a romantic weekend with my dad and his girlfriend. I was dreading it.'

Lily is startlingly pretty. Maggie is pretty too – she's got a great figure, and the kind of bone structure that can carry off a short pixie haircut. But Lily, even though she hasn't brushed her long blond hair and her green eyes have mascara smudged under them, is stunning: tall and slim, with flawless tanned skin and a heart-shaped face. It's almost a relief that she's dressed in such a nondescript way, in a navy hoodie, ripped jeans and trainers. Otherwise she'd be too much.

'So,' I say, when we're sitting on the plane. 'What do we want to see first?'

'Some sunshine,' says Maggie, yawning. She's spent the day in her lab, tending to her bacteria cultures, before trekking across town to Stansted, but she still looks ten years younger than she did when we met at New Year on the skiing holiday. Breaking up with her boyfriend obviously suits her. She's wearing a beautiful trench coat, a striped top from Petit Bateau and skinny grey jeans. I always think she dresses like a French girl: very chic.

'Pizza!' says Lily. 'And I want to ride on a Vespa. It's one of my life's ambitions.' We start laughing, but she shakes her head adamantly. 'No, it really is. As long as I ride a Vespa and eat some good pizza, I don't care what else we do.'

'How about you, Rachel, what do you want to see?' asks Maggie.

'This might sound ambitious, but . . . I was thinking that we could do the Colosseum and the Forum this evening when we arrive, and then on Saturday we could do the Trevi Fountain, the Borghese Gallery and St Peter's. On Sunday we won't have that much time, but if we get up early we could fit in the Capitoline Museum.'

Maggie and Lily are both looking at me with identical alarmed expressions.

'What?'

'Nothing!' says Maggie quickly. 'But . . . that sounds hectic. I'm sure we can see most of . . . some of those things, but we want to have fun as well.'

'People-watch,' says Lily. 'Have coffee outside, sitting at a table. Get some sun.' She shivers and puts on some socks she's brought for the plane. 'London seems so cold now,' she adds plaintively.

'I wouldn't mind doing some shopping,' says Maggie.

'And we have to have a big night out,' says Lily.

'OK – we don't have to go overboard on the sightseeing,' I say, feeling like a nerd. They're too nice to say it, but they're obviously thinking that I should have just booked a Saga holiday if I wanted to tick off sights in my sensible shoes.

And I'm sensitive to being made to feel like a nerd. Even though I know it's ridiculous, that feeling of being too keen in class, or liking the wrong music, or not knowing the cool places to go to, is still very vivid in my mind. But I'm not fifteen any more, I remind myself. I've survived adolescence and these people are my friends.

'We will see sights, definitely,' says Maggie tactfully. 'But maybe we won't wear ourselves out trying to see them *all*. And we can all do our own thing. I've brought my trainers and I'm going to go for a jog every morning.'

'Are you really?' I ask, fascinated by how different people are. 'It would never in a million years occur to me to bring my runners on holiday.'

'What are runners? Do you mean trainers?' asks Maggie.

'Oh, yeah. It must be an Irish expression.'

'It sounds as if you're bringing a load of little running people with you.' We both start laughing, with that kind of giddiness you only get on holiday.

I had no idea 'runners' was an Irish thing. It's sad when I think of all the expressions I've dropped, one by one, because I know that people won't understand them and it makes me self-conscious: your man, giving out, desperate, herself, cop on . . .

Lily, meanwhile, is deep in thought. 'You know that Hot Priests calendar?' she asks. 'Hot Priests of the Vatican or something? Do you think those guys are actually priests, or are they models?'

'Models,' says Maggie. 'Anyway, don't you have a boyfriend, miss?'

'Yes,' says Lily. But from the way she frowns and stares out of the window, I can tell there's a reason why she's thinking about Vatican hot priests. I wonder why she's not spending Valentine's Day with her boyfriend.

I suppose she might be wondering the same thing about me. But Oliver had to work; it can't be helped. Suddenly a flicker of doubt passes across my mind, as I remember what happened with Jay. He also said he had to work one weekend . . . and it later turned out he was with his *other* girlfriend. Or rather his girlfriend, because he and I were always a 'let's not put labels on this' mess. I've never felt so stupid in all my life.

But that was completely different. I can trust Oliver. Just because he had to duck out of Valentine's Day does *not* mean that he's seeing someone else. Or that he's losing interest.

To distract myself from these paranoid musings, I get out my guidebook and continue reading about Rome. Maggie gets out *One Hundred Years of Solitude* by Gabriel García Márquez.

'Isn't that—?' I ask, before I can stop myself.

'Yes. It's the same book I was reading at New Year. I *am* going to finish it, even if it takes me all year.'

'It'll take you a hundred years at this rate,' says Lily. 'Why don't you start something else?'

Maggie shakes her head. 'Once I start a book, I have to finish it.'

The airport, of course, is about an hour from Rome itself –

that's why our flight was so cheap. But the journey goes quickly, and soon we're heading towards the centre. My first impression of Rome is that it's like a giant open-air museum where past and present are randomly piled up together. We pass the Colosseum and the Forum, and hills topped with palaces, side by side with Zara shops, ads for mobile phones and people on Vespas.

We get off the bus and start to walk, following the directions I've printed out. We're on a street called Via della Propaganda, which seems funny and also extremely Roman. Everything we pass, almost without exception, is beautiful. The buildings are pink and orange and ochre, with tall wooden doors framed with stone arches; every few minutes there's an ivy-covered building housing a quaint little bar or antique shop. A girl goes by riding a moped in high heels, her black hair streaming in the breeze. I think of the Italian guys who work in Starbucks on Finchley Road near my flat. How can they stand it?

'It's so *sunny*,' breathes Maggie. She stops to take off her trench coat and puts on a big pair of sunglasses. Three Romans in leather jackets give her an appreciative look as they pass by, before checking out me and Lily.

'*Ciao, biondina,*' says one of them, smiling at Lily, before they wander on.

'Somehow it seems more acceptable coming from handsome Italians rather than out of a white van,' I say thoughtfully. 'But maybe I'm just being a snob.'

The others laugh. We pass an elegant cobbled square with a tall ancient column. The square is doubling up as a car park – more evidence of how casually Romans seem to treat their classical past. After walking down a street full of very fancy shops, we find ourselves in a big piazza, with palm trees dotted here and there and a marble fountain in the middle. A vast flight of flower-filled steps sweeps up to a church with two towers. There are people sitting all over the steps – teenagers, tourists and locals, chatting, smoking and sunbathing. Sunbathing!

'This is the Piazza di Spagna,' I say, consulting my map. 'Our hotel is on this square.'

'O to the M to the G,' says Lily.

Il Palazzetto is fairly well hidden away, but eventually we

locate the brass plate and climb the steps to the private terrace overlooking the Piazza di Spagna. We can barely contain ourselves with excitement as we're shown inside and taken to our rooms. The hotel is tiny, but both of the rooms are bigger than my entire apartment (which wouldn't be hard) and have balconies overlooking the piazza. Everything is decorated in creamy white and gold – it's like an expensive dessert.

'Aaah,' says Lily, flopping on to their bed. 'That's what I'm talking about. Can you book all my holidays, Rachel?'

Maggie is already unpacking quickly, like a neat whirlwind. Lily and I watch as she hangs her clothes in order of colour, type and probably star sign, lines up her shoes underneath according to height, and then starts sorting underwear and accessories into different drawers. I happen to know that when she's at home, she changes into 'lounging' clothes, to keep her day clothes nice.

'What's the plan, ladies?' she asks. 'It's six thirty now. Do we want to chill out here for a bit and get changed, or head out for a little drink on our private terrace?'

'I could handle a drink on our private terrace,' I say. 'And then we could go on somewhere else.' I open up my *Time Out* guide and start reading out descriptions of bars nearby. I can see Maggie and Lily exchanging glances.

'Let me guess. Not spontaneous enough? You'd prefer to wander?'

They both nod mutely, and I laugh. It's a good thing I don't take offence easily.

Hearing a buzz, I reach for my phone and see that I have three messages welcoming me to Movistar, and one from Oliver: *How is Roma? Hope it's great. Just arriving in Bristol and heading out for some beers with Laura and the others. X*

Smiling, I tap out a quick reply to say that we've arrived safely and that the hotel is gorgeous. I'm surprised by his mention of beers: I hadn't realised the Friday evening was just social. But I suppose that's the nature of conferences. Though I don't really see why Laura, his glamorous orthopaedic colleague, merits a special mention.

'So are we going out-out now?' asks Maggie. 'Or are we just going out for a quick snifter? If it's a quick snifter, I won't get changed, but if we're going out-out then I'd like to get dressed up.'

It hadn't occurred to me to dress up. I'm wearing my favourite V-neck black top, a denim skirt and flat black boots; those will take me from day to night, as the magazines say. But judging from Lily's expression, I can tell that for Maggie, it's more of a process.

'Let's say it's a quick snifter for now,' says Lily. 'We can come back and get changed if we want to.'

Lily and I brush our hair, Maggie makes some minute adjustments to her make-up, and then we go out on to the hotel's terrace. We have a bird's-eye view of the piazza, lit up by the setting sun. On the other side, I can see a large complex of buildings that I think might be the Vatican. Oh God, I completely forgot the Vatican! There's so much to see, it's almost stressful. Then I think of how silly that is, and start to laugh.

'What's so funny?' asks Lily.

I rub my face. 'I was feeling stressed out about how much there is to see in Rome. I know, I know. I've been working so hard, and I'm used to tackling everything as if it's a work project. I need help.'

'That sounds like Paris Syndrome,' says Maggie. 'It mainly afflicts Japanese people who go to Paris with massive expectations and then get overwhelmed and develop culture shock. It can lead to palpitations, paranoia, even hallucinations.'

Lily hoots with laughter. 'You're making that up.'

'No, really. I read about it in a psychiatric journal that my flatmate subscribes to. But don't worry, Rachel,' she adds reassuringly, 'you probably just need a holiday.'

We order three glasses of white wine, which arrive promptly – ice-cold, with a thoughtful little bowl of nuts and pretzels. I thank the waiter, who answers, '*Prego*.' Lovely.

'To Rome,' says Lily. 'And to our Roman Holiday!'

We clink glasses and I sigh with happiness. This is the life. I don't even need my jacket!

'Gosh, it's nice ordering a glass of wine and not being ID'd,' says Lily. 'I was so flattered at first, but then I realised it happens to everyone, even if you're fifty. It's a pain in the neck.'

'How did you end up living in LA?' I ask.

'It was very random. My cousin lives there – I went out for her wedding last October, and I got a job and never came back.'

'It must be nice to have family there. What does your cousin do?'

'She works in publishing. Her husband's American; he's a film agent.'

'Wait a minute. Is your cousin Alice Roberts?'

'Yes, she is! Do you know her?'

'Yes – I'm a good friend of your other cousin, her sister Erica. Do you know her friend Poppy as well? She's a friend of mine.'

'Yes! That's amazing!' Lily says, beaming at me and peering over her sunglasses. 'Such a small world.'

'Wait! Does that mean your Poppy,' Maggie looks at me, 'is the same as *your* Poppy? What are the odds?'

We discuss the ins and outs of who knows who how, and all get confused, but I conclude by saying, 'It just goes to show, there are only ten people in London.'

'And they do the rest with CGI,' says Lily.

The sun is properly setting now; the whole terrace is bathed in warm evening light and the steps are filling up even more. I love the way people are strolling around, chatting and forming different groups. It's as if the whole square is a big sitting room for Rome.

Beside us on the terrace are two very eye-catching women. They could be any age from forty to eighty, and both are sporting pencil skirts, silk blouses and lots of jewellery. One of them has dark hair in a beehive, with very red lipstick; the other has blond hair, blow-dried in waves, with her eyebrows carefully pencilled in. It's a lot of look, as they say, but they look great.

'I hope I look that good when I'm their age,' Maggie murmurs.

'I don't look that good now,' I say. The other two rush to contradict me, but I honestly wasn't fishing for compliments. I just don't think I could ever be bothered to go to the effort that those two women clearly have. I explain this to the girls, adding, 'Seriously, some mornings I barely have time to brush my teeth. And I always end up doing my make-up on the Tube. Don't look like that, Maggie, I have a happy life really.'

We briefly discuss work and our commutes before somehow the conversation turns to boys and whether or not you should ask them out.

'I admire people who can do it,' says Maggie. 'But I couldn't. I would be too embarrassed. I really feel for guys, I don't know how they do it.'

'Oh, I can do it all right,' I say. 'But I've never had good results from it. Either you go out once and you never hear from them again, or else they say yes at first and then they cancel. I'm equal opportunities in every other area, but not for asking men out. It's a waste of time.'

'I'm a firm believer in "everything but",' says Lily.

'What's that?' I ask, tickled. 'It sounds like what the girls at my convent school used to do.'

'It means that you can offer every encouragement short of asking a guy out,' Lily says. 'You can drop massive hints, like "Oh, I'd love to see that film" or "I'd love to try Burmese food" or whatever. You just can't overtly ask them out. Well, you can, but I agree that it doesn't work.'

'You can lead a horse to water, but you can't ask him out,' suggests Maggie.

'Exactly,' says Lily, and we all laugh.

'Is anyone getting hungry?' asks Maggie. 'It might be nice to go and have some dinner at some point.'

'I could do with a snacketino,' I agree. 'A snacketito.'

'Me too, but does that mean you'll want to get changed?' Lily asks Maggie sadly. Which was exactly what I was thinking, but I haven't known Maggie as long as Lily has so I wouldn't have had the nerve to ask.

We agree a strict time limit of twenty minutes to get changed; long enough for me to pull on jeans and a jacket – it's getting a tiny bit chilly – and for Lily to put on some more eyeliner. Maggie changes into a very cute off-white dress with a low neck that she wears with a denim jacket, cognac boots and bare legs.

'Oh no,' says Lily. 'You've raised the game! Now I look like a slob. I'm going to change.' And she swaps her white T-shirt for a tighter blue one, and her hoodie for a black-and-white-striped blazer. So I decide to swap my flat boots for my ankle boots, which have a low heel, and add some eyeliner as well.

'I didn't raise the game,' Maggie protests, as we go down the stairs. 'I didn't even change my make-up, just added lipstick.'

'You're a great one for doing all different kinds of make-up. I've worn exactly the same make-up every day since I was about twenty,' I say.

We walk through the lobby and out into the Roman evening, which is full of an indefinable excitement that . . . well, I can't keep comparing it to Finchley Road, but it is so different.

I suddenly realise that Maggie is looking at me in horror. 'Have you really, Rachel? Every single day? But . . . it's not that you don't look lovely, but you're missing out on so much fun!'

'I never thought of it like that,' I admit. 'I suppose I've found something that works, so I don't want to experiment in case it looks hideous.'

'You could never look hideous,' says Maggie. 'But could I do your make-up while we're here? Please?'

'You should let her,' says Lily. 'She's good.'

We're wandering through the big square now, looking at all the people sitting outside, drinking, smoking, chatting. The other two girls are walking slowly; I keep on having to slow down from my usual London pace. I'm always rushing somewhere – to work, from work, to the gym. Sometimes – and I know this is bad – if I'm stuck behind someone who's walking very slowly, I secretly want to punch them in the back of the head. God. What kind of a monster am I?

'What about that place?' says Lily, indicating a little restaurant tucked down a side street, with an awning and ivy-covered walls.

'Lovely,' agrees Maggie.

I'm worried that we're going to a random restaurant without consulting a single guidebook. What if it's awful? But it's too late now. The waiter makes a big fuss of us, showing us to a table outside where we can watch the world go by. I also can't believe that it's warm enough to sit outside, but it is.

We all choose pizzas and Maggie and I order a carafe of red wine to share. Lily asks for a Coke with fresh lime juice, which she communicates to the waiter with the aid of a dictionary app on her phone.

'The hard stuff,' says Maggie, sounding impressed. 'I never drink Coke, only Diet.'

'Coke is so much nicer,' says Lily. 'Honestly, try it.'

We all take a sip and exclaim. The lime juice gives it the most incredible kick and the Coke itself is delicious.

'You're right; it's so much nicer than Diet,' I say. 'And with the lime! It's fantastic.' I decide I'm going to drink this from now on; to hell with the calories.

'Jesse introduced me to it. He said he'd rather have a Coke once in a while than Diet Cokes every day.'

'Is Jesse your boyfriend?' I ask.

She nods. 'He lives in Colorado, and I'm in LA.'

'He's the whole reason she moved there!' Maggie says, snapping a breadstick. 'It was a whirlwind romance; she went over for the wedding, met him and that was that.'

'Jesse wasn't the whole reason,' Lily says with a frown. 'I got a job, and I loved it over there – I would have stayed even if it wasn't for him.'

'OK, Lil, I didn't mean to grind your gears,' says Maggie.

'No, no, you didn't,' Lily says immediately. 'Sorry.' She sighs, and Maggie and I exchange glances before changing the subject.

Maggie starts telling us about her forays into internet dating, which seem to be going well; she's got a date lined up already for next week.

'He teaches kids with special needs and he's got one blue and one green eye. Isn't that cool?'

'Very cool,' says Lily. 'What's the standard like generally? Are there lots of hotties, or is it slim pickings?'

'A bit of everything really,' says Maggie. 'Loads of snowboarders, for some reason. Half the guys have a picture of themselves holding a snowboard.'

'What are the other half holding?' Lily asks, and then goes into a fit of giggles, which sets us all off. 'Sorry. Very immature of me,' she sighs.

Maggie continues, 'And then about ninety per cent of them say they're passionate about travelling, which . . . meh.'

'What's wrong with that?' I ask.

'Nothing. Except travelling is something you do for a few weeks, a year at most. And it seems sad if that's what you're passionate about, rather than anything in your normal life.' She starts laughing. 'One guy I was emailing was the opposite, though. He said he would only date someone who lived within walking distance. It turned out that I was just outside his catchment area, so we never met up.'

'So even if he met a kind, friendly, intelligent Brazilian super-model who was an amazing cook, she'd still have to be within walking distance? Men are so weird,' I say.

Our pizzas have arrived; the thinnest, crispiest ones I've ever seen, blackened around the edges. I'm having pepperoni and mushroom, which is what I always order. And this is the best one I've ever had in my life. Maggie's ordered a mushroom one, and looks carefully – at Lily's suggestion – to double-check that there's no meat before tucking in.

'Remember that school trip to Paris when you told them you were a vegetarian and they gave you a salad with bacon?' Lily says. 'They couldn't believe that was a problem.'

'Were you two at school together? Is that how you know each other?' I ask.

Lily shakes her head, her mouth full. Maggie says, 'Next-door neighbours. She's three years younger than me anyway.'

'But we've made the relationship work in spite of the age gap,' Lily says.

'We went to different schools as well,' says Maggie. 'Yours was definitely more fun, or it sounded more fun. How about you, Rachel? Did you like school?'

'I went to two secondary schools. Local school until I was sixteen, and then a posh hot-house school in Dublin. It was fine.'

I won a scholarship, but that's not worth mentioning. In fact, those two years in Dublin are not worth mentioning. I lived with my aunt; I had no friends, no social life except my trips home to Celbridge every few months. I put my head down and studied like a thing possessed. A girl who was at school with me came up to me in my first term at Trinity and complimented me on how much weight I'd lost. In fact I was still the same size ten I'd always been; I'd just spent the previous two years swathed in tracksuits.

'How about a quick nightcap before we go back to the hotel?' Lily suggests, once we've finished dinner and paid the bill.

'Sure. But this isn't our big night out, is it?' Maggie says, stopping dead as she puts on her denim jacket.

'No!' Lily and I reassure her.

'It's just that if this was our big night out, I wouldn't have worn this dress.'

'I promise our big night out will come with full warning, and ample dress-up opportunity,' says Lily, giving her an affectionate poke.

We pass a bar with tall picture windows opening on to the street, and decide to go in. We prop ourselves up at a table by the entrance, and I buy a round of white wines; it's so cheap, in fact, that I decide I may as well get a bottle. As soon as I've poured out the wine, I excuse myself for a minute to send Oliver a quick text, to say hi and to tell him I miss him. I've never actually said that yet.

'Is Jesse at the birthday party yet?' Maggie asks Lily.

'Oh yes. It lasts all weekend. It's his mother's sixtieth,' she explains to me. 'I'm kind of in trouble for missing it. Alice and Sam are there and everything.'

'Sam is Jesse's cousin,' Maggie tells me, 'and he's married to Lily's cousin Alice, if you can follow all that.'

'Yep. We're all practically related,' Lily says. 'It's not weird at all.'

'Long-distance must be difficult,' Maggie says. 'It puts a lot of pressure on.'

'It really does.' She puts down her glass of wine. 'And I'm worried that we want different things. Jesse wants to settle down and I want to go travelling. He wants to get up early and go hiking, and I want to stay up late and go out dancing . . . It was fine at first but now we just keep clashing.'

'That's hard, when you want different things,' Maggie says, with feeling.

'Yeah. It's our age as well – I'm twenty-four, and he's twenty-eight. Part of me wishes I could meet him in six years' time, you know? He's talked about applying for jobs in LA, and it makes me feel guilty because what if he moves all that way and uproots his whole life and we end up breaking up?' Her eyes are filling with tears. 'God, I can't believe I'm sitting here talking about us breaking up.' She puts her face in her hands, and wipes her eyes. A few people are staring at us.

Maggie puts down her drink and gives Lily a sideways hug. 'Don't cry, hon,' she says. 'I know it sounds lame but it will all work out for the best. And you musn't feel guilty. Jesse is a grown-up. He'll be OK.'

'I know,' says Lily. 'He's a catch. Any girl would be thrilled to go out with him.' She blows her nose on a paper napkin. 'One of his teacher colleagues has a big crush on him, I can tell. Her name is Maudie and she's really cool and writes comic strips in her spare time and wears beanies when it's cold and has three thousand followers on Twitter. I guarantee that if we broke up,' her face wobbles again, 'he'd be married to her within a year or two. And I hate that idea, but that still doesn't mean we're right for each other . . . Anyway,' Lily exhales noisily. 'I didn't mean to wreck all of our buzzes.' She stands up. 'I'm going to go and repair my face. Do I look a total state?'

'Of course you don't,' says Maggie. 'But I do have some eye-make-up remover wipes if you like.'

This makes us all laugh. 'God, I've missed you, Maggie,' says Lily, accepting some wipes before going off to the bathroom.

Maggie and I look at each other and sigh. 'Poor Lil. It's never easy, is it?' she says.

'No it's not,' I agree. It's on the tip of my tongue to tell Maggie about my worries over Oliver, but I decide not to. We've had enough drama this evening.

Lily comes back a few minutes later, looking totally composed aside from a slight pinkness to her eyes. 'Right! Shall we head?' she asks, draining the last of her wine.

'Are we going back to the hotel or for another drink?' asks Maggie.

'Hotel,' says Lily, at the same time as I say, 'One more drink?'

We decide that as a compromise we'll have a drink on the way back. It's still warm; it feels as if we've travelled forward a season. I'm beginning to get the hang of this whole wandering thing.

When we pass by a little door that looks as if it leads down to a cellar bar, it seems the most natural thing in the world to potter down the stairs and investigate. Just before we descend and lose mobile reception, I check my phone – nothing yet from Oliver but I'm sure he'll text soon.

It's a funny little place, dimly lit, with dark red stone walls that look as if they'll start dripping with condensation later in the night. There are lots of Roman hipster types, and a DJ is playing a remix of some old gospel or soul number about the walls of Jericho tumbling down.

'What do we think?' I ask, looking around.

'I like it! It reminds me of the jazz bar in *The Talented Mr Ripley*,' Lily says.

'Here's a table,' says Maggie, moving towards a dark corner.

'Wait a sec. Let's not hide ourselves away,' says Lily, indicating a table that's got no seats and is more centre stage.

'Ladies. Can you help us settle an argument?'

We turn around and see a pair of guys our age. The taller man, who's just addressed us, is in black tie, with a camel coat thrown over his shoulders. He looks like something out of a Brat Pack movie – James Spader or Andrew McCarthy. His friend is also cute, but in a different way: dark, jowly and bearded, with circles under his eyes, wearing a hooded sweatshirt, jeans and a T-shirt.

'What argument?' asks Maggie.

'We were wondering if you were Brits or Yanks,' says Black Tie. He himself has an American accent, but a sort of old-fashioned drawl; he talks the way they do in 1940s films. 'Joe here thinks you're English, but I'm getting a transatlantic vibe.'

'You're both sort of right,' says Lily. 'Maggie and I are English, but I live in LA. And Rachel is Irish.'

'Delightful,' he says. He shakes all our hands. 'Carter DeWinter. This is Joe – my cousin – visiting from San Francisco. What are you gals drinking, anyways?'

'Thanks. I'll have a beer,' I say.

'Nonsense,' he says. 'Three spritz all'Aperol, coming up.' And he sweeps off to the bar. His cousin looks at us for a minute, and then trails after him, obviously seeking safety in numbers.

227

'They're so strange,' Lily whispers as soon as they're gone. 'Do you think he's live street theatre or something?'

'He can't really be called Carter DeWinter,' I say. 'It sounds like a law firm.'

'Well, they've bought us drinks so we're committed to them for at least fifteen minutes,' says Maggie.

'No we're not,' I say. 'It's not payment, it's a gift.'

The guys come back with our drinks, and Lily starts talking to Joe while Maggie and I chat to Carter, who tells us he's doing a PhD in art history and spending a semester in Rome. The spritzes are bright orange and very tasty; they go down like lemonade, but they're obviously very strong. After a few sips, I feel wasted.

'Our *palazzo* is right next door to the one where Shelley used to live. It's a bit stuffy, but we've tried to make it homely by hanging up our art and so forth. We've got one Picasso over the bath.'

'Where's the other Picasso?' I ask.

He raises an eyebrow. 'We only have one. We're students.'

'Where are you guys staying?' says Joe, looking longingly at Lily. When we tell him, he says, 'Why are you staying in a hotel? That's, like, old school. You should do Airbnb.'

'Airbnb,' Carter says, rolling the unfamiliar tones on his tongue. 'What is that?'

Joe laughs. 'Oh man! You never heard of Airbnb? It's where people rent out rooms in their houses. The houses are always awesome and it's so cheap. These two dudes just thought it up in their bedrooms and now they're millionaires,' he adds, obviously wishing that he was one of those dudes.

Carter frowns. 'So these strangers take you into their homes? It sounds very . . . biblical.'

'Twelve o'clock,' Maggie says out of the corner of her mouth, while Carter DeWinter is momentarily distracted. 'See? Doesn't he look like Fabrizio Moretti from the Strokes?'

He does: a very handsome young guy, obviously Italian. But Fabrizio, though he keeps staring at Maggie, makes no move to come over. I think he's being put off by Carter DeWinter and Joe. Carter is now talking about shopping in Rome.

'Of course Saddlers is the only place for moccasins,' he's saying.

'Why are you in black tie, Carter?' I ask.

'Drinks at the Embassy. I'm afraid Joe has been blackballed,' says Carter.

He's so ridiculous, but he's also very cute and he smells nice – something I always notice in a man. In fact, I'm finding him bizarrely attractive. What is wrong with me?

Joe has suddenly come alive and is talking to Lily about his flat in San Francisco.

'It's right by the ocean . . . My neighbours are the seals, man. They make a sound like this.' He snuffles expressively. 'The seals are mellow.'

Lily's cracking up and Maggie and I are exchanging 'I don't get it' looks.

Joe does impressions of more marine life, before concluding, 'But the seagulls . . . the seagulls are my kings, man. They're my kings.'

'You'll have to excuse him,' says Carter DeWinter. 'West Coaster.'

'Hello.' Fabrizio Moretti has suddenly materialised beside us, clearly intent on talking to Maggie. They chat briefly, and then they disappear off to the bar together – leaving me having a one-on-one with Carter DeWinter. Lily is still in fits of laughter at something Joe's saying.

'So . . . what's your PhD about?' I ask.

He starts telling me, and to my surprise, it's fascinating. He's writing about a female Jewish-Italian artist who was involved with the Resistance during the war and painted pictures while she was in an internment camp. Carter seems to have been very active collecting funding from various bodies – though I'm guessing he's not short of a few pennies himself.

Then he looks in alarm at some people coming in. 'Shuffle me this way,' he hisses, and before I can say anything, he's put an arm around me and has whirled me into a corner of the room.

'That woman keeps trying to get me to read her screenplay,' he says in a stage whisper.

I'm beginning to suspect he's properly crazy now. Either that, or this is a ruse for him to get me in a corner by myself. Maggie is now on the dance floor going great guns with Fabrizio Moretti. Lily is at the bar with Joe, having what looks like another Aperol spritz. Carter still has an arm around me . . . and then he leans in to try and kiss me.

229

I step back immediately. 'I have a boyfriend,' I explain at the top of my voice.

Carter takes it well. 'My mistake,' he says, gallantly.

Suddenly Lily rushes up to me. 'Can we get out of here?' she says urgently in my ear. 'Like, now? Where's Maggie?'

'OK. Carter, we have to go – thanks for the drink!' We hurry over to Maggie, who's now kissing Fabrizio Moretti. As soon as they stop for breath, we drag her away and the three of us race right out the door.

'Why did we have to leave? I was having a good time,' Maggie complains, once we're outside.

'I'm sorry,' says Lily. 'I had to get out of there or something would have happened with Joe.'

'Lily, please tell me we're not going to have to spend all weekend fleeing your admirers,' says Maggie. 'I'm not up to it.'

'I almost kissed him,' says Lily, sounding scared.

'But you didn't,' Maggie points out. 'And that's the main thing.'

'Did you get Fabrizio's number, Maggie?' I ask. She shakes her head. 'What would be the point?' she says happily. Fair enough. I'm feeling as relieved as Lily. The moment of madness with Carter was just that.

As we walk back towards our hotel, Lily starts to laugh again. 'I was thinking of something Joe said.'

'What?'

'He said . . .' She deepens her voice and does a brilliant impression of Joe's stoner drawl. 'I study every drug I take very carefully. VERRY CAREFULLY.'

This makes us all crack up. We're nearly back at the hotel now. The piazza is still full of people although it's well after midnight, and the roar of conversation rises into the mild night air. I check my phone to see if Oliver's replied, feeling ready to text him a very passionate message, but there's nothing. Frowning, I decide he'll probably reply in the morning.

I set my alarm for 8 a.m. with the intention of getting up early to fit in all our sightseeing, but I must have slept through it, because it's well after ten when I'm finally woken by a feeble knock at the door.

'Come in,' I call.

The girls both shuffle in, looking white and drawn, wearing their fluffy hotel bathrobes.

'I am never drinking again,' says Lily.

'And it wasn't even supposed to be our big night out,' says Maggie.

'Do you think we can get breakfast in bed here?' yawns Lily. 'Or coffee?'

'I'm not sure. Did you want to have your jog first, Maggie?'

She shakes her head. 'I need a cup of tea.'

I'm much less hung-over than they are, so I volunteer to ring reception to find out about breakfast. I put down the phone with a grave face.

'Bad news. We have to go to another hotel for breakfast.'

'Aaarrrggh,' says Lily, burying her head in my pillows. 'Can't deal.'

'Why don't we go to a café?' Maggie suggests.

Once we're showered and dressed we feel better, and we have the energy to go outside. It's a beautiful day: blue skies with a few little clouds scudding overhead. It rained in the night and the cobbles of the square look freshly washed. We find a table outside a café and order cappuccinos for me and Lily, tea for Maggie, and croissants. Lily puts on her sunglasses very slowly and theatrically. Maggie is huddled in her trench coat, still looking a bit green. There's a light breeze, but it's going to be a sunny day; the silver zinc table is already warm to the touch.

We discuss last night all over again and swap impressions of Carter and Joe. Lily thinks the funniest part was when I asked Carter where the other Picasso was.

'Like one wasn't enough for you,' she says.

'I was confused! He said they had one over the bath, so I assumed there was another one somewhere. I think Joe and the seagulls were funnier.'

'I'm so glad I didn't go there,' Lily says soberly.

'What was the appeal?' Maggie asks.

'He made me laugh,' she says.

231

'Intentionally?' I ask, and we all laugh.

Our waiter arrives with our croissants and drinks. My cappuccino is the best I've had since I was last in Italy: short and dense and rich, totally different to the watery, milky froth you get in London. The croissant is rich and flaky, with an unexpected but very tasty custard filling. The only disappointment is Maggie's tea, which is a cup of warm water with a tea bag floating on top.

'Oh,' is all she says, sadly. 'Just like France.'

'Let's find out the Italian for boiling water,' Lily suggests. She looks it up on her dictionary app and signals to the waiter.

'Anyway, as I was saying. I also liked his beard,' she says, once he's gone.

'Who, the waiter?'

'No, Joe. I love a good beard.'

'Your dream man is Russell Brand, isn't it,' says Maggie.

'He is my dream man. Or Jesus,' says Lily. 'I love that bearded Messiah look.'

'I'm not keen on beards,' I say. 'Or tattoos. Or jewellery. Those are all deal-breakers.'

'Really?' says Maggie. 'I don't mind jewellery. Fabrizio had a thin gold chain; it was quite sexy.'

'I like tattoos,' says Lily. 'So many people have them in LA. It's more of a hipster thing there. The girl in my local coffee shop has tattooed sleeves, and she's training to be a pre-school teacher.'

'So your ideal man is a bearded, tattooed prophet,' I suggest. 'With piercings?'

'And yours is a Ken doll,' Maggie says. 'Do you like them to have that bit of plastic moulding between their legs?'

We all laugh at that, though I'm remembering that Jay did in fact have a sort of wooden necklace thing. He used to wear it with a low-cut V-neck T-shirt. A bad sign. Oliver would never wear anything like that. Speaking of Oliver, why has he still not replied to my text?

'Does Oliver have any piercings in funny places?' Maggie asks, reading my mind.

I shake my head, smiling. 'No. No tattoos, beards or metalwork. Though he did recently cut his own hair.'

'What?' the girls say.

'Only because he didn't have time to go to the barber's and it was driving him crazy,' I explain. 'I think he thought, how hard can it be? If you're used to cutting bones and things, hair probably seems simple.'

'Does it look OK?' Maggie asks.

'It's fine – his hair's wavy anyway so you don't notice it. That was only when he was pushed for time. Most of the time he goes to Mr Topper's, beside the hospital.'

I'm sort of wishing now that I hadn't mentioned it: it is a bit embarrassing, and makes Oliver sound mad. Jay used to go to some place in Kensington where Kate Middleton supposedly goes. I think that's mad as well. But surely there's some middle ground between Kate Middleton's hairdresser and Mr Topper's?

Maggie's tea has now reappeared; this time, it's a cup of hot water, with a tea bag floating on top.

'Bit better,' she says, frowning and pushing the tea bag down.

The clock of a nearby church starts striking. A flock of pigeons, startled by the noise, fly off from the flight of steps. Twelve o'clock: how did that happen? I feel a surge of mixed adrenalin and anxiety as I think of all the things we've got to see today; starting, of course, with the Colosseum.

I'm about to suggest to the girls that we get a move on when I see how relaxed they are: leaning back, legs outstretched, sun on their faces, watching the people go by. Well, when in Rome, I suppose. We can spare another ten minutes.

And it is fun people-watching. There are crowds of Italian kids with Invicta backpacks on a school trip; a group of Japanese tourists listening to a guide with an umbrella; American tourists dressed in full hiking gear as if they're about to climb the Matterhorn; and three guys who are obviously English. One of them is wearing shorts; that's the giveaway. The other two are in jeans and quilted navy jackets. Such clones. Jay had a jacket like that. In fact one of them looks a bit like Jay. Same height, same blond hair, same Ryan Gosling-type profile—

Oh God. It *is* Jay.

'Shit.' Stunned, I shrink down in my seat. 'Guys – can we go? Now?'

'What is it? Don't tell me we're hiding from your admirers as well,' says Maggie.

I'm about to explain, but it's too late. Jay is looking straight in our direction, and now he's seen me. He does a double-take, and then smiles and leads his friends in our direction.

'Rachel,' he says, approaching our table. He doesn't look or sound sleazy or smug or like a cheating bastard, as he should. He sounds nice, and normal – even a little embarrassed. 'Small world! What brings you here?'

Without meaning to, I'm standing up and actually receiving his kiss and hug. I don't think he deserves a hug, but I also don't want to look as if I'm sore and sulking.

'I'm here for the weekend,' I say. 'Maggie and Lily, this is Jay.'

Jay introduces his friends: Henry, his blond clone, who looks posh and empty-headed, and Rob, the dark-haired one in shorts. We swap small talk about where we're staying and for how long – the boys are in a nearby hotel until tomorrow evening, like us. I wonder if the other two are lawyers from his new firm. Jay and I used to work together, but he left last October – thank God.

'Do you . . . sorry, I could be totally wrong,' Rob says to Maggie, 'but do you live in Fulham?'

'I do! Why, do you?'

'Yeah. I feel like I've seen you around. Do you go to the Nuffield gym?'

'Yes, I used to. But I've joined a new one . . .' They start swapping notes on Fulham gym facilities.

'We should let you get on with your holiday,' says Jay once they've finished their discussion of which place has the fluffiest towels and the cleanest machines. He adds, glancing at me, 'Unless . . . Where are you girls planning on going out tonight?'

Maggie says, 'We haven't decided. Do you have any tips?'

'We heard about this . . . I suppose you'd call it a pop-up club, that's happening in the gardens of the Villa Borghese. You need a password to get in.'

'That sounds amazing,' says Lily immediately.

'I'm sure I could get you in, if you wanted,' Jay says, looking at me enquiringly.

I can't help it; I *am* mildly flattered by this. And if he's in

Rome with the boys, on Valentine's weekend, then he must have ended it with Tabitha or Tatiana or whatever her name was.

But that's irrelevant. *I'm* not single, and I'm not wasting an evening on Jay.

'I'm not sure,' I say. 'We've got dinner plans with some other friends, and it might end up being a late one.'

Jay seems to get the hint. 'Of course,' he says. 'It was great bumping into you. And nice to meet you, Maggie, Lily.' He has a great memory for names. He went to charming bastard school.

As soon as they're gone, the girls turn to me.

'Who was that?' Maggie asks. 'His friend was cute! I think I have seen him in my gym. Or maybe in Waitrose. Nice legs.'

For a minute I consider telling them the whole story. About how Jay and I were 'together' – never boyfriend and girlfriend – in a gut-wrenching on-and-off way for six months, until I found out he had an actual secret girlfriend. Which explained all the mystery illnesses, the weekends he had to work, and the real reason I couldn't find him on Facebook.

I should have keyed his car or something when I found out. But I didn't want him to know how badly he'd hurt me, so to save face I went along with his fiction that we had been just friends and work buddies all along. I even sponsored his moustache for Movember – God help me.

But it's too pathetic to explain all of that, so I say, 'Oh, I had a thing with him. It didn't end so well.'

'Oh no,' says Maggie. 'I'm sorry. When was that?'

'It ended last September.'

'Well of course we won't go out with them then,' says Lily decisively. 'We shouldn't even have been talking to them.'

'Are you sure?' I ask, feeling bad. The secret garden party rave did sound interesting. Typical Jay: he always found the best places to go out, damn him.

'Of course! Hos before bros,' Maggie says, which is so unexpected and un-Maggie-like that we all start laughing.

'Where are we going, girls?' asks Lily, when we've subsided.

'Oh.' The encounter with Jay has thrown me completely off course and I can't even remember what we were meant to be doing today. 'I'm trying to think – I think it made sense for us to see the Forum first, and then the Colosseum. Let me check my guidebook.' I rummage in my bag. 'Shit! I left it back at the hotel.'

The girls look at me mutely; I can tell they're hoping I won't suggest going back for it.

'OK! We'll wander,' I say, reluctantly. 'But tomorrow, can we definitely see the Colosseum?'

'Of course!' says Maggie. 'I want to see it too.'

'Shuffle me this way,' Lily says, turning left down a side street. Ever since I told her about Carter saying it to me, she's become very taken with this expression.

'Any particular reason?' I ask, as we trail after her.

'Because it's sunny?'

Following her, I feel dubious. I want some sun too, but I don't want to spend too long wandering aimlessly around these narrow streets, endless ochre and orange and pink facades punctuated by wooden shutters and souvenir shops. We could spend all day doing this and never see a single sight.

'Oh!' says Lily.

We've come to the end of the street, which has opened up into a square dominated by a huge round building of ancient reddish stone with crumbling columns. It's obviously been there for so many centuries it's sunk several feet deep into the ground. A Latin inscription is set across the pediment. It looks like part of ancient Rome dropped into the middle of a modern square. There are hardly any tourists looking at it; in fact nobody seems to be paying it any attention.

'I know this sounds ridiculous,' says Maggie, 'but that looks *old*.'

'Let's have a shufti,' says Lily.

We go inside and I see from the holy water font that this is now a church, and bless myself automatically. The interior is dark, except for a column of light filtering down from a round hole at the top of the dome. We wander around, absorbing the hush and awe of the place, with its marble floor and mosaic walls. The silence is only broken by the shriek of a toddler escaping from its parents before being instantly snatched up again.

'This is the Pantheon,' Maggie tells us in a whisper, having got hold of a leaflet. 'It was built as a temple dedicated to all the gods during the reign of the Emperor Augustus, about two thousand years ago.'

The Emperor Augustus. For a second I get a glimpse of what it would have been like: lit by candles probably, with softly moving robed figures and strange chants and incense rising up towards the domed roof. And two thousand years later it's still here, with people walking past with their iPhones and Prada bags and gluten allergies. After a while, we drift back out in unspoken accord towards the exit.

'That was amazing . . . and it wasn't even on my list,' I say.

Lily and Maggie don't say anything but I know they're thinking: there she goes again.

'I'm not wedded to the list, you know,' I add, as we turn down a pedestrian side street lined with shops. 'It's just, I want to make sure we see Rome.'

'But we are seeing Rome!' Lily says, waving her arms around. 'This is Rome!'

I laugh, because she's right. I'm in a lather to get out and see the place, but we're here already. I take a moment to look around, absorbing everything: the buildings, the people, the special kind of light, the smell of coffee from a nearby bar, the warmth of the sun on my face, the man walking past shouting into his mobile phone . . .

Which reminds me: Oliver still hasn't texted me back. Of course he's probably mid-conference, or else his battery has died and he forgot to take his charger to Bristol. But couldn't he borrow a charger? This is how it began with Jay: the cancelled plans, the silences, the texts I had to feed through an Enigma machine to decode. What if this whole conference is a cover story, and Oliver's actually gone away for a romantic weekend with Laura? I tell myself not to be an idiot, but there's a deep-seated fear there that's very hard to shake. The sight of Jay has obviously rattled me.

To distract myself, I stop to look in the window of the shop next door, where a very fitted raspberry-pink dress has caught my eye – except I don't know when I would wear it. Maggie's looking in the window of the shoe shop next door. She casts us both a hopeful look.

'OK,' Lily and I say together. We go inside, and after a quick wander around, we sit down like two boyfriends, while Maggie tries on about twenty pairs of identical-looking high-heeled ankle boots.

'What happened to those suede boots you got at Christmas? Do you still have them?' asks Lily, leaning forward. It's as if she hopes that reminding Maggie about her other pair will end the shopping expedition.

'You sound like my mum,' says Maggie. 'Just because I already have a pair doesn't mean I don't need more. Anyway, they're already wrecked. I'm never buying suede boots again.'

Lily leans back again, resigned. 'Are you a shoe person?' she asks me.

I shake my head. 'Not really. I have to be in the mood to go shopping. And I never understood the whole Carrie Bradshaw shoe fetish thing. Maybe it's because I'm tall, but I'm just not into heels. Are you?'

'No,' says Lily. She pokes out her foot, with its Nike trainer. 'I wear these all the time now. They're so comfortable. Once you get a taste of trainers, it's hard to go back to normal shoes, let alone high heels.'

'Don't listen to them. They don't understand,' Maggie says to her boots.

Ten minutes later, after many goodbyes and *ciao*s from the staff, we're walking out of the shop, complete with ankle boots.

I look at my watch. 'Guys, if we're going to see the Colosseum, I think we should probably head over there now.'

They turn around reluctantly. 'OK,' says Maggie. 'Which way is it?'

'I can probably find directions on my phone,' says Lily unenthusiastically.

'Could we have lunch first, though?' asks Maggie. 'I'm getting hungry already.'

They both sound so forlorn, as if I'm making them do homework, that I laugh and shake my head. 'OK, fine. Lunch first.'

After more wandering, through crowded side streets, past the half-open doors of huge palazzos flanked by box trees, we come to another square, where a flower market is taking place: not just flowers, but an incredible array of fruit and vegetables. Even the leeks and lettuces look bigger, greener and glossier than they do at home. We make our way to a restaurant on the edge of the square, which I've realised is the Campo dei Fiori. So it counts as a sight.

Maggie and I are happy to sit anywhere outside, but Lily insists on choosing the restaurant with the maximum amount of sunshine, and then the table with the same. While she roves off to look at what other people are having, I check my phone one more time. Still nothing from Oliver. God damn. I am sure there's some reasonable explanation, but still, it's not great.

A priest walks by us, his black soutane flapping in the breeze. Which automatically makes me think of how excited my granny would be that I'm so near the Vatican, and how she would expect me to go to a papal mass or something.

Oddly enough, that's something that Oliver understands: his family is Catholic too. In all other ways they couldn't be more different from mine. They own a farm in Oxfordshire – two hundred acres or something – and have lived there for generations. Whereas I grew up in a grey pebble-dashed semi in Celbridge, County Kildare, which has been our ancestral home since the late 1970s. And my dad is an electrician, and was unemployed for two years after the French electrical factory he worked for closed.

In other respects, though, Oliver's family isn't what you'd expect. He was the first in his family to go to university – both his brothers went to agricultural college instead. Whereas my parents were always obsessed with school, homework and exam results. When I got into Trinity to study law, you would have thought I'd been made president. If I picture our families meeting each other – even being in the same room – my brain feels as if it's going to explode.

'I'm having spaghetti carbonara,' says Lily. 'And to drink . . . hm. Shall I have a glass of wine? I can't decide.'

'Let's get a bottle of Prosecco,' I say suddenly. To hell with Oliver. I am going to stop thinking and worrying about him, enjoy every minute of this weekend and really let my hair down.

Though I generally wear it down anyway; ponytails get on my nerves.

We order our bottle from the waiter, who happens to be very, very handsome, and each decide on spaghetti carbonara as well, to counteract the alcohol. It still ends up being a very leisurely, boozy lunch.

'This is the best,' says Lily happily, twirling spaghetti on to her fork. 'So delicious. If I lived in Italy, I really would be too fat to go on Valentino's yacht.'

'Oh God, not Valentino's yacht again,' says Maggie.

'Have you been invited?' I ask, bewildered. The other two start laughing.

'It's just this crazy thing Lily says. Tell her, Lil,' says Maggie.

Lily explains that she came across this saying in the auto-biography of some celebrity's daughter; a glamorous friend of her mother's told the girl that she was too fat to go on Valentino's yacht, and Lily was struck by the concept.

'I used to use it as motivation, back in my stupid days. I prob-ably *am* too fat for Valentino's yacht now,' she says. 'I've put on weight since I moved to the States.'

'A little, but I think it suits you,' says Maggie. 'It's all gone in the right places. Sorry, that sounds sleazy. You know what I mean.'

'I must say,' says Lily, wiping her plate with bread, 'it is nice not to worry about being thin for auditions.'

'Do you miss acting at all?' I ask her.

'I do. Sometimes when I see people in cafés reading scripts I feel envious. But then I remind myself of all the other shit they have to go through, and I don't mind so much. Soon I'll be too old to play babes anyway. Maybe I'll come back to it when I'm old enough to play moms.'

'Moms and babes,' I say. 'How depressing.'

'There are three parts for women in Hollywood. Babe, district attorney and *Driving Miss Daisy*,' says Lily, arching an eyebrow. It occurs to me that even if she's not doing it at the moment, she's an actress to her fingertips. Everything she does – her gestures, the way she says things – is a little bit more amped up than other people's.

240

Maggie has her new shoebox on her lap, and is gazing inside at her purchases and stroking them lovingly.

'Aren't they gorgeous?' she asks us. 'Look at the stitching here. And the leather is so soft. They'd be twice the price in London.'

'Did you ever want to work in fashion?' I ask her.

'Instead of doing microbiology? God, no. I mean, I love exercise but I wouldn't want to be a professional athlete.'

'I love kissing boys but I wouldn't want to do it for a living,' says Lily.

We all laugh – I laugh much longer than the others and I realise that I've drunk most of the bottle of Prosecco by myself. To round off lunch in a healthy way, we order three tiramisus, coffee for the others – and a glass of red wine for me. 'I should have worn my eating pants,' I say.

'What are your eating pants?' asks Maggie.

'They're brilliant. They look quite smart but they're elasticated – I always wear them for Christmas dinner,' I confess.

Our tiramisus arrive and before long we're all moaning in ecstasy; they're so sweet and damp and spongy . . . and boozy.

'Good?' asks the handsome waiter, pausing by our table.

'Very good,' says Lily. 'Thanks. Hey, can I ask you a question?' she adds, as he's about to leave.

Maggie and I look at each other, wondering what Lily's up to now. But she's asking him about places to go out dancing this evening. He says that Rome is more geared to bars than nightclubs (or 'dance bars' as he calls them, which makes us all smile).

'You could try La Maison – or Art Café in Villa Borghese,' he suggests.

'Oh,' says Maggie. 'Is that the temporary one, where you need a password?'

His eyes widen. 'No! You have been invited to that? You should go, for sure.' Hmm. Maybe we should have taken Jay up on his offer after all – but never mind.

'Isn't he dreamy?' Maggie sighs, when the waiter has left. 'I'm so into foreign men these days, it's like an illness.'

'I'm sure you can meet foreign hotties online,' says Lily.

'I need to refresh my online photo portfolio,' Maggie says. 'I

241

have no nice pictures of myself. I'm either all sweaty after a race or else red-eyed in a bar. And Leo is in every single one.'

'Let's make sure to take some nice photos today,' says Lily.

'What are you wearing tonight?' Maggie asks.

'Well,' I say. 'I did spot a dress earlier . . .'

Half an hour later, we're back in the clothes shop we passed earlier, and I'm trying on the raspberry-pink dress that I saw in the window. It's very fitted, but ruched at the same time. It's got a high neck and crossover straps at the front and a cut-out detail at the back, but it's so tight, I can get away without wearing a bra. I don't normally wear such bright colours, or such revealing dresses. But shopping while tipsy – which I definitely am – is a very good way to break out of a style rut.

I come out to show the girls. 'What do you think?'

Lily, who's in the middle of sending a text, drops her phone. 'Aaaaahhh!' she says, waving her hands around. 'Love it! You have to get it!'

'It's amazing,' says Maggie, walking around me. 'It's like a Hervé Léger bandage dress. And wasn't one of your New Year's resolutions to wear more colour? How much?'

I strike a slightly unsteady model pose. 'A hundred and twenty. I'm not sure where I'd wear it, though . . .'

'Anywhere,' says Lily immediately. 'To a wedding. To a restaurant. Get it!'

What happens next is a bit like the shopping scene in *Pretty Woman*, if Julia Roberts was drunk. Maggie gives me a ton of things to try on, most of which I would never have picked myself. But I love them all, and I end up buying a slinky dark blue shirt in a see-through snakeskin print, a matching dark blue silk camisole top, a pair of gladiator sandals in the softest brown leather, a pair of silver pumps with a low heel *and* a pair of coral skinny jeans. And a couple of perfect white T-shirts, which I tell myself piously will be useful for work.

'You know how I said I have to be in the mood to go shopping?' I say to Lily, as we weave our way back to the hotel, bags in hand. 'I obviously just need to have most of a bottle of Prosecco first.'

'Do you still want to go and see the Colosseum?' Maggie asks innocently.

'Um . . .' I feel a twinge of conscience before saying, 'No, it's OK.' I'm not going to feel too bad about the Colosseum. I'm on holiday.

Back at the hotel, Lily reminds Maggie about her fashion shoot idea. 'Come on, do your make-up and we'll take some pictures on the terrace.'

'Only if Rachel does it too,' says Maggie.

I don't argue: I'm only too happy to help Maggie *and* capture all my new clothes for posterity. Maggie throws on a clingy peach jersey top with a pair of navy shorts and heels, and I put on the snakeskin shirt and my new skinny jeans and silver shoes. Plus sunglasses. Lily takes a dozen pictures of us, together and separately, standing on the terrace with the piazza in the background.

'Nice, girls, nice,' she says. 'Let's have a change of location!'

So we go down and continue our shoot on the Spanish Steps. And then running down them, scattering pigeons and dodging guitar-playing students. Then, giggling, we run over to the fountain and drape ourselves on the edge of it, do mock-model poses, and even stand on the rim. People are staring at us, but it's so much fun, I don't care. I've never done anything like this in my life.

'Are you guys famous?' a very young American girl with braces asks, approaching us.

'Yes,' says Lily. 'They're very big in Japan. I'll take a picture of you with them if you like.'

So we end up being in a random tween's photo. Then we decide to sit down for some coffee in the sun – and some gelato, because the tiramisu and the wine are wearing off.

We're all silently appreciating the gelato – I'm having pistachio and coffee flavour, which is divine – when my phone buzzes with a text. Wondering if it will be Oliver, I check it and see, with a start, that it's from an unfamiliar number. It's unfamiliar because I deleted it, but I know exactly who it is.

Rachel. So good to see you earlier. Have you thought any more about tonight? Some things I'd love to say to you. Jx

Hmm. Some things he'd love to say to me? It would be long overdue. I will admit, it's fairly soothing to my ego that he's so eager to talk to me. Unlike Oliver.

I wish Oliver would text me soon, so that I can stop thinking about stupid Jay. And comparing the two of them. At first I loved the fact that Oliver is so genuine and down to earth. But now I can't help thinking: he would never take me to a secret club. He hates fancy clubs and restaurants, and he prefers old man's pubs to nice bars. I want to go away to Bali or somewhere this time next year, and his idea of a holiday is more like a wet fortnight in Wales, camping or something. I don't camp. Our skiing holiday was luxurious, but he didn't plan it; his friend did. Left to himself, Oliver probably would have booked us a week's ski boot camp in Scotland. With home-made skis.

'Was that Oliver?' Maggie asks. I told her earlier that I think his battery must be dead.

'No, Jay.' I shrug, licking the remains of my ice-cream cone. 'He seems keen to meet up later. I'm not so sure.'

To my disappointment, they don't argue.

'OK,' Maggie says. 'We could go to that La Maison place?'

'It got some mixed reviews on TripAdvisor,' says Lily. 'We should've asked Carter DeWinter. I bet he knows the places with the best Aperols.'

'Well,' I say casually, 'I suppose we *could* go to that secret garden place. We don't have to hang out with Jay once we're there. I know this is your year of saying yes to things, Maggie, so I want you to be able to meet Rob,' I add, feeling weaselly.

Maggie glances at Lily, then at me.

'But you don't want to go, do you?'

'I don't mind going just for an hour or so. To show I'm not sulking. That's if you guys were keen.' And I'm mildly interested myself to hear what he has to say. And to show him what he's missing, i.e. my new dress and me inside it. Not shallow at *all*.

'Well, I did like his friend,' says Maggie frankly. 'How about you, Lily?'

'I'll go anywhere,' says Lily. 'Does he have good taste in clubs, this Jay?'

'That's the one thing he does have. It's bound to be a very cool place.'

So I send Jay a quick text saying we'll go to the club though we might not stay very long. He texts back immediately: *You've made my day. Just getting the address.* He texts it to me, then adds: *See you outside at 9. Jx*

Two texts in the space of two minutes. How different from the time when he used to take hours, or even days, before sending me a text that I would pore over like the Dead Sea Scrolls. I wait a while – let him sweat for a change – before replying: *OK.* Short and sweet. It feels good to have the upper hand, for once. Not that I'm getting into any kind of thing with Jay again; I'm just happy to be able to show him I don't care about him.

After enjoying the sun for a little longer, we decide to go back to the hotel for Maggie to have some quiet time, and for me to have a disco nap to recover from all the lunchtime Prosecco. When we all reconvene, around seven, Maggie decides it's time to give me a makeover and produces an enormous case full of brushes and eyeshadows.

It's ironic that she and Lily both have one older brother, and yet they know more about make-up than me, with two sisters. My sisters and I were enthusiastic about make-up rather than skilful. A slick of Rimmel Heather Shimmer, all-over fake tan and maybe some hair mascara, and we were ready for the bright lights of Celbridge. We never wore blusher: sure, why would we want our faces to look redder than they were already?

'What do you think?' asks Maggie when she's finished, sitting back.

'Wow! I look so different.' Really, really striking and sort of . . . smouldering. I've never seen my eyes look so big, or dramatic. And for the first time I can see the point of blusher.

'I love it!' I tell Maggie, who looks delighted.

We get dressed – in the girls' room, for company – and it's like being fifteen again as we all jostle for room at the mirror, with Lady Gaga playing on Lily's phone. They both look fantastic: Lily in a striped-and-floral midi dress that she describes as a Man Repeller, and Maggie in a lemon-yellow chiffon strapless number.

When I compliment her on it, she tells me it's from the Kate Moss Topshop collection, and she got up at 6 a.m. to buy it online. That's dedication. Lily lends me her black-and-white striped blazer to wear over my raspberry dress.

None of us can face getting to grips with public transport here, so we ask the hotel to call us a taxi. And ten minutes later, we're speeding along through the streets of Rome towards the Villa Borghese.

When I see the queue at the entrance to the darkened park, my worries about being overdressed disappear, and instead I start to worry that I'm going to be *under*dressed. I've never seen such a glamorous crowd gathered anywhere. The men are all in dark suits and the women are all in tiny designer dresses, Fendi baguettes dangling from manicured fingers, striding effortlessly in sky-high heels. Everyone is smoking and talking non-stop while also simultaneously seeming very bored.

We're walking to the back of the queue when I hear my name being called. I turn around: it's Jay, with his two friends.

'Rachel,' he says, as we walk towards him. 'You look *fantastic*.' He looks me up and down with a smile before kissing me on both cheeks.

Jay looks good too. He's wearing a dark jacket over a white shirt, and dark blue jeans and polished brown loafers. Very simple, but he's in great shape so his clothes always look good on him. He's an amateur boxer; he took it up when white-collar boxing became popular among City guys a few years ago. His dark blond hair is slicked back, showing off his profile, which always reminds me of Ryan Gosling's . . . but I'm not thinking about that right now.

We join the queue, and he reintroduces his friends: Henry, the posh, vacant-looking one, and Rob, the dark-haired one who Maggie liked.

'So this should be quite fun,' Jay says, as we reach the head of the queue. 'At least I hope so . . . should be better than Infernos in Clapham, anyway.' He winks at me, and I laugh as I remember a hellish night out we had there for a colleague's birthday. He gently puts his hand on the small of my back to move me forward. I step away, but I have to admit, part of me likes it.

Being seen with him, in fact, is another guilty pleasure. It makes me more confident, especially in such an über-glam setting. I picture what all the people who thought I was a nerd in school would think if they saw me beside Jay right now, in my Hervé Léger-esque dress, queuing for a secret cool club. They probably wouldn't even recognise me. But I'm still relieved when the man on the door, instead of turning me away, lets me in with the others.

Now we're walking along a gravelled path in the darkness, on the edge of a lawn in a park. There are a few little lanterns strung up here and there, but aside from that it's pitch dark; everyone's giggling and bumping into each other as they walk along. I'm suddenly nervous; I hope it's not going to be some kind of *Eyes Wide Shut*-style orgy and that we're not going to be given a rubber mask and a whip when we get to wherever we're going.

I'm certainly not taking part in an orgy, whatever Jay thinks. And I also want him to know that I haven't forgotten what happened between us. I want to play it cool, but I'm not above a pointed hint.

'How's Tamara or whatever her name is?' I ask him levelly.

He looks blank for a minute before saying, 'Tamsin? God. Rachel. That is so over.' He shakes his head. 'She was . . . That was *not* a good idea.'

I'm about to ask him more, but we're nearly at the dance floor. I can hear music getting louder; it's a souped-up dance version of 'Mambo Italiano'. I suppose that's his version of an apology; I'm happy to leave it there for now. We can talk later. I can also hear Maggie talking to Rob – good – and Henry trying to chat up Lily; her Man Repeller dress obviously isn't repellent enough.

Finally the path turns a corner and we've arrived. The first thing I notice is that on the other side of a lawn there's an amphitheatre, floodlit, packed with people dancing; not just on the base of it, but on the steps, the better to show off their tiny black dresses, gold jewellery, bandeau tops and hot pants; or in the case of the guys, tight white T-shirts or shirts with half the buttons undone. We're standing in the garden, which is obviously the chill-out zone. It's lit by lanterns, with sofas set out under topiary hedges, a pop-up bar, and a platform where more people are dancing. There are floodlit fountains and hot tubs. Hot tubs! A guy goes past us wearing a pale blue suit with a pocket square, and sunglasses. At night!

'Let's grab these seats and get a drink,' says Jay. 'Ladies, what can I get you?'

Within moments we're all lounging around on a low white sofa under a tree, drinking Campari and soda, while cool trance music plays in the background. God, he's smooth. A disloyal thought pops into my head: Oliver would never have brought me somewhere like this, or been able to find us a table or drinks so quickly. He probably wouldn't get into a place like this. Whereas Jay . . . I shelve that thought. Though I wish Oliver would *help* me shelve it, by texting me.

The others are all chatting, about Rome and what a relief it is to finally see some sun.

'This time next year, I've promised myself I'm going away somewhere in February,' Jay says. 'To get some winter sun before I develop rickets.'

'Oh my God,' I say, unguardedly. 'That's exactly what I was thinking. Long-haul break to Bali or somewhere.'

'Went there on my gap yah,' says Henry. Lily, Maggie and I exchange discreet glances and I can already predict that this comment is going to join the quotable quotes of the weekend.

'Hate to tell you, mate,' says Jay, 'but Bali is over now. You know that book, what's it called . . . *Dance, Pray, Sing*? *Pasta, Pizza, Pilgrims*? Help me out . . .' He clicks his fingers, pretending to be at a loss.

'*Eat, Pray, Love!*' we all chorus, laughing at him.

'That's the one. Ever since she wrote about the hippie town of Ubud, it's been swamped with Americans finding themselves. There's even a Starbucks now.'

'How awful,' I say, genuinely relieved that I've heard this before booking my own flight.

'The place to go now is Lombok,' says Jay.

'Isn't that a furniture shop on Tottenham Court Road?' says Lily.

'Yes! But it's also an Indonesian island,' says Jay.

I'm pleased to see that though he smiled at Lily's wisecrack, he's not drooling or staring at her; he's directing all his comments at me. I've demonised him so much over the past six months, I've forgotten how nice he can be. He's sharp and sophisticated, but he doesn't take himself too seriously. We don't talk about anything heavy, the way I do with Oliver. We discuss restaurants, holidays, even clothes – it turns out he went shopping today.

'Did some serious damage at Diesel. Great dress, by the way,' he adds, eyeing my outfit. When I tell him I got it here in Rome, he says, 'I can tell.'

Meanwhile, Maggie is chatting away to Rob, and poor Lily is stuck with Henry, who's going on about his boss, of all things.

'He's got a good brain on his shoulders,' I hear him say. Lily has an 'I'm fascinated, tell me more' expression on her face, but I can tell she's bored out of her mind. I should rescue her, but I am enjoying talking to Jay. I can't help it.

'You know where I haven't been back to in ages, though?' Jay asks me. 'Floridita.'

I smile. Floridita was where we had our first ever date. Although . . . it's also where I went to have a meltdown after I found out he was cheating on me. I thought he said he wanted to talk to me about all that. I'm trying to think of a casual way to bring the topic up when the music changes to 'Mambo No. 5' by Lou Bega.

'Come on!' says Lily, jumping up and away from Henry. 'Let's dance!'

We walk down the steps of the amphitheatre and squeeze ourselves on to the dance floor, which is now even more jumping: people are crowded above us on the steps, grooving and gyrating or just strutting catwalk style. The other boys are doing a very typical restrained boy-dance, where only their bottom halves are moving. But Jay can really dance, and he's totally unselfconscious, whirling and twirling me around expertly. And I'm having the time of my life, jiving back and forth with him. There's nothing inappropriate about it; we're dancing together. That's what people do! It's social, like tennis.

'Come on,' he says, when the music changes. 'Let's get you another drink.'

I'm not sure if I should be leaving the girls, but I suppose he wants the opportunity to apologise properly, so I agree. We fight our way away from the dance floor, Jay quickly gets us drinks – I ask for an Aperol spritz because I prefer it to Campari – and then we wander away from the others towards a secluded garden seat beside one of the hot tubs.

Hmm. He doesn't think we're going skinny-dipping, does he? I should probably tell him that I have a boyfriend. But he's not coming on to me. We're just talking, which we needed to do ages ago, for closure. Except Jay's not talking about what happened between us; he's talking about Albania, which seems to be his next holiday.

'Albania?' I ask, momentarily distracted.

He nods. 'Totally unspoilt, dirt cheap.'

I nod, but there's something about the way that he says 'dirt cheap' that gives me the icks. And something else occurs to me. Here we are in Rome, but Jay's already talking about Lombok, and Albania. And when he goes to those places, he'll be talking about Ibiza, and Miami. And so on, and on. It's kind of gross, isn't it? I've also noticed that at some point while he was at the bar he decided to unbutton his shirt halfway down so that I can see his man-cleavage. How alluring – not.

Now he's back on work gossip, talking about a couple we both know who've split up after buying an expensive house together. He's pretending to look sad but actually looking ghoulishly happy at having that news to share.

God. Was he always like this? Was I so infatuated I didn't notice? I remember thinking he was a bit of a gossip, but I thought it was . . . sweet. Sweet? Sure, in the way that a poisonous spider is sweet. Or a rat. And he doesn't look anything like Ryan Gosling; he just has a long nose.

'So. You said there were some things you wanted to say to me?'

He smiles, that slow smile that used to make my heart race. 'Yes, of course. I wanted to say that, well . . . it's good to see you, Rachel. I miss you.'

'Right. I thought you might have some kind of explanation about what happened. You know, with that other girl.'

'Oh, that. Well, it was difficult for me too.'

I nod, before I can actually process what he's saying. Him cheating on me was difficult for him too? What?

'I was having a nightmare at work . . . I was confused, and I did the wrong thing. But now, maybe . . .' He gives me the slow smile again, charmingly uncertain. 'Maybe it could work?'

It's the scenario I fantasised about so many times: Jay wanting me back. But now that it's happening, I feel nothing, because Jay is a twat. I once thought I wasn't cool enough for him, and maybe that was why he cheated. But now I realise there is *nothing* wrong with me. And Oliver is one hundred, no, one billion times the man he is. I would rather be in the grottiest old-man pub with Oliver than in the world's best nightclub with this . . . fuckmuppet. And I never swear!

'Either way, Rachel,' Jay says, 'I don't want to lose you as a friend.'

Urrrrrggggh. The F-word! *This* was how he got away with it. He could do anything he liked because we were so much more than a boring old boyfriend and girlfriend; we were friends. It sounded so sophisticated and mature but it was just bullshit.

Lily and Maggie have left the dance floor, trailed by both the guys, and are standing nearby, at the bar. They're watching me and looking concerned. I'm so glad they're here to see this.

I smile sweetly at Jay. '*Of course* we can be friends. And maybe more? Nothing too complicated? No strings?'

He's practically drooling now. 'Yes. Definitely! You know, Rachel, you always were a goer.'

A *goer*. A goer! With that one word, his fate is sealed. I keep my smile in place as I say, 'By the way, I love your jacket. Where did you get it from?'

He shrugs. 'Armani, I think. Or no, sorry. Hugo Boss. The jeans are Armani.'

'It's gorgeous.' I stroke his shoulder. 'Do you want to play a game?'

His eyes light up; *of course* he wants to play a game. Because he is a *player*.

'OK. Stand up, and come over here . . . closer . . . Now hand me your mobile and your wallet.' I put down my drink and hold out my hands for them. 'Great. Now . . .' And before I lose my nerve, I push him as hard as I can, backwards into the hot tub, where he lands with a beautiful and satisfying splash.

'What . . . the . . . FUCK?!' He bobs up, spluttering and dripping all over; his half-unbuttoned shirt is clinging to him, and his jacket and his artfully done hair are ruined. 'You crazy bitch! What the fuck was that for?'

'It was for being a GOBSHITE and cheating on me. Now button your shirt up!'

Then, giggling madly, I drop his stuff on the grass and sprint off towards the girls, who are standing beside the bar with the two guys, all of them open-mouthed. Catching my breath, I manage to gasp out, 'RUN!' And we run as fast as our heels and hysteria will allow us, shrieking and laughing like maniacs.

'Oh shit! They're coming after us. Hide!' says Lily. 'This way!' We zigzag off the path into the trees, and sneak along SAS-style until we're safely out of sight and back on the gravel path, stumbling towards the exit.

'Oh my God, Rachel,' Lily says, gasping for breath. 'I cannot believe you did that. I don't know what he did, but I bet he deserved it. Respect.' She holds up a hand for a high-five.

'I've never seen anything like it in my life,' says Maggie. She's much fitter than me and Lily, so she's breathless with laughter rather than from the running. 'Rachel, you pushed him into a *hot tub*.'

This makes us all laugh again; I'm actually doubled over in pain, I'm laughing so hard. 'I know . . . wasn't it great? In fairness, I did take his wallet and phone from him first so they wouldn't get wet.'

'I absolutely love it,' says Lily. 'You pushed him into a hot tub, but in an organised, sensible way. Brilliant.'

'Yes! It could have been a fountain, but that would have been dangerous.'

'Anyway, it was his fault for taking us to a nightclub with hot tubs,' says Lily. 'What was that about?'

'Exactly!'

'But Rachel,' Maggie says, 'what did he do? I mean, seriously – what happened?'

So I explain: about our sadistic six-month relationship that wasn't, because we were 'friends', and how he cheated on me.

'Can I point out as well that his real name is Jason?' I add. Not that there's anything wrong with being called Jason, but it's typical of Jay that not even his name is real.

'That's awful,' says Maggie, looking stricken. 'If we'd known about all that, we *never* would have come out to meet them.'

'It was my fault, I should have told you earlier. I'm just sorry we had to leave early if you were having a good time.'

'God, no,' says Lily. 'The place was fun, but I was taking a hit for the team. The team being you and Rob.' She points at Maggie.

'Did Rob ask for your number?' I ask Maggie.

'Yes, but I won't answer if he calls. I don't like the company he keeps. It's my year of saying yes to everything, but not to *anything*.'

'Woohoo! You are on fire this weekend, girlfriend,' says Lily. 'You too, Rachel.' She starts to laugh to herself, and I can tell she's thinking again about me pushing Jay into the hot tub. It is a beautiful memory. I wish I could have taped it.

'Hmm,' says Maggie. 'How are we going to get back to the hotel?'

This is an excellent point. We've left the park now, and we're on a dark street with no shops or bars and nobody going by. I didn't bring my guidebook, which was stupid of me, and Lily's phone's not working.

'We could always go back to the club and see if someone will call us a taxi,' suggests Lily.

'No!' I say, panicked. 'I don't want to run into Jay again. Oh God! He's bound to be on his way out himself – he'll have to go home and change.' I look back desperately over my shoulder. 'We have to get out of here now!' Not that I think Jay will turn violent, though he is a boxer, but he might threaten to sue me, or make me pay for his dry-cleaning. Either way, it won't be fun.

'But how?' says Maggie.

We're looking around in an aimless panic when there's a roar of mopeds, startlingly loud in the quiet street. We all turn around, and we're relieved – at least I certainly am – to see that it's three girls on Vespas. As they're going past us, one of them slows down

253

and calls out something in Italian. We shake our heads, and she stops.

'Are you all right?' she says, in English. I can see blond curls under her helmet. 'Do you need directions?'

'Yes, thanks – we're trying to get back to the centre. The Spanish Steps . . .'

'We're going to the *centro storico*,' one of the others says. 'Do you want a lift?'

Lily, Maggie and I exchange glances before saying, 'Sure!' And we hop on the back of the Vespas with the girls.

'Hold on,' says one of them, and then we're off, hair streaming in the wind, skimming dangerously close to the ground, or so it feels. Sights are flying by us. I see an ancient Roman theatre; a tall column with intricate sculptures all over it; a gigantic baroque-looking edifice covered with statues of soldiers, horses and flags. My new friend calls out over her shoulder, giving me the names of the landmarks as we go. I've realised that there is way too much to see in Rome to even try and remember all the names, so I don't bother. I just soak it in: my first ever Vespa ride!

Eventually things start looking more familiar: we're back in the same streets that I recognise from our first evening exploring. The girls stop their Vespas and we all climb off, breathless and exhilarated, stumbling a bit now that we're back on solid ground.

'Thank you!' we chorus. 'That was great!'

They wave and kick-start their Vespas again, buzzing off into the night.

'Wasn't that fantastic? Like *Charlie's Angels*,' says Maggie. 'They rescued us.'

'I can't believe I just rode on a moped without a helmet,' I say. '*And* I haven't looked at my guidebook all day.'

'Rachel, you also just pushed someone into a hot tub,' Lily points out. 'I think that's worth mentioning too.' Our giggles ring out into the empty streets.

We set off in what we think is the direction of our hotel, but soon we're completely lost again. I'm about to ask Lily whether her phone is working when we hear music.

'Ooh,' says Maggie. 'Are you hearing what I'm hearing?'

It's Destiny's Child. We follow the music and find ourselves at the door of a scuzzy little bar. It's small and dark; the floor looks sticky. It's a world away from the Playboy mansion we just left. But we don't even need to discuss it: we thrust some notes at the guy on the door, and charge in, desperate to get to the dance floor before the song ends.

What follows is the best night out dancing I've had in years. We dance to 'Jumpin', Jumpin', 'Get Lucky' and back to Destiny's Child with 'Independent Women'. We dance to 'No Diggity', and then, for a change, 'Sexyback'. It's as if someone's put his iPod on shuffle and plugged it in. In fact I think that's what the DJ's done; I see him lounging against the wall chatting up a gorgeous girl in a white dress.

'I want to buy a drink but the music's too good, I don't want to miss a song!' screams Maggie.

'I'll get you one!' I hurry to the bar and order three Peroni beers, which we swig until 'We Are Never Ever Getting Back Together' by Taylor Swift comes on. Which means we have to run back to the dance floor, beers in hand.

'This is the best night ever!' Lily sings, or rather screams, along to the music. 'Ever, ever, ever!' Maggie is doing air guitar.

Then to make things even better, 'Hey Ya' comes on.

'I haven't heard this in YEARS!' yells Maggie, spinning around in uneven circles and shaking her rear energetically.

When we stumble out of the club, hours later, we're sweaty and dishevelled, our feet are sore and our throats are raw from singing. It's great.

'That was fantastic,' says Lily. 'So much fun. God, I'm so hot and sticky.'

'Me too, boiling,' says Maggie. 'Now where's the hotel gone?'

'I think it's that way,' I say, pointing vaguely.

But once we've stumbled down the narrow alley, we're not at the hotel. We're in a little square that is almost entirely filled by a massive ornate fountain. Lit by floodlights, it's an incredible marble concoction of columns, alcoves, arches and statues with billowing robes, all set above a foaming turquoise pool full of coins. Although it's 1 a.m., a few people are still here, having their photos taken or flipping yet more coins into the water.

'It's the Trevi Fountain!' says Lily. She rummages in her bag and hands us each a euro coin. 'If you throw a coin in, it means you'll come back to Rome.'

'But that doesn't make any sense,' I object. 'Surely it's up to us whether we come back to Rome? Wouldn't we be better off saving our euro and putting it towards air fare?'

They both look at me and then we all start laughing.

'OK, fine. That was a bit pedantic,' I admit.

'You can just make a wish,' suggests Maggie.

So I close my eyes and flip. I don't even have to think twice: I wish for Oliver. I hope things work out between us . . . and that his phone really has died.

As we turn away from the fountain and start walking home – in the right direction this time – I say, 'You know what the difference between Oliver and Jay is?'

'Jay is a dickhead and Oliver is lovely?' suggests Maggie.

'That goes without saying. But also, they're like Batman and Superman. Batman looks really flashy from the outside, but if you take away his car and his weapons and his castle and his business empire, he's just some guy. Whereas Superman looks like an ordinary guy but inside he's a superhero.'

'I like it,' says Maggie, nodding. 'Let's always date Superman from now on.'

I've realised something else. One of the reasons I was so fixated on Jay was because I was scarred by the memory of being geeky and friendless in school. And I thought that Jay made me cool. Whereas I resisted Oliver at first not because I didn't like him – I always did – but because I was worried about what the choice of him would say about me. I didn't want us to be the geeky couple.

But now I don't care. I'm going to embrace my inner nerd. I love my job, and I like talking about politics and watching Sky News while doing my ironing, and I wear flat shoes ninety per cent of the time. And that's OK! Oliver still likes me. At least, I'm pretty sure he does. I still haven't heard from him but I'm going to blame that on his ancient phone.

'Are we nearly there yet?' asks Maggie, plaintively. 'My feet hurt.'

'Yes! It's around this corner.' Soon we've reached the piazza, and we're crossing it again to get to our hotel. I'm sad to think it's for the last time.

'I can't believe our weekend's nearly over,' I say suddenly. 'It's been so great . . . Thank you both for coming.'

'Thank you for suggesting it,' says Maggie.

'Group hug!' says Lily, and we obey, laughing.

We let ourselves in through the front door of our hotel, and tiptoe up the stairs so as not to disturb the other guests, who all seem much older and earlier-rising than us.

'So where are we going on our next trip?' asks Maggie.

'I won't be able to come – I'll be in the States,' says Lily sadly.

'But not for ever,' says Maggie. 'Or maybe we'll come and visit you there.'

'Yes! Please come!' Lily says, practically jumping up and down with excitement. 'Come to LA – or we could all meet up in New York.'

Suddenly an angry head is poked out of one of the doors. 'People are trying to sleep!' it hisses.

'Sorry!' we all whisper. The door closes and we start giggling, but quietly, and say goodnight in stage whispers.

The next morning, we have a very late and leisurely breakfast in the same café as yesterday. I'm fairly sure Jay won't reappear, and even if he does, I genuinely don't care. My head is sore, though: I must have been much drunker than I thought last night. Lily and I have our usual cappuccinos and croissants. Maggie asks for boiling water, a tea bag and two cups, and finally assembles a satisfactory cup of tea for herself.

'Yay,' she murmurs, as she adds milk. We all applaud.

'Hey, I just realised something,' I say. 'Today is Valentine's Day.'

'Oh yeah,' says Lily, yawning. 'Happy V-Day.'

'Happy Valentine's Day, girls,' says Maggie, clinking her teacup against my coffee cup.

'Hey, Rachel,' says Lily, looking at me over her sunglasses. 'I have a question.'

'What?' I ask, hoping she's not going to bring up Oliver.

'Where's the other Picasso?' she says, and creases up with laughter.

'Lily, I hope you study every drug you take . . . verrry carefully,' says Maggie.

We take a last walk around, do some window-shopping and Maggie buys a scarf. All too soon, it's time to go back to the hotel and pack, and then queue for the airport bus. On the bus, we swap reminiscences about the weekend: the cellar bar, meeting Joe and Carter DeWinter, our epic lunch at the Campo di Fiori, the photo-shoot, the crazy amphitheatre club, me pushing Jay into the hot tub . . . then our ride home with the Charlie's Angels, and dancing to Destiny's Child in that sweaty little bar. We packed in much more than I thought.

'Though I never did see the Colosseum,' I add.

'And I never did go for a jog,' says Maggie.

'I rode on a Vespa,' Lily says happily.

We all fall asleep on the plane. Maggie's copy of *One Hundred Years of Solitude* drops under the seat in front of us and has to be rescued by Lily.

'You'd better have finished that by the next time I visit,' Lily says, handing it to her. 'Or start a new one. Life's too short.'

She's totally right: life is too short. There and then, I make a decision. I'm not going to stay mute and hide my feelings with Oliver, the way I did with Jay. I'm going to tell him I'm annoyed that he hasn't been in touch all weekend. Not in an angry, needy way; in an open, level-headed and sensible way. We're grown-ups. It's time.

Finally we land and travel to Victoria, where it's time to say goodbye. Maggie is going west, Lily is heading south to her dad's place, and I'm going north to Finchley Road.

'Thanks, girls,' I say, hugging them both. 'It was a great weekend.'

'I'll find you on Facebook,' says Lily. 'And I'll send you my email address, and my phone number in the States. Are you on Skype?'

'Let's get together soon,' says Maggie. 'And good luck with, you know, everything.'

She means Oliver. I smile, but as I sit on the bus home from

Stansted, I'm feeling more and more worried about everything. Oliver and I have never been out of touch for this long. By the time we arrive at Finchley Road, I'm thinking: what if he breaks up with me, the way Jay did? I don't think I can handle another fracture of the heart. The weather is adding insult to injury: it's dark and freezing all over again, as if we've gone back in time to the depths of winter. It's hard to believe that this time yesterday, I was prancing around without a jacket on.

I turn in to the path to my building and trudge along towards the steps, head down. Until I hear someone say my name.

'Rachel.'

I look up and blink in the dark, wondering if I'm imagining things. But it's him. He's sitting on the steps of my building, holding a bunch of purple and orange carnations and Michaelmas daisies. His suitcase is beside him.

'Oh,' I say, unguardedly. 'What are you doing here?'

'I thought I'd surprise you. Was that not a good idea?' He stands up. I'd forgotten how tall he is. And how sexy. 'I'm sorry I haven't been in touch this weekend. My phone died, and I forgot to bring my charger. And the others all have smartphones, so none of their chargers worked for me . . .'

I have every intention of saying calmly, as I'd planned, 'That's fine, but I was annoyed at the time.'

But I'm tired and hung-over, and coming down from the weekend, and instead what comes out is, 'I thought you were ignoring me.' I have a catch in my voice that soon turns into real tears. 'And it was Valentine's Day!' And now I'm sobbing for the whole street to see, and totally mortified. I must look like the most pathetic drama queen in West Hampstead.

'Oh my God! Rachel!' He drops the flowers and pulls me into his arms. I breathe and gulp, inhaling his familiar scent and feeling the wool of his coat against my cheek. 'I thought you didn't care about it! We said we wouldn't do anything.'

'No! We said we would do something low-key. And I know you had to work, but it still sucked that you changed your mind about it.' I'm still gulping and sniffing in a very undignified way. I scrabble in my pocket for a tissue, and find one from the café in Rome.

'Honey,' he says, leaning back and looking at me. He's never called me that, or anything like it, before. The tenderness in his eyes almost makes me start crying again. 'I *did* do something low-key. I sent you a card. But then I missed you, so I came back from Bristol early. I would have gone to the airport to meet you, but I couldn't remember which one you were coming through.'

'But that's crazy! You could have been waiting hours.' I start laughing, but it turns into sobs again. Oliver hugs me, and then kisses me through my tears.

'Come on. Inside,' he says. He hands me the flowers, picks up my suitcase, and holds the door open for me once I've unlocked it. He stops at my pigeonhole and takes out a card, and hands it to me as well. He's not afraid to boss me around sometimes. And once in a while, when you've been making decisions all day, that's what you need.

'How was Rome, anyway?' he asks, as we toil up the four flights of steps.

'It was fine,' I say, but I'm still feeling irrational and sulky, and I can't help adding, 'How was lovely Laura?'

'Who? She's fine! Rachel, what are you . . .'

I say nothing as we go inside my flat.

'Look, I'm sorry I had to go to Bristol,' he says. 'I really am. But I thought you didn't mind. We agreed to do something low-key for Valentine's Day – like sending a card.'

'Well I thought we agreed to do something low-key together,' I say, dully. I'm sick of the whole subject of effing Valentine's Day now; I never want to hear it mentioned again.

Oliver is still staring at me. I can practically hear the wheels clicking.

'I didn't think you cared so much . . . about Valentine's Day,' he says.

'I don't give a shit about it! I only care about *you*,' I say, blowing my nose again.

'Do you?' he says, a smile breaking out over his face. I nod.

'Well, I love you. What do you think of that?' he says.

I'm laughing *and* crying now. 'I like it. I mean, I love you too.'

He kisses me again, and we look at each other, grinning like idiots at what's just happened. And in that moment I realise that

I could tell him absolutely anything. I could even tell him about meeting Jay, though I can't be bothered yet because Jay is so boring. And I know that it's all going to be OK.

Oliver sits down in my armchair and pulls me on to his lap. 'Tell me about your weekend,' he says, stroking my hair. 'What did you do?'

'Well, we didn't do much sightseeing. But we had a lot of fun. It was gorgeous weather, T-shirt weather. I bought some clothes. We met these crazy Americans, and I kept forgetting my guidebook . . .' I want to tell him everything, and I will, but there's something I want to ask him first. 'Oliver. How would you feel about going to Bali with me sometime? Or somewhere like that?'

'Sure.'

'Really?'

He nods. 'Of course. I'd go anywhere with you,' he says, matter-of-factly. 'Except Bicester Shopping Village. One of my worst childhood memories is of my mum dragging me around Bicester Shopping Village. Never again.'

I kiss him again, bubbling over inside with happiness. It's not even that I care about stupid Bali, it's the principle of the thing. Although the one attraction is that at least we wouldn't run into Jay there.

Before we get completely carried away, I remember about the flowers. He stands behind me as I fill a jug at the sink, grabbing my waist and kissing the nape of my neck. I dodge him, laughing, and put the flowers in water.

'D'you like them?' he asks doubtfully. 'There wasn't much left at Paddington station. I wasn't sure what to get.'

'Yes!' This isn't a fib. They're the most hideous flowers I've ever seen, and I love them. I turn around and kiss Oliver again, thinking that February might turn out to be my favourite month after all.

7 March
From: Lily
To: Maggie

Well, I did it. I picked him up from the airport, and waited till we'd got back to my place and were walking on the beach – near where I first saw him, in fact. He's just left; he's going to stay with Sam and Alice tonight and fly back tomorrow. I phoned Alice when he was on his way over and she's going to make herself scarce and come and hang out with me. I hope it won't be too awkward with Sam's family. We should really be on a documentary: *When Cousins Break Up*.

It felt really shitty to make him come all this way, but I couldn't get to Boulder for the next two weekends because of work stuff, and I couldn't do it over Skype. He was sort of fine about it – said he wasn't surprised and he'd been thinking himself that we were at 'different life stages'. But Maggie, he looked so sad. And I'm so sad too. I know it's horrible to be dumped, but it's horrible to break up with someone too. It was fine with Calvin – he barely noticed when I broke up with him. But Jesse . . .

I just hope he'll meet someone else who really loves him the way he deserves. Actually, you know we were meant to be going to see Calexico together? I was going to pay him for the ticket in case he couldn't find anyone to go, but he said he might go with Maudie, that teacher friend of his. She likes Calexico. (Not as much as she likes Jesse, if you ask me, but that's another story.)

How are you? How was your date with the special needs David Bowie? (I mean the teacher with different-coloured eyes.). Have you joined Tinder yet?

Love Lily xx

PS You know one person who will be happy that Jesse and I broke up – aside from Maudie, that is? His mum, Diane.

She is probably cracking open the champagne as we speak. And she doesn't even drink.

PPS Can you give me Rachel's email address? She sent me a really nice message on Facebook, but I hate writing in that tiny blue box.

8 March
From: Maggie
To: Lily

Hi Lil,

That does sound really sad, I'm sorry. But if you're sure, then it's best to do it and let him move on. And at least you were honest with him and didn't just start being flaky and cancelling weekends.

Flakiness seems to be the number one disease affecting young London professionals right now. I've been Tindering a couple of interesting guys. The standard is much higher than on the internet, I think, but it's equally bad for mixed messages and lack of follow-through. Last week I met Bruno – half-Portuguese, gorgeous, imports wines (!). We had the most fabulous evening in Fernandez and Wells. I learned quite a lot about wine too. Do you remember that amazing rosé we had in Delphi, when we were backpacking in Greece? And then we got a bottle to take home and it was like drinking pink apple juice? Well, Bruno said that's because wine is all about the moment. Isn't that interesting?

In any case, he was super keen, telling me all about how we'll have to meet up again and how we must go to this Filipino restaurant in Peckham, etc. – and I haven't heard from him since. Zip, zero. So either he met the love of his life on his way home on the Tube, or else he is FLA Positive (Flaky).

There have been a couple of other guys like that recently – all texts and no trousers. I felt so invincible right after I broke up with Leo, and in Rome, but now I think my run of luck is coming to an end. Or maybe it's something I'm doing wrong. That special needs teacher guy was fine, but

263

there was no spark, and every time I made a joke he said 'Hilarious!' But maybe I'm being too fussy and I should see him again. What do you think?

Mxx

PS Sorry for all the moaning when you're having an actual break-up, but I know you won't mind.

15 March
From: Lily
To: Maggie

Hi Mags,

I wouldn't worry about it. You know, maybe Bruno is all about the moment too. He was great when you were sitting on a terrace overlooking the Sea of Olives, but if you took him home in your backpack, he'd be like pink apple juice. And no, I don't think you should meet Hilarious again. His princess is in another castle.

Sorry for the late reply; work has been busy and stressy this week. We lost one of our big clients, an 'imports-exports' guy (probably drugs, who knows) with six kids who throws them all the most OTT parties. He's cancelled the Under The Sea-themed birthday party for his youngest's Big Six. In a way it's good, as she wanted real mermaids and the insurance was going to be a nightmare. Still, it's worrying – poor Gretchen hasn't looked this ill since she did that Goop detox in January.

This is just a quick one as I'm going over for dinner at Sam and Alice's. I thought Sam would be cross with me, but he's actually being really nice about it all. I think Alice had a word with him.

Lots of love,
Lily xx

15 March
From: Poppy
To: Lily

Hi Lily,

Got your mail yesterday – I'm so sorry to hear about Jesse. But I'm sure it was the right decision. Sometimes it's not enough that you're both nice people. I remember you saying when you were over in February that he had his little nest, or flat, that he'd built and now he wanted to move you into it, and move on with the next stage of life.

And that's perfect for him, but not for you. Now is your time to have flings with unsuitable men and lose your flip-flops in Mexico. In fact, you've just done a massive public service – you've released an eligible man back into the wild, with his taxi light firmly on (mixing my metaphors here but you know what I mean). The women of America will thank you.

How is work and everything? And when are you coming back again? We miss you!

Pxx

27 March
To: Maggie, Rachel, Poppy
From: Lily
Subject: POWER RANGERS ASSEMBLE!!

Hi girls,

Hope you're all well. Guess what? I've been offered a free stay at the Mercer Hotel in New York for me and three friends for three nights!!! I'm good pals with the concierge there, and he's giving me a freebie. I have to go to New York for a VIP event on Saturday 19 April – it's very exclusive and hush-hush BUT I can get you all in. And we can all stay at the Mercer from the 18th to the 21st.

PLEASE COME!!!!!!!

I know it's very short notice, but there are some reason-

265

able flights for that weekend . . . and you will stay for free! Plus, I am really nervous about this event and I'd love to have you there for moral support. And I miss home and I need to see some friends! I'll do whatever it takes to get you all over here! Please come, let me know asap!

Lily xxx

From: Maggie
To: Lily, Rachel, Poppy
Subject: RE: POWER RANGERS ASSEMBLE!!

I'm in.

From: Poppy
To: Rachel, Lily, Maggie
Subject: RE: POWER RANGERS ASSEMBLE!!

What the hell – me too! Rachel?

From: Lily
To: Rachel
Subject: RE: POWER RANGERS ASSEMBLE!!

Yes – Rachel? I hope you're up for it. Otherwise we won't be afraid to use peer pressure. Or do passive-aggressive reply-alls saying 'Oh. That's a pity' if you say you can't come.

OBVIOUSLY I'm just joking. But it would be really great if you could make it. Let me know!

Lxx

266

RACHEL

London is the greatest city in the world.

I mean, no disrespect to Rome. Or Méribel. Or indeed Celbridge, County Kildare. But London takes my breath away. Especially on a night like this – standing in the viewing gallery of the Paramount bar at Centre Point, looking down at all the lights beginning to twinkle in the spring dusk, from east to west, as far as the eye can see.

'Pretty good, huh?' I say to Oliver, who's right beside me. We're both leaning forward on the floor-length window, our heads almost touching, arms and foreheads pressed against the glass. We've got the whole city at our feet, and neither of us is scared of heights.

'Gorgeous,' he says. 'Stunning.'

I turn to him, smiling. He looks so handsome, with his dark hair all ruffled, eyes crinkled up in a grin.

'And the view's not bad either,' he adds.

I groan, punching him on the elbow, but he grabs my hand and it turns into a kiss. We're away from the main bar, in one of the hidden viewing nooks, so I don't mind. We've come here to celebrate our three-monthiversary – a concept that would have made me puke before I met Oliver. We might be celebrating it two weeks late, and semi-ironically, but we're still celebrating it.

We walk back to our seats, and Oliver picks up the drinks menu. 'This looks good. But do I have the nerve to order one?'

'What – a Twinkleberry Fizz? Sure. Why not,' I say, laughing. 'Make it two.'

Sighing happily, I watch him lean on the bar, looking very

smart in his new cords, red-and-cream check shirt and boat shoes. Oliver, who coped fine as a volunteer medic in Nairobi, where electricity came and went and the public toilets were controlled by rival gangs, gets stressed out by department stores. So I've introduced him to the magic of online shopping. He somehow didn't believe that the things would really come or that anything would fit, but they did. We did a big blitz over Chinese takeaway, and got him everything he needs from shirts to underwear. Now he's delighted with himself and I'm delighted that he no longer has to wear jumpers, or shoes, with holes in them.

Of course, these decrepit items haven't been thrown out, which was going to be my next suggestion. Like aged family retainers, they're living out a peaceful retirement in a corner of his wardrobe. But that's OK. Baby steps. I've realised that there's nothing wrong with Oliver being, as Lily put it in a recent email, a 'fixer-upper' – which is what Americans call a dilapidated old house that you lovingly repaint and restore. Especially since it turns out he's more than willing to come to the occasional fancy bar with me.

As I sip the remains of my Prosecco, I marvel at what's happened to me. I'm playing personal shopper to my boyfriend and celebrating monthiversaries and talking about how 'we' saw the new Batman film or went to a farmers' market on the weekend. We've turned into one of *those* couples; the ones that used to make me sick. And I've never been happier.

Oliver's still waiting for his drinks, so out of habit I check my BlackBerry. Three work messages I probably didn't need to be cc'd on . . . and a message from Lily. Through a forest of exclamation marks I make out the subject line: POWER RANGERS ASSEMBLE!!

What does that mean? Confused, I scroll down and read the email chain, starting with Lily's message about not being afraid to peer-pressure me and then catching up with her New York scheme.

'Something interesting?' Oliver asks, setting down our drinks.

I smile and put my BlackBerry away. 'Red alert from Lily – she wants us all to come over for a weekend in New York in April. She's got a freebie with some hotel. It sounds great. Her email's very high-octane. Very Lily.'

'That reminds me,' Oliver says. 'News from New York. Guess who's just got engaged?'

'Brad and Angelina?' Oliver looks blank. 'Never mind. Who?'

'David and Nina.'

I blink at him. 'David and Nina who we went skiing with? David who used to go out with Zoë?'

He nods, his smile fading; he must have forgotten temporarily about David dating (and dumping) my friend Zoë.

'But they've only been going out for five minutes!'

'Six months,' Oliver says. 'It is quite soon, I suppose. But there it is. He rang me the other day to tell me the big news. Sounded very happy.'

Gosh. Zoë's ego might be a little bruised but she will survive – she's madly in love with her boyfriend Max. And now that I've adjusted to the shock, I'm happy for David too. And for the mysterious Nina, a girl of few words but many charms, it would seem. But there's one obvious question.

'What is Jenny going to do?' I ask, lowering my voice. 'Has he told her yet? He can't have. We would have heard the explosion.'

'I think that may have been part of David's thinking. He wants to make things very clear.'

I frown. 'You mean he got engaged to Nina to get rid of Jenny? That's extreme.'

'No! He's head over heels in love with Nina. But he *might* have had an added incentive to make things official with her. And Jenny will just have to cope.'

She will indeed. If a transatlantic move and an engagement aren't clear enough, I don't know what is.

'But you know what?' Oliver continues. 'I bet that now David's off the market, she'll actually get a boyfriend of her own.'

'You're probably right.' Thinking of Zoë, I add, 'What is it about David that makes these girls go so nuts for him? I don't see it myself.'

'That's good to know,' Oliver says, smiling. 'Anyway, the wedding will be somewhere in Ireland – they haven't set a date yet, but I'll be best man, so we'll have to go.'

'That's great! Congrats!' I say, clinking my glass against his; I can tell he's pleased to be asked to be best man. 'Thank God. I thought for a minute there you were going to say the wedding was in New York. My credit card was about to start weeping to itself quietly.'

'Why – because you've got a girls' weekend to fit in there as well?'

'Oh. No, I'm not going to go with them.'

'How come?'

'Because I've had two holidays so far this year. And work is really busy. I'm going to have a big deadline around then . . .' I don't add the most important reason, which is that I hate the idea of spending a whole weekend away from Oliver at the moment. Our weekends are the only real time we have together; if I miss one, it means I don't see him properly for a fortnight.

But it's hard to fool Oliver. He says, 'But work will always be busy. That's why you need the holidays. Wasn't it one of your New Year's resolutions to travel more – as well as widening your social circle?' His eyes twinkle.

'Ye-es.' This is why you should never tell people your New Year's resolutions; they come back to haunt you.

'And didn't Lily recently break up with her boyfriend? What was his name, Jimmy?'

'Jesse. Yes, she did.' I should have thought of that sooner. I take out my BlackBerry again and re-read her message. Poor Lily: the phrases 'I am really nervous' and 'I miss home' jump out at me. As do the phrases 'VIP event' and 'stay at the Mercer'. But that doesn't change the real reason, which I'm going to have to admit to him now.

'I know it's pathetic, but it would mean we wouldn't see each other properly for a fortnight. And that just seems like a long time.'

'We do see each other during the week sometimes,' Oliver points out, though we both know that our weeknight dates are really just sleepovers because we both finish work so late. Not that there's anything wrong with that. Oliver's got plenty of energy, and . . . Anyway. Enough said.

'I know it would be fun,' I say, referring to the weekend away. 'But I've got other priorities.'

Oliver shrugs. 'Fair enough. It's up to you.'

Hm. Now that he's agreeing with me, I'm not so sure. I don't mind being one of *those* couples, but I don't want to be *that* girl . . . the one who drops all her friends when she gets a boyfriend. I've made some great friends in the past six months, and I've become much more spontaneous. It's not that I don't want to put Oliver first, because I do, but I don't want to slip into a couple coma either.

'Actually, you know what? I am going to go.' I put down my drink, excited at the thought of New York – Manhattan! Central Park, the Metropolitan Museum, shopping on Fifth Avenue – and a mystery VIP event. Why was I ever going to say no to that?

'Good idea,' says Oliver. 'And you know, about the other thing. I mean the whole seeing-each-other-enough thing. Logistics thereof.' He looks almost nervous, but he's smiling too. 'Maybe it would help . . . if we moved in together?'

THE GIRLS TAKE MANHATTAN

Thirty Things To Do Before You're Thirty.

Shuddering, I put the magazine quickly back on the rack. I've read those articles before. They all tell you useless things like 'acquire one perfect white shirt'. I did acquire that one perfect white shirt, thinking it would make me look like Katharine Hepburn instead of a crumpled barmaid at the end of her shift. Don't get me wrong: I, Poppy Desmond, am not in a flap over turning thirty. I just don't want anyone to know it's happening next week. Or read a stupid list about all the things I should have done by now.

Instead, I'm going to write my own list. Number one: 'Go to New York for the weekend with three girlfriends for mystery VIP event.' Tick tick tick! I'm at Heathrow, about to jet off to Manhattan with Maggie and Rachel. We're meeting Lily at the Mercer, a swanky hotel in SoHo, where she's managed to swing us three free nights. She's refused to give us any details about what the event is, but who cares? It's in New York!

'Hey, beautiful. I'd recognise that ass anywhere,' says someone behind me in a terrible American accent. I turn around to see Rachel, her hair unbrushed and her denim shirt buttoned up wrong, looking exhausted and wired at the same time. As soon as we've hugged hello, she starts dancing around, singing tunelessly, 'Rum rum rum, rum rum rum rum, do doodle dee . . .' She tails off. 'No?'

'Sorry, darling, I give up. What is it?'

'*Sex and the City*!' Rachel exclaims. Her BlackBerry buzzes and she whips it out eagerly. 'Sorry,' she mutters as her thumbs dart around at bewildering speed. 'I'm overstimulated. Big case on at the minute. I've been up all night working and drinking Bed Rull, I mean Red Bull. Can we get a coffee? Where's Maggie? Where do we check in? We're going to New York!' She tries to stuff her BlackBerry in her pocket, drops it, retrieves it and jumps up and down again.

'OK, calm down,' I say, guiding her towards Costa. 'We're meeting Maggie here, remember? I need coffee too. I never sleep well before a flight, plus my mum rang me at six a.m. You won't believe what she was on about . . .'

'What, what?' Rachel asks breathlessly. 'Let's sit here. No, here. No, here! Here's the best!'

I don't think now is the time to discuss my manic mum with my manic friend. Instead, I hold the table while Rachel buys our cappuccinos, and close my eyes and take deep yoga breaths as I recall my conversation with Mum this morning.

In an attack of unprecedented madness, my mother has decided it's her duty to remind me that the women in my family tend to have – urk – very early menopauses. Hers began at thirty-five, apparently. And she thinks I should celebrate my thirtieth birthday by sharing this fact with my boyfriend.

'That reminds me,' she said innocently this morning, after giving me her views on ObamaCare, which was already a bit much when I was half-asleep. 'Have you had a chance to talk to Charlie yet?'

'Seriously, Mum!' I growled, sitting bolt upright, my happy dream of marshmallows and Michael Fassbender gone for ever. 'For the last time. We have been together *ten months*. Charlie is *twenty-six* years old. I can't start telling him about my menopause!'

'Well, I don't think it's a very good sign if you're afraid to have the conversation. But if you are—'

'Afraid! The only thing I'm afraid of is *being mental*.'

'If you are,' she continued relentlessly, 'I'd be more than happy to talk to him myself and make sure he knows the situation. I'm friends with him on Facebook, you know. I think you can get one cycle of IVF free on the NHS, but ideally—'

I stood up, clutching one hand to my head. 'Oh my God, Mother. If you dare bring this up with Charlie, I swear to God I will never speak to you again.' I knew this wasn't the best way to handle the situation, or put her off, but I was so incensed I couldn't think straight. Why couldn't I just lie, like a normal daughter? 'Yes, Mum, I've briefed Charlie about the state of my ovaries and he is on-message.'

Mum is obviously nuts to be worrying about my menopause. But the really annoying thing is, there is a grain of truth amongst all the crazy. Charlie is over three years younger than me – twenty-seven in June. In a week's time, we'll be in different decades. He might not want to settle down – or think about a family – for at least ten years. How can I possibly bring it up with him? It's way too soon. But if I don't . . .

Aargh. I am evicting my mother from my head. Thank God Charlie didn't stay the night and come with me to the airport, as he'd suggested. Imagine if he'd overheard our conversation! Early menopause: classic seduction tool.

'Hey, where's your steamer trunk?' Rachel says, plonking down two cappuccinos, three giant pastries and about twenty paper napkins, sugars and coffee-stirrers. 'Did you donate it to a museum?'

I roll my eyes at her. 'Of course not. It's been repurposed as a bedside table. I will admit, this wheelie thing is a tad more practical.'

'I'm not sure what I've brought,' says Rachel, swallowing half her coffee in one gulp and biting into a pastry. 'I packed quite quickly. I know I brought my swimsuit. Maybe a few swimsuits. Oh look, there's Maggie. Maggie! Over here!' She waves frantically before adding in a loud voice, 'What the hell is wrong with her?'

Maggie is trudging towards us, head down, pulling a wheelie suitcase that's the size of Rachel's and mine put together. Normally so chic and well groomed, she looks as if she got dressed in the dark: baggy leggings, pink trainers and a very unflattering green sweatshirt. Her pixie-cut hair is flat and messy, and she's not wearing make-up. This wouldn't be too odd with anyone else, but Maggie is a person who wears eyeliner to the gym. Maggie without mascara? Are these end times?

'Hi,' she says, sitting down heavily.

'How are you, darling?' I ask. 'What's the matter?'

'Maggie, cheer up,' says Rachel. 'Did you not hear? We're going to New York.'

'I did hear,' Maggie says. 'And you know what else I heard? Leo is officially dating that obnoxious Jenny.'

'How did you find out?' asks Rachel.

'I had my suspicions when I saw that they'd entered the London Marathon together. And last night I got this.' Maggie holds out her phone to both of us, to show us a text message from Leo: *Hi, just so you know, it's official now between Jen and I. Hope that makes you feel better about everything.*

'Hope that makes you *feel better* about everything?' I repeat.

'Patronising git,' says Rachel, banging the table so hard I jump. 'Idiot! Plonker. Knobhead. Loser. Gobshite!'

'Also his grammar's wrong,' I add. 'It should be "between Jen and me". Very common mistake.' I can't help it; I am a grammar nerd.

But Leo's grammar is the least of Maggie's problems. 'And that's not all,' she continues. 'I was stood up last night, by an internet date. I sat in bloody Pearl Bar in Covent Garden for twenty minutes before I finally texted him. He said he couldn't come because it was his birthday recently and he had to write thank-you letters.' She shakes her head. 'Leo has a new girlfriend already, and I'm being rejected by people I've never even met.'

Rachel, like me, is obviously trying to think of something positive to say.

'If he's never even met you, he's not rejecting you,' she says. 'And he's an idiot. Though a very polite one.'

'What about Leo, then?' says Maggie. 'What does it say about me that he'd prefer to go out with Jenny, who is officially the worst person in the world?'

'I don't know that she's *officially* the worst person in the world,' says Rachel judiciously. 'I mean, what about—'

'She is pretty bad, though,' I say, giving Rachel a discreet kick

275

under the table. 'But don't forget, you dumped Leo. Jenny is just . . . having your leftovers. Your congealed, scummy, mouldy leftovers. Out of the bin.'

Maggie's not listening. 'I don't get it,' she says. 'Even Hitler was married. What's wrong with me?'

'Nothing's wrong with you, darling,' I say, ignoring the Hitler thing and pulling her into a sideways hug. 'You're gorgeous and lovely and brilliant. And men are idiots.'

'No they're not. What about Sylvain?' Her face wobbles. 'I feel like Sylvain was the last bit of good luck I had. I should have stayed in the Alps. And you know the other annoying thing?'

We shake our heads, afraid to ask.

'All the married women in my lab telling me how lucky I am to be single. If it's so great, why don't they try it?'

'But they're right!' Rachel says. 'Being single is great. You don't need a man to be happy.'

'Oh no you don't,' Maggie says, pointing a menacing finger at her. 'I am not taking "you don't need a man" advice from someone with a lovely boyfriend.'

'Being single isn't all it's made out to be,' I agree. 'And it's not made out to be much.'

'Look. I know what you need to do.' Rachel is bouncing her leg so energetically that I have to grab my coffee cup to stop it from falling off the table. Maggie looks at her expectantly.

'Come to New York with us!' Rachel finishes, waving her empty coffee cup. 'Have a fantastic weekend and forget all about those two losers.' She makes an L sign on her forehead.

'Oh,' Maggie says sadly. 'I thought you had some real advice.'

Maggie turns down the offer of a tea and we head towards the check-in desk. Rachel, still wired, is chattering away non-stop about the case she's been working on and some new book she's been reading about how to talk to the head of your firm when you're stuck in a lift together. She's normally quite softly spoken, but not this morning; people in the queue are turning to stare at us. I decide to use the time to send an olive-branch text to Mum: *Sorry about being narky this morning, I know you mean well. Talk soon. Xx*

276

'I can't believe I got lash extensions for him,' Maggie is saying. 'Speaking of which . . . Shit! Don't tell me . . .' She bends down and starts rummaging in her bag.

I'm not sure if she's talking about Leo or the internet date, but I decide it's best not to ask, and make soothing noises while sighing internally. With Maggie in a dating quagmire and Rachel developing ADHD, this isn't exactly a dream weekend so far. Just as I'm thinking this, my phone buzzes with Mum's reply: *Good news! I've checked and it's three cycles of IVF that you can get on the NHS, not one. Xx Mum*

'Aaaaaaargh!' I drop my phone in a rage.

'Morning, ladies,' says the girl at the check-in desk. 'Is everything OK?' She's not looking at me, but at Maggie's woebegone face.

'Not really,' says Maggie. 'I got stood up last night, and my ex of four months has already got a new girlfriend.'

'Oh dear,' says the check-in girl – Patrice, according to her name badge – with polite sympathy and seen-it-all-before weariness. She's incredibly done-up for this time of the morning; even her eyeshadow is wearing eyeshadow.

'And I've just realised I've left my entire make-up bag, with all my favourite products, on the Tube.'

'No,' breathes Patrice in horror. 'Your entire bag? You poor thing! Mine would cost me *hundreds* to replace.'

'I know! Mine is going to be about that,' says Maggie. 'Brand-new Chanel Vitalumiere foundation . . . all my lipsticks . . . my Suqqu cheek brush—'

'A Suqqu brush?' the girl says, clutching her hands to her cheeks in horror. 'No! You poor, poor thing.'

'I should have insured it all really,' says Maggie.

'I tell you what.' Patrice leans forward and lowers her voice conspiratorially. 'Don't tell anyone, but . . . I think this might cheer you up.' She taps at her computer before issuing us with three boarding passes.

'Are you upgrading us?' Rachel asks, in her extra-loud voice.

'It's the least I can do. And good luck, darling! At least you're going to the right place to restock.'

* * *

We try to act nonchalant as we stroll away, but it's probably clear from the way we keep clutching each other and giggling that something's afoot.

'I'm SFU!' Rachel says, checking her boarding pass and jumping up and down. 'SFU! This is a life's ambition! Suitable for upgrade,' she explains. 'Do you know what this means? We can go to the first-class lounge!'

'I'm going to duty-free,' Maggie says. 'I've got to start replacing stuff. But where do I even start?' She looks panicked.

Together we persuade Maggie that it will be cheaper to buy make-up in New York, and we head to the first-class lounge. It's heaven: spacious, sun-drenched and calm – or at least it's calm before we get there.

'It's so quiet and peaceful here!' says Rachel loudly. 'And look at all the snacks! They're free! And coffee! I was just thinking I'd love a coffee!' She runs over to the breakfast buffet and starts loading up. Maggie and I sink into the huge, comfy chairs, hoping nobody realises we're with her.

'There's even an Elemis spa!' says Rachel, coming over with a tray piled high with enough mini pastries, cold cuts and cheese to last a week. 'We could all go and get pedicures and a hot stone massage!'

'I don't think we have time for massages,' I say, taking the tray from her before she sends it all flying. 'Rachel, why don't we sit down and have a little quiet time? Look, here are some magazines. Let me take this coffee away – I think you've had enough for now.'

The magazines and food keep her busy for a while. I start to relax and think that, given a few almond croissants and a Buck's Fizz, Mum's text and my impending menopause will soon be distant memories. I've also had a very sweet text from Charlie: *Fly safe, babe. I love you. Xxxxxxxx* He always puts about eight x's in a text, which I find incredibly endearing. In fact sometimes we exchange text messages that just consist of x's. It's all pretty sickening. Sighing happily, I decide that this is going to be a great weekend after all.

I've never turned left on a plane before. There's no queuing or shoving; we each glide to our own white-draped throne – it's more of a bed than a seat, with a lovely white blanket that feels like cashmere and that I'm very tempted to steal. And more Elemis products, which I discreetly snaffle after I rub in the luxurious hand cream and – miracle of miracles – lie down.

'Look! I'm lying down *on a plane*,' I tell Rachel. The whole experience seems to have overawed her; she's been quiet for least five minutes.

'I'm not sure I can ever go back to normal flying again,' she says, sounding worried.

Soon we're in the air. Maggie's trying to read, but Rachel and I are lounging in our seats in a lordly fashion, rubbing ourselves all over with Elemis and chatting and giggling manically about our good luck. The businessman across the aisle is giving us an odd look, even more so as I start working my Elemis hand cream into my hair.

'Flying is very dehydrating,' Rachel explains to him. He nods and retreats quickly behind his *Financial Times*.

On Rachel's other side, Maggie still has her book open – *One Hundred Years of Solitude* – but she's not reading it; instead she's staring into space.

'You know what I've decided?' she says suddenly. 'I'm not going to talk to a single man for this entire weekend. I'm serious. Not a waiter, not a . . . a taxi driver, nothing. I'm having a mancation. A *hombre* holiday.'

'A bloke break,' suggests Rachel.

'Are you sure, darling?' I ask. 'After all, we are going to this VIP event. What if you meet Ryan Gosling?'

'Yeah, about this event,' says Rachel, drumming her fingers on her little side table. 'Do we have any clue yet what it is? Has Lily said anything to you, Maggie? Also, if she lives in LA, why is she doing this thing in New York?'

'Not a word,' says Maggie. 'She's being extremely mysterious.'

'Maybe it's a strip club,' says Rachel. She slaps her knee. 'Lily's opening a strip club . . . and we're the acts.' She's bent over with laughter, delighted with herself. Maggie and I stare at her, puzzled.

'I think it's probably just some product launch or other,' says Maggie.

I'm not so sure. Lily is an events manager, and she's worked on some very high-profile launches and is Twitter friends with a number of A- and B-listers. I'm guessing it's a private screening of a new film, with the stars and directors. Which wouldn't be awful. As long as Rachel calms down by then; in her current state, I could see her leaping straight into Mark Ruffalo's lap.

'Would you like some champagne, ladies?' asks the air steward, beaming at us.

Rachel and I say yes please. Maggie grabs my arm and nods at me urgently. Of course: she's not talking to men. This is going to be a pain.

'She'll have one too,' I say. The steward looks puzzled.

'She's taken a vow of silence,' Rachel explains, taking her glass and half-draining it in one swallow.

'You know you might have to talk to a man at immigration, don't you?' I ask, once he's left.

Maggie sighs. 'Fine. As long as he's in a Perspex box.'

'Can I have another champagne?' Rachel asks the steward.

I've lined up two films and three episodes of *Parks and Recreation*, which should get me through the flight, but before I'm half an hour into the first one, I feel my eyes closing.

After what feels like ten minutes, I wake up to the sound of an announcement about landing.

'Landing?' I say, yawning and looking around blearily. 'What? Landing where?'

'Where do you think, Atlantis?' says Rachel, bouncing up and down in her seat. 'New Yoik, baby! You slept the whole time. Not us. We were awake, weren't we, Mags?'

Maggie nods, looking stony-faced.

'Thank God you're awake. She's been talking non-stop for the past six hours,' she hisses to me, while Rachel goes to the loo. 'I couldn't watch a single film! First she was going on and on about all the things she wants to see in New York and about how she's going to climb the stairs in her office building instead of going to the gym. Then she started talking to the guy across the way about how, when you find your soulmate, you just know.'

'What?' Looking at the businessman across the aisle, I can see he's shrunk deep in his seat, headphones clutched protectively to his ears.

'Oh, and she was also telling him she's a . . . master of the dark art of tort law? I really hope they don't sell Red Bull in America,' Maggie says.

The queue for immigration is as hellish as ever; this is one guest list Lily couldn't get us on. And I'm nervous when Rachel starts quizzing the man in the box about the finer points of immigration law. But eventually we're safely out and queuing for a taxi. Although it's only April, it feels like summer and we're all peeling off layers – Rachel tries to remove her denim shirt before we remind her she's got nothing on underneath.

'Is it OK if I do the talking?' I ask, as we queue for cabs. 'I've got our directions all planned out, so we don't sound like tourists.' I also don't want the driver noticing Rachel's state in case he refuses to take her.

Rachel interrupts. 'Hold on one cotton-picking second,' she says in her terrible American accent. 'What have we here?'

She points over to a massive red convertible with a shonky home-made sign beside it: 'Ride to the Big Apple in Style in a 1958 Chrysler Convertible with Jim's Tours. Only $200 per trip.'

'Isn't that a bit – expensive?' 'Tacky?' Maggie and I say in unison, but Rachel has already charged ahead and is thrusting dollar bills at the driver. We shrug and pile in after her, giggling and putting on our sunglasses.

Unfortunately, our luggage won't fit in the tiny boot, so the three of us have to squash into the back with all our bags on top of us and Maggie's case in the front seat. Plus, Jim of Jim's Tours looks about fifteen and stalls twice before we've even left the airport.

'Hi, ladies, it's my pleasure to take you to Manhattan,' he says as we join the freeway. 'Let me start by telling you about the history of our great city. Founded in 1624 by the Dutch fur—'

Rachel interrupts him. 'Have you got an iPod dock? I made a New York playlist!'

Jim, getting the message, abandons his commentary and sticks on Rachel's playlist, which starts with 'Hot in the City' by Billy

Idol. As we drive through Brooklyn, hipsters in beanie hats look at us pityingly – what with our teenage driver, Rachel dancing in her seat and all of us singing along to the theme music from *Working Girl*, we're not cool.

Then the view we've been waiting for comes into sight, and we all scream in excitement. Before us is Manhattan under the blue April sky, its towers shining in the sun, and right ahead, the Williamsburg Bridge with its elegant red lines and double-arched tower.

'Quick! "Empire State of Mind"!' yells Rachel. Jim obliges, and as we speed across the bridge, we're all singing along at the top of our voices, though none of us really know the words. When it gets to the chorus, Rachel takes off her seat belt, and, despite our yells of protest, stands up in the moving car and thrusts her arm in the air, hair whipping in the breeze. Not knowing the lyrics, she settles for 'Da da da da DA DA . . .' before falling sideways into my lap as Maggie and I scream hysterically.

'Miss! Sit down, please!' yells Jim, swerving in alarm. 'I'm not insured! It's my dad's car! He'll kill me if I do anything to it!'

'What? That's outrageous!' Rachel says indignantly, whipping off her sunglasses. 'Is your name even Jim?'

Maggie and I manage to calm her down, and then we're over the bridge and driving along through the Lower East Side, Chinatown, Little Italy and SoHo. The traffic's slowed to a crawl and Maggie's trying to take pictures of everything at once. Meanwhile, the Chrysler's attracting plenty of attention all of its own: tourists are filming us and Rachel is giving regal waves from behind her sunglasses like Jackie O. She's also keeping up a running commentary on how she's getting rid of her Oyster card and buying a convertible when we get back to London.

'It just makes so much *sense*,' she keeps saying.

I'm ignoring her and concentrating on the New York sights: the green and white street signs, the brownstone buildings and the trees, the men in baggy shorts and baseball caps and the actress-model-whatever types loping along sipping iced lattes. All too soon we arrive at the corner of Mercer and Prince streets in SoHo. Jim boots us out, but not before Rachel insists on taking pictures of us all with him and the car, while traffic piles up behind us hooting furiously. I tip Jim an extra twenty dollars and he skedaddles, thrilled to get rid of us.

'So much for us not seeming like tourists,' Maggie says as we watch the Chrysler drive off, leaving a crowd of gawpers in its wake.

'Now we need to find the hotel,' I say. 'It's somewhere on this corner.'

Rachel's looking up, teetering around in circles and craning her neck. 'I think the hotel . . . *is* the corner,' she says, in tones of profound insight.

Examining the wall with her fingertips like a blind person, she finds the revolving entrance and crashes through with such force that she manages to go around twice before falling into the lobby. Maggie and I hurry after her, dragging her suitcase, which she's abandoned on the pavement outside.

'Would you look at this place! It's like a library. Look at all the books arranged by colour! Ooh, that chair looks comfy.' She flings herself down on a giant armchair, legs stretched out in front of her. I've just spotted a miniature vodka bottle sticking out of her handbag. It's five in the afternoon; I hope we don't get kicked out before we've even checked in.

'Guys! You're here! How was the flight?'

It's Lily. She runs over to hug us all, looking very glamorous in an oversized black mesh top, with her long, slim legs in tight grey jeans. She's wearing sky-high black platform heels, and her blond waves are falling around her face.

'It was great! Maggie lost her make-up and we flew first class!' Rachel announces at top volume, jumping to her feet to greet Lily. 'And I almost fell out of the car! How are you? I'm so excited! New York!'

Various fashionista types are now looking up from their laptops and cocktails in polite horror. I make 'Get her out of here' signals to Lily.

'I tell you what,' Lily says, 'let's go straight up to our rooms. I've already got the keys. Rachel and Poppy, you're sharing one room, and Maggie and I are next door.'

Before Rachel can object, we drag her to the lift and bundle her upstairs to our room. It's gorgeous: neutral sleek decor, two gigantic beds, lofty ceiling. There's a handwritten note welcoming us to the Mercer, and even a complimentary bottle of Pinot Noir, which I quickly stash in the bathroom cupboard before Rachel spots it.

'What's happened?' Lily whispers, following me into the bathroom.

'Nothing. Maggie's lost her make-up and Rachel's lost her mind.'

'Whoa,' Rachel says, from next door. 'I feel sort of weird suddenly.'

We rush back into the bedroom. She's sitting on her bed, fingertips pressed to her forehead. We make her lie down, pull off her shoes and find her some salted pretzels and mineral water.

'Do you feel sick at all?' Maggie asks, putting a stainless-steel bin beside her.

'No, I'm just . . . crashing. Think I was on a bit of a high earlier,' she says indistinctly. Within seconds she's asleep, a half-chewed pretzel on the pillow beside her.

'Oh, thank God,' whispers Maggie, as we tiptoe out of the room. 'What was that? You don't think she's got a drug problem, do you, Poppy?'

'No. But I definitely need a drink.'

'Me too. Let me just . . .' and Maggie opens the door of their room, shoves her bag inside and closes the door. 'Ready!'

'Seriously? You don't want to unpack and change first?' Lily asks, bewildered. Maggie normally likes to move in and unpack fully once she arrives somewhere, and have a full costume change between events.

Maggie shrugs. 'What's the point? You look great, though, Lily. Are you . . . How come . . .?'

Lily throws back her head and laughs. 'How come I look presentable, you mean? I had a meeting. Come on, let's head to the bar.'

Downstairs, the bar is already filling up with shoppers wielding big bags and people having civilised afternoon drinks. I tell myself that nobody remembers us from earlier, though this is probably wishful thinking. We find a table and order a round of Cosmopolitans

– Lily's suggestion. 'I know it's a massive cliché, but this was part of my New York fantasy,' she explains. 'The four of us together, having Cosmos! Though I didn't think we'd be one man down so soon.'

'Could I see some ID, miss?' the waiter asks me.

'Oh my God! Are you serious?' I ask, thrilled. 'Of course you can!' I show him my passport, before stuffing it away in my bag so the girls don't see my date of birth. This holiday is going to be a birthday-free zone.

'If it isn't my favourite English party planner! How are you, Lily? Everything OK?' A dark-haired guy in a cream suit has breezed up to us: very handsome, with beautifully waxed eyebrows that put mine to shame. Lily jumps up to hug him.

'Girls, this is Christian, who's hosting us here at the Mercer. Christian, these are my friends Poppy and Maggie.'

'Lovely to meet you,' I say.

'I adore your hair,' Christian says to Maggie. 'Very Jennifer Lawrence.'

Maggie just smiles and raises her eyebrows expressively. Christian looks puzzled, but continues, 'I hope Luis comped you these drinks? Great. Anything at all you need, let me know. Oh, I almost forgot. My stylist friend said she could pull a few outfits for you tomorrow. I'll leave them in your room, yes?'

At this, Maggie's eyes widen and she looks mutely at Lily.

'Wonderful! That is brilliant, Christian. Thank you! Can you stay and have a drink with us?'

'I would love to, but I've got to interview some pet pedicurists. Have fun, girls!' And he's gone.

'Look at you, Miss Well-Connected,' I say admiringly, taking a sip of my Cosmo. 'How do you know him? Has he got something to do with your mystery event?'

'No. He used to be the concierge at Chateau Marmont – which is the sister hotel of this place, in LA – and we've worked on a ton of events together. So when I told him I was coming to Manhattan, he said we had to stay here.' She shrugs. I'm impressed: Lily's only lived in Los Angeles for six months, but she's obviously got the States sewn up, coast to coast.

'But what was he saying about outfits? I was dying to ask him, but I couldn't,' says Maggie.

'Oh, yes. He's got some dresses for us, because it will be very glam. I knew you'd bring lovely dresses of your own, but I thought it could be fun for you to have some real red-carpet stuff.'

'What about you?' Maggie asks.

'I've already got a dress.' She shivers with excitement. 'I hope it goes well! I've never been so nervous before an event.'

'Not even when you organised Chris Pine's birthday party?' Maggie says.

'Oh God, it's bigger than that.'

'Does it involve Luther Carson?' I ask. He's a big star, and Lily knows him.

'In a way, yes. Him and others.'

'Is it a performance?' Maggie asks.

'Um – I suppose so. Yes.' Lily wriggles in her seat. 'But please don't ask me any more questions or you'll spoil it! The whole thing's completely confidential.'

'Can't you even tell us where it is? Or when?'

'Downtown, tomorrow at five o'clock. Near Wall Street. And that's my last word.'

Maggie's peering at herself in the mirror behind the bar. 'God. Is that what I look like without make-up? I'm like a mouse.'

'Don't be silly, darling, you look lovely,' I say. 'But you can borrow some of my stuff if you want. I've got fake lashes and everything.'

'Thanks . . . I can't believe I've lost all my make-up just as I'm attending my first and last red-carpet event. I presume there will be photographers at this thing, Lily?' Maggie asks.

'Yes,' says Lily. 'But bring your own cameras as well. And that is positively the last question I'm answering. The actual event will only last about an hour, I think, and then we can go out afterwards. And before you ask, Mags, *tomorrow* is our big night out. I'll want to celebrate once this thing is safely done. Now, where do you want to have dinner?'

The next morning, we meet in the lobby at nine thirty. I slept pretty well considering the time difference, although I woke up a few times and took the opportunity to check that Rachel was still alive. Lily's back in her usual jeans, white T-shirt and trainers, and Maggie is looking more like herself in a striped Breton T-shirt dress and ballet pumps, but is still make-up free.

'You know, I really like your no-make-up look,' I tell her. 'Your skin is so amazing, you should go bare more often.'

'That's what I was saying!' says Lily. 'It's very off-duty model.'

'Hardly,' Maggie says, patting her cheeks cautiously. 'I look washed out. But it'll be good for me – take me out of my comfort zone. No men, no make-up.'

'Where's Girl, Interrupted?' Lily asks.

'Rachel? She's fine. She was in the shower when I left.'

'Morning,' says a hoarse voice. We look up to see Rachel approaching us slowly, wearing a sequinned long-sleeved black top, green linen Bermuda shorts and orange sports sandals. Her wet hair's in a bun and she looks dazed.

'How are you feeling?' asks Maggie mischievously.

'Like I've been tumble-dried,' says Rachel, sitting down and looking at us apprehensively. 'How long was I asleep?'

'About fifteen hours.'

She winces. 'I am so, so sorry about yesterday.'

'It's OK, Rachel,' says Lily, patting her hand. 'We know about the amphetamines.'

'I wasn't on amphetamines!' says Rachel, at which the business meeting beside us looks up. 'Urgh. My throat is sore from talking so much yesterday. What . . . what was I saying?'

'You were going to buy a convertible because it makes more sense than an Oyster card,' I tell her.

'And you had a lot to say about soulmates to that guy on the plane,' Maggie says. 'And do you remember standing up in the car, on the way from the airport? You almost fell out.'

Rachel buries her face in her hands as we all giggle mercilessly.

'I'm so sorry. It's this Hennings case, it's been a nightmare. I had eleven Red Bulls on Thursday night, and with all that champagne on the plane . . . I must have gone temporarily mad. I'm so embarrassed.' She plucks at her sequinned top. 'And I seem to have taken a lucky-dip approach to packing.'

'It's not much weirder than my outfit,' I tell her. I'm wearing a green and yellow printed 1950s dress with Clarks brogues and heart-shaped sunglasses. 'Come on. Let's get some breakfast into you.'

Breakfast at the hotel is probably great, but we want to see as much of New York as possible, so we decide to go out to a café called Jack's Wife Freda on Lafayette Street. It's a gorgeous sunny morning, and the air is full of that New York buzz. The sky is blue, the air's fresh and as we wander through SoHo, everyone's smiling – us most of all.

'Look, the magnolia trees are coming into bloom,' says Rachel.

'Look, the new collection has landed at Marc Jacobs,' says Maggie.

The café is lovely, all leather banquettes and marble tables, and sunlight streaming through the windows. They're playing Rufus Wainwright's cover of 'Across the Universe' by the Beatles; one of my favourite songs. Four glasses of iced water are plonked down in front of us as soon as we sit down; Rachel drains hers in one swallow.

'I hope they can manage a decent cup of tea,' says Maggie. 'Oh no, it's a man. Poppy, can you ask him for me?'

'OK,' I say, sighing. 'What are the instructions again? And Maggie, I can't be your interpreter for ever. You'll have to start speaking to men at some point.'

The great thing about America, though, is the way they're willing to cater to the most mad requests. So when I ask the waiter for boiling water and an empty cup, he says, 'Sure!' Everyone watches Maggie assemble her cup of tea with the tea bag she brought, and we all applaud when she finishes it off with a dash of milk.

'Ah, breakfast in America,' I say happily, drizzling maple syrup over my pancakes. 'I could quite easily spend all day eating breakfast here.' I remember to take a picture for Charlie; like me, he's a pancake fiend.

'What is our plan, though?' asks Maggie, grinding pepper on to her veggie omelette. 'We've got to get to the thing by five, did you say, Lily?'

'A bit before if that's OK. Quarter of,' says Lily.

'Quarter *of*?' says Maggie. 'You really have gone native.'

'I have to!' Lily protests. 'They don't understand me otherwise. I once arranged to meet someone at half-two and he thought I meant one thirty. And don't get me started on pants.'

'You like it here, though, don't you?' says Maggie, wistfully.

'I don't like it,' Lily says. Swallowing a giant bite of her breakfast burrito, she pauses dramatically before saying, 'I *love* it. I mean, I miss you guys, but I love Los Angeles, love living by the ocean, love the whole thing.' She waves her coffee cup to illustrate her point; the waiter comes by and gives us all a refill. 'See? Coffee refills. What's not to love?' she finishes.

'So you really prefer LA to . . . Bromley?' Maggie shakes her head. 'You might have Beverly Hills, but we've got The Glades shopping centre.'

We all laugh, but Maggie looks sad. 'You know how you're organising this event here? Does that mean you might be moving to New York?' she asks hopefully. 'That would be much closer than LA.'

'No, this thing is a one-off. Anyway, I wouldn't want to live in New York. It's cool, but it's too frenetic and angsty for me. Everyone looks so stressed out. LA is much more relaxed.'

Rachel has already finished her pancakes and taken out a guidebook with a forest of Post-its stuck into it. She's indestructible; her caffeine hangover is obviously a distant memory. 'So for today,' she says, 'I was thinking we could start with the Guggenheim and the Met, then walk across Central Park and get the subway up to the Cloisters.' She reads from her guidebook: '"This medieval art museum is a little-known highlight of the Upper West Side, with scenic views all over the Hudson."'

Lily and Maggie are looking non-committal. 'Hm,' says Rachel, laughing. 'Do I detect a case of the Colosseums?' I know she's referring to their holiday in Rome, when she wanted to march them around a load of sights and the others were having none of it.

'We can always divide and conquer. I'll do some culture with you, Rachel, while the others grab New York by the carrier-bag handles,' I offer.

'Mmm, shopping,' says Maggie, rubbing her hands.

'Are you sure you want to go shopping, Mags?' asks Lily, less enthusiastic. 'Aren't you meant to be saving for a deposit for a flat?'

Maggie shakes her head. 'I've given that up. I'm going to be renting for the rest of my life, so I may as well do it in style.'

'So you've abandoned the beach hut scheme?' asks Rachel innocently. We try to keep straight faces, until Maggie starts laughing and we all join in. I'd forgotten this mad idea of hers.

'I know, I know. It seemed genius at the time, but I hadn't thought through all the practicalities. Like plumbing. And heating. Little things like that.'

'But imagine waking up every morning to the sound of the waves,' Rachel says, which sets us all off again.

We pay the bill and say our goodbyes, with Lily giving us some last-minute info. 'Don't forget, Christian's got some outfits for you to wear if you want to. He'll leave them in our room. Oh, and I've booked you all a Town Car for four p.m. I've got to be there early, so we can just meet at the venue. Maggie has the address.' She looks very keyed up; she's obviously extremely nervous.

'No further questions,' says Rachel. 'Let's get to it!'

'Good luck, darling. I'm sure it will be fabulous,' I say, giving Lily a hug.

We arrange to meet Maggie back at the hotel at three, and Rachel and I head off towards the Guggenheim – on foot, so I can walk off my pancakes.

'That's the only way I can stay ahead of Charlie's cooking,' I explain as we head uptown, in the general direction of Central Park. 'I walk to and from work every day. Otherwise I'd be the size of a house.'

'You're lucky he's such a great cook. Oliver's idea of cooking is pasta and Dolmio sauce,' Rachel says. I smile. She often pretends to complain about her boyfriend, in the same way she complains about all the hours she has to put in at her law firm. But she doesn't fool me: she loves them both.

We're at the Guggenheim for an hour and a half, spending almost as much time admiring the incredible snail-shaped building as the art inside. Then we decide that's enough culture, cross Fifth Avenue and head towards Central Park. Looking at the lines of horse-drawn carriages, the pretzel sellers and the hot-dog stands, I sigh happily. Work, London, my angst over turning thirty all seem a long way away. As does my impending menopause.

'What are you laughing at?' says Rachel.

'Doesn't matter. I'll tell you when we're sitting down.'

We get hot dogs and two bottles of water, and take them into the park. After strolling for a while, we find ourselves by the lake, which is looking stunning, with floods of white cherry blossom reflected in the water, and the skyscrapers of New York floating up out of the greenery. We take turns seeing how many we can spot: the Empire State Building, the pink Trump Tower, and of course, the Chrysler building. Though we might have got a few of them wrong.

'I'm going to send these to Oliver and make him jealous,' says Rachel, taking about a hundred pictures.

'How is Oliver?' I ask, as we sit down under a cherry tree.

'He's fine,' Rachel says. She looks so blissfully happy that I'm not at all surprised when she adds, 'He's asked me to move in with him. It is very soon, but it might be sensible – you know, we could sell both our places, get something better *and* see each other more often. We both work such long hours, it's awkward travelling back and forth . . .'

'Very sensible,' I agree, smiling. 'So it sounds like Project Rachel is all going well?'

She nods. 'Project Rachel is showing good deliverables in the key areas of work, relationship and home. Finally. What about Project Poppy?'

'Um . . .' I was all set to tell her about my conversation with my mum but it seems ridiculous, on this sunny spring day, to start talking about my biological clock. 'I'm fine! Work's fine, flat's fine, Charlie's fine. He's talking about leaving publishing and setting up a café, did I mention that?'

'Ooh, that sounds fab,' says Rachel. 'He could start with a supper club, couldn't he?'

'Yes, he's mentioned that.' I pause, and force myself to continue. 'I suppose . . . I do worry that we might be on different time frames. In terms of settling down and, um, having a family. But it seems way too early to bring it up.'

'No it's not. Talk to him about it,' Rachel says immediately.

I nod, but I realise suddenly I don't want to, for the stupidest reason: because it would be unromantic. I don't want him to feel he has to settle down because his elderly girlfriend is putting the thumbscrews on him. I want him to be the one to suggest it – the way Oliver's suggested the next step to Rachel. Otherwise how will I ever know that it's what he really wants?

'God, look at the time,' Rachel says. 'We'd better get back to the hotel for our red-carpet treatment.'

Since we're running late, we decide to get a cab, and before long we're back at the Mercer, where Maggie is contemplating a rail full of dresses and boxes of shoes and accessories.

'What a great job perk,' says Rachel. 'This almost never happens in law firms. That's funny . . . they're all different shades of blue. Isn't there anything black?'

'There must be some kind of dress code, or theme,' says Maggie, who's in heaven rifling through the dresses. 'What about this one? With maybe these booties? Oh my God, it's Elie Saab!'

'Has Lily left already?' I ask. 'Did you help her get ready?'

'No! She insisted she didn't want me to, and she left without me even seeing her. I've never seen her in such a state.'

'Did she give you invitations or anything?' I ask, holding up a petrol-blue halter-neck number against myself.

'No. She said she'd wait outside for us. Oh, no.' She's holding up an exquisite pale blue minidress, with long sleeves, lace-appliquéd all over. 'This is so pretty. But it won't work with my no make-up vow.'

'Maybe you're being overambitious – with no make-up and no talking to men,' Rachel says.

'How about if I curl your lashes and add tinted lip balm?' I suggest. 'That won't count, and it's honestly all you need.'

An hour and lots of costume changes later, we're all set to go. Rachel's hair has been backcombed into a high pony, and she's in a blue printed poplin dress with black leather sandals. Maggie's wearing her Elie Saab minidress, and I'm thrilled with my floor-length halter-neck dress from Halston Heritage. We're so busy taking pictures of each other we almost forget about the Town Car, and they have to ring us from the lobby to remind us.

'I'm quite nervous,' says Maggie as we drive off. 'Is that really sad? I keep on wondering what to say if I meet someone famous. Do you think it's better to pretend not to know who they are, or to say you love their work?'

'Love their work, definitely,' I say, checking my reflection in my little gold compact mirror. 'Will you tell me if one of my eyelashes comes loose? I don't want it to drop in my champagne just as I'm chatting to Hugh Jackman.'

'I probably won't know who anyone is anyway,' says Rachel. 'Did I tell you about the time I met what's-his-name . . . Dominic Cooper? It was at a party. I asked him if he'd been in anything I'd seen, and he said he was the fiancé in *Mamma Mia*. I said, "Really? But that guy was really buff!" He was incredibly nice about it, though. Cute, too.'

'But you won't have to worry about talking to Dominic Cooper,' I remind Maggie. 'You've taken a vow of silence with men, remember?'

'Dammit!' she murmurs. 'Damn. Ooh, I think we're here.'

The car has stopped outside a big stone building. It looks very grand from what I can make out from the window – a flight of steps, and pillars at the top.

'Where's the red carpet?' asks Maggie, as we climb out and walk up the steps.

'There are lots of people going in and out,' says Rachel. She looks up and reads the sign outside the building. 'New York City Hall. Hm. Are you sure this is the place?'

'Yes! Look, there's Lily,' Maggie says, pointing to the top of the steps. Then she stops dead. 'Oh my God.'

We look up to see Lily coming slowly down the steps towards us. She's wearing . . . I blink. A fifties-style white dress, with a sweetheart neckline and a full skirt. And silver pumps. She's carrying a bouquet. And wearing a veil.

This can't be what I think it is. This is a new trend, right? Wedding chic. Maybe it's a Japanese craze that's spread to New

York. Or she didn't pack anything smart so she borrowed a wedding dress. And a veil. That must be it.

'Bridesmaids,' Rachel says, clutching my arm. She indicates our dresses. 'That's why the colours match. We're bridesmaids.'

'Hi, girls!' Lily says, stepping down towards us. 'Perfect timing. You all look great!'

'Is this a film? Do you have a part in something?' Rachel asks. We all look around hopefully. There are plenty of other people here – that is, other couples, in dresses and suits, surrounded by friends and family taking photos. But no movie cameras. Lily shakes her head.

'Are you and Jesse getting married?' asks Maggie. 'That's it, isn't it? You're back together and you're getting married!'

Lily puts back her veil with a sigh. 'No. That would have been easier, but I wouldn't have done that to Jesse. I am getting married, though.'

'You're getting married,' Rachel repeats. 'To whom?'

Before Lily can reply, Maggie bursts out, 'But you said there were going to be VIPs! I've been practising my Hollywood small talk!'

Lily indicates us. 'You're the VIPs! I couldn't get married without you here.'

'Lily,' Rachel says in a deliberately calm voice, 'is this a visa marriage?'

'Of course,' says Lily. 'Look, the truth is, I've lost my job. My boss has decided to cut back, and she's letting me and another girl go. It's nothing we did wrong; we were the last ones in . . . Now I've got ninety days to leave the US. And I can't do that. I love it here. I want to stay, and this is the only way to do it.'

I think we're all in shock; we all want to shake her and tell her she's crazy, but we're too stunned to even know where to start.

'But can't you get another job?' I ask. 'You said you had a meeting yesterday?'

'That was an interview, and he said he liked me but he can't justify paying for my visa. That's what I keep hearing. The only way is to marry a US citizen.'

'Shh! Keep your voice down,' says Rachel. 'Come on, over here.' And she marches us all down to the bottom of the steps. One family group after another is walking up and down past us; we have to stand aside to let a couple pose while people throw confetti. Little do they know a crime is being discussed just out of shot.

'Who's the guy?' I ask. 'And what's in it for him?'

'That's the great thing,' says Lily. 'You see, he's in the military. And he gets better quarters and leave if he gets married. And they go easy on people in the army, so no one is ever going to ask him. I've researched it all and it'll be fine.'

'I'm sure you have, but it's not happening,' says Rachel.

'What do you mean?' Lily asks.

'I mean we can't let you go through with this,' says Rachel. 'You're talking about committing a crime, Lily. It's called marriage fraud and they take it very seriously. You'll be deported. You could even go to prison. Either way, you'll have a criminal record and you won't be allowed back into America. Ever.'

Like spectators at a tennis match, Maggie and I swivel back at Lily to see her reaction.

'I won't,' she says calmly. 'Honestly, Rachel, it's foolproof. An Australian girl I know in LA married a soldier in a set-up like this, and that was five years ago and she's got her green card now. They always turn a blind eye to soldiers, especially if they've got exemplary records. *My* fiancé has a medal.'

She sounds almost proud, and with a sinking heart I realise she's getting into character; she's going deep. We swivel back over to look at Rachel.

'You know that even once you've got married,' she says, 'you won't get the visa right away? They'll make you go back to the UK and apply for it from there.'

'They won't! There's an exception for military spouses,' Lily says triumphantly.

Rachel continues, 'And they'll investigate your relationship with this guy – they'll want to see details of your history together, where you met, email exchanges, airline tickets, everything. God almighty, Lily,' suddenly she sounds very Irish as well as agitated, 'have you never seen *Green Card*?'

'We've figured all that out,' Lily says. 'He can fake letters to and from his base. He's been in Afghanistan. They're not going to say boo to him.'

There's an awful silence, broken tentatively by Maggie.

'Maybe you could call off the wedding for now,' she suggests, 'and sort of get to know this guy instead? If you hit it off, maybe it will become a real thing . . . you know, it could be . . . romantic?'

Poor Maggie. I know she doesn't really believe this will happen; she's just hating the tension, as am I.

Suddenly Rachel laughs, and shakes her head. 'OK,' she says. 'I've said what I think, and now it's up to you. If you want to do this, and potentially go to prison or get deported . . . I can't stop you.'

'Right,' says Lily. 'Thanks.' She seems nonplussed, as if she'd expected more of a fight. She looks at me. 'What do you think?'

'Honestly, babe, I think it's a completely insane idea. And I can't bear to think of you in prison. You'd have to have a mullet, and a prison wife, and wear the same knickers for months.' Lily smiles, which makes me even more irritated. It wasn't a joke!

'How about you, Maggie?'

'Lily, *surely* there's another way. You got one job; you could get another one. Or become a nanny, or something – but don't do this marriage thing. *Please* don't do it.'

But Lily is adamant. 'None of you have to come if you don't want to, but I'm doing it anyway. We did the paperwork here yesterday, and we're all set to go.'

'What's the guy's name?' Maggie asks.

'Ryan,' she says promptly. 'Lance Corporal Ryan Bruckner, of the US Marine Corps. Mrs Lily Bruckner; it's got a ring to it, hasn't it? Speaking of which . . .' She holds out her left hand to show us a vintage-looking ring with white and blue stones. 'Ryan bought it for me in Dubai, on his way home from Helmand last Christmas. Isn't it perfect?'

You would think that anyone with half a brain would march Lily straight off to the police, but instead we follow her back up the steps of the building, as if we're sleepwalking. She's completely in character now, giving us the whole backstory of her whirlwind romance with Ryan and how they met (at a bachelorette party in Miami, apparently). I grab Maggie's arm as we're about to enter the building, and pull her behind a pillar for a quick confab.

'Maggie!' I hiss urgently. 'She's your best friend. Can't you talk her out of this?'

'I honestly don't think so,' Maggie says. 'I've known her since she was nine. Once she's set her mind on something, it's impossible to stop her. And I know it sounds insane, but if anyone can get away with something like this, it's her.'

'But we've got to be able to stop her. It's three against one. You're sporty, aren't you? You could take her! She's a skinny thing!'

'You think?' says Maggie. 'I think if the three of us tried to carry her out of a public building, kicking and screaming, people would intervene. Then we'd be the ones getting arrested.'

'What is she like?' I say, suddenly furious. 'Why did she have to put us through this? It's a fucking nightmare!' A mother-of-the-bride going past gives me an odd look, and I hastily plaster on an 'Isn't this lovely?' smile.

'I don't mean to make excuses,' Maggie's saying, 'but the thing is, Lily is younger than us. She's only twenty-four.'

'Only twenty-four! This would be a stupid stunt to pull if she was *fourteen*! I'm going to take her aside and try and talk some sense into her. You and Rachel see if you can come up with some kind of plan B.' And we go inside to catch up with the other two.

We're in a vast marble lobby, with a high ceiling and a flight of steps leading to more floors above. It's a mixture of business-like and bizarre: people in suits with briefcases, who obviously work here, and couples in white dresses and tuxedos getting photographed by tearful relatives. I've never seen so many women in wedding dresses in one place; it's like a bridal convention. Rachel's sitting on a bench, thumbing furiously at her phone. Lily's disappeared.

'What are you doing?' I ask, panicked. 'Where is she?'

'She's in the loo. I'm reading up on marriage fraud,' she says. 'Here's my plan so far. We interrupt the ceremony and say we don't think they know each other well enough to get married.'

'Would that work?' asks Maggie.

'I'm not sure, but it should cause enough of a diversion to stop the wedding from going ahead.' Rachel sighs. 'Unless we tell them that it's a visa marriage, in which case she probably *would* get arrested. But that might be better, because they'd let her off more lightly if it was only attempted . . . I think. Oh God, this is worse than my finals.'

'Are you sure she's in the loo?' says Maggie. 'What if she's already gone ahead with it?'

'Shit!' Rachel jumps to her feet and we all start scurrying frantically around the crowded lobby as best we can in our extra-high heels. We must look like such idiots, all dressed up to the nines and running in circles while dodging photographers and couples left, right and centre.

'Too many girls in white dresses! It's like looking for a needle in a fecking haystack!' snarls Rachel.

'Look! She's over there,' I say. 'I think she's made some friends.'

We hurry over to where Lily is sitting on a bench, holding court with three tiny old ladies, who are oohing and aahing over her ring. One of them has pink-rinsed hair and a pink tracksuit, and is wearing glasses with winged corners like Dame Edna Everage. The other's got a blue rinse, a blue dress and a cane, while the third lady has purple hair and a gigantic badge with the American flag on it.

'Oh, hi, girls,' says Lily, looking up. 'Meet Estelle and Marie and Dolores. They come here every week to see the weddings!'

'Call me Dolly, dear,' says the blue-rinse lady, in a real Noo Yoik accent.

'I was just telling the ladies about Ryan's medal,' Lily continues.

'That's wonderful,' says Dolly. 'I so admire the men and women of our armed forces. You must be very proud of him, huh?'

'Oh, I am,' says Lily piously.

'Are you having music at the ceremony? What's your something blue?' asks Purple Rinse.

'Garter belt,' Lily says. 'And we're having "Up Where We Belong" – the theme from *An Officer and a Gentleman*. I watched it when I was missing Ryan really badly, on Valentine's Day.'

Maggie looks over at Rachel, and they both roll their eyes: they were with Lily on Valentine's Day, and I take it she wasn't watching Richard Gere films. But the ladies all love this detail.

'Oh my! I love Richard Gere!' says Purple Rinse. 'That scene where he comes into the factory, and she's wearing her little flat cap, and he carries her out . . . I swoon every time.'

'These are my bridesmaids, by the way.' Lily indicates the three of us, all standing above her stony-faced and silent.

'Nice to meet you,' says Dame Edna, looking at us dubiously. She turns back to Lily and says in a loud whisper, 'They don't seem very happy for you, dear.'

'Why don't their dresses match?' says Dolly.

'It's the new trend,' says Lily, going pink. 'Maggie – will you take my picture with the ladies?'

'Don't, Maggie! It's evidence!' Rachel hisses.

'I think she's jealous,' Blue Rinse says to Lily, also in a stage whisper.

'So what's your something borrowed?' asks Purple Rinse.

'These shoes,' Lily says, holding out one silver pump. 'Jimmy Choos. Borrowed from my cousin Alice.'

'Does she know what you've borrowed them for?' I ask her pointedly.

'Oh! Look at the time,' says Lily, pretending not to hear me. 'I think Ryan might be waiting upstairs. Shall we, girls?' And she says goodbye to her new friends, and races up the stairs before we can stop her.

'Wait! OK, here's our plan,' Rachel says, grabbing both our arms. 'We play along, encourage her, reverse-psychology like mad – and then when the ceremony starts, I'll sabotage it. Got it?'

'Got it,' we reply, and hurry upstairs. Thank God for Rachel. I'm never going on holiday with Lily again without a lawyer present.

The waiting room is packed with couples of every stripe: gay, lesbian, straight, some in full-on bridal regalia and some in leggings and T-shirts. There's a very charged atmosphere; tense yet festive. A big old-fashioned number counter hangs on the wall, and people are getting paper tickets from a dispenser, like at the post office.

'Look, there's Ryan!' says Lily.

I think we all hoped, right up until now, that Ryan wouldn't show up and somehow it would all go away. But here he is, large as life, in full uniform: black with red piping, and a black and white hat tucked under one arm. And he does indeed appear to have a medal – and a sword. Ryan himself is less impressive than his uniform. He looks about nineteen, with straw-coloured hair, angry red acne all over his face and neck, and white eyelashes.

'God, he's no pin-up,' mutters Rachel.

'I'm not marrying him for his looks,' whispers Lily tartly.

'No, your love goes deeper than that,' Rachel says, just as Ryan reaches us.

'Nice to see you again, Lily. You look very pretty,' he says in a Southern drawl, kissing her on one cheek while shaking her hand in a very formal way. Jeez. Subterfuge much?

'Ryan!' hisses Lily, looking around her in a paranoid fashion. 'We're meant to know each other really well. And be madly in love.'

I would have thought you'd have to pass some sort of intelligence test to get into the Marines, but Ryan's making me wonder. Still, he's looking delighted at the opportunity to express his love for Lily.

'Oh yeah. Right. I can't wait to be married to you, babe,' he says. 'I can't wait for our wedding night.' And he grabs her, *dips* her and engulfs her in a lengthy snog. As he props her upright again, I catch a glimpse of her face. Her expression is literally indescribable.

'I've got the rings, baby,' Ryan says, patting his pockets. 'We are good to go.'

'Hi, Ryan,' says Rachel, stepping forward. 'I'm Rachel. None of your comrades able to make it today?'

'No, ma'am,' says Ryan, looking shifty. He obviously wasn't expecting Lily to bring backup.

'Let's get you crazy kids organised,' I say, grabbing a ticket for them. 'Here we go – lucky three hundred and forty-one!'

'I can't wait to catch your bouquet,' says Maggie.

Lily's looking bewildered at our change of heart. In fact she's looking generally dazed as we all squeeze on to a bench to wait our turn. Ryan is sitting with his legs so far apart, he's squishing her and me, and he keeps fingering his acne and adjusting his trouser crotch. No wonder he needs a visa marriage. Who else would have him?

'Three three nine,' someone calls. 'Three hundred and thirty-nine . . .'

Lily almost jumps out of her skin, then wipes her palms on her skirt, yawning.

Maggie whispers in my ear, 'She's terrified. She always yawns when she's scared. Can't we do something to stop this happening?'

'No. We've got to stick to what we decided,' I whisper back. Although I'm not sure whether Rachel's plan is even going to work. What if they kick us out of the ceremony room and carry on regardless?

Number 340 is up now. We're next. Weren't we meant to be spending this afternoon sipping cocktails at a VIP event, rather than being accessories to a bloody crime? I could honestly strangle Lily. Although at the same time, I really don't want to see her go to jail. What if she does get arrested? She'll be thrown into a cell with a load of knife-wielding drug dealers, and they'll cut off her hair to sell it on the black market . . . Here my knowledge of prisons runs out. But it won't be good.

'Three forty-one,' says the disembodied voice.

Looking despairingly at each other, we all file into the ceremony room, which is small and fairly low-frills: a man with a moustache leaning on a small pulpit, a microphone and a gavel, and a short blue carpet.

'Have you got a photographer?' asks the officiant.

Maggie steps forward, holding her phone aloft. He shows us – the 'wedding party' – where to line up, and instructs Lily to take Ryan's hand, which she does very reluctantly. And then the ceremony starts. It's happening.

I keep looking at Rachel, but she hasn't said a word yet. Shit. Has she forgotten her master plan? I'm really worried now. And so is Lily: her legs are shaking below her white skirt and the veil is bobbing up and down. The officiant is doing his bit with great relish, dwelling dramatically on certain words.

'If there is anybody *present* who knows any *legal* reason why this couple should *not* be married,' he's saying, 'speak now or *forever* hold your peace.'

Finally, Rachel's opening her mouth to say something. But before she does, Lily manages to put up her hand. We all whip around to stare at her.

'Yes, ma'am?' the man says, looking at her. She doesn't say a word but shakes her head a few times.

'Are you saying that you *don't* want the ceremony to go ahead?' he says, enunciating slowly.

Lily nods frantically.

'Are you here *against* your will? Is there *anything* else you need to tell us?' the officiant asks eagerly. I sense his day has just got a lot more interesting. Now Ryan is the one who looks nervous.

'I don't want to do it,' Lily croaks. 'I haven't done it yet, have I?'

'No. This marriage has not and will not take place.' He bangs his gavel, making everyone jump.

'Thank God.' And Lily runs from the room as fast as her Jimmy Choos will permit.

'Oh, hell no!' Ryan says, throwing down his hat in a rage. 'No you don't!' He's about to run after her when Maggie, to our amazement, leaps at him and trips him up, pinning him to the floor. All her triathlons have obviously paid off.

'Ooh, sorry. Are you all right?' she asks breathlessly, ruining the effect.

'Order! Order! Vacate this courtroom immediately!' says the officiant, banging his gavel over and over again and looking thoroughly overexcited.

'We're going!' says Rachel, and the three of us frogmarch a protesting Ryan out of the courtroom, under the fascinated eyes of the waiting couples, some of whom start taking pictures. This is the second time we've been papped since arriving in New York; I hope it's the last.

'Now you listen to me,' Maggie hisses to Ryan, once we're out of the room. 'You get out of here, and don't ever go near her again!'

'That's right, and delete every email you've ever had from her – unless you want us to report you to the police right now. Don't think we won't do it,' adds Rachel.

'Get off of me!' Ryan splutters. 'Crazy bitch wasn't worth the trouble anyway!' And he shakes us off and marches away, punching his hat back into shape.

We rush over to the window that overlooks the front steps.

'Is he gone? I won't breathe until he's gone,' says Maggie, wide-eyed.

'Yes! He's gone. Phew. Let's go and find Lily. What's that?' Maggie's holding out a piece of paper.

'It's the paperwork they did yesterday,' she says. 'I took it from her before we went in, and now we can destroy it.'

'Thank God for that,' says Rachel.

Like last time, it takes us a while to find Lily, but eventually we locate her huddled on a bench downstairs in the marble-floored lobby. She looks up at us from under her veil, terrified.

Rachel says, 'It's the Runaway Bride!'

'Congratulations, darling,' I say, ripping up the paperwork and throwing it over her head. 'There's your confetti.'

Lily picks some scraps of paper out of her veil before saying in a small voice, 'How angry are you all?'

'Out of ten? Only about twenty,' says Rachel, sitting down beside her.

'I am incandescent with rage,' I say, sitting on her other side. 'I've always wanted to use that phrase. You're a bloody idiot, Lily. And you nearly ruined our holiday.'

Lily looks up at Maggie.

'Very angry,' Maggie says simply. 'That was really stressful.'

Lily lowers her head. 'Is he definitely gone? And did I definitely not get married?'

'Yeah, he left. He was waving his sword around and saying something about how he's going to "make that bitch pay"? Was that it?' Rachel asks me.

'She's joking!' Maggie reassures Lily.

'Don't worry,' says Rachel, grinning. 'He's left, and you're one hundred per cent not married. Did you pay him any money, Lily?'

'Not yet. I was meant to pay him three grand after the ceremony. But I paid thirty-five dollars for the licence. Oh, and I bought the ring.'

'You were bloody lucky,' I tell her.

Lily starts to cry. 'I'm so sorry, guys,' she sniffs. 'I'm so sorry I put you through that. Oh God, I don't have a tissue.'

'Use your veil,' suggests Rachel.

Maggie reaches for Lily and gives her a big hug.

'It's OK, Lil,' she says. 'We forgive you. It didn't happen.'

'Girlfriend, he is NOT worth it,' says an unfamiliar voice. Two stray wedding guests have stopped to look at us; they obviously think Lily's just been jilted.

'Mm-HMMM,' says the other, hand on hip, before they move on.

Lily stares after them, and says, in a small voice, 'I'm going to miss America.'

We charge out of the building, nearly hysterical with relief.

'What do you want to do now, Lily? It's your wedding night,' I say.

'Let's not stay around here – it'll be full of wedding parties,' she says. 'I'd better get de-brided.' She switches her engagement ring to her right hand, and takes off her veil.

'Are you crazy? Keep it on!' says Maggie. 'Free drinks!'

'No thank you,' Lily says, folding her veil up and stuffing it inside Maggie's handbag. 'I've had enough of being a bride. Can we just get a cab and drive somewhere? Quick, before he comes back!'

We end up getting a cab to take us the nearest bar, which turns out to be an old-fashioned subterranean wine bar near Wall Street. We cause quite a stir by crashing in at six in the evening in all our finery, plus there's the fact that we're practically the only women in the place, which is full of old men in suits. After reassuring Maggie that she won't have to talk to any of them, we commandeer a booth, and get a round of cocktails to toast Lily's non-wedding.

'Here's to the Runaway Bride,' says Rachel, holding her martini aloft. 'I mean Miss Havisham. Let's see, what else can we call her?'

'The Bolter!' I exclaim. Looking at their blank faces, I continue, 'Nancy Mitford? No? Oh well.'

'But Lily, what made you decide not to do it?' asks Maggie.

'I just . . . It didn't seem such a big deal in theory, but when I had to stand up there with him . . .' She shudders. 'And I felt too guilty. I knew that technically it wasn't legal, but when I saw everyone else – all the gay couples especially – I realised I was making a mockery of something important. I felt like a horrible fraud.'

'You're sure it wasn't the prospect of your wedding night with Ryan?' asks Maggie.

'There was that too,' Lily admits. 'I'm not gonna lie.'

'That's what we should have done!' I say, smacking my palm on the table. 'We should have told you the authorities would want to see DNA evidence that you and Ryan had done the deed.'

'No problem for Ryan,' says Rachel. 'I don't know what you thought the arrangement was, Lily, but he definitely thought he was getting a bride with benefits.'

'Please,' says Lily faintly.

'I bet he had a Holiday Inn booked, with the full honeymoon package,' says Rachel. 'Rose petals all over the bed, chocolate-dipped strawberries, champagne in a bucket.'

'He was well up for it,' Maggie says. 'The second the ceremony ended he was going to scoop you up and carry you out of the building. Kicking and screaming.'

Rachel drops her voice, being Ryan. 'I can't wait to be married to you, babe. I can't wait till our wedding night.'

'Ew! Noo,' says Lily, laughing and clapping her hands over her ears.

I'm wiping tears from my eyes. 'Oh darling, your face. After he dipped you in that Hollywood kiss – I've never seen anyone look so frozen stiff. You were like a rabbit in the headlights. I wish I'd caught it on camera.'

'I did! I did!' Maggie shrieks, attracting stares from the old men in the booth beside us. 'Look!' She gets out her phone and shows us the photo of the happy couple just after Ryan's kiss. He looks like he's on cloud nine, and as for Lily – she's like that painting *The Scream*. It is priceless.

'You are going to have to destroy all those photos,' Rachel says, glancing at the men behind us. Then she starts to laugh again. 'But that one you should keep.'

We're still giggling helplessly when the barman comes over with another round of cocktails for us.

'What's this? We didn't order these,' Maggie says.

'Sshh,' says Rachel, quickly distributing them.

'From the gentlemen at the bar,' says the barman.

'Really? I thought that only happened in films,' I say.

'It happened to me once in a hotel bar in Liverpool. But he thought I was a hooker,' says Rachel. 'Those guys seem legit, though.'

Two very clean-cut Wall Street types in suits, standing at the bar, are giving us a discreet wave.

'I think they're looking at you, Mags,' says Lily.

'No, they're both looking at you. Guys like that do not go for short-haired brunettes. They're all blond, all the way.'

'But you can't talk to them anyway, Maggie. Don't forget your vow,' I remind her, sipping my Cosmo. They might be a cliché, but they're very delicious.

'Wait a second!' says Rachel. 'You broke your vow already, remember? You spoke to Ryan!'

'Aaargh!' This seems to call for another round of screams, as we realise what's happened. We really are popular in this bar now.

'The spell is lifted,' says Lily. 'Go forth and chat.'

Maggie shakes her head.

'I don't feel like it,' she says. 'Why should I? I know what will happen. We'll get chatting, they'll say British dentists are awful, we'll say Americans are obsessed with air conditioning, I'll end up snogging one of them, we'll go on to some club together, and then he'll get annoyed because I won't sleep with him. Or else I will sleep with him and it will be fine but I'll feel hollow inside the next day. Why bother?'

There's a silence; no one seems to have a ready reply.

'Well, when you put it like that . . .' says Rachel.

I'm a little concerned. Maggie's way too young and beautiful to sound so cynical. But then I decide this isn't the time for a big debrief about her love life. Also, I don't want anyone to start asking about mine.

'OK then,' I say, draining my Cosmo. 'Time for a change of scene. Where to next? We've got a non-wedding to celebrate. Let's take Manhattan!'

I wake up with a pounding headache, and crawl across the room to the minibar. It takes for ever before I figure out how to open it, and scrabble frantically among the bottles. Gin, vodka, whisky, Pepsi – oh, thank God. Water. I open the bottle and drain it dry.

'You don't mind, do you?' I croak to Rachel, who's already awake and texting someone – Oliver, no doubt.

'Knock yourself out,' she says. 'I'm not thirsty.'

'How can you not be thirsty? Are you bionic?' I ask. 'Are there robot legs under those covers? How much did I have to drink last night?' I collapse back on the bed.

'Not as much as Lily or Maggie. Or Vinnie.'

'Who? Oh! Him.' Now I remember. After going to an awful sports bar, we ended up in a jazz bar in the East Village, where we met a double bass player called Vinnie, who decided he and Lily were getting married that evening. 'You're dressed for it, I'm dressed for it, why not?' he kept yelling over the music. Then we collected more of his friends, and their instruments, and we all ended up taking a cab to another dive bar – with a detour to Times Square, because for some reason the guys were convinced we'd never seen it before. I have a memory of Vinnie and his friend Ricky taking turns trying on Lily's veil, and then it goes blurry.

'Did we do karaoke?' I ask, frowning.

'Yes. You and Ricky sang the theme from *Beauty and the Beast*, don't you remember?'

'"Tale As Old As Time"! Oh goodness, so we did.' I think we did it quite well, actually. I wonder if anyone filmed it?

'Do you think Maggie stayed away from the boys? They were coming at her with all their instruments.' Rachel chuckles. Now

I remember: she and I crawled home at 1 a.m., but Lily and Maggie were still partying hard.

But Maggie, when we go next door, insists she didn't go near the guys. 'Unlike her,' she says, nodding towards Lily. 'She brought Vinnie back here for a nightcap, and they were snogging in that cupboard.' She points at the walk-in wardrobe.

'What? It was my wedding night,' says Lily.

'You're looking very, um, fashion-forward, Rachel,' says Maggie.

I'm so hung-over I've only just noticed Rachel's get-up: a white lace shirt and yesterday's green Bermuda shorts. With cowboy ankle boots.

'I know, I know. Don't pack under the influence,' says Rachel. 'I seem to have brought about twenty swimsuits, but no clothes. And my orange sandals broke.'

'You're not going commando, are you?' asks Maggie. 'Oh good. In that case, I can lend you something.'

Maggie gives Rachel a quick restyle – cut-off denim shorts that actually look quite cute with the shirt and boots – and we head out to a diner nearby for a restorative Sunday brunch. There's a queue – this seems to be a rite of passage with breakfast in America – but before too long we're sitting down, sipping our iced water (so civilised not to have to even ask for it) and drooling over our menus.

'Hmm. I think I want the pecan pie French toast,' says Maggie. 'But then what about the buttermilk pancakes with blueberries?'

'I want the pancakes,' says Lily. 'But I also want a banana and walnut sticky bun. To hell with it, I'm having both. This might be my last breakfast in America.' She sighs heavily. I think we'd all like to contradict her, because of course that's not true, but none of us wants to encourage her into believing she's going to stay here if she can't.

When the food arrives, we eat in silence at first, partly because we're all hung-over and partly because it's so insanely good. I take a picture of my *huevos rancheros* for Charlie, before realising that all of my pictures so far on this trip are of food. Oh well.

'Oh my God, this French toast is to die for. I want to marry this French toast.' Maggie looks at Lily apologetically. 'Oops. Sorry, Lil. I didn't mean to say the M word.'

'Oh no!' Rachel says, putting down her knife and fork. 'It's been at least twelve hours since we made a wedding joke!'

'Quick, someone!' I say, snapping my fingers. 'Let's see, um, wedding bells, honeymoon . . . Nope, can't think of one. But when I do, I'll be sure to share it with you.'

'Ha, ha, ha,' says Lily, slowly mopping up the last drops of maple syrup with the last scrap of pancake.

'Shit,' Rachel says in a different tone of voice, staring out of the window. 'Don't look now, but . . . Ryan's over there. Across the street.'

Lily gives something between a shriek and a yelp, dropping her fork with a clatter, and then she actually ducks under the table, peering out of the window in a petrified way. 'Is everything all right?' asks the waitress, coming over.

'She's fine!' says Maggie, patting Lily on the shoulder. Lily's face changes and she starts laughing, giving Rachel a shove as she sits down again. 'You are *evil*,' she says. 'Oh my God. I actually thought he'd followed me all the way to brunch.'

We're all laughing so hard, it's a while before Rachel can say, 'I didn't think you would fall for it. Oh lord.' She wipes her eyes. 'Don't worry, Lily, you're grand. He hasn't the wit to follow you anywhere.'

'I don't think he was a real Marine,' says Maggie. 'He was too easy to tackle. And his uniform looked fake, like it was from a fancy-dress shop.'

'Maybe. They did ask him about some army paperwork he didn't seem to have. But enough about stupid Ryan,' says Lily, clapping her hands together. 'Listen, guys. Today I have a surprise for us all!'

We look at her in silence.

'Another surprise?' asks Maggie, in a voice filled with dread.

'Let me guess. We're robbing a bank,' says Rachel. 'One last heist before you retire for good?'

'No! It's a real surprise, and it will be fun. Christian at the Mercer set it up for us and I'd feel really bad if we said no. All we have to do is wear something that we don't mind getting wet.'

'No,' says Rachel immediately. 'Sorry, Lily, but once bitten and all that. I'm not letting you take me to a second location.'

'First rule of being kidnapped,' agrees Maggie.

'Fine! I'll go by myself. It's something I've always wanted to do – and now that I'm leaving the States, it's probably my last chance.'

We all exchange glances. 'You can get tattoos in the UK too, you know,' says Rachel.

'No, it's not a tattoo! It's a speedboat trip to the Statue of Liberty.'

'Oh, bless you,' I say before I can stop myself. 'You mean one of those family-splash adventures, where you have to be a hundred centimetres high?'

'No, Christian's arranged a private one for us,' Lily says, sounding injured. 'And he made reservations for us to go inside the statue too. But don't worry about it. I can meet you all later.' She slides out of the booth to go to the loo.

I'm such a pushover. I know she's caused havoc, but I feel sorry for her now that her crazy schemes have all come crashing down around her head.

'Come on, guys,' I say. 'Let's do it. It'll only be an hour or two, and it's her dying wish before she leaves the States.'

'I'm not convinced,' Rachel says. 'It could be a trap. How do we know she's not luring us on to a cruise boat or a whaling ship or something?'

'I feel so disloyal, but me too,' says Maggie. 'It's like, if the boy who cried wolf invited you to a surprise party, would you go? No.'

'Don't be silly. It won't be a trap,' I tell them both firmly. 'And the sea air will be good for our hangovers.'

An hour later, we arrive at Battery Park, where we're meeting our skipper, Dallas. He leads us to the mooring and shows us our vessel: a sleek little red-and-white speedboat with brown leather seats. For someone with such a fun, outdoorsy job, Dallas seems very downbeat. He's short and stocky, with a hipster beard and very short legs, which must be convenient on a boat.

'OK, ground rules,' he says, in depressed tones. 'No standing, smoking, alcohol or nudity in the boat, please wear your lifejackets at all times. Any questions?'

'Can I just confirm we're going to the Statue of Liberty and straight back, yes?' says Rachel, climbing aboard. 'We're not going anywhere else – like Canada?'

It's another gorgeous sunny day and it's an exhilarating feeling to be skimming across the water, with the skyscrapers of Manhattan glittering behind us and the Statue of Liberty on the horizon before us.

'I'm not – a big – fan of – getting my – hair wet,' I say breathlessly, as we bump along. 'Or of things that go really fast through cold air. But this is so cool!'

Lily seems to have revived as well. 'I'm the king of the world!' she screams, holding out her arms.

'*Titanic*,' Maggie explains to Rachel, who's looking mystified. 'Ooh, we need sunscreen.' She starts scrabbling in her bag, dislodging a very bashed-up-looking paperback: *One Hundred Years of Solitude* by Gabriel García Márquez.

'I adore that book,' I say, but my voice is drowned out by Lily's laughter.

'Oh my God, Maggie. Are you *still* reading this?' She holds up the book to us. 'I need witnesses. How long has Maggie been trudging her way through this?'

'You had it in Rome, didn't you?' says Rachel, who's looking a bit green. 'And at New Year. Though you said you'd been reading it for a while then.'

'It's been about a year. But I'm on page fifty! I'm making progress,' Maggie says, defensively.

'No you're not, you're bored stiff with it! Here. I'll summarise it for you.' Lily flips through it, pretending to skim-read. 'The man lived for a hundred years and was very lonely. The end. Maggie, this book is holding you back. I'm confiscating it for your own good.' And she puts it in her bag.

'Give it back!' shrieks Maggie.

They scrap over for it for a second before Lily chucks it to me. Unfortunately, I'm completely uncoordinated; I bat it away by mistake, and *One Hundred Years of Solitude* lands with a splash in the ocean.

'Oops,' says Lily. 'Book overboard! Can we go back, Dallas?'

Dallas isn't very pleased with us, but he does stop the boat and turn it around. Although we do a few circles, there's no sign of *One Hundred Years of Solitude*.

'Lily, you absolute brat! You drowned my book!' Maggie says, staring at the waves behind her as we chug off again.

'I'm sorry,' says Lily. 'But now you can start reading something you actually enjoy.'

'Are you OK, Rachel?' I ask, suddenly noticing that she's very quiet.

'All this – bumping isn't – good for – my hangover,' she says, looking green. 'Urrgh. Oh no. I'm going to be . . .' And she leans over the side of the boat and is noisily sick.

'I think we've finally discovered Rachel's kryptonite,' I say, reaching in my bag for tissues.

When we disembark at Liberty Island, my legs start to wobble the way they did after Charlie made me go on the Tower of Terror at Disneyland. Rachel's still feeling queasy, so Maggie offers to stay with her while Lily and I climb up inside the statue.

'Ever since that skiing trip, I haven't been so keen on heights anyway,' she says.

Lily and I slowly approach the Statue of Liberty, craning our necks as we stare up at its vast green height and spike-crowned head. Tour groups are milling around taking pictures, while guides with loudspeakers give commentaries describing the people arriving in crowded ships over the centuries, desperate for a glimpse of America.

'She looks good for three hundred and whatever it is,' Lily says.

We have to go through a million scans and ID checks before starting the slow climb up the dizzying spiral staircase.

'Boy, this is brutal,' pants Lily, after we've been climbing for five minutes. 'Three hundred and seventy-seven steps!'

'I know. But just think: by the time we get to the top, you'll have worked off half a pancake.'

Eventually we reach the viewing area, which is smaller than you'd expect, especially with all the tourists crammed inside it. But the view from the top, of the whole island of Manhattan and

New York harbour, is utterly breathtaking. We spend a while glued to one of the square panel windows, staring at it.

'I can't believe I'm going to have to leave all this,' says Lily, a catch in her voice. I look over to see she has tears in her eyes. 'Sorry,' she says, wiping them. 'Being a drama queen. But I love it here so much, Poppy. Everything was going wrong for me at home, ever since . . . well, since the accident.'

I nod, thinking that I've never heard poor Lily say the word 'died' in relation to her mother; it's always 'the accident'.

'And then I came here and things just fell into place. It wasn't always perfect, but I was so happy here. And now it feels like everything's falling apart again. I can't stand it. I don't want to go home.'

'Honestly, Lily, if you want to stay here, I bet you can. You have so much to offer. Not to mention your cousin is married to a film agent – can't Sam help you? I'm sure he could help you get a job as an assistant, or a runner, or even a nanny, like Maggie suggested.'

'I don't know if you heard, but the last time I tried to use Sam's connections, it wasn't a big success,' Lily says.

'But wasn't that because you stole his address book and talked your way into his client's house using a false identity? I'm sure if you asked him for help, it would be different. Have you even told them you've lost your job?'

'No . . . I suppose I could ask,' she says.

'Of course you could! Come on, Lily. Don't give up. You might have to go back to the UK and apply for jobs from there. But I'm positive that if you want to stay in Los Angeles you'll find a way – a legal way. You're that kind of person.' For some reason this makes her cry again, so I pass her the second half of my packet of tissues (Rachel has the other half).

'Thanks, Poppy,' she gulps. 'For you to have faith in me, after what I did yesterday – it means a lot.' She blows her nose. 'I really have learned my lesson, I promise. I can see there's a difference between going after what you want and full-on insanity. In future, when everyone around me is telling me the same thing, I will pay attention.'

'I know what you mean,' I say, as we start walking down

the steps again. I've decided to listen to the advice of my mother and Rachel. As soon as I get home, I'm going to talk to Charlie and broach the whole subject of The Future. God, it sounds ominous, like some Michael Bay movie with a sweaty Channing Tatum running away from a giant CGI explosion. Mm, sweaty Channing Tatum . . . I snap myself out of it and join Lily, who's buying green plastic souvenir crowns.

We go back outside to find the others parked on a bench near the water. Rachel's slumped over one edge, sipping Diet Coke and looking green. Maggie's staring thoughtfully across the bay. Dallas is moping away at a distance, eating candy floss.

'How was it?' Maggie asks.

'Good. Climby,' says Lily. She sits down beside Maggie, and presents her with her crown, while I put Rachel's on for her. 'What's been happening here?'

'Not much,' says Maggie. 'I was chatting to Dallas. He was telling me he just broke up with his girlfriend of eight years.'

'Oh, no wonder he's so depressed,' I say. 'I'm glad we bought him a crown.'

'Yes. He's put on ten pounds since it happened, apparently. And it got me thinking . . . things could be worse. I am so much happier than I was with Leo. And of course I'll meet someone at some point. You both did, didn't you?' She points at me and Rachel.

'Of course we did!' I say.

Rachel nods weakly.

Maggie continues, 'I suppose it doesn't seem such a big deal any more. I don't know why, but I'm feeling optimistic about the future.' She stretches out her arms and looks over at the skyscrapers of Manhattan shining across the water. 'It's hard not to be optimistic looking at a view like this, isn't it?'

'I agree,' says Lily, smiling at me.

'What do you think?' I ask Rachel.

She gives us a pathetic look, her crown askew. 'I can't do that boat again. Do you think we could call a helicopter?'

Back at the hotel, we decide to have a little down time. Rachel goes to have a sauna – her favourite hangover cure – and Maggie sets off for a run in Central Park (madness). Lily is meeting Christian for a drink. After reading and relaxing for a while, I decide to Skype Charlie. It's a Sunday, so I'm expecting him to be in his shorts and football T-shirt, as per usual. But to my surprise, he's looking dapper in his best Liberty shirt. Dapper, but anxious. Why is he anxious?

'Poppy! Finally,' he says. 'I've been texting you, and leaving messages at the hotel.'

'Have you really?' I look at the phone beside the bed and see a blinking red light. 'Sorry, babe. I can't get texts here. And we've been out a lot. How are you?'

'*I'm* fine, but what about you?' he says.

'Me? What about me?'

'Poppy! Come on. Your mum told me. She messaged me on Facebook asking for my number, and then she left me a voicemail . . .'

Oh no. Oh no, no, no no no no no. She is a *dead woman*. And I should never have let her join Facebook!

'I can't believe you didn't tell me, Poppy. You know you can tell me anything. Especially if it affects both of us.'

'Really?' I can't believe how seriously he's taking this. I'm torn between being impressed, and mortified that my mum has been sharing details of my biological clock with him. 'I didn't think it was necessary yet. Mum's overreacting.'

'Overreacting! If I'm going to be a father—'

'You're going to be a *what*?'

'A father! Isn't that what she meant? You're pregnant, right?'

'Good grief! Of course I'm not! What on earth gave you that idea?'

'Your mother did! In her message! It was a bit crackly, but she was talking about my responsibilities and your, um, reproductive health' – now he's blushing – 'and her future grandchild! What the hell was I supposed to think? And then I couldn't get hold of you, and I couldn't reach her either – I've been going out of my mind.'

I can't even find the words to set things straight; I've covered my face with my hands. My mum has created some chaos in her time, but this takes the absolute chocolate-covered, cream-filled double-decker biscuit. Charlie still seems to believe that I'm pregnant though I've just told him I'm not, and he's going on about all the thinking he's been doing, and how he wants to be there for me.

'. . . so I went and got you this.' The screen jerks and he disappears.

'Charlie?' I say, peering. 'Where did you go? Come back! I can't see you.'

'Oh, sorry.' Hands reach to the screen, and now I see him: he's on the floor. On one knee.

'I love you, Poppy, will you marry me?'

A giant hand is coming towards me holding out a ring. Solitaire diamond. White gold. Red box.

'Oh my God! Charlie! You have got to be joking!'

'What?' He puts the ring down and peers back into the screen, looking offended. 'I'm not joking! Will you marry me?'

'Charlie, stop it! Listen, for the last time! Mum was talking nonsense. I'm not pregnant, OK?'

'You're not?' He looks bewildered. 'Not even a little bit?'

Oh my God. Men!

'No! You can't be a little bit pregnant.' I take a deep breath. 'Look. I'm really sorry Mum gave you such a fright. What she was trying to say . . . not that she should have said *anything* to you, but that's another story . . . was that women in our family tend to . . . um . . .' Nope. I could tell Charlie anything, but I can't say the M-word. 'We have to try a little earlier if we want a baby. Like, before we're thirty-five. That's all.'

'Oh,' he says. The poor thing; he looks totally shell-shocked. 'I see. That's good to know.'

We stare at each other wordlessly. He's obviously adjusting to the whole she's-not-pregnant thing. While I'm catching up with the whole he's-just-proposed thing. I can't believe he did that. It was obviously ridiculous – like something out of a 1950s kitchen-sink drama, with him doing 'the right thing'. But I am touched, as well. And I'm glad we've begun the whole discussion about The Future. To be continued when we're back in the same room, and time zone.

'It's funny,' he says. 'I was shit-scared when I heard her voicemail, but now . . . I'm almost disappointed.'

'Really?' I say, even more touched. 'That's – wow! That's nice.' Good God! I might not need to do The Future with him after all. Is he actually broody? Am *I* even broody? Now I'm the one running scared from The Future, with its CGI clouds gathering on the horizon and things exploding behind Channing Tatum.

The picture blurs for a minute, and when Charlie comes back, his face is showing a mixture of emotions I can't identify. 'Well,' he says. 'We could do it anyway, right?'

Now it's my turn to be bewildered. 'What do you mean?' Does he want to knock me up right away? This is all happening rather fast, isn't it?

'You know. It's sooner than I thought, but Poppy . . . you know I love you. Will you? Marry me?'

He holds the ring out to me again, as if I need a visual cue. I stare at it for a few minutes before I can speak.

'Are you serious? You want me to make a huge, life-changing decision, just like that, over Skype?'

His face changes. 'Is that a no?'

'Yes! I mean, no! I don't know. This isn't the movies! You can't just spring this on me and expect me to reply off the top of my head.'

'Why not?' he says. 'I know how I feel about you.'

Aargh. This is so messed up. I wanted to discuss The Future with my boyfriend, and now he's proposed and I'm saying no. But honestly! What does he expect? With a huge effort, I get my voice under control. 'Charlie, I don't want to talk about this any more. Not on Skype. We can talk when I get back.'

'Fine,' he says curtly.

'Fine!' I say.

We glare at each other and I can tell we're both trying to think of a killer line to sign off with. But we can't. We're such saps.

'Enjoy the rest of your weekend in New York!' he snarls.

'Thank you! I'll see you when I'm back!' I snap. And our call ends with the incongruous 'bloop' sound effect.

*   *   *

I sit on the floor in a state of shock, trying to process what just happened. Then I see a note that must have been shoved under the door at some point while I was being proposed to.

Dear Poppy,
   One last surprise. Meet us at 7 p.m. at 42 East 20th Street.
Dress smart.
   Love, the Girls.

'Too many!' I shout, crumpling it up in my fist. 'Too many surprises!'

What has got into everyone? What with Lily's shotgun wedding and Charlie's Skype proposal, this weekend is like an episode of *Lost*. What are they planning now? Is Maggie going to turn into a smoke monster, or is Rachel going to reveal that Oliver is her long-lost twin brother and they have to split up? Actually, that is a genuine fear of mine. You always read about sperm donors' kids who meet not knowing that they share a father, especially when he made hundreds of donations.

Aargh. Why am I thinking about sperm? Now I'm back in the whirlwind of Charlie, my mother and this debacle of a situation. I cannot believe Mum's ability to wreak havoc in my life from two thousand miles away. And Charlie – I can't believe he thought that the best solution to a set of life-changing decisions was an Argos ring and a Skype proposal.

I suppose I should make an effort and dress up, but that requires a degree of concentration that I don't have, so I pull on a Hawaiian print dress and add red lipstick. That will have to do.

Outside the hotel, I hail a cab and give the driver the address. I have no idea what to expect – a topless bar? A tattoo parlour? – but it looks normal. An elegant brownstone building with a round awning and lettering above it – it's the Gramercy Tavern! Finally things are looking up. I hurry inside and find the girls at a fantastic table in the centre of the dining room, waiting for me.

'What a great surprise! I've always wanted to come here!' I say, giving them all a hug in turn before sitting down. 'Thank you!'

It's a classic New York place: the kind of place where Harry might have taken Sally on a date. Wood-beamed ceilings and white plaster walls; white tablecloths and candles on the round tables. Best of all, the food is meant to be amazing: classic dishes perfectly executed, according to the *New York Times* review I've been drooling over.

'How did you get us a table? I tried to book online, but it was impossible!'

'Please,' says Lily. 'If I can't get a table in a restaurant, there's no hope for me. I *might* have given the impression you were the model Poppy Delevingne,' she adds in an undertone. 'But it's too late now, we've got the table. And we *look* like VIPs anyway.'

They really do. Lily's in a black-and-white strapless silk dress, with her hair teased into a big mane, wearing blue drop earrings. Rachel's looking gorgeous in a pink shift dress with an orange belt – it turns out it belongs to Maggie, who's wearing a very cute blue ruffle top tucked into a floral miniskirt. She's also got fabulous smoky eyes and nude lipstick.

'I had a little session in Sephora,' she admits, when I compliment her. 'The whole no-make-up thing wasn't really me.'

'Fair enough, darling. So how did you know I've always wanted to come here?' I ask.

'Charlie told us,' Maggie says. 'And he also told us . . .'

They all exchange glances, and Lily nods to the waiter, who approaches with a bottle of champagne. No. They can't be . . . he can't have . . .

'He told us it's your birthday next week! Happy birthday!' they chorus.

Oh. I put my hand over my mouth, suddenly feeling a mixture of emotions. Horror at turning thirty; happiness at having such great friends; and gratitude to my wonderful, idiotic boyfriend.

'Oh my God,' I say unguardedly. 'I thought for a minute Charlie had told you . . .'

'Told us what?'

'That he proposed.'

Deafening shrieks ensue. 'That's amazing!' 'Congratulations!'

319

'Fabulous!' They all start pouring champagne and toasting me at once.

'No, no, stop!' I protest. 'He . . . It was a mess. My mother gave him the idea I was pregnant . . . which I'm not! And he misunderstood and he proposed, and when I said I wasn't pregnant, he suggested getting married anyway.'

Now everyone's looking confused. Maggie's champagne glass is hovering in mid-air, as if she's not sure whether to sip it or not.

'And so I said no,' I finish, really regretting telling them now. 'No big deal! Now, what's everyone going to eat?'

They all open their menus and pretend to read them, but they're obviously wondering whether they can ask more questions.

'Why did you say no?' Rachel asks, bluntly. The others put down their menus, looking relieved.

'Because it's a huge decision! I can't say yes on the spur of the moment like that. And we've only been together ten months. That's not long enough.' I look at them all doubtfully, and find myself adding, 'Is it?'

'Don't ask me,' says Lily. 'I'd only known Ryan a day. But I will say,' she adds thoughtfully, 'I think it would be long enough. If you really loved someone.'

'And it's not just about time. Leo and I were together a year and it still wasn't right,' Maggie says.

I look at Rachel, hoping she'll come up with something sensible.

'I don't know,' she says. 'I used to think there were set rules – move in after a year, get married after two or three. But now I think: when you know, you know.'

Great. Now they're all making me feel really unromantic. But I *am* a romantic! I'm a hopeless romantic!

'If you're not sure about Charlie, then you definitely shouldn't rush into anything,' Maggie says helpfully.

'It's not that,' I say, realising I'm being completely illogical. 'I am sure about Charlie. I know I want to spend the rest of my life with him. I just wasn't expecting an impulse proposal over the internet.'

'I'm sure it wasn't an impulse,' Rachel says seriously. 'He loves you. I'm sure he's thought it through.'

I don't say anything, because deep down I agree with her. Charlie's spontaneous, but he's not an idiot. Not really.

'It seems so soon. And he's only twenty-six! Twenty-seven in June, but still.'

'My dad was married by the time he was twenty-seven,' Rachel says.

'Mine too,' says Lily.

'But men are different these days! It's evolution in reverse. Anyway . . . I shouldn't have mentioned it. Let's drop it and order some food.'

'Of course! Happy birthday dinner,' says Maggie quickly. 'Why didn't you tell us it was your birthday this week?'

'I was being an idiot,' I admit. 'I just felt really old.'

'Don't be ridiculous! You're a spring chicken!' says Lily, though she really can't talk. I'm sure she thinks I'm ancient.

'You're younger than Cameron Diaz,' Maggie points out.

'You're only as young as the man you feel,' Rachel adds, cackling to herself as I roll my eyes. They are right: I was being stupid. Obviously the whole thirty thing had hit me harder than I thought. But now that I've come out about it, it doesn't seem so bad. Especially when Maggie plonks down a pink gift-wrapped box in front of me.

'What? Guys, you shouldn't have!'

'Come on, open it.'

I open it up to find, under layers of white tissue paper, the most beautiful jewelled hair comb. It's silver, decorated with tiny seed pearls, and looks like it's from the 1930s, if not earlier.

'We thought it was very you,' says Rachel.

'This is gorgeous! Oh, I don't believe it! Thank you so much.' I give them all a kiss, and put it in my hair, feeling almost tearful at how sweet they are.

After sharing a starter of scallops with Lily, I have steak and triple-cooked chips with Béarnaise sauce, which is probably the best steak and chips I've ever had. I can't help imagining

321

how much Charlie would love it here. Suddenly I find myself remembering the first meal he ever made me. He spent the day cooking up an amazing feast for me, and carried a bag full of Tupperware containers across London to my flat because I was stuck at home with a twisted ankle. And we weren't even going out then – he was wooing me.

Enough! No more Charlie thoughts. I take another sip of red wine and try and concentrate on the conversation about where to go after dinner. They're discussing a place called Tenjune, which is meant to be good, when Maggie says, 'I had a sort of a tip just now, from a guy I met.'

'What? When did you have the chance to meet a guy?' I ask, looking around the restaurant in confusion. What has been happening today?

'When I went out for my jog in Central Park this afternoon. He was jogging too. He came over and asked me for directions.'

'Ah,' says Rachel. 'It's an old one but a good 'un.'

'I was wearing my Royal Parks Half Marathon T-shirt, so we started talking about that – he's done it too. He lives in London, he's English. Over here on holiday. His name's John.'

'Great name,' says Lily. 'Very retro. What was his tip?'

'He said he and his friends were going to this place called Le Bain tonight. I think it's in the Meatpacking District. It's meant to have a rooftop bar and great views over the city.' Maggie shrugs. 'It could be fun.'

'That's great!' says Lily. 'We have to go!'

'No, we don't,' says Maggie. 'This is our weekend. If we don't go, it's fine, I'll just send him a text or something. If it's meant to be, it's meant to be. And if it's not, it's not.' She sounds very serene; I'm impressed. Seconds later, she adds, 'I would quite like to, though.'

'Sure, sounds great,' I say, absently. *If it's meant to be . . . when you know, you know . . .* These are things I believe, so why am I not acting on them?

I keep thinking about Charlie and his proposal. Yes, it was impulsive and a bit ham-fisted – but it was sincere, and passionate, and generous: all the things I love about him. I don't really think our age difference matters. Or how long we've been together. So why did I say no?

'Ladies, are you ready for some desserts?'

I'm so distracted, I pick a dessert at random from the menu, something I've never done in my life. And this is dessert at Gramercy Tavern!

'I think I've made a mistake,' I blurt out, once he's gone.

'Do you want me to call him back?' asks Maggie. 'Or you can share my caramel cheesecake if you like.'

'Not with dessert. With Charlie. I do want to marry him! I just . . . I didn't think it would happen this way.'

'You mean, you had a romantic notion of how you'd get engaged and this isn't living up to it?' Rachel asks innocently. Damn, she's good.

'Maybe,' I admit. 'I certainly didn't think it would happen online or feature garbled phone calls from my mum and us being on different continents.'

'Come on, tell us your engagement fantasy.'

I say instantly, 'Moonlit gondola ride in Venice on our second anniversary. God! I'm such a cliché.'

'Nice,' says Rachel. 'Mine is a skiing holiday – New Year's Eve, champagne in front of the fire, ring hidden in a box of chocolates.'

'I always thought I'd like to get engaged at the top of a mountain,' Maggie muses. 'Now I think it's been done to death. Every second couple seems to get engaged on top of a mountain.'

Lily's looking at us all as if we're insane.

'Tell us more about the proposal, Poppy,' Maggie says. 'How did he do it?'

'Well, he asked twice. The first was when he thought I was pregnant. He disappeared from the screen because he went down on one knee. And then he reappeared and said, "I love you, Poppy, will you marry me?"'

'Oh.' Maggie has clasped her hands in front of her and Lily looks dreamy; even Rachel is blinking something back.

'Yeah. Then the second was after I told him I wasn't. And he said something like "Why don't we do it anyway?" and waved the ring around again. Not really a story to tell your grandchildren.'

'What was the ring like?' Lily asks.

'I couldn't see very well. But it was a diamond solitaire, white gold. Very conventional. Not what I would have chosen at all.' I shrug, feeling mean for criticising Charlie's ring choice. 'Oh, and he was wearing his best shirt.'

This seems to be the final straw. They make a collective 'Awwwww' sound.

'The ring doesn't sound like you,' says Lily. 'But the rest of it sounds romantic!'

'What kind of ring would you have liked?' Maggie asks.

'Oh, I don't know. Something with character. Vintage. Not a diamond, necessarily. Something like your one, actually,' I tell Lily.

'Have it,' she says immediately, pulling it off her finger.

'What? Why?'

'You don't think I want it, do you? It's always going to remind me of when I was a visa bride.' She passes it to me. It's gorgeous: shaped like a lightning bolt, made of small white and blue stones that Lily says are topazes and sapphires.

'So Ryan was meant to have bought this in Dubai, was he?' Maggie says, looking puzzled.

'That didn't hold water, did it? No, I bought it in a vintage store in LA. It's art deco, or so they said.'

'It's beautiful.' It fits perfectly, even though Lily is half my size. I turn my hand, watching it catch the light. I think I have an idea. Charlie may have botched his proposal – but I've still got a shot at mine.

'Could I borrow it?' I ask Lily.

'Of course! I'm telling you, you can have it. It's your other birthday present! Why do you want it?'

I take a deep breath. 'I'll explain later. But I'm going back to the hotel to Skype Charlie – again. I'll see you girls later at Le Bain. And wish me luck!' I stand up, fishing dollars out of my purse. Rachel tells me not to worry about it.

'It's your birthday. Anyway,' she says, when I protest, 'we got out of buying this one a wedding present,' indicating Lily. 'Call this an engagement present.'

'Oh, don't say that. Not yet,' I say, suddenly nervous.

'You could use my phone to Skype him,' says Maggie. 'They might have WiFi here.'

I turn around. 'Thanks, Mags. But weird as it sounds, I think it would be more romantic on a laptop.'

In the cab on the way back to the Mercer, I'm buzzing with impatience. It's after midnight in London; Charlie might have fallen asleep over his game of Minecraft. Or he might be out drowning his sorrows with his brother; he might not even want to talk to me. I call him on my mobile as soon as I get into the cab, but there's no reply. I'll have to try again from the hotel.

The traffic's terrible, so as soon as I recognise our surroundings, I pay the driver and get out of the cab. I rush back towards the Mercer through the springtime dusk, feeling exhilarated. I meant it when I told the girls that I wanted to spend the rest of my life with Charlie. The rest of my life is starting sooner than I thought, that's all.

Back in my room, I fire up my laptop and wait for the connection. He's not online, so I have to ring his landline. I get a grumpy reply and he agrees to Skype. As soon as he appears on the screen, my heart melts. He's sitting up in bed wearing his comfort hoodie – the ancient extra-soft one he wears when he's feeling blue and wants to curl up and be sorry for himself.

'Hey,' I say, brimming over with love. 'Were you asleep?'

'No,' he says gruffly. 'Couldn't sleep.'

'Oh babe. How come?' He shrugs, so I continue, 'I'm sorry about earlier. You just caught me off guard a little.'

'Fair enough,' he says, sounding subdued. 'Look, let's drop the whole thing.'

'Actually . . . let's not.' I hold out my hand, and uncurl it slowly to reveal Lily's ring. Suddenly my heart is hammering, and I'm absurdly nervous. How do men do this? I clear my throat. 'Charlie, I love you. Will you marry me?'

He stares at the ring for a minute, before a smile breaks out across his face. 'It's a bit small for me, babe.'

I laugh, and wave it at him. 'No – it's for me to wear. If that's what you really want.'

'Of course it is,' he says. 'Don't make me start singing the Spice Girls. I would love to.'

Now we're both grinning like idiots. He said yes!

'This is the drawback of getting engaged over Skype,' he says. 'We can't have engagement sex.'

'You say the most romantic things,' I reply. 'We can when I get home. Gosh. When do you think we should tell people?'

'We'll get our PR people to put out a joint announcement. By the way, be honest: do you hate the ring I got you?'

'I don't *hate* it . . .'

'It's OK. I knew you'd prefer something more unusual, but I didn't know where to start. So I ran to Oxford Street and got a holding ring. If you prefer that one you've got, then go for it. I want you to have whatever makes you happy.'

'You're sure?' I look down at the lightning bolt ring. 'I do love this one. You wouldn't feel hurt if I wore it instead?'

'Nah. I can give the other one to my next fiancée.'

I stick out my tongue at him, wondering how it's possible to love someone this much.

After spinning out our goodbyes for another minute or so, we finally end the call. I flop back on to the luxurious bed and exhale in a sigh of perfect happiness. I love Charlie; he loves me; we're getting married. I have everything I could possibly want.

Except maybe some Ben and Jerry's AmeriCone Dream ice cream. There's some in the minibar freezer, and I never did get my dessert this evening. In fact, I'm very tempted to skip Le Bain and curl up here, watching films and vegging out. It's been a physically and emotionally exhausting few days. I think my body is telling me it needs rest. And ice cream. The girls will understand.

Turning on the TV, I find an old episode of *Sex and the City*. Perfect. I'm about to take off the Hawaiian dress and get into my PJs when I stop short. Wait a second. It's nearly my birthday *and* I just got engaged! Why would I stay in a hotel room watching *Sex and the City* when I have the real thing outside my door?

*   *   *

326

Half an hour later, I'm clattering across the cobblestones of the Meatpacking District on the way to Le Bain, dressed to kill (or at least lightly injure) in one of my favourite outfits: a black jumpsuit with a low-cut neck, sleeveless and backless. It's an original number from the seventies, very fitted and slinky. Lots of black eyeliner, metallic heels and a fake snakeskin clutch round things off nicely, and I'm wearing my new jewelled comb in my hair.

There's a queue, but on the off chance, I ask if we're on the guest list. We are! Reflecting that I would hire Lily if I could afford her, I go straight to the rooftop bar. The view is spectacular: the lights of Manhattan, and all along the East River to New Jersey. The crowd is a mixture of Eurotrashy-looking types, suburban kids on a big night out, and some very sleek and sophisticated people behind the velvet ropes to the side. And they're playing disco music! Something tells me this is going to be an excellent night.

'Poppy! You're here!' I turn around: the girls are standing at a little table the size of a tray, drinking champagne. I run over and hug them all.

'You look fantastic!' Maggie shouts over the music. 'I love that jumpsuit!'

'What happened?' asks Rachel eagerly, handing me a champagne flute.

'Well . . . we're engaged!' I hold out my left hand and they all exclaim over it, although they've obviously seen it before. 'And Lily, I love the ring. Thank you.'

'I'm really glad! I owe you, after everything I did. Just maybe don't tell people exactly how you got it,' says Lily.

'No! I want the world to know that Charlie proposed over Skype and I said no, and then I proposed with my friend's bogus engagement ring from her fake wedding. It's romantic.' Lily is looking freaked out, so I tell her I'm joking.

'Congratulations to Poppy and Charlie,' says Rachel, and we clink glasses. Maggie insists on taking a photo to capture the moment, and we all check and approve it. Then Maggie turns to Lily.

'Tell Poppy your news!' she says.

'Oh my God, more news?' I ask, alarmed. 'What now?'

'I checked my email while you were gone . . .' Lily does a little twirl, and starts dancing around in a way that makes it clear she's had a head start on the celebrating. 'I've been offered a job by a wedding planner in LA and she's happy to sponsor my visa!'

'That's amazing!' I give her a huge hug. 'Fantastic, darling, well done!'

'And I spoke to Alice and she's going to put me in touch with her lawyer. I'm going legit.' She starts bopping to 'Young Hearts Run Free', one hand in the air.

We all clink glasses and toast my birthday, our engagement *and* Lily's new job.

'What a weekend,' says Rachel, looking at us all in wonder. 'What a year! Fabulous trips, new jobs, not one but two weddings . . . I can't believe I thought I was the one with the scoop, with Oliver wanting to move in with me.'

'I can't believe I thought Leo getting together with Jenny was news. That was just, like, a tweet,' says Maggie.

'A tweet or a twit?' asks Lily.

'Both,' says Maggie and we all giggle.

'Hey, where's your bloke?' I ask her. 'Did he make it?'

'He's over there,' she says demurely. 'I said I'd come and chat to him later, once I'd had a drink with my friends.'

I take a discreet look over my shoulder, and I know immediately which guy it is without her even telling me. He's tall and sporty-looking and handsome – not as handsome as Charlie, obviously, but still. And I instantly know that this is going to become a thing. I don't know why – maybe it's Maggie's air of confidence, or the fact that this John guy can't stop looking at her. But I know. If Leo was a tweet, this man is a whole novel.

Lily obviously agrees. 'I have a good feeling about this, Mags,' she says. 'And do you know why? Because we got rid of your *Hundred Years of Solitude* book.'

'Don't start on that. I'm still annoyed, you know,' Maggie says.

'No you're not! Think about it. That book represented your past. You needed to let it go and move on.' Lily does another twirl and head wave to the Jackson Five.

'Maybe you're right,' Maggie says. 'It was a good book, but it wasn't for me. I need to move on and meet the right book.'

We all clink glasses again, and this time we toast our engagement, Lily's new job *and* to meeting the right book.

'So are you going to move in with Oliver?' Maggie asks Rachel.

She nods. 'I think so. Not yet, though. I'm going to suggest September. What about you, Poppy? When's the wedding?'

'I have no idea. But I am going to wear something fabulous.' I grin as it hits me all over again: Charlie and I are getting *married*. 'And you'll all have to come!'

'Please let me help organise it! Oh my God. Do you know what this means?' Lily says. 'Hen paaaartaaaaaaaaaay!'

'Oh wow, Lil, my ears,' says Maggie, giggling.

'She's right!' says Rachel. 'Poppy, this is officially your hen party. Your New York hen, anyway. We'll have one in London too, with penis straws and strippers and everything. And your mum can be guest of honour for getting the ball rolling.'

'Of course she can come, but can we keep that part quiet, please?' I'm already planning the official version of our engagement story, and it does *not* feature my mum, Facebook or my menopause.

At that moment, the music changes to 'Love Train', which is possibly my favourite song ever. It's so crowded now that we have to fight our way on to the dance floor, and as we do, pieces of metallic confetti start falling on us. I don't know where it's coming from because we're in the open air, but it's flying around, covering everyone with silver scraps. I notice one girl picking it out of her glass. 'This is a LAW SUIT waiting to happen,' she tells her friend.

Lily's taking a different view. 'Glitter!' she says, jumping up and trying to catch the confetti as it falls. 'This is the best night ever!'

'And we're just getting started,' says Maggie, twirling around in a very slinky way that I'm sure isn't lost on John.

'Exactly,' Rachel yells over the music. 'It only gets better from here.'

And we all start dancing, whirling around and generally

having a fantastic time. I feel like I could dance all night, and maybe I will. All three of the girls are totally right. This is the best night ever, and we're just getting started: it only gets better from here.

POPPY

If you'd asked me how I thought I would spend the evening before my wedding, I probably would have imagined having a calming aromatherapy massage, or sitting around with my female relatives and friends, laughing over herbal tea as we painted each other's toenails. Instead, I'm on my knees in my mum's living room in Brighton, holding a glue gun and trying to follow an online tutorial to create thirty mini burlap bows.

I really have been laid-back about everything – guest list (all my friends in return for all Charlie's random relatives), food (jerk chicken and rice and peas made by local caterers according to my grandma's secret recipe), venue (my mum's friend's garden), even my dress – but I did want the flowers to look nice. I set my heart on having huge masses of summer wild flowers overflowing from jam jars on every table. But they're already wilting and frankly look like bunches of weeds. I secretly wanted to go back to the flower market for more this morning, but Maggie and Lily and my mum were looking tired and I didn't want to be a bridezilla.

'What on earth are you doing?' says a voice behind me. It's Mum, already in her pyjamas though it's only nine o'clock. She's also wearing her favourite home-made honey face mask. I thought I was the one meant to be having an early night and a face mask?

'Nothing!' I say quickly. 'I just thought the flower arrangements looked a bit sad, so I found this tutorial online to decorate the containers . . .'

'Poppy. Put. Down. The glue gun.' Mum marches into the

room, taking in the scene: the blue glow of my laptop, the glue gun and the piles of burlap and twine I've accumulated over the past few weeks. Whoever said DIY arrangements were cheaper was talking nonsense: I could have bought Kew Gardens with the amount I've spent on these doo-dahs.

'Now leave those flowers alone. They are absolutely fine. Honestly, Poppy, I thought you were a sensible girl. How on earth are you going to manage married life if you lose your head over a few weeds?'

'So you *do* think they look like weeds!'

'They do a bit, but nobody will notice them anyway, I promise you. The only people who notice flowers at a wedding are the people who are planning their own weddings. And sometimes not even them. Now come on, love, pull yourself together. Pass me all that string, I'll use it on my runner beans.'

Feeling indignant, but also secretly relieved that I don't have to make thirty hand-tied burlap bows, I hand her the twine.

'Really,' Mum says, folding it up neatly, 'your generation are so bourgeois. We never had any of this fuss. Down the registry office, pub afterwards . . .'

'I know, I know,' I interrupt her. 'You wore Doc Martens with your wedding dress and had your honeymoon in a caravan in Wales. While I'm wearing a vintage dress and going on honeymoon to Italy. I'm such a capitalist swine.'

Mum's expression softens. 'No you're not. You're a good girl, Poppy.' In one of her typical switches from lecturing to sentimentality, her eyes start to tear up. 'I'm proud of you. And I just want you to enjoy tomorrow and not fret over silly things. It will go by so fast!' And she gives me a big hug. Now I'm starting to tear up as well. We're as bad as each other.

'Right, that's enough wallowing,' Mum says briskly, releasing me. 'Now here's what's going to happen. I'm going to clear all this nonsense up and then I'm sending you out for a drink with Charlie. Remember him?'

Instantly I start to panic again. 'But that's all wrong! We're not supposed to see each other the night before the wedding!'

Mum's response is to raise her eyes, and her hands, to heaven. 'Did I bring her up to be superstitious?' she asks an unknown listener somewhere on the ceiling. 'Or to be an independent-thinking feminist?'

I think the 'superstitious' accusation is a bit rich considering Mum's devotion to homeopathy, but I decide not to go there. 'I don't even know what he's doing,' I point out. 'He might be out with his dad and brother for all I know.'

In response, Mum pulls out her phone and instructs me to get dressed. When I come back five minutes later, she tells me, 'You're meeting Charlie in the King Edward and I want you back by ten thirty. No later.'

'OK,' I say, quite happy for once to feel about fourteen.

Twenty minutes later, Charlie and I are sitting holding hands in the pub down the road from the B&B where he, his best man and his brother are staying. To hell with superstition: after just five minutes with him, I feel calmer and saner. After one look at me, Charlie asked if I'd eaten dinner, and when I said not really, promptly ordered me a burger and chips.

'I am glad Mum sent me out,' I admit. 'I was one glue gun away from a total meltdown. Which is ironic really, given that we wanted something simple and DIY.'

'I think we confused "simple and DIY" with "easy and stress-free",' says Charlie. 'They're not the same thing, are they? I'm glad you talked me out of doing the catering, by the way. The cake was plenty.'

I squeeze his hand as I remember all the trial icing, hair-tearing and stress that went into Charlie's creation. At least I got to eat the mistakes. 'I just hope everyone has a good time. And that the flowers don't look too ropy. And that my dad doesn't say anything too weird in his speech.'

I was in two minds whether to ask my dad to do a traditional father-of-the-bride speech. After all, he did drop the ball when he moved to Saudi when I was twelve, and he hasn't exactly been Father of the Year since then – sending me oddly age-inappropriate presents like anti-wrinkle cream when I was fifteen. But I figured I was already snubbing him by having my mum walk me down the aisle, so it was a sort of peace gesture. As was letting him bring his new girlfriend, who judging from Facebook looks younger than me. I can't even start to imagine what kind of chats she'll be having with my mum.

'He'll be fine,' says Charlie. 'And at least my grandma's not giving a speech.'

Charlie's Grandma Flo is a sweet little white-haired lady who is also quite racist. I've warned Mum about her, and she says she's just relieved that *my* grandma, who's now retired to Jamaica and doesn't like to fly, can't be there. It's one less thing to worry about.

'You two all ready for tomorrow?' asks a passing woman carrying a clutch of pints. I recognise her as one of my mum's many cronies from the bead shop, which is her local hangout.

'Enjoy it,' she adds. 'It all goes by so fast!'

We smile and nod, but as soon as she's gone I turn to Charlie. 'Have you noticed everyone keeps saying that? It goes by so fast! Blink and you'll miss it! Over in seconds! Honestly, it makes me wonder why we're bothering with this at all.' I break off, realising that I've just put my foot in it. But Charlie is grinning.

'You know I didn't mean that,' I add quickly.

'It's OK,' he says. 'I'm just thinking how much I'm looking forward to hearing you rant about stuff for the rest of my life.'

I lean forward and kiss him. 'Me too.' And suddenly I realise that all the squabbling relatives and wilting flowers in the world aren't going to spoil what's happening tomorrow. I've met the love of my life and we're getting married!

The next morning, when I wake up in Mum's spare room (my old bedroom for a few years while I was home from uni), it feels like Christmas or a birthday when I was small. It's normal, but also not. I'm just smiling to myself at the thought of Charlie seeing me in my dress, and wondering what he's doing now, when I feel something throbbing on my forehead. It's as if I've been bitten or stung. Worried, I hop out of bed and go to the mirror to investigate.

It's a huge spot, literally right in the middle of my forehead, glowing red like a traffic light. I don't even get spots that often: I've never had anything like it before in my life. I've never *seen* anything like it before in my life.

'Really?' I say aloud. 'Really, universe?'

I try to dab at it with my Rimmel cover stick, but it's one of those spots that laughs at concealer and emerges triumphantly from even the heaviest layer of make-up. I can't believe I thought wilting flowers were a problem. I've got a spot that would survive the Apocalypse. And it dominates my whole face. Never mind my mum or dad: my spot will be walking me down the aisle.

'Poppy? Your friends are downstairs. And I've brought you some breakfast.' After a knock, Mum comes in bearing tea and toast. 'Ooh,' she says, putting down the tray and staring at me.

'It's pretty bad, isn't it?' I ask.

'Not *too*,' she says unconvincingly, her eyes fixed a few centimetres above mine. 'Just let me get at it with some tea tree oil . . .'

'Mum! No! Don't touch it! That will make it worse!' I back away. The last thing I want is Mum attacking my face with her home remedies. She might have great skin herself, but this is a medical emergency.

'I know,' Mum says. 'Why don't you make a feature of it? Like a bindi? I've got some sequins . . .'

'Mum! No!' Now I feel fourteen again, but in a bad way. Spots, fights with my mother; am I going to my wedding or a school disco?

There's another knock at the door. 'Poppy? Can we come in?'

'Yes,' I say, mournfully.

Alice and Lily step into the room, their words of wedding excitement dying on their lips as they're struck speechless by the sight of me. And not in a good way.

'You don't have to say anything. Or pretend not to notice it,' I tell them. 'It's like another person in the room.'

'It's really not that bad,' says Alice. 'Honestly. You just need a bit of concealer on it.' Which is all well and good coming from someone who's glowing with Californian tan and not a trace of jet lag since she and Sam arrived last week.

Lily, meanwhile, is rummaging through a bulging bag. I told her I was doing my own make-up, but she's clearly brought an extra arsenal and I can't help feeling glad.

'This,' she says, waving a stick aloft. 'This is what you need.

They use it on set in the movies. It covers scars, tattoos, everything.'

She presses it on using a brush, and they all stand back and study me. 'Well?' I ask.

I don't even need to look; their faces tell the story. The spot is concealed at the edges, but the centre is already starting to emerge from the cover-up. It's literally indestructible. And I know it's really shallow of me, but I can feel tears coming to my eyes. All the time I spent choosing my dress, and my shoes, and deciding to have my hair down not up, and I'm going to be foiled by a stupid spot?

'This spot is going to be the third person in our marriage,' I mutter, trying to make a joke of it.

'Look, don't panic, Poppy,' Lily says. 'I promise we'll think of something. For now, why don't you have some tea and toast before it gets cold? You really need to eat.'

I let them fuss over me and feed me tea and toast while I try telling myself that I'm thirty years old and I shouldn't be losing my mind over a spot. I have a faint hope that it might die down once I've had a shower, but no: it's still burning brightly even when Mum brings me an ice cube and I press it to my face for five minutes.

'I know it's not much consolation, but remember Photoshop,' says Alice. 'It's a force for good as well as evil.'

'Yes! We'll remove it in post-production,' says Lily. She glances at her watch. 'Poppy, you'd better get into your dress. You'll feel better once you have it on anyway.'

'It is the most beautiful dress,' says Alice encouragingly.

It really is. It's an ivory silk 1930s number with a draped bodice, a fitted dropped waist, delicate lace cap sleeves and a little puddle train. It's very *Downton Abbey*, but I can actually get into it *and* wear a bra, which is really rare with vintage numbers. I adore it. As my mum buttons me up, I start to feel calm again. What's so bad about a spot, anyway? It's not like anyone will be looking at me up close.

Until I see the others staring at something under my arm.

'Oh God, what now?'

'Nothing,' says Alice in a strange voice. 'Just a slight . . . hole situation.'

'What?' I race to the mirror and see for myself a rash of little holes all down the left side of the dress, which make a lovely contrast with my brown skin underneath.

'Oh dear,' says Mum. 'I didn't think the moths would get up to your bedroom, love.'

A few responses come to mind – among them 'You have MOTHS?' – but I bite my tongue. It's not worth it. I may as well accept that this is just not my day. I'm going to have to go up the aisle in a moth-eaten dress, with a huge spot, and pretend to be happy because otherwise everyone will say I'm a bridezilla when I'm not. I'm the opposite of a bridezilla! I hate the wedding! I wish we'd just got married in jeans with strangers off the street as witnesses!

'It's fine,' I say, trying to keep my voice steady and make a joke of it. 'Charlie has to marry me anyway, right? No matter what a sight I look?'

'Don't panic,' says Lily. 'Here's an idea. Have you got a teddy or a camisole?'

'I don't have anything here! Unless you count my combats from my All Saints phase when I was nineteen. The only teddy I have here is Mr Bear.' And in the state I'm in, I might need him soon for moral support.

'I do!' says Mum. She rushes off and returns a few minutes later with a short ivory camisole which is nearly the exact colour of the dress. It's a bit too big for me, but it fits under the dress, and when I lift my arm you can't see a thing.

'That's amazing,' I say, shaky with relief.

'And that's not all,' says Lily. 'I've got an idea for your, um, face problem. Flower crown!'

'Flower crown?' I repeat, dazed.

'Yep. Like this?' She produces a beautiful boho concoction made of white flowers of different sizes; they look so real that I have to touch them to see that they're silk. 'You could wear it on the back of your head, but if we try it low down on your forehead, Kate Moss style, then . . . *voilà*!'

It's a miracle. The crown just hides my spot, and it goes perfectly with the dress, making it look effortlessly chic rather than costume drama; I don't know why I didn't think of wearing something like this before.

'And you just happened to have this in your bag? Along with industrial-strength concealer?'

She nods. 'It's useful for hair-mares. And obviously also for spots. I should have thought of it earlier really. And I'll also make a note to have a spare camisole.'

'Lily, I don't know what they're paying you in your wedding-planning biz, but it's not enough,' I tell her, awed.

'Oh, they don't pay me much, don't worry. Now you've got two something borroweds!' says Lily. 'Something old is the dress, something new is your shoes – not that you have to bother with all that,' she adds, obviously not wanting to stress me out further. 'But what's your something blue?'

'Have you forgotten?' I wave my engagement ring with its sapphires at her, and Lily blushes.

'What's this?' asks Mum.

'Oh – Lily helped Charlie with the ring,' I say smoothly. It's mostly true – and after Lily's just saved my bacon, I'm not going to tell Mum about her near-brush with marriage fraud.

I slip on my low silver shoes – bought from a professional dance shop, because I want to be able to dance the night away – and do my make-up while Mum and the girls get into their dresses. I'm not having bridesmaids, but I've asked Alice, Maggie, Lily and Rachel to be an informal bridal posse. I can't wait to see them all today. In fact I can't wait for today – all of it. I don't care if the cake gets smashed to bits or if the flowers look like pondweed: as long as Charlie and I actually get successfully married, I'm happy. And we're all going to have a good time, and if anyone doesn't, that's their problem.

I flip through my iPod until I find 'You Never Can Tell' by Chuck Berry, which is going to be my first dance with Charlie. I woke up in the middle of the night recently worrying that the reference to teenagers getting married might make people think of the age difference between me and Charlie, but now I don't care. I hop up and start demonstrating the moves we've practised while the girls all cheer and clap, and when we've finished I yell, 'Let's get married!'

Everyone was right: it does go by really fast. It seems only seconds later that I'm in the Regency Room at the town hall, walking in to 'What the World Needs Now' by Burt Bacharach. I thought I would start crying when I saw Charlie, but actually we're both beaming and tearing up at the same time. The whole thing feels like a dream; it's hard to believe that all the people we love are really together in one room for us, and that this packed, excited space is the same place where we had our rehearsal last week. And it's hard to believe that we're saying the words that make us husband and wife, but we are. It's happening. And then the registrar, who like everyone in Brighton is a friend of my mum's, says, 'You may kiss the groom' and everyone laughs.

The confetti doesn't quite go according to plan because everyone's still waiting for us in the lobby, rather than on the steps as we'd planned. So Charlie's best man Dave has to shoo them outside and we have to go inside and come back out again. But it doesn't matter. We're floating on a wave of happiness that takes us out of the town hall, down the street and towards the square where the party is happening.

One of Mum's friends happens to own a house on Park Crescent, a Georgian terrace with a beautiful private garden surrounded by white wedding-cake houses. She's very kindly let us use it for the day. Lily has been working away with Mum and the caterers to set up some tables under a big white tent hung with pink and white paper streamers made by me and Mum. And the sun is shining; it's actually blazing down from a blue July sky, the perfect day for strolling around on the lawn and drinking champagne.

'You look stunning, Poppy! And by the way, I *love* your flowers,' says a friend from work, hugging me. I smile, remembering that she's also engaged. I had totally forgotten about the flowers, and I couldn't even tell you if they're on the tables or not. I'm so busy taking in all the things I *hadn't* planned. Like Alice and Sam playing with my little cousins, and my mum having what looks like a very civil chat with Dad's new girlfriend, and Dave making Charlie pose for photos beside his cake, which is a total triumph – chocolate Guinness, three tiers, vanilla buttercream icing – and worth all the stress and late nights.

The only thing is that everyone else seems to have a drink except me. I'm in ten different conversations at once and I'm having too much fun to go to the bar. Except I would quite like a drink now.

'Champagne for the bride?' says a voice behind me. I turn around, thrilled, to see Rachel and Maggie carrying a bottle and a cluster of glasses. They both look great, Maggie in a blue lace dress and Rachel in a very snazzy fuchsia jacket and black-and-white skirt, which is just the right side of eighties chic.

'You stars,' I say, gratefully taking a flute. 'How did you know that was just what I wanted?'

'I've been to too many weddings where the bride doesn't have a chance to have a drink until the speeches, practically,' Rachel observes, pouring champagne with one expert hand. 'It's probably a good thing from the point of view of pacing yourself, but I would want a drink, personally.'

'You look absolutely stunning, Poppy,' Maggie says. 'Just perfect. And this place! It's like a Richard Curtis film. Speaking of which, let us know if you have to go and get pictures taken or something like that. I always feel guilty talking to the bride at a wedding, in case she needs to talk to more important people.'

'Don't be crazy! *You're* the important people. Anyway, we did the pictures before the ceremony; makes life a lot easier. Where's John?'

'He's over there,' she says, pointing. 'Having a manly chat with Oliver about bikes, I think.'

I smile. Bikes are one of the few things John gets chatty about; he's the tall, strong, silent type, and does something complicated in IT. He's very different from Maggie, but ever since they met in New York, they've been inseparable. They've even shared their Gmail calendars, whatever that means. I have a feeling that Maggie could be the next one to have a meltdown over her flower arrangements. Unless Rachel beats her to it, of course.

'I love this,' Maggie adds, touching my flower crown.

'Oh yeah,' I say, laughing. 'It's actually hiding a massive spot. Lily magicked it out of her box of tricks this morning. She's been unbelievable – she helped Mum find the caterers, the tent and the booze, all from Los Angeles.'

'Did I hear my name?' says an excited voice, and Lily bounces up to us. Rachel pours her some champagne and says, 'Poppy was just saying what good work you did with the wedding planning. You're obviously a natural. How's the new job going? Not so new now, I suppose.'

'It's brilliant,' Lily says happily. 'I love it. I thought at first it might be a bit tame, but a wedding is a lot more meaningful than a product launch for some new eye cream.'

'And how is it going with your rock star?' Rachel asks. Rock star might be pushing it: the story I've heard is that Lily met this guy while he was busking outside her local coffee shop. From what Alice has told me, he's not exactly marriage material, but I don't think that's what Lily is looking for either.

'Elijah? Well, he's not a star *yet*,' Lily says, completely seriously. 'But he's really, really talented. I'll send you a link to his YouTube channel.'

'You know you could have brought him, right?' I say, suddenly feeling bad that Lily's the only one here without a date.

'Oh, he could never afford the air fare,' she says, sounding almost proud.

'Another glass of champagne?' Maggie asks, seeing I've drained my glass.

'OK, but this is my last one – I am giving a speech later on,' I say, accepting a half-glass.

'Champagne is good for speeches,' says Lily. 'By the way, I've vetted your best man's speech for you and it's totally fine. It's quite the bromance – all about how he and Charlie bonded over Pokémon when they were six – but nothing to frighten the horses.'

'You and my mum together could run the country,' I tell her, sincerely.

'Your mum certainly could,' says Lily. 'She is *owning* that red dress. And look at her being chatted up by that silver fox.'

I turn around, and then whip my head back to the girls. 'That silver fox is Charlie's dad,' I say faintly. 'They do get on well, but . . . You don't really think they're *flirting*, do you? We couldn't handle it if they . . . Urgh.'

'Of course they won't,' Maggie says soothingly. 'Your mum is way too sensible. But a bit of mild flirting is no harm. That's what weddings are for.'

'It's so nice to finally have a date to bring to a wedding,' says

Rachel suddenly. Then she looks at us. 'Sorry. Did I say that out loud?' We all laugh. 'But it is!' she protests. 'This time last year I was dating Jay – at least that's what I thought I was doing, though there was a clue in all the weddings I went to on my own. Plonker.'

'This time last year I was single and miserable,' I say. 'Charlie and I got together a year ago next week.'

'I was miserable too, but not because I was single,' says Lily.

'I was in a couple and miserable,' says Maggie. 'And I hadn't made friends with you two yet!' she adds, gesturing to me and Rachel.

'What am I, chopped liver?' asks Lily, but she's grinning. I notice our photographer hovering nearby and beckon him over; I want to make sure he gets this on camera.

'Let's have a toast,' I say, holding up my flute. 'Here's to bringing a date to a wedding, being single and happy . . . and to old and new friends.'

And they all raise their glasses and chorus, 'To old and new friends!'

NICOLA DOHERTY

The Out of Office Girl

Alice Roberts is having a rubbish summer.

She's terrified of her boss, her career is stalling, and she's just been dumped – by text message. But things are about to change . . .

When her boss Olivia is taken ill, Alice is sent on the work trip of a lifetime: to a villa in Sicily, to edit the autobiography of Hollywood bad boy Luther Carson. But it's not all yachts, nightclubs and Camparis. Luther's arrogant agent Sam wants to ditch the book entirely. Luther himself is gorgeous and charming but impossible to read. There only seems to be one way to get his attention, and it definitely involves mixing business with pleasure. Alice is out of the office, and into a whole lot of trouble.

978 0 7553 8685 7

headline
review

NICOLA DOHERTY

If I Could Turn Back Time

What if you found The One, then lost him again?

Or not so much lost him as became the neurotic, needy girlfriend from hell. The girl who tried to make him choose between her and his job, and got seriously paranoid about his relationship with his female best friend . . .

Zoë Kennedy knows she doesn't deserve another chance with David Fitzgerald. But if there's the tiniest possibility of making things right, she'll snatch it. Even if it means breaking the laws of physics to do so . . .

A fabulously funny, romantic read about falling in love, falling on your face and finding the one you're meant to be with.

978 0 7553 8688 8

headline
review

Now you can buy any of these other bestselling titles from your bookshop or *direct from the publisher.*

FREE P&P AND UK DELIVERY
(Overseas and Ireland £3.50 per book)

The Summer Guest	Emma Hannigan	£7.99
Don't Want To Miss A Thing	Jill Mansell	£7.99
If You Were Me	Sheila O'Flanagan	£7.99
A Special Delivery	Clare Dowling	£6.99
Spare Brides	Adele Parks	£7.99
The Proposal	Tasmina Perry	£7.99
A Place for Us	Harriet Evans	£7.99
Wild and Free	Wendy Holden	£7.99
Destiny	Louise Bagshawe	£8.99

TO ORDER SIMPLY CALL THIS NUMBER

01235 400 414

or visit our website: www.headline.co.uk

Prices and availability subject to change without notice.